BEYOND THE MACROCOSM

INTERACTIVE SHORT STORIES
OF DREAD AND WONDER

Written by: Konn Lavery

Edited by: Cara Flannery

reveal BOOKS

Ebook ISBN-13: 978-1-990542-03-9

Print ISBN-13: 978-1-990542-04-6

Published in Canada by Reveal Books.

Book artwork and design by Konn Lavery of Reveal Design.

Photo credit: Nastassja Brinker.

Printed in the United States of America.

First Edition 2022.

Find out more at:

konnlavery.com

AUTHOR MESSAGE

Beyond the Macrocosm houses a collection of shorts that belong to an expanding universe. Like the first volume, the stories take place within the Macrocosm which is a large-scale expansion spanning across many genres and literary styles to tell a greater storyline.

An interactive timeline on my website at konnlavery.com showcases the novels and shorts along with major events that alter the Macrocosm's universe. There's also a Wiki on my website which explores characters, locations, eras, languages, items, and more.

The stories within this volume have been previously published in some form. Most have been revised from their original state, making them richer and strengthening their linkage within the Macrocosm.

PREVIOUS STORY PUBLICATIONS

- *Summer Giver*: Originally published in the Prairie Gothic anthology by Prairie Soul Press in November 2020, edited by Stacey Kondla.
- *Death Shot*: Originally published in Terrace VI Forbidden Fruit anthology by The Seventh Terrace in June 2021, curated by Robert Bose and Sarah L. Johnson.
- *Sway*: Originally a submission for the first round of NYC Midnight competition requiring three themes. Genre: Romance. Subject: A Membership. Character: An Appraiser.
- *The Smell*, *Taylorism*, *Natural Cosmos*, *Unlocking Immortality*, *Work Out*, *Ash*, *I Love You*, *Aureate Rise*, and *Archean II*: Originally published on my blog from May 2020 to January 2021.
- *Will of the Shaper*, *Draconem Revival*, *Nature's Apex*, *Nature's Design*, *Promises in Sand*, *Transhumanism*, *Bioringer*, *Post Religionism*, *Ice Face*, and *Blood Will*: Originally featured on my Patreon as part of the monthly short story from February 2021 to June 2022.

THANK YOU

I've been consistently writing short stories, starting on my blog, since May of 2018. They started as an experimentation with the writing craft and over time they evolved into key pillars of the Macrocosm.

The shorts range from character origin stories, prequels to novels, sequels, and standalone tales. They've helped string together important events within the Macrocosm, exploring how the universe shifts from the fantastical fantasy world into the gritty modern times, and finally into the mysterious futuristic sci-fi universe.

None of this could have been possible without the readers who have joined the progression of the Macrocosm over the years. Some of you have been reading since my first novel's release, *Reality*, back in 2012. I'd like to thank everyone who has been following my writing since then and onwards, even through the various genre jumping and rewrites.

A special thank you to the monthly Patreon subscribers who have been a part of the journey during the writing of this collection. You all rock!

Cheers to: Dan Harrington, Kristopher R Manabo, Christopher Jenson, Brenda Lavery, David Luecke, Kyle Lavery, and Lindsey Molyneaux. You all helped make the Macrocosm.

A big thanks to Jim Jackson, Stacey Kondla, Robert Bose, and Sarah L. Johnson for working with me on previous publications, it was a lot of fun contributing to the fantastic collections. Thank you to S.L. Baker for sponsoring the contest entry which created my first romance story.

Thank you to the beta readers, Lex J. Grootelaar, Sarah Burrows, Sydney Fiske, and Lindsey Molyneaux for the feedback and pointers, and my editor, Cara Flannery, for polishing this collection.

Last, but not least, I want to thank my mother, Brenda Lavery, for years and years of support ever since I was a small kid. Back then, I drew characters with crayons, sculpted clay figures, and wrote backstories for terrible, unbalanced boardgames which neither of us knew would serve as the Macrocosm's Big Bang, creating the superverse it is today.

SYNOPSIS

The Nameless One and their ghoulish companion are locked in an endless loop. They attempt to undo the catastrophic cosmic event known as the sky rip which threatens to consume the fabric of reality and erase everything that has happened, is happening, and will happen.

Unfortunately, the Nameless One doesn't remember what, how, or why this occurred.

You, the reader must make the right choices, navigating through the "pick your destiny" collection of 22 short stories to gather clues and discover out how to break the time loop. Enter the fantasy-rich past with reptilians and paladins; fast-forward to the future with DNA-shifting robbers; witness the modern world of gritty horrors.

Each short story explores award-winning author Konn Lavery's expanding Macrocosm, sharing the same universe as his previous novels such as the horror novels *Rave* and *Cultivate*, the dark fantasy series *Mental Damnation*, and thriller *YEGman*.

Only you, the Nameless One, have the power to save the Macrocosm before the sky rip destroys everything, taking you and all the outlandish, cosmic and wonderous things with it.

TABLE OF CONTENTS

BEFORE WE BEGIN . . .

Welcome, reader, to *Beyond the Macrocosm*. We're about to set forth on an abnormal interactive journey. Unlike the usual fictional written word, we're not buckling down in a linear progression from beginning to end, story after story.

What does that mean? Well, it simply means you get to participate in the book. Throughout the shorts and the overarching storyline, you'll be prompted to act at the end of each section. Keep watch for text like this:

Wave your arms wildly! (Turn to Page 50)
Fold your arms. No one tells you what to do. (Turn to Page 44)

And so, you'll flip to the page as instructed by one of the two options, which will take you to the next part of the story you chose. The above doesn't lead anywhere and is just an example. If you try to read this collection linearly from beginning to end, I am afraid to say you're going to find it a jumbled mess of confusion.

If you want to read only the short stories, use the table of index at the beginning of the book and jump to where your heart desires.

In some sections of the book, you'll be faced with two or three choices, while other times, you have one option. If you find there is no action to take at the end of a scene, that means you can turn the page just like any regular book.

Sound fun? Let's dive into a universe of the outlandish, cosmic dread, and wonderous!

Oh, before I forget, I did mention this book is interactive, right? There's more going on within these pages than just making a choice. There are important fragments scattered throughout these pages. Make a good note of that detail. Keep your wits about you while exploring the Macrocosm, or everything is doomed to be infinite.

WELCOME BACK?

___/\/\/_repetition creates a sense of déjà vu. You have been here before, yet you can't quite place when. It's a strange feeling of familiarity deep in your gut. Perhaps this is simply a dream. Or perhaps you have lived past lives, and your soul is remembering details of your previous journeys. Here's another theory . . . you're overthinking it.

After all, you are going about your daily business at the grocery store just as everyone else does. Up and down the aisles you move, under the beaming fluorescent light. You are passing the produce department with a basket in hand, for you don't need many items today. Deep down, that gut feeling won't shrug off. Nonsense. This is new! You're here and now.

An old man is picking through the pile of apples down the same aisle you pass. Your presence catches his attention, and he gives a crooked smile that raises his wrinkles. His hand is shaky, but he manages to grab the perfect shiny, unbruised, crimson apple.

"Always pick the right one," he says in a high-pitched, croaky voice.

You're unsure if you smile or not, hurrying on with your shopping.

"If you just pick the easiest one pulling you in or at random, you'll end up with a bad apple. You want the good one, the unlikely choice.

Boy, they should keep these signs organized. It's all out of order. Meaning you have to keep track of the letters of each sign yourself and move them around to know what order they go in . . ." His voice fades as you pass him, making you realize he is talking to himself more than you. Plus, in your life, you can't stop and chit-chat with every old man you see. What about you? You certainly have enough going on already, right?

Onwards, you pass the produce department, going past an end cap full of sour candy boxes with big bubbly white letters stating "Chewz." Below the title is the flavour, "NUT GRAPE." You're unsure why this catches your eye, but it does, and you focus on the overly optimistic wide-eyed blue ghost on the box.

The ghost's black tentacle-like hair and white eyes are rather horrifying for a candy mascot, but it keeps you transfixed. You focus on every curve of the linework and the dark to light blue shading that make up the form. While you're being pulled into this mascot's hypnotic power, you fail to realize that your basket is now missing.

A high frequency rings in your ear, damping out the top 'retro 90's' playlist on the radio. In fact, the whole grocery store begins to liquify as if it were wet paint. You don't care if the whole room is missing or not because this cartoon character keeps you entranced.

There's only the NUT GRAPE Chewz box and you in this dripping space. The gaze you have on this box is so mind-sucking that you'd think you're about to enter a deep slumber. The whole grocery store melts together, mixing its colours with each other, creating a mucky grey as they fall endlessly below you.

This is abnormal from a daily experience. Is it familiar? Only you can answer that.

Your whole view of the grocery store and the NUT GRAPE Chewz box is gone, and your eyes close, leaving you in black. It isn't possible to tell if you're standing or sleeping. You take deep breaths, slowly letting the oxygen in and out of your system, feeding the brain.

As you drift off into the depths of your mind, you get a complete understanding of your system before your consciousness is freed.

Your body is stiff and your eyes are dry with the lids applying heavy pressure. You'd think you had run ten thousand kilometres for how exhausted your body is.

It's okay to let your mind drift away, leaving the rock-of-a-body behind and slipping from your reality, free from the daily worries. There's no strange old men or NUT GRAPE Chewz boxes. Any thoughts you've had, the concerns, the joys, none of it matters. It's a fair wonder if you're having a stroke on the grocery store floor. These could be your final moments.

Or perhaps this is a dream after all. You certainly feel asleep now. There's a weightlessness to your form as the spacial awareness around you dissolves entirely. The body shifts from your normal state, transforming into something more robust, almost godlike.

Now you're unsure if your body even exists. Is that damn NUT GRAPE Chewz box responsible for this? Maybe it's a simulation and the box was a glitch breaking the false world, and you're awaking in the real one.

That stroke theory is also quite probable.

Whether you're dying or experiencing astral projection, one thing is for sure: you no longer have a body. Your soul is flying beyond the physical limitations of your flesh.

A deep reverberated voice echoes around with no natural origin for the sound. It speaks in two voices simultaneously with a lower-pitched tone as if two beings are talking together. It says, "Nameless One, snap out of it. Come on, get up."

One might use the word demonic to describe the sound. Still, you cannot pinpoint the origin, just like you cannot figure out where you are or if you have a body. You still have some form of control of *something* and try to speak.

"Hello?" you say, with your own voice echoing into the void.

"There you go," the being says. "I was wondering when you'd finally stop ignoring me. Ambling about your daily activities. Do you only pay attention when you dream?"

"Who is this?" you ask.

Your voice echoes again, and there's no reply from the mysterious voice.

You wait . . .

Waiting.

Still waiting, and nothing.

A crackling boom explodes from above. Flashes of lightning cast dark swirling purple and blue clouds. In the brief moment of light, you see an ocean of black with a white horizon all around and no land in sight. Darkness returns, preventing you from checking to see if you have a body.

Another thundering snap erupts, giving you a clear view of an alien world. Directly below you is a rocky, charcoal plateau. The blackness returns, and you see nothing. The impending force of gravity grips your system, pulling you down to the formation. Your stomach tenses, feeling acid rush up your esophagus. You're falling.

Some vomit reaches your mouth as your heart skips the odd beat while the wind breezes past your skin and hair. Another tremendous boom comes from the sky, and the light permanently stays as you fall past a swirling vortex of clouds. Grey-and-green rotten faces and hands reach out for you through the violent winds. Their jaws open, exposing mouthfuls of brown teeth. Their eyes are gone, with only black sockets, exposing their souls as the bony hands attempt to grab you.

A hand rockets towards your face, moving right through as you fall past a violent vortex and the flying undead. You keep falling, further down, heading straight for the ground. You look up, trying to think if you can do anything to save yourself from the impending doom.

The faces and hands swirl endlessly into the black vortex, surrounded by colourful clouds. Lightning frequently strikes, highlighting the depth of the storm. Far above the vortex, behind some of the sky, is a jagged tear spreading across the gloomy atmosphere for thousands of miles. The edges of the rip burn with bright white smokeless fire. Inside the shape is a mirror reflection of the black ocean and plateau.

The sky-copy isn't a perfect likeness. Each time you look elsewhere, the visuals in the mirror distort. The ocean below and the plateau morph disproportionately like a funhouse mirror. What's that? Some of the black ocean in the rip shifts tones and shapes so drastically that you see people in them. The shapes change too swiftly; you can't pinpoint what or who they are, but you saw eyes and faces.

Another morph elsewhere catches your eye. The ocean shape turns into a hard, metallic cylinder with beaming blue propulsion beams coming from it. It shifts into black scales and extends into a large muscular body with wings until a tidal wave washes it away before completing its transformation.

Another transformation occurs, closer to the plateau in the rip. It forms a strange pale humanoid creature with sharp fangs. It's completely hairless and tries to roar but is warped into flowers, then an office chair, and back to the black ocean.

You look down, realizing how close you are to the rocky surface. Gravity is accelerating, and you're going to collide directly into the ground with devastating force. You try to blink but are unable to. You have minimal control over this body as you reach the ground and move straight through the stone with no resistance.

Every layer of the ground is visible while descending further into the earth. You fall into a cavern, moving past the stalactites and colliding with an unconscious body on the ground, deeming your journey an end. This body you recognize because it's you. No way.

You scurry backwards on the sand in an erratic motion, exhaling rapidly. A jolt of energy zaps throughout your entire system, and you gasp for air, springing upright, covered in sweat, limbs shaking. Drool and stomach goo drizzle down your chin. Your fingers and toes are ice cold to the touch.

"Again?" comes the reverberated voice. This time, it has an origin right behind you. "You chose this, again?"

You spin around, realizing you have complete control of your body. It's energetic. Amazingly, you leap up with ease and wonder if this body is even you. It feels like you, but foreign. It's as if you were you on the very best day of your life tenfold.

"If only we could both recall . . . Look, let's stay focused," the voice says.

You turn to face the voice. Little did you expect to see a genie-like creature hovering right in front of you. Black and blue smoke disintegrates into open space below its torso. Further up the body, the form compresses into lean muscles and folded arms ending with three sharp claws. Each wrist contains scars of a cross. The black and blue smoke forms two distinct layers within this creature. An outer translucent blue layer and a blacker inner core, almost like an egg yolk.

The creature's white eyes are locked on you. Its extended muzzle stretches its lips from cheek to cheek, exposing the razor-sharp teeth. There is no hair, only black tentacle-like extensions on the scalp that defy gravity, floating in space, just as its whole form does.

You gasp, realizing it's the NUT GRAPE Chewz mascot! You back away, stumbling onto the sand and skidding down the hill.

"Really?" the being sighs, hovering towards you.

"What are you?" you ask, gaining control of your breath.

You're still shaking, disoriented, and spit out the remaining acid in your mouth. But you didn't have a body when vomiting; it doesn't make sense. The only rational conclusion is that it isn't real.

"This is a dream, an overly realistic dream." You say out loud, unsure why you do. Maybe it is to reassure yourself that this is indeed made-up.

"Pull yourself together, understand?" the being says. "We don't have time for your ridiculousness."

"Understand? This isn't real." You slap your face, trying to wake yourself up somehow. The wild thought of trying to piss yourself comes to mind. Urinating in dreams can wake people up sometimes. Unfortunately, there's no pressure to give. Hitting yourself isn't providing any help either. So, you stand up, brushing the sand off your legs, seeing you're wearing the exact same clothes that you had on in the store.

"It's me, Malpherities," the being says.

It is a dream, you think. Yes, this is all some completely ridiculous figment from the depths of your imagination about the NUT GRAPE Chewz box. Unfortunately, you sure feel a lot in this dream. Things like this happen to people all the time in their sleep. They can even recall pain. Thankfully, you have not felt that, other than the slight sting of slapping yourself.

"Great." Malpherities rubs his forehead. "We're going through this once more."

The being hovers past you, soaring down the hill towards a pathway leading deeper into the cavern. The more you look at this Malpherities character, the more the sense of déjà vu rises. That same deep gut feeling returns. You have no memory of him other than that damn box. In fact, your whole memory is foggy now. You were at the store, but before that? Nothing.

A rumbling thunder comes from outside and you say, "Wait up!" You hurry to catch up with the being, skidding down the sand.

"Of course, you follow, as always," Malpherities says while moving into the dark tunnel that descends deeper into the caverns.

"Sorry?" you ask.

"It doesn't matter. Because we go through this again, and again!" Malpherities chuckles in self-pity. "We've really made a big mistake, haven't we?"

"What mistake?"

"I'm wondering if this can even be undone."

Another crackling boom comes from the sky with a deep trickling rumble, shaking the entire cavern. Rocks and dust tumble from the ceiling. A deep, ear-ripping tear erupts all around, forcing you to cover your ears. A foot-long stalactite falls just behind you as you try to keep up with Malpherities.

"The rip is expanding, hurry!" Malpherities says, turning a corner.

"Wait!" You make the turn and freeze.

Malpherities keeps moving, past another being who looks strikingly familiar to Malpherities. This one is finer; the upper torso and arms are lean. The face has larger white eyes. It tries to scream. The voice is more feminine than Malpherities's, but the sound is identical to a damaged tape recording. The body of the being pulsates violently, reshaping and blending into and out of the cavern wall. It's disturbingly similar it is to the mirrored world you witnessed inside the sky rip.

Malpherities is a good twenty paces ahead of you, moving down the descending hall into a wide-open space. You pick up your speed, running right past the tortured creature. You spot another one; this one is much larger, with a broad torso and thick jawline. It, too, is crying in agony as the body mixes in with its surroundings. You can't stop and overanalyze it. Whatever is going on here isn't good, and this Malpherities might have some answers.

"You dropped the damn orb again," Malpherities says.

Another eruption shakes the entire cavern, and you try to remain upright.

"What orb?"

Malpherities halts in the centre of the dome, beside a black ball on the ground. Further ahead is a large opening to the cavern at sea level. The black ocean waves are violent, splashing against the rocks and splattering onto the ground.

"Here," Malpherities says, picking up the polished sphere. The motion makes the golden glitters swirl around inside it. The object vibrates rapidly in his claws. His arms shake, trying to control the energy as it glows orange.

"Nameless One, quit messing around and take it!"

You reach Malpherities, looking up to see that the ceiling goes all the way up, possibly to where you first woke up in this strange space.

"The Midway is collapsing," Malpherities says. "Quickly, activate the portal!"

MAKE ONE OF TWO CHOICES:

This is just a bad dream. Try and wake yourself up again.
(Turn to Page 23)

Say, "What do I need to do?" (Turn to Page 25)

None of this can be real. There's no way you're on some alien rock with a black ocean and talking to a floating ethereal being from a candy box. It's pure fiction! And so, you deem this is just an obscure sleep to laugh about later. You must be stressed, or you ate something wrong. Yeah, there must be some rational explanation for what you're experiencing. The grocery store couldn't have collapsed all around you. And so, you decide to slap yourself again, harder this time.

Your palm hits your face, and the pain burns your skin, lasting several seconds.

"What was that for?" Malpherities asks, still struggling to hold the orb.

The ground shakes, giving you a sickening realization that this is not a dream at all.

"We don't have time for this! We have to find the fragments and break the loop," Malpherities says.

"This can't be happening," you mutter to yourself, stepping back to look at the whole cavern.

Malpherities slams the orb into your chest, and you're forced to grab it with both hands. The orb stabilizes, and your body tenses. The skin and flesh on your fingers melt, yet you feel no pain. The liquid-like flesh fuses into the orb, coating it entirely.

Your vision brightens, so bright you can barely see the ocean behind Malpherities. His voice is distant, identical to the dream state you first heard it. "Nameless One, you must make a choice, navigate to find the fragments for you have the seeing eye. With any luck, this is our last."

Malpherities and the cavern are nowhere to be seen. There is whiteness all around as two swirling vortexes appear before you, with violet and blue clouds around the edges. In the centre of each space is pitch blackness. You keep melting as your consciousness descends to and from your hands, leaving the body behind. You and the orb are one and the same, moving towards the two portals.

"Trust yourself and bring order to the fragments," Malpherities says.

The orb-you continues to move towards the swirls. It may not be your body, but you do feel control. Yes . . . you can navigate the direction of the orb into either portal. To what end remains a mystery. Malpherities chucked this orb into your hands before you could get a straight answer about why you're here.

Glimpses of landscapes phase inside these portals, morphing shapes and tones like the sky rip. The portal on the left shows a foggy forest deep within the mountains. There's an abandoned school bus. You hear screaming. There's an office cubical in the right portal with fleshy tubes running all along with the carpet flooring. Groans and cries echo as syringes appear, squirting translucent liquid.

Trust yourself. Malpherities's words replay in your mind. The orb naturally gravitates left. You can still control the sphere, giving you the command of where you go next.

MAKE ONE OF TWO CHOICES:

Embrace the orb and levitate towards the left portal.
(Turn to Page 27)

Seize control and levitate the orb towards the right portal.
(Turn to Page 39)

This whole scenario is a bad dream, but you decide to see what it is about. After all, it feels so real; you cannot do anything other than accept it as such.

You say, "What do I need to do?"

"Find the missing fragments and break the loop."

"What fragments? Loop?"

Your answer is chucked aside as Malpherities slams the orb into you, forcing you to catch it. Upon your touch, you feel a humming pulse run through your body. It has an unmatched power that causes you to tense. Little do you realize that your fingers begin to fuse into the orb. By the time you notice, your arms and torso are melting into this strange shape.

What? you think.

There is no pain in this transformation. The body you once had is nowhere to be found as you and the orb hover as one. Even though it's an electrifying command, you can feel a sense of control over the hovering sphere.

The cavern, the black ocean, and Malpherities dissolve into a bright white similar to the grocery store. Out of nothingness, two swirls form in open space and expand with a black portal inside each.

"Trust yourself and bring order to the fragments," Malpherities says, his voice distant like the first time you heard him.

Purple and palace blue clouds form around the edges of the black spaces, swirling inwards, sucking you and the orb in. You still have control and can move this orb left or right, depending on your desire.

Inside the black void to your left, you spot wilderness, mountains, and an abandoned school bus. The faint screams of a girl are heard. There's a cubical office space with tacky burgundy carpeting to your right. Mechanical and flesh-like tubes run along the floor into each cubical.

The orb is being sucked into the left portal. Remember, you can navigate this new form of yours. *Trust yourself.* Malpherities's words echo in your mind.

MAKE ONE OF TWO CHOICES:

Embrace the orb and levitate towards the left portal.
(Turn to Page 27)

Seize control and levitate the orb towards the right portal.
(Turn to Page 39)

You believe letting go the best option, and the orb gravitates into the left portal, hitting you with rapid acceleration and sucking you deep into this new world. The closer you get to the swirling vortex, you can feel the gentle touches from mountains' mist in the dark forests. You pass the purple and blue clouds surrounding the portal, getting a clearer look at the wilderness.

You can sense, feel, and experience everything except that it isn't you . . . Your sense of the orb, of yourself, and everything you believe dissipates. Your thoughts are thrown aside as you're locked into a strange seat of observing.

WILL OF THE SHAPER

Keeping a secret is never easy. It'll weight down on your psyche. Well, at least for normal people. Lucky for me I have a poor short-term memory. If you tell me something, I'll forget like that. There's not a lot of secret-keeping in my hometown, Fort Nelson, thankfully.

The peaceful small-town life is wonderful for me and folks who don't want a lot of trouble. It's also close to the Canadian Rockies and Muncho Lake, letting you get away from the busy life. Well, that was the case until about six months ago. There's a creature out there in the woods. Some seriously strange events started happening around the holidays just before school started up in the new year.

Kids have been reported missing, and I know why. My friends, Wesley—also my brother—and Curtis, are on the same page as me regarding this monster. The other folks here think we're making it up for attention. They think we're just high school troublemakers trying to rattle the town's chains. We're not! This thing is out there; it's tormented—or she, rather—it's conflicted. She'll watch you when you're not looking and then strike. I escaped lucky, unlike her other victims.

I've been ill fortuned to witness her in her prime, twice in fact. Once was from a distance and the other . . . let me tell you how it all happened. It's a rarity to see her. When she's near, you can hear her croaky moaning. It's like an old door swinging or the type of sound you make from the back of your throat, trying to mimic a dolphin.

You can find her footprints in the mud and snow since she's barefoot and has nasty three long toes on each foot. I had thought to myself, *Who the hell goes around barefoot up this far north? You'll freeze!* Fort Nelson is far colder than anywhere else in British Columbia during the winter. These tracks are easy to follow, and after a while, they just stop—no sign of anything. It's like she vanishes into thin air. We don't have any footage of her either. In the moment of fear, I never thought about pulling my phone to record her.

We originally pieced together that it is a she because that eerie croaking has a womanlike touch to the sound. Our theory was confirmed after I saw her the first time, and the second. She preys on teens—like us—for the most part, targeting boys . . . one girl did go missing.

Wesley, Curtis, and I have gone to the RCMP, telling them about *her* and the missing teens. They know these kids are dead in the back of their minds, but they don't care, I think. Missing people happen all the time, and unless there is a body, it is a missing person report and not a homicide. People can be flagged as missing for years, and that's where the RCMP leave them.

Alright, let me explain how I first saw her. Wesley showed me this wicked abandoned bus down by the river years ago when we were kids. He is more adventurous, into parkour, which keeps him thin as a corpse. Most of the time, he goes out at night, too, like some vampire kid. Mom complains about him not having enough sunlight and to stop playing his 'angry noise,' which is actually called industrial music. He wasn't always this way, but he's changed. We all do while growing up.

Wesley, Curtis, and I like to drink out in the woods on that old bus. That's where we first heard *her*. Our buddy, Garett, was with a couple of other kids and us. We were kicking back in that bus with the beers that Curtis got from his dad's liquor store.

Curtis is a year older than us and has a wicked taste in music. He's introduced me to so many black metal bands—you can get why Wesley is friends with him. Industrial and metal go hand-in-hand. The guy has a bit of a temper, so don't mess with him. Oh, Curtis is a Satanist, too, doing all the rituals. He lent me his Satanic Bible for me to read. I'm not much of a reader, but I am giving it a shot. It would be so cool to brag about being a Satanist. That'd really piss off the folks of Fort Nelson.

Anyways, back to her.

There we were, laughing and smoking cigs like we would any other time when Garett decided to go for a piss. That's when we heard her. The shuffling in the nearby bushes, and then the croaky moan . . . it's not like a sexy moan either. The sound starts off quiet and gets louder until it morphs into a rattling hiss.

She made just that sound, followed by Garett screaming at the top of his lungs. God, I've never heard someone shout like that. The agony he must have felt before she got him. Then, all sounds stopped—no creaky moan, rattling, or screams. We ran out to look for him. We couldn't see anything. At first, we figured the doofus ran home— maybe he drank too much, but he didn't come to school the next day, and we've never seen him since.

It's messed up. Some of the other kids talk about it. For the most part, no one takes it seriously. As a rule, people stay out of the woods anyways. There's an active grizzly in the area. Let's not forget the mountain lions or the wolves. Fort Nelson is a busy place with wildlife, and people would rather be safe. Let me tell you, though, that bus is awesome—totally worth it!

The RCMP eventually interviewed everyone in school about Garett. Wesley, Curtis, and the other kids told them straight up what happened. Not much came of our statements. The cops investigated the bus and the area but didn't find anything. She's cunning . . . and able to cover up her attacks. There's just those footprints, moving through the mud before stopping abruptly.

31

Nehom, the girl I hung out with in math class, believed us. She's cool and was new to our town. Her parents moved in on an acreage just outside of Fort Nelson. She said they moved to Fort Nelson to get away from the old life, start new where no one knew them. She's apparently lived in over a dozen towns across the west coast.

I still remember the first time we met. I was late to math class and Mr. Ramirez shifted the desks around to accommodate the new student. I was pissed off because my spot was taken by one of the bookworms. It was rad, way off in the far corner in the room. Nehom spoke up, offering the empty seat next to her, in the middle. Mr. Ramirez was cool with us sitting there since Nehom was shy, and I could help her get familiar with the school. I was good with it because it was either Nehom the new girl or sitting way up in the front.

I was taken aback by her poor fashion compared to the other girls in the school. She wore cargos, hoodies, and basic sneakers and nothing new. Her eyes were amazing—like a radioactive green. Plus, the blonde streaks and pale skin forms a perfect punk look.

Right away we hit it off. Nehom was well-versed in black metal and thought Curtis's copy of the Satanic Bible was dope. Nehom said she was familiar with the religion and read the book herself to understand who she was. I guess I'm doing the same thing; the whole scripture is about self-empowerment.

I also forgot her name right away thanks to my poor memory. No matter what I do, I cannot remember the names of people, movies, bands, anything. Nehom had me write her name down several times, and her name stuck with me. Bam. Nehom. She poked fun at me for forgetting her name—I love it when a gal can rip on you. She called me Fish-head and the name stuck.

Nehom was chill and could kick back with a drink. She ain't afraid to go in the woods like some of the other kids. Man, this one time—about a month after Garett—Curtis and I tried to throw a party out by the bus, and most of the kids were too chicken-shit to join us. Only the hardcore kids went. That's when the second kid went missing—another boy.

We heard that croaky moan again. As always, it starts gentle then rises to that throaty crackling, and finally the rattling hiss. That killed the party vibe fast, and we all booked it. Nehom wasn't with us, and neither was Wesley—I'd hate to lose my brother or Nehom . . . what a cutie, minus the odd taste in clothing.

After that party kill, Curtis, Wesley, and I decided to go to the RCMP and get serious with them. Two people were gone! The officers knew we were trouble. Curtis has been caught drinking underage, me with cigs, and Wesley with dope. They usually let us go on a warning. Still, with our backgrounds, they noted our stories, and that was all. I mean, we were the last to see Garett and that other kid—I'm forgetting his name. See? Horrible memory.

I can count about six people she's taken, one being a girl and the rest boys. The girl, Vanessa, was a real piss-off. I started flirting with her in social class, and things were getting fly. Look, I liked Nehom, and I think she liked me, but Vanessa, damn, I heard she was into hooking up. That's a no-brainer.

Vanessa and I went out by the old bus after school, like, on a Thursday. We had smokes, and I kept a six-pack out there from another night with Curtis. We were smoking our own cigs, flirting a lot, and she even kissed me before asking for a drink. It was all looking good. The only problem was that the six-pack was missing. Like, wow. Curtis probably took it. Thankfully I had another stash just outside the bus. I told Vanessa to hold tight as I left the bus.

The croaky moan began slow and gradual, coming from deeper in the woods. The soft gravelly voice rose into the rapid rattling. I figured she was coming for me since I was a good fifty paces away from the vehicle. Oh no. I saw *her* creep around from the back of the bus's rear bumper, crawling towards the vehicle door. I must be the only person who has ever seen her and lived to talk about it.

She was on her hands and feet, naked, pale, and hairless with a bright sheen against her plastic-like skin. It looked like that weird dangly creature from that fantasy movie everyone loves. Is it based on some book? Toads of Rings or something? I don't know, it doesn't matter. Damn memory. *She* looked skinny and dangly like in the movie while crawling into the bus.

Vanessa screamed, and I ran to her. Her shrieks followed with tormenting cries of agony. The glass windows smashed and the bus rocked violently. Another window shattered as I ran up the step.

Too late. She was gone. A bit of blood trickled down the back window. Outside were the long-toed footprints in the dirt. They went into the woods for about three dozen steps before disappearing. No blood, only a couple of black feathers on the ground where the prints ended. Vanessa was officially a victim. That gal was ready to take her panties off too! I swear.

I'm still a bit pissed about Vanessa, and there's nothing I can do about it. Maybe I should be more sympathetic to her family, but seriously, I hadn't been laid since before the holidays. There was nothing I could do. *She* is too swift and cunning.

You never know where she is going to be or when she'll strike. I told Curtis, Wesley, and Nehom. Curtis swears he never took the beers, as does Wesley. So, neither were out there before Vanessa and I arrived. Nehom was a little irritated that I took Vanessa out there. She kept digging her nails into her arms. Maybe I should have made a move on her sooner, because she started to distance herself from me for a bit. All four of us didn't see a point in telling the RCMP this time—they didn't care. Vanessa would be filed as a missing person by someone else, and that would be the end of it.

This brings us to when I saw *her* the second time. Curtis was disturbed about the bus and stopped going. He still gave us some beers, and we hung out. Wesley and I went to the bus again and nothing happened.

Nehom came with me this one time, three victims after Vanessa—being about six months since that terrible evening. We were hitting it off well. I think she got over the jealousy of me taking Vanessa out there. She was back to her regular old self, cracking good jokes and hanging out with me.

Nehom and I were a few drinks in, slurring a bit, and we kept scooching closer to one another. Her crooked smile and constant eye contact was pulling me in. I took this as a sign and went in for the kiss. She seemed surprised at first, stiff, but didn't hold back. The moment held . . . and I pushed further, grabbing hold of her. She gave in and took my face with both hands. My fingers slid under her shirt to cup her tit as a croaky moan picked up. The noise wasn't outside. Goosebumps trickled my forearms, piecing together the impossible.

The sound was coming from Nehom's throat. That moment, as our lips held and I let go of her breast, I realized what was going on. Nehom was *her*. Her eyes were open as I stared at her twitching throat. It shook like a vibrator being jammed in the esophagus.

Nehom broke free, and her eyes teared up. She kept saying she was sorry, over and over, and that she thought she could control it for another few days. She rambled on so fast with her vibrating voice I couldn't make it all out. Nehom said she was fond of me, our similarities, jokes, and didn't want to feast on my flesh. She didn't think I'd kiss her. Emotional energies ignited the monster's will, leaving her powerless. She begged me to run. I told her I could help. She begged some more. I tried to reason with her, until she started shouting at me with the voice-rattling, "R-R-r-r-U-U-U-u-u-U-U-N-N-N! RUN D-A-A-a-a-a-A-M-M-N YOU!"

I dashed towards the bus's door. Nehom kept telling me to escape until her voice mutated into full-on croaky growl. Her face squished into a scowl as her eyes dabbed black—as if ink droplets fell inside. She pounced towards me, knocking the wig off her scalp. Her fingernails sprouted into claws as tiny white spikes pierced through her skin. They ran down her limbs and back, shredding her clothes and shoes to scraps. The toes elongated into rabbit-like feet, scraping against the metal floor.

My foot slipped on the muddy entrance to the bus, and my jaw biffed the floor. I bit my tongue in the process, causing blood to seep out of my mouth. Nehom's dangly naked form was on top of me in no time, her throat vibrating and the flesh swollen wide past her jaws. Her claws pierced my wrists as her toes coiled around my legs, overpowering me. All I could do was shout for help in gurgling sounds due to the blood in my mouth.

Her mouth opened slowly with her bottom jaw splitting in two, revealing a mouth full of razor-sharp spikes. All of them vibrated rapidly as a slithery black tentacle wormed its way from the depths of her esophagus towards me. The jaws continued to expand, stretching the skin outward until each half was the size of my body, ready to envelop my flesh.

For some reason, I shouted her name, "NEHOM!" thinking I could reason with her, spewing blood. Damn, I was right. It must have shot her back into reality for a split moment. Her pure-black eyes sucked back into her beautiful green irises. The jaw gradually constricted back into her mouth. The vibrating slowed down, the neck's flesh deflating, giving her the freedom to talk.

Nehom freed my wrists and legs, telling me to run again. She said she couldn't control it for much longer. The craving was too much. She was tired of being alone and apologized again while crawling off me, butt naked, saying she was a fool. She retreated into a corner, curling up into a ball as the gravelly groans escalated once more.

I wanted to do something, anything for her! But I knew she was *her*. I ran. My wrists were fucked, and my tongue kept bleeding down my chin, but I didn't stop running. My legs were wobbly, stomping into the mud, but I never looked back. I didn't stop. Never.

She didn't come back to school. The RCMP made another missing person's report. Apparently, they visited the acreage too, and it was an abandoned home—kind of like the bus. Maybe that's why she liked hanging out at the bus, because she gravitates towards the forgotten and abandoned . . . like her victims . . . or her, who drifts through life alone. I don't know. I'm still trying to make sense of it in some poetic summary.

About a month later, after my wrists and tongue healed, I did get a sign from her while I was walking home, about thirty days later. I had noticed a pattern with her attacks. A month goes by after she mutates into that thing and feeds.

There was this crow sitting on the fence, staring at me. Of course, I walked by it as it cawed. The animal flew towards me and sat on the fence again, cawing. I ignored it, and the crow did the same thing a third time. I stopped and stared at the bird.

A droplet of white entered the crow's eyes . . . ink . . . and it morphed into a human-like state. They turned white with toxic green irises—Nehom. The crow's throat vibrated briefly, and I could make out the bird's chirp, "Fi-eh-heah, Fi-eh-heah," as the eyes shifted back to all black and the animal flew away. Maybe I was reading into it, but it certainly sounded like "Fish Head" to me.

People in Fort Nelson stopped dying—or going missing—and life returned to normal. Curtis and Wesley believe my story. I mean, Nehom just stopped showing up to school, and I have scars on my wrists. Those are two clear signs that she was that monster the whole time. I still think about her, and she had a soft spot for me.

The three of us try to hypothesize what she was. A demon, shapeshifter, or maybe an alien. We can't come to any conclusion. Nothing in folk tales or mythology mentions anything close to her. Obviously, from what she's told me, she doesn't know what she is either. I wonder if "the monster" she mentioned is a part of her, or possesses her. Or it is two souls in one body? We dubbed her a Shaper as if we're explorers who discovered a new creature. We kind of did, but she's not an animal. She's another being like us, only not human. One thing is for certain, I'll never forget the name *Nehom*.

Awake from the observing state. (Turn to Page 47)

Your gut tells you to command the orb's direction, and you seize control of it through sheer willpower. The orb is obedient, and you move towards the right portal. The swirling purple and blue shapes of the portal consume your entire view. They stretch, expanding into infinity as the distorted blips of the strange office environment takes over everything you see.

The sense of you and the orb fade away. Your five senses are returning, except they aren't familiar at all. They clearly belong to someone else. You have no control of these new senses or this new body and are simply observing while experiencing everything that isn't you.

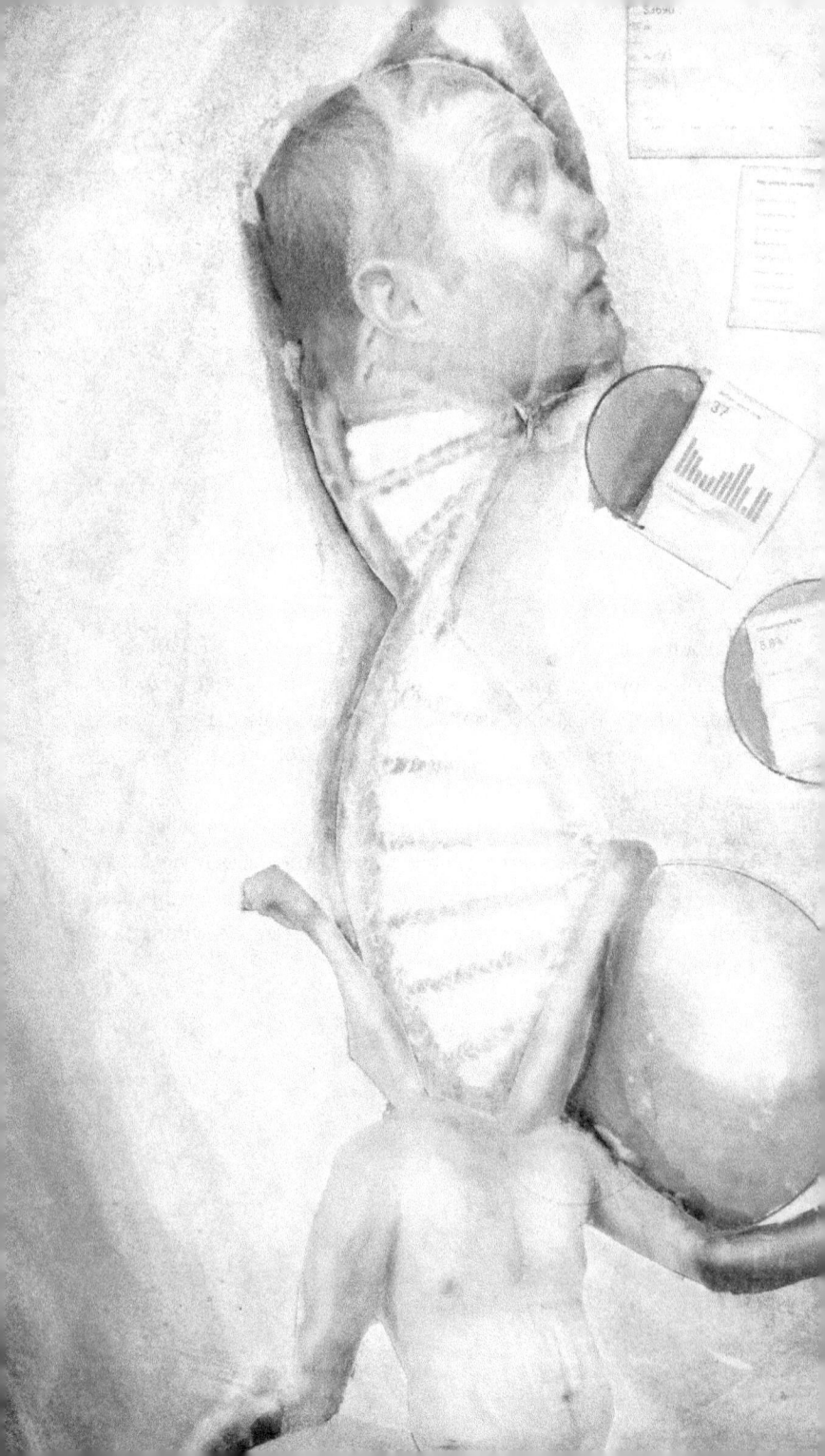

TAYLORISM

If you're reading this, it means you got out and you're no longer one of the gears. I'm running out of e-paper, and good luck finding *any* type of paper now that everything syncs into Manageficient Enterprises. Forgive me for glazing over details of how humanity entered the C.H.I.T. age. Protect this document, for it may be the last archive of the truth, not the fictionalized retelling.

Back in the before times, when we were still human, I was like any other white collared working class person. Each morning I grabbed my cup of coffee from the café across the street from the office, chatted it up with the barista, and headed to work. The boss didn't mind if I was late sometimes. The relaxed work schedule was a good model as long as the work was completed.

This policy lasted until the buyout all those years ago, making the creative work environment with lucid roles a thing of the past. Manageficient Enterprises had been in the process of absorbing design and engineering firms for years. They own practically every company in the industry in one way or another. They've cleverly positioned themselves as an umbrella corporation, working in the shadows and letting the smaller businesses appear independent. You see it all the time in big biz because it lets them branch out into other industries.

Manageficient Enterprises' primary philosophy is maximizing process potential. The C.E.O. has public opinions about *synthesizing workflows by capturing human capabilities*. It sounds like a bunch of techy corporate jargon if you ask me. But, I've seen the synthesized workflows put into place, and they are far more effective than loose work hours and lucid roles. After half a decade, Manageficient Enterprises championed the C.H.I.T. age. Conditioning Human Initiation of Transcendence. Yeah, now things shift from techy corporate buzzwords to a techy new-age cult.

Machines. Productivity Software. A.I. Milestone Tracking. Workflow Processes. Single-Task Functions. The list can go on. This corporate empire had revamped our office like they did the world with their brilliant hardware engineering and software integrations.

They patented unique energy solutions, allowing robots to run for weeks before recharging. This upped their mobility and high processing neural network deep learning. The damn machines were installed on every desk, in every car, store, phone, and computer. They existed both in the physical world and the digital when you signed onto any type of computer. Their purpose: tracking employee progress on a micro-milestone-level.

I once believed that working diligently gave you respect amongst your peers. Hard work would help you avoid trouble. Discipline got the job done more efficiently. I thought I had a strong work ethic until these machines analyzed every move we made during work. The "fitness cuffs" weren't just to track our personal steps and heart rate. Those sleep cycle reports went straight to head office, and I quickly learned that's how HR analyzed our efficiency.

The organic process of multitasking didn't fit within the automated reporting systems that fed the machines. If you didn't meet that *rewards-stretch-goals* or some quote *personal function improvement moonshot* un-quote wasn't satisfying, they would mark it on your quarterly A.I.-driven review. You could say bye-bye to a salary increase in a year's time. Well, that was when salaries were still needed.

The world experienced an improvement in productivity, cooperation, and peaceful trading since Manageficient Enterprises synthesized the working world with automated A.I. There was one problem, though. Humans. We weren't effective in this polished engine. We were unpredictable. Emotional. Animalistic, one would say. The health cuffs said so.

Now that I look back on it, the machines weren't terrible. They were a part of the initial company buyout, at the very beginning of the C.H.I.T. age. Manageficient Enterprises pivoted its focus towards the medical industry. They had begun consulting with spiritual leaders and doctors as the turn of the decade closed. See? Techy new-age cult. I didn't pay too much attention to their consulting at first, until the law got involved.

The government announced cooperation with Manageficient Enterprises and the spiritual leaders of the world. Together, the three sectors had discovered a way of improving human life. They said the flaws in us were obvious and could not be corrected by biological means. Violence, crime, and war were inevitable as we destroyed the planet with our gluttony and pride.

I remember watching the broadcast live as these spearheads revealed their grand solution: a pill. It wasn't any pill though. This one was loaded with a complex solution that was the start of our demise. Manageficient Enterprises said the solution was developed from their molecular biology department. Their team pulled in the best minds our planet had to offer. The corporation's tech far surpassed older gene editing tech like RNA and CRISPR.

It's amusing to recall my health cuff beeped at me to calm my heart after I heard the news since I was burning unneeded energy due to the fear of what was to come.

This pill, once ingested, would navigate through a body's bloodstream, squeeze into organs, identify and deploy needed repairs or chemical imbalances. They helped people's well-being, combated depression, and could even alter DNA strands, modifying our very makeup. This was all fine and dandy for futurists who welcomed the coming age when man transcended itself. Other people weren't when it was required by law.

Riots, protests, and rebellions formed. They didn't last long, or they went into hiding, because the triad of evil had the world in its grasp. The pills proved to need multiple intakes. It wasn't a catchall in one swallow. The body needed multiple doses of this solution to further complete the full human experience. The pills occurred twice a year, quarterly, then weekly. At this point the pills were re-purposed into direct injections—it's far easier to poke and instill than to pin someone, who screams for liberty, to the ground and make them swallow.

People's personalities changed. Their individuality started to dwindle. I began experiencing long periods of the day where I thought like everyone else, finishing people's sentences as they did mine. Traffic was a non-issue, as each person could read the other person's mind.

Our species had officially leaped into the C.H.I.T. age.

Those pills and injections weren't just to combat depression and make us good workers. Oh no. We were so wrong. A decade of tweaking our biological makeup continued, manipulating our brains, and changing the way we see the world. We became numb to our emotions as our thoughts focused on milestone tasks. Our limbs began to weaken. Some of us couldn't walk. The machines were pleased, and the health cuffs sent good reports to head office.

I didn't need to get my cup of coffee every morning. Hell, I didn't even see a point in leaving work to go home. None of us did. Money was pointless since the machines fed and cleaned us at our desks. No one enjoyed the simple recreational aspects of life. We had become worker ants, never questioning our function within the colony.

We're all connected to tubes which aid our bodily functions. Chewing and swallowing exhausts too much energy. I wonder why human workers were needed at all. Then again, the human mind doesn't work in ones and zeros—no matter how many artificial neural networks an A.I. has. The machines need our brains. That is my theory.

The pills and the tubes made us an organic extension of the machine. Living gears, if you will. Of course, organic material has its downfall. Some human genes didn't react well to the solution. They burned out quickly, spewing blood and leaking fluids out their orifices. The machines would simply install a new human at a desk to keep progress intact.

Losing a human didn't matter since no individual was unique. We all were the same and a worker could easily be replaced with a new one, like a new gear. We've been reduced to mechanical pieces, easily replaceable with no talent or edge.

Let me correct my analogy: we're cells a part of a larger organism. Single-function entities that assist in feeding the machine new ideas that it cannot do on its own. In a way, we're like the millions of microscopic creatures that make up the human body, unaware of the higher entity that we're a part of. I wonder what this half-organic and half-machine entity is capable of thinking.

I've reached the end of the page. Let me tell you, seeing the crystal-clear solar-panel towers from outside the glass-metropolis in the setting sun is a beautiful view. If only I could shield out the sun, those damn machines would power down. Knowing them, they have a backup energy solution.

I know they have a tracking device on me, and I can hear the humming of their drones. They're not far. They'll seize me, seal up my wounds from whence I cut myself free from those tubes, and they'll inject me with more solution of obedience. I'll be fused to my pod so I can carry out my one function for the higher entity. Who knew humanity would have assimilated into a single organism in the name of corporate efficiency?

Fragment: T

Awake from the observing state. (Turn to Page 67)

The state of observing ends, and you're sprung from the backseat and into the captain's chair. Every smell, touch, taste, sight, and sound return as your own. The white abyss with two portals is gone, and you're in the dark cavern beside the black ocean waves moving up and down.

The strange creature, Malpherities, is hovering beside you with his black and blue smoke dissipating to the ground. The tentacle-like hair floats effortlessly as the pure white eyes gaze at you.

The sudden shock of senses causes you to gasp, and you drop the orb. The black ball hits the ground with the golden glitters moving in every direction. It rolls a couple paces away until it hits a rock, leaving it stationary.

"What was that?" you ask.

"An observing state," Malpherities says in his haunting doubled voice.

"Observing? I felt, thought, and experienced everything. I was that person!"

"Haven't we been through this in another life?"

"You keep saying stuff like that. I have no idea."

"No, you don't."

"Who was that? Those people, the . . . the creature it—"

Malpherities cuts you off, saying, "Did you find any clues?"

"What? What the hell is going on? I just lived the life of some kid in British Columbia."

"You are useless."

"And what are you doing? Just standing here? And what is this orb?"

"Oh, I was with you. You just weren't paying attention because you're being a diva."

"Diva? Fuck you! I felt my wrists get punctured!"

"You would. That's what observing does. You live a full life belonging to another."

"Why would you chuck that orb into me? I don't want to live through that."

"We need the fragments. We need to reassemble them in their right form to break the loop. Did you see any of these fragments in the observation?"

"I don't even know what I am looking for."

A tidal wave from the black ocean soars towards the entrance, splashing against the rocks and stalactites. The black droplets splatter everywhere. One of them lands on your back hand. It has an incredible oil-like texture.

"Don't get that in your eye."

"Why not?"

"The orb is made of the same elements. The liquid will take you to new observation and witness anyone's life from any point in time."

"As I just did? Witnessing someone's life?"

"Yes, which is why you felt like you were in the shotgun seat and not in control of what you experienced. Too much of the liquid will transport you entirely from here and into the new life forever."

"I don't want that!"

"Hmm, yes. I must manage my own expectations of you, Nameless One. I forget you are mortal and handle the observations with shock and fear because you are so stuck in your own body. It's arrogant, really. You also don't handle crossing realms well, passing from the mortal realm to here."

"And where is here?"

"The Midway. It serves as a base for my kind, the ghouls, to break space-time and enter different worlds."

"To find these fragments?"

"Ah, good guess. Fragments only matter now. Before, we used it to feed on death. Look, I'd love to give you a history lesson and everything. I truly would. This all feels bizarrely familiar to me. I'll give you a summary to get your head in the game. The vortex just below the rip in the sky is known as Death's Vortex. It is the resting bed for all souls."

"This Midway, is it the afterlife?"

"In a sense, from your perspective, yes."

"Feeding on death, like the Grim Reaper?"

Malpherities groans. "The parallels are uncanny. Now, you probably saw a couple of my colleagues phasing in and out of existence back up in the cavern. Unfortunately, the great rip in the sky is destroying all of reality. That includes the Midway, Dega'Mostikas's Triangle, or Hell if you like to call it, the Heavenly Kingdoms, the mortal realm that you are from, and every other realm in existence. This includes Death's Vortex, meaning every soul that ever lived will cease to be."

"And there are these fragments in these other people's lives? From this orb?"

"Yes."

"And I have to put them in order?"

"Yes. It's quite simple, really. Maybe you'll get your memory back then too."

Malpherities's words dawn on you; you really don't recall anything about yourself. Your name, where you were beyond the grocery store, your parents, all of it is gone. You remember the old man, the NUT GRAPE Chewz box, the cartoon Malpherities, but nothing significant. How can that be?

You want to say something or scream. Before you can, thundering cracks come from above, causing the entire cavern to shake. A massive stalactite snaps at its base and descends upon you and Malpherities. The ghoul snags the orb, grabbing you with him, and pushes you clear of the danger as the giant rock collides with the ground, shattering into hundreds of pieces.

Dust flies everywhere while Malpherities's shaking claws place the orb in your hand. He says, "Just like before. Now, Nameless One, hurry."

"What clues are we looking for to stop the rip?" you ask while the orb begins to fuse with your melting flesh. The humming energy from the object surges through your veins as your fingers and arms become goo, wrapping around the sphere.

Malpherities and the cavern bloom into bright white as he says, "The rip has locked us in a time loop as it continues to expand, engulfing everything."

"We're in a loop?" you ask. It's the last thing you can say as the entire cavern dissipates to pure white. Two portals appear in the open. You and the orb meld into one and are sucked into the portals. Stormy clouds form around the edges of each one, separating the two portals and letting you glimpse into the worlds they offer.

Malpherities's voice is distant as he says, "Break the loop. We will find the clues."

You see a metropolis city on the left side, flashes of a gym, a handgun, and a nail. The visuals blend into the Midway, and you see Malpherities. He forces the orb into your hand. The visual washes back into the city before you can see anymore. The second portal showcases a dark warehouse at night, another handgun, and the man with the bloody nose directly under a lamplight.

The gravitational force pulls you to the portal on the left with the gym. You can still control this orb, dictating where you will go.

MAKE ONE OF TWO CHOICES:

Navigate to the left portal with the metropolis. (Turn to Page 53)

Turn to the right portal and enter the warehouse. (Turn to Page 59)

WORK OUT

Always exercise . . . every day, every . . . single . . . day. I never stop. If I did, well, things would start to get ugly. I've spent too much time trying to pull myself out of the gutter, and there's no way I am going back in that dirt. I lift, cardio, and repeat. My old friends say the ridged routine has made me dull, or I can't ever loosen up. Yeah, well, too bad, bro. This is the new me. Guess we'll go our separate paths.

I take selfies, so what? The engagement I get online is crazy. Not to get like, egotistical (because my life coach says it's a toxic path for the heart and mind), but it's a real motivation booster seeing those numbers go up from all the gals. Maybe I can be a life coach one day too. My followers get what I am trying to do, not like my old pals. My friends, or ex-friends I should say, and I were into some serious shit. Partying was a regular thing. Then the drugs came in. Eventually, we got roped into selling the goods. You need money to keep partying, and what's a quick way to get cash? You sell the drugs. Man, we knew that right away after watching our own pockets burn before our very eyes. Long story short, I got out, they didn't. It's sad seeing them wither away.

About a year went by. I thought they wrote me out of their lives, but one found me. When an addict needs their goods, it turns out they'll try to leech off anyone, no matter how far back or removed they are. It was Tweaky-Trav, or Travis rather. I try not to use our old nicknames for each other. It's degrading.

Anyways, Travis was standing outside of the CrossFit gym just off 124th Street there. I get there pretty early, so I didn't expect to see anyone other than the pro bros pumping. Travis was unrecognizable, bony, tattered clothing and all. He was rubbing his arms excessively with his hood up. If he didn't call me by my nickname 'Roadkill' (long story on that), I would have walked right past him in the parking lot. Roadkill. What a name.

Anyways, the sight of my old party bud was upsetting, but I stuck to my guns and asked him what he wanted. The man was pathetic. I still can't believe I used to be like him. Travis started talking, saying he got mixed up with the Crystal Moths. I heard about that gang on the news, after a big scandal about a corrupt sergeant and some vigilante who went by hashtag YEGman. It was short-lived, minus the heat the police took. Social media is funny that way. Everyone loves sensationalizing something one moment, and then they forget about it the next.

I don't. I remember the Crystal Moths from that horrific video that girl took with the sergeant and hashtag YEGman. That video was violent, proving the Crystal Moths weren't to be messed with. Unfortunately, it looked like old Tweaky-Trav got himself involved with these guys. Sorry, *Travis*, said that he was needing my help with distributing some of the drugs he had. If he didn't get rid of them this week, he would have to pay for them all now. And if that didn't happen, well, you should look up the Crystal Moths' return policy.

Man, my heart is too big. I wish my brain were bigger. As mad as I was, I chose to help Travis. We've been through hell and back together. He's a moron, but I couldn't just leave him to get gutted by these guys. The Crystal Moths don't mess around. They're not only in Edmonton. These guys are all over, which meant Travis was dead meat even if he skipped town.

Look, it's only been about a year since I've switched my life around. I still have some contacts from when I used to deal. The other guys never had these connections. This would be a quick job. Roadkill was back in the business. You should have seen Travis's face when I told him I'd help him out. He gave me a bag full of this shit right there and then. I had to stuff it in my gym bag quickly so no one saw it. We'd meet up in a couple of days. Tweaky-Trav, relieved, booked it after.

All day, my brain kept asking me, *"What the hell you doin', man?"* My coach would be so pissed. I couldn't even get a good workout in. My mind was too distracted, being filled with negative thoughts of doubt and self-hate. Still, I had to help Travis.

I called up a few of my old contacts, and they hooked me up to their distributors. I managed to get rid of the goods down the chain of addicts and sellers. Boom, job done. There's a thrill to holding a fat stack of cash after the end of a day. Tweaky-Trav sucked at this shit.

Travis and I met up a couple of days later. He seemed nervous, even though I told him the job was done. Hell, he looked like he saw a ghost, even after I gave him the cash. He was fidgeting with his bottom lip and wouldn't say anything. He wouldn't leave either. I finally asked the guy what was up. Travis said there's more to sell.

I could have decked the prick right there and then. After a long day of working out, you have all that adrenaline, making the urge powerful. I closed my eyes, breathed through my nose as my life coach taught me, and centered myself. This was a red flag, being a slippery slope that I didn't want to go down. Travis was using me as his enabler. It took every fibre of my being to tell my old pal that I couldn't this time.

My skin went ice cold and my stomach pushed itself up into my throat. Travis's mouth dropped, eyes not blinking, his skin whiter than paper. It was like I sentenced him to death. He started to plea. I told him I couldn't. He snagged my tank-top, begging me. The guy was down on his knees! I wanted to say yes so badly, but I couldn't this time. I swatted him off, throwing him to the floor. He was as shocked as I. All I could do was storm off and not look back. I heard him cry out to me, something about turning him into roadkill. I don't know. I just kept running.

Travis didn't come back. That week I was so focused on my workouts. I needed to keep myself distracted from thinking about what I had done to my old pal. We had gone through thick-and-thin over the years until I went to rehab and got my life in order. I still can't believe I left him.

He showed up on the news not long after. I was watching it on my TV, having my post-workout evening shake. They had Travis's mugshot on the screen while the whole report focused on the Crystal Moths. Even the title was demeaning: *CRYSTAL MOTHS LEAVE SIGN TO CORRUPT POLICE ON DEAD MAN*.

That's all they saw Travis as, *a dead man sign*. This had nothing to do with the cops. It was a deal gone bad. Gotta love the news, eh? The report switched to a graphic photo of Travis's body at the crime scene. A moth was nailed into his forehead. It's so belittling. I felt sick and could barely finish downing my shake. He died because of me. What kind of friend was I? If I had only . . . no. I can't think that way.

My coach worked with me on my mindset to get out of that life, and I can't run these thoughts through my head. That's how my old pals and I stuck together. We manipulated each other into thinking we needed a brotherhood to survive. It's toxic codependency. Still, I can't get it out of my mind. Tweaky-Trav, sorry, *Travis*, is gone because of me. The other guys reached out. Some of them are pissed. Others are trying to get me to deal again. They're persistent. They call me a murderer—which is one of the kinder insults.

The gym noticed, and we got the cops to kick them out of the parking lot. They let me know they're around. Whether it's a note on my car or a phone call, I ignore them as best as I can. Their little jabs are constant reminders of what happened to Travis. It's my fault, and I need to live with that. So, I keep working out. The repetition clears my head: exercise, every . . . single . . . day.

Awake from the observing state. (Turn to Page 57)

The man with the nail in his head morphs, shrinks and grows. The skin twists and turns while the concrete washes away.

"The Midway is collapsing," Malpherities says. His voice is distant and echoes. "Quickly, activate the portal!"

Déjà vu . . .

You have no time to think about the familiar sentence that the ghoul speaks as all senses return to you. The morphing of visuals stabilizes and becomes solid objects. The cavern is here, Malpherities is beside you holding the orb, and you can't help but think that you've been here before.

It angers you and you want it all to go away. You're not convinced this is happening. There's not a chance!

Finish your thought. (Turn to Page 23)

ASH

I hate dealing . . . I've been doing this since I was a little brat, and it's way more work than the payoff. Every day we put our lives on the line in hopes to get a bump up the ranks and a sweet pay increase. I don't have many options. In this new 'organization,' I've gotten the hint that the bosses aren't gonna give us anything more substantial. We have a role to fill, and they aren't interested in sharing the profits. Bosses need workers, and druggies need the product, and the 'company's' pocket gets thicker.

Let me tell you, when a new shipment comes in, it's time to hustle. This particular shipment came in at around, like, two A.M.—fairly common. We usually don't know what day or the time. Your phone will buzz, and you better stop whatever the hell you're doing and get down there to get your piece of the goods. If you don't, tough shit. The rest of the street-crew will take it and sell it. At times, they'll despise you for it too. Other times they're glad to take the cash. It depends on the drug, the amount, and everyone's personal bills. The game is: sell the drugs fast so the bosses don't expect you to front the cash. If you don't move the product, or pay for what isn't sold, say your goodbyes to your loved ones.

I was half-tanked this specific evening, playing pool. My girl came and visited me at my crib, staying the night. She has no idea what I do. I like to keep it that way, way less headaches. Still, when you get a phone call at two A.M. after a drunken mattress tangle, she starts to raise an eyebrow. Maybe I'll tell'r one day so she stops thinking I got a side piece.

So, I sobered up, got dressed, remembering to tie on the white rag on my arm—bosses get pissed if we don't show loyalty. What kind of name is Crystal Moths, anyways? The rag symbolizes a moth, I think. Whatever, it doesn't matter. They're the biggest players in the game and always have work, so I show up with the stupid rag. Most people would—and have—killed to be a member of the Crystal Moths. I don't ever want to lose my gig, no matter how much I bitch about it.

The drive over wasn't long, and yes, I was still sobering up. Even though Toronto never sleeps, you can get to the docks from North York fast if you know the roads' ins and outs. I'm no fool and parked my car a few blocks away. I suppose if a police bust occurred, I'd be fucked. If I had the car closer, they would get the plate. That's a minor detail. Eventually, I got to the docks to meet the rest of the Crystal Moths. Our direct boss, a couple of goons, and a higher-up that haven't seen in a long time stood with six street crew members. I was the last to arrive, it seemed, just on time too.

All of them had some representation of white clothing. Shirts, bandanas, suits, you name it. This higher-up, his name is Mastema, which I highly doubt is his real name. Seriously, think about what kind of name that is. I grew up in a hardcore religious family and remember a thing or two. If you didn't, look it up.

I know the street crew pretty well. We're all hungry to feast ourselves onto whatever product there is. The boss has been stingy on the smack and coke, and that stuff sells for top buck. I know enough junkies who are dying to get their fix. Well, that all changed after this night.

Junk and lines aren't the only product on the market. Plus, this was just another job, another paycheck to me. Everyone has bills, and you have to fend for yourself. Not to mention I got to pay for my kid's child support. Don't get me started on his mom. Whatever she likes to say, my work is no different than some corporate sleaze climbing their way up to the top, squishing everyone they can. I'm just squishing junkies.

Our boss was quiet, her hands cupped together, face still as stone. Like Mastema, she was wearing a full white blazer. What makes this pickup more interesting is that Mastema was there. I think the last time I saw the guy was when he recruited me. The Crystal Moths are stingy with who they hire, especially after that incident in Edmonton. It involved some hotshot vigilante and the exposure of our plugs in the police. Since then, Mastema personally screens everyone who is involved with the business.

Mastema kept his eye on all of us. He always looks sharp, dressing in expensive suits, his long hair neatly combed and trimmed. His skin is so pasty, and his eyes are bright, they almost look white. Hell, the guy looks like a vampire if you ask me. I'd never say that to his face. There are stories of him gutting people that say the wrong thing. Not that I have witnessed it, but I prefer not to find out.

He looked tense, fiddling with his golden rings, pacing back and forth. This isn't like him at all. There's no point in saying anything because no one talks until a boss talks. I would have loved a smoke too, ask the other street dealers how they were doing. We're semi-close. I keep them at an arm's reach, with my kid and all. Small chat wasn't on the plate that evening.

The warehouse doors were slightly open, where two other guys came out, wearing white dress shirts and holding crates. It must be from overseas or something. The two Crystal Moths dropped the wooden boxes in front of Mastema and took their place with the other goons. One of them was holding a crowbar. Mastema stopped in front of the crates.

"We have something new," he said in that creepy velvety voice he has.

His words gripped my attention, and I forgot about the smoke.

"In these two boxes, we have a particular product that is going to revolutionize our business."

A few of us exchanged glances, having no idea what the boss-man was getting at. I looked at our direct superior, whose gaze was on Mastema. He nodded at the man with the crowbar. The guy leaned onto a box and cracked it open, handing Mastema a black plastic vacuum-sealed bag.

"This," Mastema said. "Is the future. No one else has their hands on this product, except for us."

"What is it?" a street-crew gal—Sierra is her name—asked. Way bolder than I am, as I stayed silent during this whole thing.

Mastema casually chucked the bag at her. "Crack it open and pass it to your colleagues. Understand that because we have exclusive access no one anywhere has tried it before. You will need to persuade our clients. Lace it. Taste it with them. Use any method you prefer, as long as you move it."

Sierra peeled the bag open, pulling out a palm-sized charcoal diamond chip. She passed the bag around as each street-crew member grabbed a piece. It was my turn, taking out one of these new drugs. The piece I grabbed was brittle along the edges, like it was about to flake off, but it had a leathery texture in the centre, like a leaf losing moisture or something. This was organic for sure.

"It's highly addictive, so be careful. However, I encourage you to familiarize yourself with our new product."

"What's it do?" Sierra asked.

A devilish grin painted on Mastema's pale face. "It makes a Frisco Speedball look like child's play."

Silence. We were all staring at these strange diamond-shaped drugs. I had never seen anything like it. The street-crew—including myself—had so many questions about it, but most of us were too afraid to ask. I heard of Frisco Speedballs before. I don't know if the others had.

"Some of you are so young," Mastema sighed. It was a weird thing to say because the guy looks no older than me. But the way he talks, though . . . it's like he's had past lives or something. I'm not spiritual anymore, but I'm just sayin'.

"Ever shoot up a concoction of cocaine and heroin as you're about to peak on a tab of LSD?" Mastema asked.

Nothing from the crew.

"It's an exultant ride," he said.

You have to be really ballsy or fucked-up to want to do that. I haven't, despite my background—hence the child support—and there was no way in hell I was going to try this . . . this . . .

"Ash," Mastema said. "It's got the best of all and less of the downs. More cohesive, more addicting, and less burnout. We don't know the long-term effects yet, but that's why we're selling, isn't it? You grind it until it is a fine powder, self-explanatory. Snort it, smoke it, lick it, or whichever creative method works for you. The effects will vary." Mastema grabbed another plastic bag and raised it. "This is a historic moment, and you have the honour of being a part of it."

One of the street-crews, Bari, sniffed the ash he held. It had no odor. "Where does it come from?"

"Not for you to know," Mastema said.

"People are gonna ask, whadda we tell'em?" Bari asked.

"Get creative. I don't care," Mastema said.

After that, we chatted about prices and split the drugs within two crates. We were pioneers embarking on something no one has heard of. It was the last time I laid eyes on Mastema too. I'm sure he's off handling the business, distributing this stuff to other crew members across North America.

As you know, this ash stuff is taking the world by storm, and no one knows where it comes from. I still don't know where they got it from or what the hell it is. Since that night, I just sell it. No way have I tried it. I'm clean now. My kid doesn't need a deadbeat father. Most of the time, I grind it up to disguise it, which makes it just look like some charcoal or . . . ash.

"Okay Chen, how much does it go for?" the silvery voice spoke.

I say, "Well, a gram can be two-fifty. It depends on supply, and where the cops are at." My voice reverbs in the darkness. The moment holds. "Look, I told you names, everything, we change our meetup spot every time."

The elegant hand slides the Glock off the splintered table and back into the dark, away from the open black bag. I can barely see the gal sitting behind the beaming light. Christ, the brightness is annoying, and these zap straps, she's a real piece of work. Who ties them this tight? A droplet of blood falls from my nose and onto the unfinished table, soaking into it—a reminder of when she hit me in the face and put me here.

She reaches for the black bag, exposing her pasty skin and the glimpses of her blonde hair. I still can't see her damn face due to that light. The gal snags one of the diamonds and inspects it.

"You said organic?" she asks. The ash is fresh enough that she can spin the diamond between her thumb and index finger.

"Yeah," I say.

"A leaf?"

"Well, I don't know. It sure as hell isn't made in a lab."

"It's a scale," she says.

"A scale? Like a reptile?"

"Yes, dumb shit. You can have them as pets. They are in the wild?"

Belittling me . . . she thinks I'm a joke. I'm not. I'm a simple man because I choose to be for my kid. I say, "Okay, lady, why hasn't the news said anything?"

Her full coral lips smirk under the sharply cast shadow. She pulls on her hair in the dark, dragging the wig off. The real, darker, hair is a short sweaty mess as she drops the wig onto her lap and pushes the chain-linked light out of the way. Now I can see her whole face. A young gal, man, she can't be much older than my baby sister. Mid-twenties. Her cold eyes and confidence say otherwise, like she's seen shit.

She speaks, "The news knows, but they're all part of the game. Everyone is fabricating this bullshit fairy tale we live in. Give it time, and some leaks will find their way on the web."

I brush her words aside and ask, "You're clearly not a cop. What do you want?"

She leans forward, and I see a nasty bullet scar on her chest, under that tank top. "You street dealers have no idea how deep the Crystal Moths run."

Scar . . . independent studies. Mid-twenties, pasty gal. Yeah. No fuckin' way. . . "Hey," I say without thinking, eyes locked on the scar. "You're that girl, aren't you?"

The gal sits back, letting go of the light. It swings like a pendulum, casting sharp contrasts on her now stone-cold face.

"Yeah," I say, now certain in my forthcoming claim. "You exposed the cops out west with the video. The Crystal Moth bust in Edmonton with that hashtag YEGman. The reporter kid with that website everyone goes to . . . Lola."

The gal chucks a burner phone on the table, standing up, and clicks the light off. "Cops are on their way," she says, walking away.

Her boots echo in the open space as I keep shouting, "Hey! hey!" hoping she'll come back. That bitch! She doesn't listen. Eventually, a door shuts, and I'm left alone in the dark to fantasize all the possible ways that Mastema is going to kill me.

Fragment: U

<u>Awake from the observing state.</u> (Turn to Page 89)

The stale stench of industrial machinery leaves your nose. The bright sky with solar panel-covered skyscrapers is gone. All senses, the real ones, switch on instantly, throwing you from the passenger seat of another's life and into the captain's chair of your own. The strange futuristic world is gone, the orb rests in your hand, and you're standing in the cavern while the bright white space dissolves. You twitch unexpectedly, dropping the orb, and it rolls a couple feet from you, stopping by a rock. The tidal waves from the black ocean splash against the cavern entrance as another thundering boom erupts in the sky.

Malpherities is here, hovering in the air with his tentacle-like hair floating effortlessly. His arms fold with the muscles tightening. He must be impatient.

"Well? Did you find any clues to break the loop? I may have seen one, but I can't tell." Malpherities asks in his doubled voice.

"I . . . maybe? What the hell was that?" you ask.

"You sure love to ask questions. But you must work with me, did you notice anything? Fragments of matter, clues of any kind? You can see more than me, think!"

"I don't understand. What did that orb do?"

"It lets you enter an observation state. You experienced another person's life and every sense they have to offer."

"Right, I got that, but it was so foreign. Is that the future?"

"Yes, but we don't have to get into the giant history of the mankind, do we? It gets old talking about it over and over."

You point at the orb. "That thing is a time-travelling machine?"

"Right . . . Your memory is worse than mine. Damn mortals and their souls. If only you held onto every petty thing the flesh holds dearly, we wouldn't have to go through this all the time."

"The future is bleak! Why would you throw that orb into me?"

"Look, we've been through this in a whole other life, Nameless One."

"What is going on?"

Malpherities groans. "You become such a bore. Don't worry. It will all make sense once we can reassemble the fragments in the right order. Then, we'll finally break this wretched loop. Did you see any of these clues or fragments in the observation? I may have, but it's hard to tell. The orb and I don't meld well with me being linked to Death's Vortex."

"You have to slow down. This is way too out there. Where is here, this time loop?"

"We are in the Midway, which acts as a superhighway for my kind, the ghouls. We use it to travel to different times and realms to feast upon the dead. It gives us life force and allows us to maintain balance for Death's Vortex."

"Which is?"

"Well, it's the other ghouls and me. You see, Death's Vortex is a hive mind, with projections of itself acting as unique individuals. Meaning we each have our own personality. I'm sure you saw a couple of my colleagues being phased in and out of existence as we came down to this cavern."

"So, you're death?"

"You really are a creature of habit, but no. We are more like observers, feeding our life force and ensuring the universe's death rate remains in balance with life and cycles through. Souls can be a tricky currency." Malpherities pauses. "Things are not well, as you can see with the giant rip and the sky. We're stuck in this time loop within the Midway, but that rip is outside the time bubble and is expanding. Eventually, it will eradicate everything in existence. The afterlife, the Midway, the mortal realm which is your home, and even Death's Vortex."

"Then what will happen?"

"Nothing will be. And I would rather not experience that. I've been around for a very long time and happen to enjoy my existence. I'm sure you do too, whatever it includes. I'm guessing you have no memory of who you are?"

You think about his question momentarily, trying to recall any memory. Where you grew up, your first job, if you can drive, all of it is gone. It shocks you, and you rub your head, trying to think as hard as you can, but nothing comes to you. "No. I really can't remember. I—" you feel blood rush into your face and arms. It's a mix of anger and fear. You're about the scream until Malpherities speaks.

"Exactly. This has happened to you before, Nameless One, in a more simplified format. Don't get emotional on me now. We must find fragments which can help us break the loop and stop the rip in the sky."

Malpherities picks the orb up with both claws. Upon touch, his arms start shaking due to its energy. He hands it over to you, but you're hesitant to accept. The first time Malpherities slammed the orb into your hands, your fingers fused to the object and your entire body melted, becoming one with this sphere as you hovered towards two portals in a white abyss.

Following that, you experienced a horrifying futuristic world and felt every pain that the poor soul went through. Do you really want to go through that again? Malpherities certainly could elaborate more on what is happening here.

Another great crack erupts from above, causing the entire cavern to shake. One of the stalactites on the ceiling cracks, tearing free, and descends directly above you. Malpherities pushes you out of the way as the rocks slam into the ground, shattering into hundreds of pieces with dust flying every which way.

Malpherities uses both of his claws, shoving the orb towards you. "We don't have time for this!"

MAKE ONE OF TWO CHOICES:

Take the orb. (Turn to Page 71)

Swat Malpherities's claw. (Turn to Page 87)

You take the orb, locking gazes with Malpherities's pure white eyes as the powerful energy buzzes from your fingertips.

"I'll be with you. We'll look for the pieces," Malpherities says.

The skin along your fingers melts, coating the orb as your consciousness is sucked into the black sphere with golden glitters. The cavern fades into a blinding white light. You and the orb are one again. Malpherities is gone, the fallen rocks are no more, and the black ocean ceases to be.

Two black holes appear from nothingness with distorted swirls, expanding outward as coloured clouds surround the outer rims. The portals continue to expand until they take up your entire peripheral view, and you are presented with two new observations to witness.

As before, you can direct this orb, dictating where you will witness next. The right portal shows a church, with torches and men in armour. You can hear groans coming from the dark basement stairwell. The portal on the left has a small town with distant screams that are inaudible. The roads are empty.

The orb is being pulled forward, equally sucked in by both portals. You can guide it, though, and determine which observation you will witness.

MAKE ONE OF TWO CHOICES:

Steer the orb to the right portal. (Turn to Page 79)

Direct the orb to the left. (Turn to Page 73)

I LOVE YOU

"I love you" is supposed to be a phrase you use for those you hold dear. Never did anyone think that those three words would become the kiss of death. The amusing thing is a lot of people do not believe in the supernatural. They're such naïve simpleton. Some of us do know the truth. I am also relatively efficient in practicing the unnatural craft.

It's upsetting to think my former wife didn't believe. She couldn't 'see any proof' and that was as far as she toyed with the idea of otherworldly. Wouldn't she be surprised now? Not everything real can be seen with our naked eyes. Our vision can deceive us so easily, especially when we focus on the single sense. We have so many more! Smell, touch, hearing, and taste are equally important, letting us experience our world fully. Then, let's not forget about the lesser-known sixth sense—extrasensory perception.

Even then, people who believe question how effective it is. Human beings are limited in our abilities. Therefore, we must rely on trinkets and rituals which let us tune into the unearthly and harness powers that we cannot even fathom. It takes an awful lot of willpower to manifest and control something from the other side. I know this first-hand, as I tried to combat The Lover. Others have too. Christ, some of the world's most capable magic users have attempted to take control of the situation.

I could have learned so much from them if they weren't now dead. Just like anyone who encounters The Lover, she takes their soul. Everyone in the town can hear the haunting shrills of "I LOVE YOU" before she frees her victim from this world. I'm not sure what she does to them. Maybe she's harvesting souls to fill the void of her broken heart. Or perhaps she is merely eradicating people of their flesh tomb, making them ethereal like her. If she does, where are the others? We don't have a solid understanding of what she is—I mean, I have a better idea than most, but no one believes a warlock. Her presence has frightened the kingdom, and they have barricaded our town and have set up a patrol along every road, preventing anyone from entering or leaving. We are on our own.

Thankfully, most of us are farmers and can make food to last. Occasionally, several supply wagons ride into town with needed resources. Some elected townsmen stand at the barricaded roads, negotiating with the soldiers to bring us goods. We don't have any other choice. A riot would only end with the soldiers shooting us. We can't even send letters out. The kingdom doesn't want this being known to the rest of the world. Our best bet for survival is cooperating with the king's men and avoiding The Lover until they figure out what to do with us.

A portion of me wants to try and reason with her. Of all people in our town, I am the most capable. Then, I hear the shrilling "I LOVE YOU" as she takes a new victim, and the fear sinks in. I shudder, knowing that she has outdone the other great mystics. Then I think about what I know. No . . . I cannot. Fear keeps me alive and locked in my home.

I've seen her a few times. She appears as a sad woman in a nightgown. Her face is twisted inward into a knotty mess of flesh and anger. No one would ever know who she is. That poor soul is stuck between this world and the next. She is proof of undead, hovering up and down our crooked, potholed streets.

The latest sighting of The Lover was probably a couple of days ago, just before dusk. Truthfully, I've lost track of time, staying inside constantly in this bland house. My ill-fated wife's blue eyes may have kept me a little too entranced to ever notice the dullness of this place.

I remember watching from the window as the church bell rang. We use the bell to indicate when it is no longer safe to go outside because someone spotted The Lover. Her schedule is reasonably consistent, but on occasion, she has fabricated during the day.

Poor Ivan, our neighbour—my neighbour—was on his way home after picking up supplies. He was running wildly, panting with his legs flailing. Ivan was doing his damn best to be quiet while hurrying down the street. She had already spotted him, hovering atop the hill. All light in the sky turned dark, leaving us under blackness, darker than any night.

She was radiant, glowing blue and white. Those haunting eyeless sockets are something I will never forget, radiating a dark blue flame of fury. The pointy teeth stretch across her elongated mouth. I'm sure she uses them to feast on the souls once they have passed from this world.

My viewpoint was limited, peeking from the curtain. Just like everyone else in their homes, we watched poor Ivan run down the street. He was crying for help. What could we do? Physical objects go right through her, and no one else in this town practices demonology. I've dabbled in it, after The Lover, but alas it is not my specialty.

The shrilling words of "I LOVE YOU!" pierced from The Lover's open mouth. The voice projects from her throat, for her jaw does not move. The sound is too much to bear, and many of us cover our ears while she shouts. The Lover continued to scream over and over, "I LOVE YOU! I LOVE YOU!" All I can think of is my poor wife, who didn't believe my powers, crying, "I love you!" before I cast that fateful spell on her, binding her to the demon. Thus ended my attempts at demonology.

Ivan wasn't able to keep up his pace as The Lover closed in. I wanted to look away, but I had never seen her take a soul. My neighbour tumbled onto the brick road, dropping his groceries in the process. The Lover was only half a block away as the mysterious fog she brings surrounded the area. Her mouth closed, and she seemed innocent at this point. Simply a sad lady who wanted closure. Who can blame her? I felt sympathy for her only for a brief moment because, after, the fog surrounded Ivan. The Lover's jaws expanded like a snake—three times the size of her skull—as her mouth plummeted towards Ivan. His hand extended upward through the fog, begging for mercy, as she dove down onto him. Ivan's screams erupted as one more "I LOVE YOU!" boomed throughout the town.

I couldn't blink, watching the fog swirl around and around. One moment Ivan was there, begging for his life, and the next, he became the fog. I could hear his voice continue to scream for mercy. The voice changed as if he were underwater, bubbling and muffled. All the smoke pressed inwards to the single point where Ivan and The Lover once were. Then, it dissipated into nothingness.

That was it for poor Ivan. The sky returned to a familiar orange hue as the sun prepared to rest. Already, people were scurrying out of their homes to salvage whatever supplies Ivan left behind. Not I. I remained at the window, watching and wondering how many more souls The Lover would take before she was satisfied. Then, as always, an overwhelming wave of guilt rushes through me, knowing what I had done. The fear, the anger, and the helplessness. I'm sorry.

Awake from the observing state. (Turn to Page 89)

I LOVE YOU

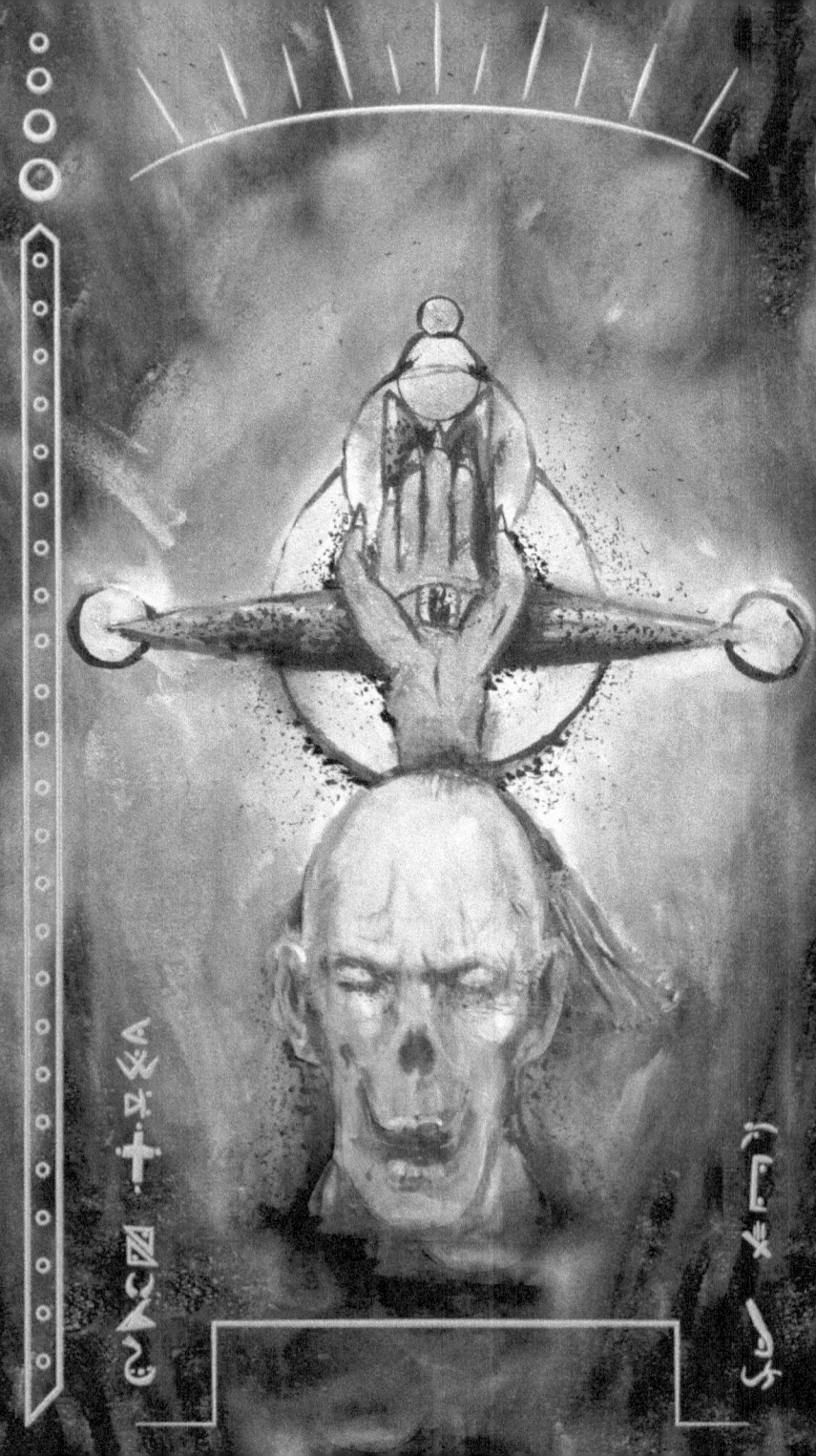

AUREATE RISE

My faith has never steered me dishonest as I obey the inner light that leads me. We all face trials of fire, testing our true nature. With guidance from above, we can walk through unscathed. Decades of focus are needed to harness the powers of the light. The Heavenly Kingdoms no longer bless mere mortals with their holy powers. Centuries ago, they once did, creating the Paladins of Zeal. A grave error, as man is incapable of handling such gifts while bound by sin.

For humans to obtain a fraction of a paladin's strength, we must earn it through vigorous determination and discipline. Of course, the words of power will never reach the feats of the former. Paladins matched the angels. A mortal corrupted by sin with tainted powers of light is deadly. Thus, it be their eradication. True holy men burned their false teachings and brought the focus on the worship of the true God. A single paladin remains alive and has proven themselves in the new Kingdom of Zingalg. They do not fight our faith in God nor enforce their old ways. This paladin simply serves. Our new religious hierarchy controls the ability a priest can have, preventing another rise from the Paladins of Zeal. We vow silence with our words of power unless granted by a higher priest to speak, demonstrating the light.

Not all remains perfect in our faith in God. I pray. My brothers of faith believe in the true God. I . . . Our sect did not stray from the truth. Others have, altering the words written of the Son, foolishly forming unholy cults. No . . . we stayed faithful to the Scriptures, never bending to the temptations of evil. I pray . . .

High Priestess Imperia feeds our holy crusades not in the form of travel on steed but in the uncharted realms of our own psyches. Our mind, body, and spirit are intertwined into a unified harmony forming the holy triangle—naturally nearing the holism of the Father, the Son, and the Holy Spirit reflected in his mighty creations. Perfectionism is all we can expect from our Lord. I pray. . .

The High Priestess had never drifted us afar. The creation of the Aureate Rise was forged from her vision granted to her by God Himself. Need I reflect upon it again? She witnessed extraordinary heights for our spiritual intelligence if we learned to unify our three elements. Her blessed vision showed blackness all around . . . with a dim golden light guiding her closer to the truth, growing the more reinforced her faith was, until a glowing golden cross appeared with a hand in the centre and a thumb on each side—totalling six fingers—and an eye in the centre of the hand.

Her vision has led us to forge the Aureate Rise taking refuge in Mount Kuzuchi, below its snowy peaks, where we have locked ourselves inside an old forgotten chapel. Deep isolation is required to venture into one's psyche and bridge the gap between the three elements. High Priestess Imperia has ordered us to descend to the basement, locking us down there. In dark solitude, we can champion our unity without the distraction of sin. Our determination is enforced by the Aureate Rise Shield, guarding the locked door to the surface.

The High Priestess remains above, focusing on ancient literature and codices that the Aureate Rise Shield crusade for, hoping to gain more insight into the chasms of our souls. The Shield are no priests. They are clerics and are not disciplined in the light. My brothers and I report the discoveries we make about the connection of the mind, body, and spirit, speaking through the cracks of the locked stone door to the Shield, then they report to High Priestess Imperia.

The mind is a terrible place. I pray. These thoughts—or trials—are purely my own. I once wished that it was evil entering my mind, tempting me . . . Now, I am not so sure. I pray . . . Perhaps the last letter I received from my old colleague, Dr. Alsroc, have fractured the barriers I have built around my fortitude. His message describes attempting to solve a brain disease known as Mental Damnation. This disease pierces the mind and sends them to Hell, where the unfortunate is ultimately consumed by the fallen souls, burning for eternity.

I wish to dismiss Dr. Alsroc's letter! Yet, the words have raised concern that I cannot shun. The disease victims are depicted as crossing from our world and into the afterlife during their dreams, returning the next day with tainted visions of the unholy. Eerily enough, the Aureate Rise and our High Priestess are guiding us through the depths of our own mental states. We eat next to nothing, we sleep little, and pray for days on end. I feel weak—so hungry . . . thirsty. The trials . . . how many years have gone by? We have no muscles, our eyes are sensitive to light. Our hair has grown far past churchly formality.

I ponder for hours, prayer after prayer, attempting to unravel what lies deep within myself. These heights that the High Priestess described seem to be a fool's dream. Are these visions from God? Or has she turned mad, bending to darkness, and enslaving us—and for what? This I do not know, and so I ponder. Are these more temptations of evil? Is this my own jealousy of what the High Priestess has created? There's reason to feel such ways. She's the higher rank, commanding us, and capable of far greater words of power than I. She's not down here in the darkness.

Dr. Alsroc's note has infected my mind, leaving me with uncertainty. I have my doubts about it merely being a brain disease. He described his last patient, Frenan Soulstone, as having similarities hauntingly foretold in an ancient book in High Priestess Imperia's study. Yes, I confess my actions of witnessing the surface, proving me disloyal to the Aureate Rise's mission. I pray . . . I ponder.

I believed the holy light unlocked the basement door, as at the time I could not fathom any other reasoning for why it opened. None of my brethren noticed who were entranced in deep meditation. Atop of the stone stairwell, I could hear my name being called . . . *Greth . . . Greth, come to the light.* Perhaps it was a trial of fire that I ignored. Regardless, I believed it to be the holy light and crept up to the surface of the chapel. Fresh air filled my lungs, and the torchlights nearly blinded me.

The light led me straight to High Priestess Imperia's study, where she was not present—possibly another miracle. My hand ran across the long black marble table. Papers scattered its surface. The first I noted were historical documents, stained with blood—of whose, I am uncertain—that accused the church of shifting to false prophets, straying humanity from the truth of the Creator—renamed to the one true God. The author claimed that the Paladins of Zeal knew the way before the Holy Book was rewritten.

These archived documents accurately describe what all holy men fear in the back of their minds as their mouths remained silent. I am victim of this. The truth is not worth the loss of life, and God will guide his loyal followers to salvation. Seeing these archive notes with the naked eye changes this perspective. All I could think about was exposing High Priestess Imperia to the church.

Further on the table were more papers that eventually took me to the far end where a large codex rested. It was the size of a small child. This massive tomb was open, letting me see the black pages and golden ink. These pages were so black that all light ceases to reflect on them. It was impossible to tell where a page ended and another began. I could touch it and move the page, feeling an unholy power channel into my veins.

The book itself is bound by a stone exterior, and I can only imagine the codex's weight. If it weren't for the papers around this monolith, I would not know its name nor be able to read the contents inside. They were the High Priestess's notes, attempting to transcribe the ancient language. On the top sheet of her papers were the words: The Book of Consulo.

The words in this codex are most unsettling. Its language is of unknown origin. With the transcription notes, I read some of the texts found within the pages. The Book of Consulo claims to have the power to undo all creationism—a great reset, one might say. In the wrong hands, and a small sliver of this book's knowledge, it can be used for necromancy. If a mortal dies, it can revert it—an unholy monstrosity.

The Book of Consulo and Dr. Alsroc's letter have crossover phrases that troubled me to my core. This Mental Damnation speaks of an afterlife, a place known as Dreadweave Pass, where the dead have been reanimated to serve a fallen god. Not the holy God, some other evil god known as the Weaver, who is locked in a prison within this realm. I believed it once nonsense until this book.

Both the codex and the letter use phrases such as the Creator, Dega'Mostikas's Triangle, and the Truce of Passing. The transcriptions from the Book of Consulo never mention the Son of God or the Holy Spirit, nor God himself. Where could have the Aureate Rise Shield found such a book? The High Priestess must know of dark deeds at play.

My view into this codex was brief, as the Shield had returned with more loot, and I could not be caught for such treason. I hastily escaped from the study and hurried to the basement. Unfortunately, the lack of food and muscles in my legs caused me to clumsily fall.

The Aureate Rise Shield seized me. I began to pray for strength, knowing that torture and punishment were soon to follow for such disobedience. The Shield took me to High Priestess Imperia, beyond the study and into her private chamber made of black stone and marble. She knelt at the end of the chamber where a gold statue stood, shimmering in the torchlight. The sculpture was the same cross seen in her vision—with a two-thumbed hand and an eye in the centre. Except this torse-sized grey and pink hand was made of flesh. It was tied to the cross from the palmar region and above the eye. The fingers gracefully stretched and contracted, it was alive with mangled flesh dangling where the wrist should be.

The High Priestess rose, turning, and approached me, with her long black-and-gold gown draping against the marble floor. Her stride was calm and expression unfazed by the fact that I have deliberately disobeyed our sect's purpose. I did not lose my gaze into her purple eyes. Beyond their surface, I could clearly see the drunkenness of power. At that moment, I lost faith. Not in the holy light, but in humanity. The documented truths exposing centuries of deceitful spitting, claiming to lead humanity out of the paladins' tyranny, have shown me that we were all fools.

High Priestess Imperia asked if I believed God guided me to the study so I could feast my eyes upon the historical documents and the Book of Consulo. I told her I believed the holy light did. She laughed at me; I was puzzled until she said she personally unlocked the door, wanting one whose faith was troubled to come forth and seek the truth behind the Aureate Rise. Through her mighty power, she transcribed words into my mind that tempted me to leave the basement.

The High Priestess ordered the Aureate Rise Shield to murder me. In a flood of clarity, I finally understood what she was attempting to do. She wanted a body—and I fell into her plan. The church would not question a disloyal priest's death. Yes, then she would be free to do what she wished through the Book of Consulo and its necromancy.

The Aureate Rise Shield drew their swords. I prayed to the light, calling upon holy powers that we deemed not speak. I broke my vow of silence and summoned a prayer of protection. The light effortlessly absorbed the failed strikes from the Shield's swords.

I spoke more words of power—of truth—smiting the minds of the Aureate Rise Shield. They dropped their weapons, falling to the ground, locked in repent for their immoral actions. With one word, I could release them. I did not. Their minds ran around and around, reliving the sins they committed until their psyches collapsed under their own weight. Their limbs fell limp as blood seeped from the mouths, nostrils, and ears.

The High Priestess's words of power, bent by the Book of Consulo, are enslaved and shattered my protection prayer. The fortitude shields I built crumpled, and her false smite smeared my thoughts. I attempted to speak a word of power to heal! High Priestess Imperia finished hers first and the unholy speech scorched my face, melting half of it away. My mind gave in, and blood oozed out of my remaining facial orifices. I, too, fell as the Aureate Rise Shield did. I wish that it ended there, and I was brought to the golden gates of the Heavenly Kingdoms to meet God. That was untrue. The Book of Consulo is more real than I could have ever dreamed.

High Priestess Imperia leaned over my dying body as the last breath of air left my lungs. My soul began to rise; I could see my body. She spoke words in an ancient tongue with pronunciations that I could not attempt to mimic myself. The power of the unholy book flowed through her vowels as liquid-like energy channeled out of her glowing fingertips and onto my corpse. The black-and-gold stream defeated all worldly rules by hovering over my body like a snake about to feast. It seeped into my mouth, eyes, and ears, fueling the body with new blood.

My soul was pulled back down, locking me into the dead flesh. I was alive again! My hands pushed me up from the cold marble—which I could barely feel. I rose, facing the High Priestess directly. I have never seen such a malevolent grin of joy spread across someone's face. I . . . I was living, yet, I wasn't. My heart failed to pump, and my cold skin was stiff. The blood is new. It's thick and made of the black-and-gold energy. She repeated this process for the men I had killed, and they rose from the ground.

High Priestess Imperia deemed us the first of her new order. I wish to resist. My soul is bound to hers, and her will is my action. The Book of Consulo has granted her powers meant for gods, not mortals. Her first command for us was to strangle the remaining priests. I was not in control of my hands as I squeezed the life out of each of my brethren, watching their helpless eyes beg for mercy. Those that fought back with words of power were eradicated with my own tainted words—infused with might from the Book of Consulo. Then, the High Priestess converted my brethren into the living dead, growing her army.

I do not know what her end goal is, as she does not share it with anyone. She obsessively studies The Book of Consulo as we await her command at the gate of the church, under the pouring rain. We do not eat, we do not sleep, and we do not tire. The words she'd learned from that unholy codex has converted us into a horror that only a warrior of light can destroy. Hope is never lost, as light always guides us, and we simple priests may have fallen victim to treachery, but there is truth. I still believe the light led me to witness the Book of Consulo, not High Priestess Imperia. In time, no secrets stay buried forever, and she will face judgement from God for her sins. That, is what I pray.

Awake from the observing state. (Turn to Page 89)

You swat Malpherities's claws as they come flying towards you. The impact has little effect, but you dodge the oncoming orb. The ghoul's shaking claws hits dead air as he spins to face you. His face crunches inward as he snarls, exposing his razor-sharp teeth.

"Nameless One, we do not have time for this." Malpherities charges at you again, trying to push the vibrating orb into your hands.

"No!" you shout, dodging the ghoul. "If it's so important, why don't you do it?"

"You must guide us. You're far more able to identify the fragments. Somewhere locked deep in your consciousness is the reason for the collapse of existence," Malpherities says.

The ghoul bolts with lightning speed, his tentacle-like hair flailing wildly as he collides with you. You managed to grab both of his wrists, and the two of you smash onto the ground with you on the bottom, skidding for several feet.

"You gotta cough up some more answers," you say, grinding your teeth.

Malpherities keeps pushing the orb down on you, his strength is immense, and you're unsure if you're able to keep the orb away.

"We don't have time for this," he repeats.

"I can be of help to you if you tell me what the hell is going on!"

Malpherities growls and rolls off you, taking the orb with him. He drops it onto the ground, and the vibrating stops. The ghoul slumps in defeat, and his tentacle-like hair drapes down in misery.

You say, "I don't know how that rip and the sky got there, or even how I got here. I saw you on a candy box in a grocery store, so this all seems like some bad cartoon. You have to work with me. Now tell me, what the hell is going on?"

"You want to know?" Malpherities says.

"Yes!" you say.

Malpherities growls in resistance and then nods. He levitates to your eye level. "You must trust me."

"You won't shove that thing into my hands?"

"No," Malpherities says. "But you will witness something most baffling, giving you insight into what we are going through."

Find out what Malpherities is talking about. (Turn to Page 91)

The observation ends, throwing you from the role of the observer and back to the participant in the Midway. The orb's power dissipates, taking the energetic current with it. You drop the sphere as you did the first time due to its immense power. You feel your fingers, seeing how this body is under your control again. It's not easy adapting to melting and fusing with that orb and living out another's life. It doesn't follow any form of logic, just like everything in the Midway.

"Well?" Malpherities asks.

"Well? What am I seeing? It's real . . . But not. I need to know what's going on here."

"There's not a lot of time, with the rip expanding and us endlessly living this over."

"And what are you doing while I'm in these other lives?"

"Oh, I enter with you, and I too am looking for the fragments. We ghouls see the world in different lights or shades. But, you are more attuned to spotting these fragments compared to me. Something locked deep inside you is responsible for everything. Now, let's make this brief, as you're proving to be incompetent and can't remember anything, ever. Let's go through a bit of the history lesson to jolt your memory, shall we?"

Continue on to learn how you got here. (Turn to Page 91)

Malpherities soars around the collapsed stalactite and to the black ocean. The waves violently splash against the cavern entrance as he scoops up some liquid from a small pool on the ground.

He brings it to you and says, "You and I have had a previous encounter, one that has been stripped from your memories. We worked together in a more linear fashion."

"Meaning?" you ask.

"When you first arrived, you presumed you had died. We could not solve what caused your arrival at the Midway. You didn't kiss death's lips, and you didn't perform a ritual, a scientific experiment, or anything of the sort. You did tell me that you had transcended from the mortal realm and into the afterlife, experiencing a euphoria, which is the usual process of reincarnation."

"Reincarnation is real?"

"Yes, but not important. You even travelled through Death's Vortex above us. That's when you witnessed a rip in the vortex that brought you here."

"A rip, like the one above?"

"It seems to fit. Your memories were also wiped, as usual, when a soul leaves its flesh. It doesn't hold onto simple things like your experiences in the mortal realm. But you returning to the Midway again, and again, is not the normal trajectory of a soul, taking some of your memory with it and scrambling it. Hence why you have no idea who you are and only have blips of familiarity."

"I noticed that. Things feel familiar, but they're not."

"At first, we thought the rip was nothing, just an anomaly in the cosmos that brought you here. We were so wrong."

"I don't remember any of that."

"You wouldn't. I do, as it was before this time loop that keeps resetting your mind. Here, let me show you our past encounter with an earlier version of you."

Malpherities approaches you and raises his claws above your head. You're hesitant and take a step back, unsure what he is about to do with that black liquid.

"What is that stuff?"

"It is the source of the orb. It's potent when not fused with gold."

"Gold?"

"Yes, there's a lot of chemistry involved that goes beyond your knowledge, making it appear like magic. This liquid enables the observing states and can even transcend you to another place entirely if you are drenched in it. When you find just the right amount, it can be quite effective." Malpherities swirls the liquid around in his claws directly above your head, squinting while analyzing it closely. "Something I've learned from our past experiences is that you mortals cannot see the visions within the liquid. Only ghouls can see where the liquid will take you."

"That's reassuring."

"It should be, as I will make sure you witness our previous encounter. Now open your eyes wide."

You take a deep breath and open your eyes, looking up at Malpherities's claws. He splits them apart as you say, "Will it hurt?"

The black liquid splashes onto your face, seeping into your eyelids, nostrils, and even into your mouth with a strong tar flavour. The sting is intense, causing your eyes to puff up red, and your nostrils ignite into a fiery burn. You attempt to wipe the liquid off instinctively, but the ghoul grabs your wrists, holding them tight enough that the skin punctures from his razor-sharp claws.

"Hold still, let me guide you," Malpherities says. His voice is ever distancing, becoming dreamlike.

Similar to the orb, the room blooms. The cavern fades to white with the ocean, Malpherities, and even you while entering a new observing state. You, with Malpherities, can move anywhere, quite similar to when you were at the grocery store, landing here in the Midway. You're soaring through open space as the white void morphs into a spectral of colours. There are so many of them. You're seeing hues that you've never seen before. The colour alters into solid lines representing sacred geometry and endless patterns. This must be the euphoria of post-death, or how people describe too many psychedelics.

A black hole pops from nothingness directly in front of you and multiplies in size. Purple and blue clouds dance around this hole. Rotten faces phase in and out of the clouds as lightning booms within Death's Vortex.

The colours are gone as the vortex's roiling tunnel consumes your view, descending deeper. A tiny slit appears unaffected by the violent storm. The rip expands so large that it sucks you straight out of Death's Vortex and into the Midway.

Malpherities appears from thin air on the plateau. Unlike the first time, you remain hovering in the sky, above the endless black ocean and the upland directly below. You see another version of you on the ground, equally confused as you currently are. This other you and Malpherities chat momentarily and then leave the plateau, down a spiral staircase, and into the cavern. Your godlike state descends below the ground and into the cavern where the other you and Malpherities reach a sandy hill. There's a black matte pedestal with a golden bowl at the top.

Malpherities dips his claw into the golden bowl to get a small bead of black liquid. He dabs the droplet into your eye, causing the other you to enter a trance. A few moments later, you come back horrified. The two of you discuss what you found in the observing state.

The ghoul's distant voice says, "We were trying to jolt your memory. As you weren't supposed to be in the Midway. We presumed you may have had a sliver of your past stuffed somewhere in your mind since you had a body you recognized. The soul didn't complete its transition, so some portions of your memory could exist. At this point, we presumed you had died still."

The other Malpherities drops the liquid into your eye again, you enter a trance and it ends. He then dabs again. At some point, you decide to drop the liquid into your eye. You both follow this process over an unprecedented amount of time until three more ghouls appear from the cavern entrance. Two of the newcomers you recognize from earlier in the cavern hall who were distorted from the rip.

Malpherities and the other you run further into the cavern, exit through a hall and follow a path wrapping around the outer column of the plateau. You and Malpherities stop, talk briefly, and you watch yourself jump from the plateau and into the black liquid miles below. The three ghouls stop by Malpherities, growling and hissing.

Before the other you hits the ocean surface, time freezes. Your godlike state hovers around Malpherities and the three approaching ghouls. Then the vision soars directly to the other you. Getting this close, you can see the fear in your wide eyes as you're about to collide with the black ocean. It's eerie getting a full three-hundred-and-sixty-degree view of yourself, locked in time, just like everything Malpherities has shown you. It is definitely you. Just like now, this you is a stronger version of yourself at a prime age.

"This is where we left off, Nameless One." Malpherities's voice echoes in your mind.

"Then what happened?" you say or think. You're not sure what's in this dream state.

"To me, or to you?"

"Both."

"Well, you woke up back to your world, with memories and all, and continued on with your silly little life in your time."

"Until now?"

"Yes, when I came back for you through the candy box."

"How did you do that?"

"I tried to send you a message through the black ocean before the loop reset the very first time, and all time and space became mangled, me included. Obviously, it didn't work, because we're going through this again."

"What was the message?"

"It's mangled."

"A candy box?"

"It wasn't my choice. Reality got jumbled up. Now watch."

The view navigates up from the ocean and back to Malpherities and the three ghouls. Time unlocks, and the other you crashes into the ocean, disappearing forever. The three ghouls and Malpherities start waving their claws around, yelling at each other. He tries to reason with them, and the argument eventually simmers. The bigger ghoul guides the other three back to the plateau and points above. Malpherities's eyes widened, and he scratches his neck.

Beyond Death's Vortex is a small slit with burning white edges. It's so tiny that if you weren't paying attention, you would most likely mistake it for being a star, mainly due to the storm directly in front of it.

"Is that it?" you ask.

"The rip in the sky. Whatever means that got you here to the Midway the first time had a colossal side-effect." Malpherities's voice becomes more apparent as the vision fades to white.

The empty space fills spottily with colour, shapes, and depth until the cavern recreates. You're still standing, blinking like mad, and take a step back. You wipe your face, hands, and eyes, trying to remove black liquid. It has entirely evaporated. Malpherities is beside you by the base of the ocean.

"That's how we got here, after we made the orb," Malpherities says.

"You didn't notice there was the rip in the sky the first time?"

"I can't know everything, Nameless One. I'm a projection of Death's Vortex with a personality twist of my own."

"Right, and the other ghouls are too."

"You and I wrote it off as an anomaly in the cosmos, and I couldn't find anything abnormal about it. I was too focused on your observations then, trying to piece it together. This is why the other ghouls and I work well as one. We see things that others cannot. I have a habit of straying from them and ignoring their calls. A rebel, if you will."

"They wanted to warn us, in that other version you just showed."

"Yes, and I thought they'd want to eat you, so I told you to jump into the ocean."

"What happened to the other ghouls? I saw two of the three, phasing in and out like the rip."

"All three attempted to investigate the rip. Long story short, don't let the white flame touch you. It's deadly," Malpherities says.

"And how does all of this work with me and a time loop?"

"Whatever you did, or whatever brought you to the Midway, is burning the fabric of existence. We need to find the fragments from whence the loop started to restore the damage it created."

"Or everything is destroyed?"

"You got it."

"And the loop started how?" you ask.

Another whipping crack erupts in the sky, this one shaking more than just the plateau. Far off in the distance, the black ocean is punctured by an invisible force, blowing miles worth of liquid into the air. The rumbling makes you snag the wall to keep upright. The distant black ocean slams back down, sending a tidal wave in all directions. That includes the plateau and the entrance where you stand.

"This won't be good," Malpherities says. "Quickly."

Malpherities hovers past the collapsed stalactite and snags the orb. He grunts while gripping the orb, which now shakes violently. You take one last look at the massive wall of liquid accelerating towards you. It'd be best to run now.

You book it, hurrying to catch up with Malpherities and the two of you dash through the hallway, leading up to where you first awoke, passing the other two ghouls who keep morphing in and out of the wall. Their voices are agonizing, begging for mercy.

Deep vibrating comes from the plateau base as the massive wall of liquid splashes against the rock formation. At the bottom of the hallway, the collision's aftermath is evident, with the black liquid flooding the entire base level of the cavern.

Malpherities reaches the sandhill beside a black matte pedestal. You run up the dune, your feet sliding slightly in the silky sand. The ghoul places a claw directly in front of your chest, stopping you from going any further. If he didn't, you would have undoubtedly fallen into the sudden drop a couple paces in front of you.

You lean over, past the pedestal, to see the giant hole leading directly to the cavern's base level, which is flooded with violent waves of black liquid. The sand is delicately cut in half, and a step further would likely cause it to collapse.

"This is where you woke up and dropped the orb," Malpherities says. You don't recall the black pedestal, but you were in a state of shock.

The ghoul says, "Now, will you work with me?" He extends the orb with both claws, his arms still shaking. "The key to detect the fragments has always been you. The orb bends to your will from your blood."

"My blood?" you ask.

"You ask so many questions, Nameless One. Take it. Its power is too great for a ghoul. Find the clues, and we will break this loop."

You're not entirely sure what he refers to with blood or how this orb was made. You're hoping that breaking this loop will help you understand how the time traveling object was created and what this rip even is. Or why Malpherities can't do any of this on his own. Damn NUT GRAPE Chewz box.

And so, you boldly grab the orb, feeling the familiar hum through your system. Your hands and body meld with the orb. The room dissolves to white, taking Malpherities with it as two portals appear from the open space, along with a third. This is new.

You and the orb gravitate towards the center rift. The one on your left showcases a laboratory with plenty of chemical equipment. There are bodies with herculean muscles. Explosions. The center portal flashes a farm in the prairies, followed by agonizing screams and fire. The third one has a forest and a logging company tearing down trees with masked figures in the woods. The choice is yours; which one will you take to uncover the secrets of your blood?

MAKE ONE OF THREE CHOICES:

Enter the left portal. (Turn to Page 101)

Embrace the centre portal. (Turn to Page 113)

Direct the orb to the right portal. (Turn to Page 131)

TRANSHUMANISM

The definition of being human varies depending who you talk to, with culture and religion playing a crucial role in their reasoning. For some, it is critical for us to return to our true selves, embracing the billions of years of evolution that got us here. Others believe being human is about adapting and overcoming our weaknesses. We certainly have done a fair amount of the latter. The proof is seen in our dominance over the planet. Not to mention our technological advancements have made us unrecognizable to our next closest relatives.

The great apes are only a small fraction of what we've destroyed from our advancements. I suppose we are simply evolving, as all creatures do. This reasoning would mean that our global supremacy is a part of our nature and not defying its intent. Or is it? The question isn't a simple black and white answer. In the past, it has led to many debates from creditable people.

I, for one, stood somewhere in the middle for many years. My career path led me to see the forefront of technological developments. I was a bioengineer. Humanity is no longer afraid to play God with our genetics. None of us foresaw where this finding could go, nor did we expect the alterations to happen so suddenly. The flip in society was similar to the rise of the net well over a century ago, where the access and speed of the internet rapidly altered how society functioned.

Being a bioengineer has had many perks. There's the usual benefits like consistent pay, healthcare, and vacation time. I had access to information before the rest of civilization, such as progression in DNA editing. The process was difficult at first, time consuming, and expensive. Gene editing has taken many different names over the years. The details of how the genes are edited matter little because the end result is what shareholders are looking for. In a world ruled by privatized organizations, results driving profit are king.

At first, we worked on small subjects like chickens and mice to see how gene editing can alter a creature. The intentions were good. We could cure diseases, alter feeble traits, and make the animals more resilient from birth. Our team determined these successful trials could be applied to humans. It's a noble, and foolish, cause. Greed is everywhere, and any good invention is a double-edged sword, fabricating new problems. If history has taught us anything, it is that technology grows from enterprises and war. We were unfortunate to have both with our miraculous discovery.

Manageficient Enterprises held the patent to our DNA modifying process. Unlike previous gene editing techniques, ours was less invasive, and the A.I. software was able to make far more accurate predictions of an edit's outcome before we made the injection. Everyone wanted to get their hands on the tech for one reason or another. We could make bigger cattle, faster growing chickens. Hell, at the time we knew we could make smarter politicians, more attractive celebrities, and longer living powerful individuals . . . like CEOs.

The corporation held back, knowing we could streamline and improve the DNA modification tech. We moved beyond small creatures and into modifying chimpanzees. We made them intelligent, tougher, and then quickly terminated them. This wasn't some foolish science fiction movie; we're aware of the dangers that come with our invention. Unfortunately, Manageficient Enterprises had their own goals in mind with the technology.

We worked on our first human modifications from "volunteers". I knew better from seeing their rugged forms, cheap tattoos, and hateful scowls. These were prisoners of some kind. Our team didn't question their origins and went to work. We were given specific instructions to make them more resilient, then to give them faster reflexes and more muscles. Soon we learned we were making super soldiers for some government with the highest bid. The pilot project was the first of many branching from the initial scope. We worked with "volunteers" of all types from around the world, letting us exploit specific human traits we chose.

One project had us improve the brain capacity of the volunteers. Another was designed for enhancing senses such as hearing and sight. A small group we made cancer free. One was purely to enhance sexual performance and self-pleasure. The intention for these projects was never fully clear. Our team made educated guesses. Still, as engineers, most of us didn't question. We were curious more than anything. Some did leave the project, taking a moral stance against our dangerous dabbling, acting as whistle blowers. Nothing came of it because the claims were lunacy from the outside perspective without proof.

I stayed. I had to see where this would take us. Curiosity is what leads humanity to new ventures, and I was at the front seat of witnessing us reaching a milestone in human evolution. Yes, we were designing our own future, something that no animal has ever done. That fact alone is what made it so enticing.

I saw the potential from day one when we improved the mice. Now, knowing that this technology was in the hands of a private organization proved my noble dream difficult. I was powerless and could only act as the hand for Manageficient Enterprises and whatever end goal they had in mind.

The prisoner—sorry, volunteer—modification contracts weren't the only form of income for the company. We worked on some grotesque solutions that moved the technology away from human modification. Generations ago, when Manageficient Enterprises was a small engineering consulting firm, they were bought by another company,

Allen Oil Site Solutions. As it was, I'm unsure who was the parent company, Allen Oil Site Solutions or Manageficient Enterprises. Big business likes to shift companies around. Umbrella companies and sister organizations matter little, as long as the businesses dodge taxes and lawsuits to maximize profits. With that, Allen Oil Site Solutions and Manageficient Enterprises were one and the same poison.

Our project for Allen Oil Site Solutions was finding a safer way to drill for what little oil was left on this planet. We modified sea creatures who could handle the pressure of the deep sea, merging them with machinery to create biomechanical drilling units. The process was clunky, messy, and didn't prove fruitful. The animals were in pain, their efforts slow, and the machines often broke, tearing from their skin and bone. We tried to reduce their pain sensors, increase their obedience, but nothing worked. Robots and human workers were better in the end, despite being more costly. Still, the project paved the way for something bigger.

Manageficient Enterprises has their hands in many industries. The CEO has specific interest in improving workflows for corporations countless times. Taylorism is the exact term. It's the theory of breaking down every task into individual components—or gears—so any employee can achieve them. With our knowledge from the biomechanical animals, we created a solution that could improve people's performance at their job. They wouldn't be distracted by simple human desires, workplace attraction for example. Sorrow, project burnout, and soul-sucking data wouldn't effect these new workers. The process was part of a larger picture: Conditioning Human Initiation of Transcendence. Also known as the C.H.I.T. age. The solution was first introduced as a pill, swallowed multiple times. Year after year people were no longer sick, sad, or felt any other need other than to fulfill their purpose for head office.

Conditioning Human Initiation of Transcendence changed everything. Manageficient Enterprises took their solution to market and corporations from around the world purchased their products. Governments obtained it for schools, hospitals, law enforcement, and eventually it became a law. The pills were adjusted to work as injections, given at birth. People didn't question these injections. Yeah, there were a few bad apples, but as a whole, humanity could see the end result—global peace. People were compliant. No one argued about religion, political views, or any minute differences. The solution reduced people to worker ants who understood the bigger picture of their new global colony.

War was a thing of the past for a good decade in the C.H.I.T. age. Governments began to merge, forming fewer countries. More companies merged or were bought out by Manageficient Enterprises. Ten years of injecting this dope rewires a person's brain and removes many of their sensors. We improved upon the failed biomechanical animal project and fused people directly with the computers to work faster. Tubes fed workers and extracted their waste. People were obedient to the alterations on their bodies and minds. They knew that their goal was to serve the greater of humanity: progress. The alterations were the beginning of transhumanism. These pale, physically slow blobs were unrecognizable to their former selves.

I hadn't taken these injections, nor did my team. We knew what we were creating with this solution. Again, this is the advantage of being at the front seat of human discovery. Manageficient Enterprises insisted that we did, but our case was strong. We have proven our efficiency time and time again, being the spearhead of the gene editing process. There were many sectors under us who were modified with the solution. They focused on specific projects and needs, making alternate versions of the solution.

Our team's purpose was to focus on the grand design of humanity. The CEO began to speak with me directly. We made specific injections for him, making him more beautiful, smarter, taller, younger, and so on—the perfect human. His colleagues, friends, and family were also given this specific injection, separating the working class from the elite. He discussed long-term planning with me frequently. The man— if you could call him that—wanted to breed these worker post-human sub species more efficiently. He wanted to increase their performance.

The CEO also knew that planet Earth wasn't going to serve us forever as our population kept increasing and we continued to strip nature from the picture. Our global colony was in jeopardy.

During our last meeting he offered me a choice for myself and my team. He was so proud of every advancement that we had achieved over the years that he wanted to offer me an option. I could join him as one of the elite, where I would be fed the injections he and the other worthy upper class took. The alternative was to take the original solution, mutating me into a happy working post-human sub species. He provided me with a fork in the road, and I had to make a choice.

The CEO told me there was no more room for humans on this planet. The new people were to rule. The workers were compliant, and willing to provide for the elite who were the best qualities of humanity. They were able to fully enjoy their senses, or sins, you could say. The downfall to the elite's embracive modifications were the negative aspects of the human mind. It was something we hadn't quite worked out yet. Anger, hate, gluttony, lust, and jealousy are powerful emotions they still had.

This meeting gave me the clarity I needed to understand that you couldn't ride the middle line forever. Eventually you would be pulled in one direction or the other. The world had been polarized for many reasons in the past, but never for our ground-zero purpose in this universe. Should humans design their own evolutionary path? I, personally, had the option to architect mine. My choice would alter future generations if I chose to have children. I could become an elite and embrace the diverged perks of being a god, or I could be forever contented helping the elite build their indulgent utopia. Transhumanism was happening before my very eyes, and my passive nature ended that day.

I chose neither path. Doing nothing is a powerful action that the CEO did not foresee. I told him that I would think about the offer, and I returned to the lab and informed my team. The fact that they also chose to stay human for so long gave me hope that they would listen to my rationality. They understood that we were given an ultimatum and we couldn't keep coasting as we had.

They agreed to follow me, and we left Manageficient Enterprises, escaping into the underground of the global nation now known as the Society, ruled by Manageficient Enterprises. We brought our families with us, taking supplies, weapons, and removing any technology connected to the global net. We built our own network on a new frequency, letting us communicate safely. We learned there were others throughout the planet that resisted the C.H.I.T. era, denouncing transhumanism. Now, there were three types of intelligences on the planet: the elite, the workers, and us—the humans.

Of course, our choice did not sit well with the CEO or Manageficient Enterprises. Naturally, a war began. We were able to rescue children, and the few people who hadn't been fully mutated by the solution. We bombed the elite's facilities and factories. We hacked their infrastructures. They sent drones and biomechanical super soldiers—that I had helped create—to eradicate us. Yet, I knew how to counter them. We created our own solutions into bio-bombs that attacked their exploited genes. All forms of warfare played out, even the nuclear, leaving us in a charcoal wasteland of extreme heat and cold of what was once a beautiful planet.

The mind's evolution plays an immense role in what it means to be human. Of all the great apes, we use our brain far more than our relatives. We had reached a tipping point that split humanity, leading to disastrous results. I suppose a species' split is the inevitable natural course. Every creature evolves into something new. Sometimes this is a clear path from one to another. Other times one evolves into multiples, as did the humans. We, the true humans, are still alive and reside under the surface of the planet. The elite went for the stars, seeing that the planet was destroyed. They took their worker subs with them.

Humanity is now trapped on a dying planet. We must leave Earth in order to survive. Unfortunately, we destroyed most cities, including the technology, leaving us with almost nothing. Human beings are resistant, and we built anew. We can dig through the scraps. It will take time. Thankfully, we have brilliant minds. We have tools. We will survive and either repair this planet or head for a new one. With any luck, we won't run into the elite and the Society. If we do, they will have hell to pay. Humanity will survive, as we always do, because we adapt as our evolutionary roots deem it so.

Awake from the observing state. (Turn to Page 109)

The orb's power diminishes, and you fly from the futuristic landscape and back into the Midway on top of the sandy hill beside that steep decline. You're still feeling the after-effects of experiencing someone's life, making you have a gut-wrenching sadness. It's almost too much to handle, and the orb slips from your hand. It lands with a thud in the sand right by your feet. Careful next time; it could have easily fallen into the black liquid below.

"Don't let the observing states muddle your mind," Malpherities says. "You do experience everything, but remember, it is not you. The real you is simply witnessing."

You scratch your head and say, "Yeah. It's just a lot to take in. I keep observing that depressing future."

"Bleakness is everywhere if you look close enough. And truthfully, everything will be in dismal if we don't find these fragments."

"Nothing really stood out as a fragment, I think," you say.

"In we go again," Malpherities says.

And so, you repeat the process by snagging the orb, melting into it, and watching the cavern turn to white. As before, portals appear. There are three of them like last time, how exciting.

A beach stretches as far as the eye can see in the far-left portal. It's no ordinary beach because there is a secondary planet in the sky beside the sun. The middle one shows brief flashes of a laboratory, syringes, and a futuristic metropolis with spaceships and plasma rifles. The far-right portal has an underground bunker with people screaming and a nasty stench.

The orb is being sucked into the portal to the right.

MAKE ONE OF THREE CHOICES:

Enter the portal to the left. (Turn to Page 157)

Engage into the central portal. (Turn to Page 173)

Let the portal to the right suck you in.(Turn to Page 217)

SUMMER GIVER

I'm not sure if this is a confession or if I am overthinking the whole thing. The prophecy. The scrolls. They were parallel to reality. Grandma's fits—or her preparation, depending on how you look at it— were clear signs.

I was adopted, as you know. A given, considering my heritage, and that the Vaans were Ukrainian. The Vaan family took me in and were quite generous. Papa—his first name was Ihor—and Mum—Maria— came here from their motherland to start a new life—the typical "sail to the New World" kind of story.

It makes one wonder why the Vaans chose this far inland. I thought at first that it was the same reason as all the others: opportunity. Coal and land. Boy, was I wrong.

At the time, the Vaans' choice to come to Alberta was a blessing. They raised me as one of their own to the point I might as well have been born in the Ukraine. I'm sure you met my grandparents, Adam, the first, and Elizabeth. Sweet, sweet Elizabeth, so keen on traditions before her health troubles.

Papa and Mum had Adam the second before I was adopted. What a strong boy. He never let the hideous animal scar on his chest stop him. I admired that about his character. He was kind, and he cared about me. I know he did. You wouldn't understand. I just wish he was more forward with how he felt earlier on. Maybe all of this could have been avoided. Maybe not.

My birth family? Well, they were neighbours to the Vaan farm. To be honest, I can't remember my biological mother and father in detail. It is like a dream—the more you think about it when you wake up, the fuzzier it becomes.

I know my birth parents were caught up in the conflict with the Canadian Militia and the North-West Rebellion, before the turn of the century. I was four when this all happened, but I know it was violent because the Canadian Militia forced their standards. They presumed we were part of the rebellion, being Métis, and despised us. I don't overthink it because I cannot change the past and I was raised as Ukrainian.

The rest of Medicine Hat was kind to us. Your father always let me see his horse whenever we were in town before the Canadian Militia arrived. They brought hell with them.

My mother and father were working on the farm when the troops showed up. I was indoors, scrubbing the floors when I heard yelling, then, the first shot. Father and Mother burst into the house as bullets soared through the windows—glass was everywhere. It didn't take long for the militia to overthrow the farm, armed with rifles and fire. Father made a distraction so Mother and I could escape. I remember crying as Mother held my hand as we ran, then, she too was shot, and I kept running. Eventually, I arrived at the Vaan farm. Grandma, sitting on her rocker, saw me.

After the death of my family, I went back to visit my old home. Only scorched ground remained and the burnt bones of my parents. Eventually, the farmland was taken over by the tall grasses, bluebells, and the small gophers hiding in the rubble. The remnants of the farm vanished. Such is the cycle of life when summer arrives.

You probably heard some of the rumours in town. Trust me. My family wasn't involved with the North-West Rebellion. My parents wanted a simple life, that was all.

Papa and Mum had a second child sometime after my family's death. Symon. He looked up to Adam, his older brother. As did I. Adam was going to take care of our family and make sure our parents could retire. He'd get married, as would I, and as would Symon. However, the lack of women in Alberta made competition tough for the boys. The lack of a real courtship dance wasn't the only thing. Education and proper healthcare were a problem. The railroad business began to grow to provide necessities and diversity to the province.

I'm rambling. I should tell you things changed when Adam proposed to move. It shocked the whole family. Mum and I were cleaning up the boiled chicken and borscht dinner at the time. We froze, waiting. You could see the betrayal and anger in Papa's eyes.

"You don't care about this family," Papa sneered.

"It isn't forever. Please," Adam said. "I would be able to build the railroad east, save some scratch."

"There is nothing but noise out there." Papa rubbed his brow. "This is why we moved here! To get away from it all." He stood up and walked away. Papa had worked all day on the farm and didn't need this from his son.

Grandma kept her head down low. She said, "Summer is coming. The gift is in you. Your grandfather would have understood. I understand."

Grandpa passed away before Symon was born. All too soon. Grandma was upset but remained a positive light in our family. We all knew she ran the farm. Papa liked to play a strong leader, but it was a mask.

Adam tried to talk to Papa again, but the talking escalated into yelling, and Papa stormed off to his room, slamming the door shut. He didn't come out for the rest of the night. Grandma stared out the window in her rocking chair, sipping a glass of vodka. Mum knitted. Symon went to bed early, because he was only a kid. Then there was Adam and me.

"Are you sure?" I asked my brother quietly as we sat in his room.

"I have to," he said. "What choice do I have here?"

"Papa can't work the farm forever."

"I know. That is why I will come back."

Adam's choice made sense. There wasn't much of a future for him in southern Alberta. Adam wanted to marry. Hell, we both did. We were of the age when our parents married, and being single for so long raises suspicion amongst the townsfolk. That's why you kept pressuring me too.

"I support you," I said, taking my brother's hands, staring into his blue eyes.

He squeezed them. "Thank you," he said. "You mean a lot to me. It makes me wonder if . . ." he paused.

"If?" I asked.

"Nothing. I'll be leaving tomorrow." He leaned forward and gave me a kiss on the forehead. It was the first time he had done that. It seemed fitting—like a "see you soon" and not a "goodbye forever."

After giving Adam a hug goodnight, I went out to the living room to find Mum had gone to bed. Grandma remained in her chair with an empty glass of vodka. She often fell asleep in her chair.

I quietly crept up to her and slid the glass from her hand. Her eyes shot open, and she looked at me with a blank stare. I froze, not sure what to do.

"Grandma? I'm just taking your glass." I said.

"Aestatis Dator," Grandma said, not blinking.

"Sorry?"

"Summer Giver," Grandma said. "He and the devoted shall sprout from the pure."

She must be sleeping, I thought. Grandma had rambled nonsense before. It scared me, but I wrote it off as an old-person thing. I was wrong, eh?

Adam didn't say goodbye to anyone. There was no point. If he did, it would have started another fight. Papa continued his routine and didn't talk all day. Mum and I went into town, taking the carriage. My mind buzzed, wondering what Adam would do while working on the railroad. He'd meet a pretty girl and start a new life. A part of me felt left behind. I felt like I didn't belong in this world at all.

Then, reality sunk in again, and I remembered we were going to buy some potatoes. The Vaan family would simply continue life. That evening, I wrote my first letter to Adam, grateful he left me an address.

Dear Adam,

I know it is quite sudden. You just left, but I couldn't wait. The farm isn't going to be the same without you. My thoughts are clouded about the future. Mum and I went into town to buy some potatoes from Liam. He was flirtatious as always. Mum was encouraging me on the ride back to accept his advances. You know how I feel about Liam.

Grandma has been as silent as Papa, just with more vodka. They both don't have much to say. Papa is doing his best with the crops and livestock. The rain is late, and we're waiting. Symon is lost without you and clings to me now. I will do my best to fill in your shoes. I know I won't ever be you.

Enough of me. How is work? How is it out east? Tell me about all of it. I cannot wait to hear from you.

Love your sister,

Terra

Weeks went by before I heard back from Adam. Papa calmed down when he had a drink. Grandma, on the other hand, was not acting like herself. Her mood began to swing. The sweet old lady who used to bake us cheesecake tarts was no longer here. Maybe she was frustrated with the drought, like the rest of us. Her bones had ached in the past when spring arrived.

Her ramblings in a foreign language continued. I knew it wasn't Ukrainian because I heard her speak it before. This was something else. Mum and Papa didn't comment. They looked unsurprised as if they had seen this behaviour before.

In Grandma's room, I found an old book clutched in her hand as she snored. It was leather-bound with an emblem of the sun on it. I knew it wasn't the Bible. I had never seen this book before. That should have been the first sign, but I didn't think much of it. We had more important things to be concerned about—like the lack of rain.

The next day I received Adam's letter.

Dear Terra,

Things are well, thank you. I didn't get the job I wanted on the railroad. I find myself in the coal mines. The company has its hands in multiple industries and had to fill a new mining camp. You know the coal business is booming in the prairies. Life has a way of not turning out the way you expect. I feel hollow inside. The mines are dark. We start early and finish late. I never see the light.

I miss you. You understand me. At night I think I can hear your voice, calling for me to take your hand. I know it is not really you. Maybe I am losing my mind? I don't know. I think about Papa, Mum, Symon, Grandma, and you. Our family. Then I dream about the sun, lush greenery. I'm flying up, holding your hand as we rise.

I hope things look up for Papa and the farm. I won't be gone forever. Trust me. I want to return. Being in the dark mines has given me plenty of time to reflect.

This isn't meant to be an offence. Maybe we're meant to be closer than just siblings. You are adopted and not a Vaan. I haven't bedded a woman and you no man. We are pure. Good was in front of us all along. You as my wife and me as your husband. I threw it all way.

Maybe I am confused. Maybe I am lonely. I would crumple this paper out and start over, but I am out of paper and ink is low. So this is my one chance to share my words. Maybe God wishes for me to express my deepest thoughts. Forgive me, Terra. I hope things improve on the farm.

I'm not sure when I will be back, but I know I will be.

Love,

Adam

He sounded lonesome. He had regret. His confession was unsettling, but not completely crazy. He was right. I was not a Vaan. We were close, and I didn't like any of the men in town. It was a lot to take in. My main concern was Adam's feelings. He was off in a strange land all on his own. He was also my brother. Immediately, I wrote him back.

Dear Adam,

I am so glad to hear from you. I pray that the circumstances you find yourself in start to look up. It is upsetting to hear that the fresh start hasn't turned out to be what you were looking for. I am afraid things haven't improved much around here. The drought is worse. I suppose you left at an opportune time. Maybe you cursed the farm? I am only joking, partially. At this point, I can only pray to God that someone is listening.

I understand your feelings. I know you better than other people. I am sure the loneliness you and I are experiencing will pass. This is normal, right? Please, I treasure you in a special place in my heart. I haven't thought of us like this before, and I understand your reasoning. You can be honest with me as I have always been honest with you. We have time to think things through. Things are difficult for us both. Maybe it will all turn around, and you will meet a beautiful woman.

Love,

Terra

The last sentence weakened my heart. I wasn't sure why. Maybe it was a way of suppressing feelings I hadn't come to terms with yet. It doesn't matter now.

Weeks went by. I wondered if Adam was mad at me, but he did mention he was running out of ink and paper. His words crept up in the back of my mind numerous times throughout the spring. He didn't sound like the strong, confident Adam that I knew.

One night, we couldn't find Grandma. She wasn't in her chair as usual. Papa and Mum went outside looking for her. They told Symon and me to wait here in case she returned.

Anxious and worried, I went back into Grandma's room to investigate. Perhaps she left a clue. I pulled open the dresser drawers, the nightstand, and the closet—nothing. I lifted the mattress. It was bare too. As I was about to leave, my foot pressed on a floorboard that levered upwards. There was a hidden compartment.

Under the floorboard was the leather-bound book with the sun emblem. There were some scrolls, a dagger, and a small bronze shrine.

It had a platform for a candle and a naked man with the face of the sun and a long line running down the middle of his torso. I flipped open the book but couldn't read the words on the pages. It looked close to English, but it wasn't. I guessed it was the same language that Grandma had been speaking in.

My search ended when the front door opened. Papa and Mum had brought Grandma back. She was in her nightgown, shouting, "The Summer Giver! He has birthed! The season is near! He awaits his devoted."

"Mum! Please," Papa said.

"Silence, you disappointment!" she hissed.

I still hadn't heard back from Adam, and the weeks continued. My frustrations grew. I had no one to talk to. Symon was too young. Papa stayed quiet and only related to his liquor. Mum buried her head, pretending none of this was happening. Grandma was off her rocker, as the saying goes.

Then tragedy struck our family. Having no one to talk to, I wrote Adam again.

Dear Adam,

Papa shot himself. You leaving the farm hasn't been easy on anyone.

The drought has continued, and the animals are dying. He couldn't take it. I think he bottled up his emotions more than we realized.

Papa's death hasn't been easy on us. Mum tries to take care of the household and keep an eye on Grandma and her fits. She has gotten worse. Symon and I take care of what is left of the animals and crops.

Liam, the potato farmer, has come by too. He was kind to donate some of his harvest to us. The drought hasn't struck him as hard. Liam tried to talk to me as he always does. I couldn't. Liam mentioned I am of age and has offered his hand in marriage. It is a tempting offer. Then, I think about you. Our history. Your heartfelt letter. I sleep with it. I told Liam I wasn't ready. Please, this one letter cannot be the only one I get from you.

I beg you, write back, so I know I am not talking to a ghost.

Love,

Terra

A part of me wondered if Adam was dead. Maybe a rock crushed him in the mines. Or perhaps he met a girl and forgot about us. I didn't know what to think. I still hadn't told the family we had been exchanging letters. I feel that would have upset them. Papa had been disturbed enough, clearly. You're the only other soul that has seen these letters.

Grandma had another fit. Mum and I went out to look for her. Symon begged to join us, but I told him someone had to hold down the fort. It didn't take long to find the old lady. She was out in the middle of a field, naked, screaming at the moon.

"Grandma!" I called out.

"Adam! Where is summer?" Grandma wailed, arms outward.

"Mum! I found her!" I yelled. But Mum had gone to the other end of the farm to cover more ground.

I put my lantern down and wrapped Grandma in the blanket I brought with me. She didn't respond, just continued to stare at the moon. I knocked over something heavy with my foot. I looked down to see the small metal shrine of the sun-headed man, the one I found under the floorboards. There was a candle in its socket. The flame had toppled onto the dry ground. Quickly, I extinguished it. The last thing we needed was a fire.

Grandma turned and stared at me. The moment was too long. She smiled and said, "Of course." She reached for my cheek and stroked my face. "How could I have not seen the devoted?"

"Grandma, let's get you back inside," I said, trying to guide her back to the house.

She resisted and wailed, "Adam! Aestatis Dator!"

I wasn't sure if she missed her husband or was calling out to my brother. Then, I swear I saw Adam in the distance. He stared at us with those blue eyes. The scar. He was naked. His head glowed brightly as lightning struck. Then, only the silhouette of a man remained.

"Adam!" I called out.

"Adam!" Grandma repeated.

This is ridiculous, I thought. Realizing that I, too, was yelling into the fields, thinking I saw someone. It was just wheat crops. I forced Grandma to move with me, leaving the shrine behind. I'd come back for it tomorrow in the daylight.

Here, this is the fourth letter I wrote to Adam.

Dear Adam,

This is the third letter I have written, and I still haven't heard from you. I am greatly worried. Please, can you forgive me? A reply would be reassuring so I know you are alive.

I think I am going crazy like Grandma. I swear I saw you in the field. Grandma was distracted, calling out to Adam. Maybe it was Grandpa or you. I do not know. But I thought I saw you. That should be a sign that I miss you. Don't you see?

Please, Adam. I need to hear from you. I haven't told anyone about our letters yet. They are between us. Come back. Mum and Symon miss you. The drought hasn't improved, and we are desperate. If it wasn't for Liam's generosity, I don't know what we would do. That stubborn Irishman, still trying to sweep me off my feet.

Love,

Terra

These letters were only supposed to be between Adam and me. They're so personal. It is like he said—life has a way of not turning out the way you expect. God, if He exists, has a strange way of strengthening faith. I would like Him to explain the sun-headed man.

The next day, I went back to find the shrine of the sun-headed man. It was gone. Grandma hadn't taken it. I know that much because we kept a close eye on her all night. Maybe it was Adam in the field after all. I don't know.

Summer was here. The rain hadn't come, and the crops weren't growing. Symon and I didn't have the knowledge or strength to save the stock. We did our best. Mum brought up the idea of selling the farm. She didn't have a plan on what to do after that, but I knew the money wouldn't last us forever. Still, it was a tempting idea.

Adam. My poor brother. I was confused. Every night I went and looked at his letter, the one about us. It tormented my mind. Maybe he was right. Maybe he made a mistake when he moved away and brought this poor luck upon us. If we had gotten married, maybe Papa wouldn't have shot himself. Maybe the drought wouldn't have happened. Even if it all had, I wouldn't have been so alone. All I have is this letter and the memory of him kissing me on the forehead.

Symon was trying, but he simply wasn't old enough. Mum had closed in on herself. She prayed to God in the same obsessive way that Grandma did.

One afternoon, Grandma was taking a nap in her rocking chair. Mum had gone into town, and Symon was working out in the fields. Curiosity struck me, and I wanted to take another look at Grandma's floorboard compartment.

Carefully, I went into her room and pulled out the planks of wood to find the familiar leather-bound book. The shrine of the sun-headed man was there. We made sure Grandma stayed in her room, but perhaps she did sneak out and get it. I don't think I'll ever have a clear answer to that.

Under the shrine, there was the dagger and the scrolls. I pulled some of the pig-skin papers out. They had crude paintings on them. There, the same naked man with a sun-head stood tall. A man and a woman lifted a baby to him as sun rays directed towards the child with a floating, flaming dagger above him, burning his chest. There were glyphs and scriptures written in the same language found in the book.

Another scroll had the sun-headed man holding the hand of a naked woman, both coming out of a baby's cracked-open chest. Flowers were in the place of the baby's guts, and water was in the place of blood. A couple of skeletons were holding the large baby up. It was quite beautiful.

Grandma groaned. I stuffed the scrolls into the compartment and placed the planks back down. That was the last time I was able to look at her storage before you arrived. This is the last letter I sent to my brother before you saved me.

Dear Adam,

I am writing my final letter to you. You haven't responded, and I can only imagine you resent me, or you have died. So, this is my goodbye letter. I felt uncomfortable after the one letter you sent me. The thought was obscure. Outlandish even. Then, the more I think about us, the more I begin to wonder if you were right. I miss you.

Things have gotten worse. Grandma makes me worried as her shouting has escalated. We've found her naked more times than clothed, dancing wildly. The larger issue is it is only Symon, Grandma, and me. Mum went to town yesterday and hasn't returned home. I'm not sure what we are going to do. Maybe she abandoned us or was kidnapped. Anything is possible. All I know is that she hasn't come back.

She brought up selling the farm. I thought it was a coward's way out. Now, I do not think so. It might be our only option.

Be well, Adam.

Terra

I don't know what happened to Mum. I was more concerned with Symon, knowing that the family responsibilities fell on me. I kept thinking about the scrolls. The sun-headed man, the baby, the two skeletons, and the lady. At the time, I wasn't sure what they were. Now, it is obvious.

That evening, after I mailed the letter, Grandma had another fit. This one was indoors. She was flailing around with a lantern, kicking the rug and chairs out of the way for more room to trot around. The ground was wet with oil. She was yammering on.

"The Summer Giver, he is on his way! Sprouted from the pure. He awaits his devoted. Summer is here!"

Symon and I tried to calm her down. She wasn't having any of it. She dropped the lantern, it crashed, and the floor lit up. I don't know how the flame grew so quickly. Grandma embraced the flame as it began to consume her flesh. She didn't scream or twitch. She raised her arms, smiling, looking up to the burning ceiling.

"Aestatis Dator!" she cried. "I bring you your devoted!"

Symon and I screamed, knowing Grandma had lost her wits. Her fate was sealed.

I attempted to guide Symon through the fire, but a beam fell and crushed him in front of me. I was trapped, coughing and wheezing from the thickening smoke. My body was scraped and scorched from the crashed timber. Alone.

Terra, my dear, came a voice. It whispered all around me. I couldn't tell where it was coming from. The crackling of the flames and the rushing wind made it impossible.

We will be united again, the voice said. It was Adam. I had to be going crazy. The heat and lack of air were melting my mind. No. I wish that were so. It was, indeed, Adam. From the flames came a bright light, moving towards me. The body of a naked man with a long, jagged scar running down his chest was below the light. The beam of light was his head, glowing too bright to see his face. The form, the scar . . . I knew it was Adam.

I am here for you, Adam said. He continued to move towards me, floating. The flames didn't touch him.

His hand extended outward. *Terra, my devoted.*

I reached for him as a voice shouted, "Terra!" This was a real man's voice. It was your voice, outside the flames, muffled from the crackling.

Terra!

"I see you!" you shouted.

I extended my hand, reaching for Adam. We touched—a powerful surge of energy pierced through my hand, channelling through my being. Adam flashed through my mind. Papa. Mum. Symon and Grandma. Our happy family. Then the sun. The naked man and I held hands, soaring out of a thick forest and into the cloudless sky. Vibra. It was familiar, a re-enactment of the scrolls and Adam's dream.

A firm hand snagged my shoulder and pulled me. It tore me through the flames and smoke, and out into the open air. I gasped, and sweat rolled down my face. My hair and dress were scorched. There were burn marks all over my arms.

"Terra! Who else is in there?" you said.

Reality began to take hold again as air filled my lungs. My vision adjusted to the darkness as the cool wind bit my lightly roasted body. My mind refreshed. The memory of Grandma and Symon burning, Mum missing, and Papa shooting himself were clear. The scrolls. Adam's dream. His scar. It was no animal attack; it was an intentional mark from that dagger.

The sun-headed man and his woman—no, wife . . . me. We sprouted from the baby. Just like the scrolls had shown. It all made sense. Adam was calling to me from beyond. His physical form was the baby. His soul was the sun-headed man, wanting to take my hand so we could be together. Male and female. Man and wife, as is the cycle of life. The skeletons—my poor family. It was a prophecy for the gift of summer. Adam was to bring it. The scrolls outlined the prophecy. Purity. Was it fulfilled? I don't think so. You intercepted it by saving me.

It was you, Liam.

* * *

"That's all I remember. I don't know what came over me," I said. "I still think of my brother, Adam." I sat across the dining table from Liam. The dim lighting made it difficult to see his expression. I wanted to know what he was thinking. It couldn't have been good. One hand was on his pistol. The other was inches from a bottle of whiskey.

"And the letters, to your . . . brother?" Liam asked.

"They were sent back to me, from the coal company. Adam's body was never found, just like Mum's. I can't help but wonder if the prophecy was real, and Grandma and Grampa had initiated something. A blessing turned a curse if it wasn't fulfilled. How else would you explain the drought? How else would you explain Papa shooting himself? Mum vanishing? Or how these letters survived the flames? The Summer Giver needs a pure soul to bless us with lush crops."

Liam snagged the bottle and chugged some whiskey. He slammed it back down and said, "Is that how you explain carving a knife down our baby boy's chest?"

I swallowed heavily. Liam was right. It was my rationalization, and he didn't understand because he never saw the sun-headed man. My confession wasn't enough. He'd see, when our boy is old enough to wed. When the flames come, and the Summer Giver sprouts.

Awake from the observing state. (Turn to Page 129)

Your eyes fly open, making you realize you've returned to the Midway atop the sandhill, beside your ghoulish companion. The orb loses its energy and falls to the floor, scattering particles of sand. You rub your head, trying to understand what you experienced. The anger, delusional beliefs, and sacrifice were undoubtedly a lot to take in.

"Any clues?" Malpherities asks. "I didn't sense any."

You shake your head. "I don't think so."

"Well, we must keep going." Malpherities leans down and grabs the orb. It wiggles rapidly in his claws. You take the orb from him, it calms in motion, and your body fuses with it. The room blooms white, and three new portals appear from the empty space.

The portal to your far left showcases a laboratory, ships, and protests. The center portal pulls you in, displaying an underground bunker with people screaming. Blood is everywhere. The portal to the right has brief moments of a deforesting company tearing down trees. There are masked people in the woods, watching the workers.

MAKE ONE OF THREE CHOICES:

Take the portal on the left. (Turn to Page 101)

Ride into the portal in the centre. (Turn to Page 217)

Enter the portal on the right. (Turn to Page 131)

NATURE'S APEX

Work, chop, Work, chop.
CHOP, CHOP.

The mundane task of tearing down the forest is no glorious job. But hey, it pays the bills, right? There's good money in ripping apart the wilderness around Prince George. The town is willing to pay a rush job, too; they aren't messing around to flip this location into a tourist trap. People complain about it, saying that it is a disservice to the environment or whatever. Well, too bad. People progress. There's so much forest out there that it doesn't matter! Plus, pulling in visitors with a catchy sign will help the economy. The new millennium is eleven years away, meaning it's time to get with the times. At least that is what Tanner tells himself because he was told that, because he needs this money, because he wants to go to college, because he is an adult now—no more mooching off his folks. Thus, Tanner works hard.

Tanner is drenched in sweat, hauling the scraps left by the heavy machinery further ahead. One by one, the trees fall. Birds fly everywhere! Some small critters are bolting for their lives, hoping not to get crushed by the machinery. Branches, logs, dirt, bushes, animal corpses—you name it. Anything that is in the way goes so the next crew can install the framework for the large town sign. Thus, Tanner cleans up.

A fraction of the town folks are pissed off about the teardown. Quite frankly, Tanner keeps his head down. If he didn't, maybe he'd side with the environmentalists—since they do have a point—but then how would he make enough cash to pay for school? He wants an education and does not want to be in the logging industry for his whole life. In this town, your options are limited. Thus, Tanner doesn't overthink it.

"Tanner!" came a coworker's voice. Tycho. He's sweating just as bad as Tanner. Tycho is new to the crew, but Tanner doesn't mind showing him the ropes.

"Yo?" Tanner asks through the loud sounds of trees crashing.

SNAP. SNAP.

CRASH!!!

Tycho says, "When is our break? I'm sweating like a pig here."

Tanner laughs. "Not for a while, man. We just started."

"Christ," Tycho says, lugging a large branch into the woodchipper.

BZZZZZZZZ!! One down, dozens more to go.

"Nasty," Tycho says, picking up a pile of dead birds. They're in a mangled nest, probably hatchlings.

"Yeah, well, tough shit for them," Tanner says.

"You think that?" Tycho says through the kerfuffle.

"Well, yeah. It's not our fault. We're just trying to get paid."

"People are gonna be pissed. You don't kill animals."

"If those tree-humpers want to get mad at anyone, it should be the mayor."

"Totally. Still, we should take ownership of what we do, you know?"

"Then quit," Tanner smirks, throwing some branches into the woodchipper.

BZZZZZ!

Tanner doesn't want to get into a stupid righteousness conversation with Tycho. The guy is too fresh to understand that the crew couldn't give less of a shit for nature. This isn't some Snow White Disney movie.

No. This is life! What was that thing people said in school? Oh, right, Darwinism. Survival of the fittest, baby! Thus, Tanner stays focused.

SNAP. SNAP. CRASH!! More trees are tumbling down.

Tycho stays quiet, keeping his hippie-dippie comments to himself, and the crew works throughout the early AM with the red horizon highlighting the area. The sooner they clear out this forest, the better. Tanner just wants to kick it back with a beer.

He eventually finds a dead deer—a small buck. It looks like a branch punctured its lungs. The muzzle is all bruised up, too. Jeez. That's going to take a few people to move. It's not like Tanner enjoys this, but man, he *really* needs that cash.

"Tycho! Hudson! Get over here. Help me move this," Tanner calls out.

Hudson gets here right away, ready to lift the corpse. Tycho hasn't shown up. Seriously? Where'd he go? Tanner looks around to see if he can spot him, but he's nowhere.

"You see Tycho?" Tanner asks.

"Nah," Hudson says. "Probably getting spooked. I tell you, there's something out in the woods."

"Shut it, man," Tanner says. Hudson is ridiculous. Look at him, scratching his bloated belly. Somehow, he's managed to gain weight over the past couple of weeks clearing this shitty forest. Throw in a dash of over-worrying with too many burgers, and you end up looking like goof here.

"I'm telling you, I've seen some weird shit. People, but not."

"Tycho!" Tanner calls out. "Get over here!"

Rustling comes from the bushes, and Tycho appears. "Yo, sorry, man."

"What gives? Stop wanking it."

"Had to piss."

"There are stations for that. Don't act like some animal. Now help us move this thing."

The three guys figure out how to move the corpse as a man by the heavy machinery shouts, "FUCKING CHRIST!"

He stops the parson loader and hops out of the operator seat, tumbling onto the ground. Another man screams, catching the rest of the crew's attention. Tanner, Hudson, and Tycho leave the deer corpse and gather with the rest of the twelve crew to see what is going on.

The first guy's eyes are popping out of their sockets, saying, "You guys see that?"

"See what?" Hudson asks.

"In the forest, fucking Sasquatch."

"Bullshit," comes a gruff voice, the foreman. He sips his Tim Horton's coffee with a loud *SLLLLLUUURRRP* and puffs on his smoke, saying, "Get back to work."

"No, it's true!" the second man says.

The guy who screamed chirps in, saying, "I saw something in there. It looked human but had an animal face, like this." He uses his fingers to emphasize ears on top of his skull.

"I told you this place is cursed, man," Hudson says.

"I said zip it, bro," Tanner says. How many times does he have to tell him?

The foreman says, "Alright! Let—"

"Look!" the first man shouts before the foreman can finish.

A tin can flies into the air with flames coming out of the top, followed by smoke seeping from it. Wait, there's another, and another! *HSSSSSSSS!* The three cans fall towards the twelve deforesters, seeping large streams of smoke. Instantly the crew starts coughing and covering their faces. These are homemade tear gas devices. The goddamned tree-humpers!

SPLAT, SPLAT, SPLAT!

The crew keeps coughing as paintball bullets splatter their vests. Blue, red, and orange colours hit them all over. These poor workers have no defence. How many attackers are in the forest? A dozen, or maybe three? It's impossible to tell with the tear gas filling up the area.

The crew is shit-scared and starts booking it, despite the foreman's attempts to wrangle them. Tanner is coughing violently, eyes watering, hurrying back as a paintball bullet hits his biceps. Ouch, that'll sting later.

Some of the crew straight up flee the scene, including that pussy-ass Hudson, bringing them down to about five guys. Two of them are roiled and rush into the forest towards the paintballs, shielding themselves with their forearms.

Tanner is with the foreman, running out of the tear gas area, trying to keep himself together. The foreman pulls out his walkie-talkie, pressing the communication button to talk.

THWMP!

A branch knocks him in the back of his neck. He drops the walkie-talkie, falling to the ground. Tanner spins to see a deer-masked deforester standing in front of him. Woah, it's one of the tree-humpers, hidden as one of their own. Clever bastards.

Tanner shouts and lunges a fist at the man. His foe is too fast and shoves the branch into his gut. It throws Tanner to the ground with a hefty thud. His assaulter raises the log and swings it down; Tanner prepares for impact! Firm hands snag the log in mid-arch.

"Vlad, what the fuck?" comes the deep voice of the assaulter, slightly muffled from the mask—clearly Tycho. The new guy . . . betrayer.

"We don't kill straight up. Mercy only," says the man. He's got to be Russian with that accent.

"I wasn't gonna kill the guy. I'm not a psycho, dumbass. Just rough him up."

"With the size of that log into his face? Think."

Tanner groans, attempting to crawl away, still on his back. He doesn't need this shit. Why did he attempt to play hero for the foreman? Maybe Hudson was right to book it. Too late now. A boot steps on his shoulder, pinning him. Tanner looks up to see this Vlad character staring at him in a rubber deer mask.

"Not so fast," the man says, leaning down to look at Tanner in the teeth. "You're going to be the message from Mother Nature's Guardians."

Just now, Tanner clues into how quiet the scene is. Either the rest of the crew ditched, or these pricks managed to get the upper hand on them. All you can hear is the *HSSSSSS* of the tear gas. Footsteps pick up, and a third deer-masked tree-humper appears.

"Hey, the others are gone. Well, I had to beat the shit out of another," says the newcomer.

"All good, Haze," Vlad says. "We got our message here. This asshole tried to help the foreman call for help."

Tycho says, "Trust me. He doesn't give a shit about what he's doing."

Vlad nods, saying, "Good. This will complement our message to the mayor."

The man named Haze pulls out a spray can and says, "Knock 'em out. Let's do it."

"Don't say shit, you got that, Tanner?" Tycho sneers. "You'll have wished the log crushed your pretty little face."

Tanner gasps. "No, wait, I—" Before he can finish his sentence, Vlad slams his boot into the side of his head, knocking him out.

Blackness.

At this point, Tanner isn't aware of anything that is going on. They're moving him . . . he fazes in and out of consciousness . . . where? Darkness fades. The scene brightens to overexposed light. Three deer-men appear in front of him, fully naked like some strange anthropomorphic creatures, laughing at him with twisted faces and fangs. Behind the deer-men are large hands made of wood. They're feminine—Mother Nature. Fire fills up the sky. Oh, her wrath!

These visuals are all a crack-dream as Tanner feels a bucket of liquid splatter his body. The substance is sticky. Blades of grass and feathers sprinkle his body. The sound of a spray can *SPSHHHHHHHHH* wakes him up as a rubber mask is placed over his head. Tanner blinks several times, gaining a grasp on reality once more. He can see through the small holes of his mask. The three deer-masked tree-humpers run from the scene, vanishing into the forest, back to Mother Nature. They are her safe keepers. Man, Tanner isn't with it. He tastes blood in his mouth.

Now, Tanner clues into the fact he's tied up against a tree. His body is wrapped in rope and cannot move at all! His mouth is stuffed with rags, making him gurgle for help. He's stripped down to his boxers, covered in red spray paint, chicken feathers, and grass. Eventually, help arrives as the crew returns to the deforestation site with the RCMP and an ambulance.

The news also shows up. They're fast buggers. Video cameras and flashing photography are all over him as the RCMP cut him free from the tree. They remove his mask, letting him see it is a rubber chicken. He's seen this mask at the dollar store. It's not 100% accurate for the animals in the forest, but hey, it got the message across.

The red paint on his chest forms a crude deer icon on his chest. Those damn tree-humpers. They made a joke of Tanner. Tycho . . . the accomplice. Chances are Tanner won't be seeing him again any time soon. He's best not to rat on the guy either. Tycho made his point pretty clear, and these guys don't seem to be shy of violence. Hudson had it right all along—be afraid and ditch your coworkers when danger arrives. For real, that's what animals do in the wild. Mother Nature's Guardians are the apex predators. Survival of the fittest. Tanner learned about Darwinism in school. Plus, in the end, all Tanner wants is some cash because he wants to go to college, because shit like this fiasco isn't worth it, because they made him into a chicken man. Thus, Tanner is looking for a new job.

Fragment: R

Awake from the observing state. (Turn to Page 139)

I s it possible? Was that one of the fragments? You awake from the observing state, returning to the real you as the orb slips from your hand. Your smile in excitement. Yes, indeed, you did see a clue. That wasn't some glitch or figment of your imagination. "I saw a fragment!" you say.

"Really?" Malpherities says. "I don't believe it."

"Was it actually . . . the letter R?"

"Hmm. Not much of a clue, is it?"

"No, not really. The fragments are letters?"

"We will make a note of it. Let's go. We're on a roll."

The excitement of the discovery fills you with enthusiasm as you seize the orb, preparing for the next observation. Your body melts with the object, and the room turns white. Three portals appear, offering new lives to explore.

The orb naturally gravitates towards the portal on the left, which shows brief flashes of an underground bunker, blood, and people screaming. The center portal has an astronaut in space, floating endlessly. The portal on the far right has a snowy mountain scene with a knight in shining armour. Golden scales belong to a giant lumbering reptile.

MAKE ONE OF THREE CHOICES:

Be sucked into the left portal. (Turn to Page 217)

Enter the central portal. (Turn to Page 223)

Turn towards the right portal. (Turn to Page 141)

DRACONEM REVIVAL

Being a remnant of the past is an uneasy path, like training a draconem. Most humans are incapable of performing the daunting task. It requires discipline, courage, and persistence. The draconem themselves are monstrous flying reptilians that hold a higher degree of intelligence than humans. Which makes one wonder, how can you tame something with greater intellect than yourself?

Large hazelnut serpentine eyes stare into the face of the hunter standing before it. This human, much like the draconem, is of a dying breed—a Drac Hunter.

The hunter pets the massive reptilian's head, gently running her steel gauntlet along the metallic-like scales. From afar, they simply look like a shining sheet of gold and brown. Upon closer inspection, you can see an array of colours on each scale, reflecting against the setting sun on the icy landscape.

The draconem snorts, exhaling a gush of hot air into the hunter's face and short brunette hair. She laughs. "Oh, Sam." Technically the draconem's name is Samantherius, the name she had before being tamed. But Sam serves the hunter now.

She's developed a special bond with this creature, for most draconem lack their former intelligence. The hunter is all too familiar with the infamous Drac Age, a time when the draconem ruled the world, enslaving all others who dared challenge them. Times have changed for the better. The old world of heroes that have brought humanity out of the Drac Age are dwindling, like the Drac Hunters and their draconem.

Kassandra, the hunter, and her loyal draconem are relics of the ill time. No different than the famous Paladins of Zeal or the Knight's Union. She could spend a lifetime reflecting on the past, remembering the former days of glory, saving her people from enslavement. After all, she is a fighter, and in times of peace, is there a home for one?

She does not know. However, she is still cleaning up the remaining rebellious draconem that challenge the new authority of mankind. She estimates there might be a dozen of them left. It's an educated guess by the frequency of reported sightings and how many draconem used to rule in the Drac Age. Her job has an end goal of making sure that another Drac Lord does not rise again. They are still out there . . . one, in particular, is the infamous Karazickle, Drac Lord of the night.

This is why Kassandra and Sam overlook the icy mountaintops of Mount Kuzuchi, far above the forestry of Zingalg below. Reports of a draconem within this rocky landscape have risen numerous times. People claim to have seen a massive draconem that soars over the moon. Some claim it is white; others say it is black. Each sighting has different descriptions of their size, making it impossible to know what is true.

At the base of Mount Kuzuchi is the vast forest of Zingalg; further down are the grassy hills with a river where a village is visible. Huts, smoke, and bridges are tiny dots from this distance. The hunter would usually ask these villagers about the draconem sightings, but this is no ordinary village. It's a village of vazeleads—reptilian men. They're harmless, just not too intelligent, and she can't waste her time with them.

"Does that thing always give you attitude?" comes a grizzly voice. There's the subtle sound of distaste in the man's tone. Against

Kassandra's will, she had to bring a Paladin of Zeal to investigate the sighting. The Council of Just willed it so.

"Sam has a mind of her own," Kassandra says, facing the paladin. The man is covered from head to toe in golden armour that radiates an unnatural yellow-and-white glow. This demonstration is only a fraction of the holy power blessed to paladins from the Heavenly Kingdoms, giving humanity an advantage over the draconem in the Drac age. The glow is most likely some protection prayer. Kassandra doesn't know nor care. She didn't want to bring the man because paladins are stubborn and aren't fond of draconem.

The man says, "They have no minds of their own once they been enslaved. You know that, right? That's the purpose of the nymphs' words of power. They're no different than those vazeleads down below."

"Llath, if only you were knew one close hand," Kassandra says.

The man, Llath, walks ahead on the icy snow, each step crunching. "I'd rather not. Their kind is responsible for everything."

Kassandra knows there's no point arguing with a Paladin of Zeal. They are probably the most arrogant people in the known world— even more so than the nymphs who are stuck in their ancient ways of nature, denying the advancing civilization. Perhaps that is why the Paladins of Zeal and the nymphs agreed over those powerful words to enslave draconem. These words, when whispered into a draconem's ear, shatter their intelligence, reducing them to a beast. They become no different than a dog—easily tameable.

That is what the nymphs' supernatural words are supposed to do to a draconem. However, Sam is different. Sam seems to be fully aware; Kassandra has witnessed it herself. The draconem responds to words and conversations. She doesn't speak, but her snorts and huffs say enough.

There's certainly no convincing a Paladin of Zeal—or anyone for that matter. It is probably for the better. If anyone were to find out, they'd either execute Sam or reapply the words of power to enslave

Sam for good. Too many words of power can crush a mind entirely. Sam's intelligence is Kassandra's secret.

Kassandra snags the leather rope dangling from the saddle atop Sam. She climbs up to the draconem's spiky back and onto the seat, engaging her to walk alongside Llath. The Paladin of Zeal refuses to ride the draconem, even though he rode on her earlier as they flew to Mount Kuzuchi to get here. Paladins . . . merely stubborn loyal followers of their higher-ups. They'll obey orders from their captains, following the chain of command leading up to the Heavenly Kingdoms. Not like Kassandra; she is a free agent.

"It shouldn't be that much further," Llath says. His reference is to the cave he spotted while they were travelling up Mount Kuzuchi.

"What do you suppose we will find?" Kassandra says.

"If the reports are true, a draconem," Llath says.

"The sightings have been mixed. Some say it's large, others small. Black . . . or white."

"There's only one white dragon left."

"Karazickle."

"Aye. Wouldn't Lord Saule be proud of us?"

Sam snorts again, and a shiver runs down Kassandra's spine. It isn't due to the cold winds and the setting sun. No. She fears that they may find Karazickle, Drac Lord of the night. There would be no chance in hell the three of them could take on Karazickle. Only fools would try in such small numbers. With any luck, the sighting is just a regular draconem, something Kassandra is trained to handle.

"Lord Saule would give you a fair promotion, wouldn't he?" Kassandra says.

"Indeed. Truthfully, I doubt we will find Karazickle. The Drac Lord has not been spotted in over a decade. You know how these sightings go. People exaggerate what they see in the sky. Watch our luck, it'll be some mountain bird."

"I suppose so," Kassandra says. "No one has gotten a good look at a draconem anymore. They're rare."

"Yes, as you and I are. The Drac Age was so long ago. Amazingly, people like you get into this profession."

"Well, my father was a Drac Hunter, and so I follow my family."

"It's a dead end," Llath says.

Kassandra doesn't reply to the remark, knowing it is true. There aren't too many draconem around. Once all the draconem are gone, she has no idea how she will maintain a living. Perhaps she will become a mercenary for hire, taking on odd jobs just to stay alive. It certainly wasn't what she had hoped for with her life. Owning a draconem is not an easy expense. They need to eat an astronomical amount of food. Then there's housing one. No ordinary stable can hold such a beautiful creature. At the end of the day, there is no way she would abandon Sam.

"There," Llath says, pointing to a cave in the near distance. The wind picks up, blowing snow into their faces. "That must be it."

Sam huffs, pointing at the ground. Kassandra spots what the draconem is referencing—large pawprints in the snow. Another draconem is nearby. They are on the right track. Llath doesn't comment on Sam's observation, which is a clear sign of the draconem's intelligence, and the three venture over the rough, jagged landscape towards the cavern. The closer they get, the larger the cavern becomes. The entrance is over double the size of Sam, who was already three times as tall as any human.

Giant stalactites and icicles run along with the ceiling of the cavern. The pawprints in the snow lead directly into the entrance, disappearing into the dark charcoal interior. The prints are twice the size of Sam's. It appears they'll be wrangling a monstrous draconem today.

The three enter the cavern, leaving the windy mountaintops behind. They adjust to the darkness with the only light radiating from Llath's armour. All outside sounds muffle the further they go as the temperature warms. The snow tracks of whom they stalk dissipate as the cave descends deeper . . . and deeper.

The group slows their pace to a crawl, making sure not to make any noise. Unfortunately, due to Sam's size, she cannot help the sounds of her giant paws pressing into the rocky ground. Kassandra dismounts and pats Sam on the head. "I need you to stay guard here."

Sam snorts, the eyes going back-and-forth as if she is reading Kassandra's posture. Yes, Kassandra is slightly slouching, eyebrows slanted, indicating she is worried about Sam's safety. They need stealth, and Sam is just too large to go any further. There's also the concern that draconem can sniff each other's presence. It's a double-edged sword which makes them effective at hunting their own kind.

"Let's go," Llath whispers. "We don't want to stay around too long. We aren't aware if those tracks are fresh or not."

"Keep watch, Sam," Kassandra orders, standing upright.

Sam flairs her nostrils and sits, watching as Kassandra and Llath venture further down the cavern. Kassandra doesn't want to leave her, but there is no choice. She grips the handle of her sword strapped to her belt, ready for action. Llath already pulled out his spiked mace and a previously strapped shield from his back.

The cave slope comes to an end, and they make a right turn to see a warm glowing light coming further inside. Someone is home. No words are exchanged between Kassandra and Llath, as they are both fully aware of the dangers that await them.

The light comes from another right turn, and the two carefully creep up to it, keeping their backs close to the rocky walls. But not too close, as there are jagged, razor-sharp edges all along the wall.

They make the turn and enter a massive underground dome, large enough to house an entire village. The path spirals downward, leading to the dome's base, where a dozen cages are visible under numerous torchlights. The cages contain humanoids. They have tails . . . extended muzzles, brown scales, and feathers on their scalps. These are vazeleads. There are a couple of wooden tables with shackles and chains draped over them. Trays with various operating tools are prepped for surgery.

A human-sized glass tank filled with a light-grey mist rests beside one operating table. On the wooden surface of the table, a vazelead is cuffed with rusty metal chains. The reptilian does not look like the other vazeleads. Most of the scales are gone. Those that are left are dark charcoal running along the neck down to the whip-like tail. What remains of the naked body is smooth leathery skin. The vazelead is far taller, muscular, and the muzzle is shorter. The eyes are closed, and the gut has been sliced open, exposing the organs inside. Jars of their black blood rest on a tray.

"What is this?" Llath says.

"Some sort of experiment," Kassandra says. "No draconem is capable of such delicacy."

"No," Llath says. "Could this be a rogue Drac Hunter?"

It's a possibility. Draconem are too large to perform intricate surgeries—or experiments—on small creatures like vazeleads or humans. Yet, a Drac Hunter has no need for vazeleads. They're harmless villagers. Whatever this is, it is meant to be a secret. The question is, why?

"Should we go?" Llath asks.

Kassandra says, "Let's investigate further. We need some answers on whatever horror this is. So far, there doesn't appear to be any draconem, and we can handle some fool and their mad experiments."

"Aye," Llath says, taking the lead. The two carefully go down the spiralling slope and into the dome. Kassandra doesn't like this but needs to scope it out—that's their mission. Who has a laboratory deep within a mountain? What is that mist? Perhaps this inhumane autopsy is related to the mixed reports they had received.

The two reach the bottom of the slope and are ground-level with the laboratory. The dome goes further into the mountain, disappearing into the dark. Most of the vazeleads in the cages are sleeping, shivering. One of them starts to sniff. The black feathers along its scalp puff upwards. It looks at them as its yellow eyes widen. A toothy smile spreads across its face.

"Humans!" it says, standing upright. "A paladin, yes!"

Kassandra takes the lead.

Llath's says, "Don't waste your time with it."

She doesn't listen and is tired of Llath's superiority complex. She creeps up to the being, resting against a rock to avoid being exposed in the open. Up close, she can see that the vazelead is bony, indicating it hasn't eaten in days. Its claws grip the bars of the metal cage as its tail sways side to side in excitement.

"We don't have long," the vazelead says.

"What is this?" Kassandra asks.

"My people are in trouble, please. Warn everyone. The banishment!"

"From what?"

"The metamorphosis fumes! He's discovered the potency of the underworld . . . what it does to us—turning us into monsters."

"Fumes? What?"

A deep thundering roar bellows from the darkness, silencing the vazelead and Kassandra. Llath hurries over to her side as giant black reptilian wings flap, blowing gusts of wind into the dome from the dark. Four paws appear from the shadows, landing on the ground, sending a treble ripple beneath Kassandra's feet. Pebbles fall from the ceiling as a monstrous draconem comes into the light. The black scales glimmer from the torch flame while the neck leans forward. It sniffs aggressively, eyeing the laboratory. This draconem is about a head taller than Sam, not capable of those paw prints seen earlier in the snow.

"Escape," the vazelead says. "Warn everyone."

"What are they doing?" Kassandra asks.

Llath raises his mace. "Let me stun this draconem. You can tame it, Kassandra."

"Don't do that," the vazelead says.

The draconem lets out a bellowing growl, loud enough to silence the three's conversation and make them cover their ears. It stomps towards them, sniffing excessively. It knows there are visitors.

Llath dashes from the rock and raises his mace. "God, our Saviour, help us to follow the light and live the truth. Grant me flame so I may reveal what lurks in the shadows. Amen!" He shouts the Prayer of Power as a bright light beams from his spiked mace, projecting into the draconem's eye, temporarily blinding it.

Kassandra charges to the draconem, knowing the standard procedure to tame a beast. The paladin disorients it. She gets to the creature's ear and whispers the words of power to shatter its mind. Yet, something isn't right about this draconem, for it does not speak. Nor does it seem to observe. It is merely angry, hunting, like an animal. It's as if it has been tamed already by the nymphs' words of power. Her guts tell her that they need to re-evaluate, but there is no time as Llath keeps shining the light into the beast's face, causing it to roar with frustration.

The draconem's tail swings violently, barely missing Kassandra and knocking some laboratory equipment to the ground. She dodges the attack, rolling out of the way, and leaps towards the tail as it recovers. The hunter clings onto one of the large spikes that run along the creature's spine and tail.

Their opponent stands on its hind legs momentarily, then soars downwards. Llath leaps clear of being stomped on. The light diminishes from the mace, and the draconem's sight returns.

Kassandra is halfway up the creature's back as it lashes out violently, storming into some of the cages. The gigantic paws collapse the metal rods, including the vazeleads inside, crushing them. The draconem continues to move viciously, attempting to shrug Kassandra off.

Llath gets up with both hands, swinging his spiked mace at the ankles of the foe, piercing into the scales. The draconem yelps, allowing Kassandra to bolt up. She runs along the creature's spine and leaps for the neck, climbing up to the back of the skull. The ear hole is beside her, and she starts to whisper the words of power.

The animal groans as it sways side to side, the eyes are rolling back. Yes, the words of power are working!

"Enough!" comes a thundering strident voice from deeper within the cavern.

The command stops Kassandra from speaking. The draconem freezes, and Llath pants, freeing his mace from the creature's ankle.

From the darkness comes a man. He, too, is in golden armour with long black hair, ending by his shoulder blades. His hands rest behind his back, just above the deep red kilt. The calmness of his stride is odd, making Cassandra feel more on guard.

"Lord Saule," Llath says as he lowers his mace, kneeling.

How? Kassandra thinks. Nothing here is adding up. She's never seen Lord Saule in person and could have never identified him.

"Stand, loyal paladin," Lord Saule says, coming to a stop. "You and this Drac Hunter are simply obeying orders. Loyal and admirable. You know not what is in place here."

"And what is that, Lord Saule?" Kassandra asks. "This draconem appears tamed already."

"That it is," Lord Saule says. "This is the business of the Council of Just. Not of your concern, and you should leave."

Kassandra says, "But the Council of Just sent us here . . . there are draconem sightings on Mount Kuzuchi."

"It is simply my loyal draconem here. Thankfully, I intercepted you before reapplying those words of power. You could have crushed whatever is left of his mind."

The vazelead whom they talked to earlier hisses. "Lies!"

Lord Saule scowls.

"What of these vazeleads?" Llath asks.

The vazelead shouts, "Karazickle!"

Another draconem roar erupts from the dome entrance. It's familiar. Sam. The golden dragon leaps from the upper tunnel and soars towards Lord Saule. Her teeth are fully exposed, snarling at her opponent.

"Sam! Down," Kassandra orders. This is a perfect example of Sam having her own mind, for draconem are supposed to obey their Drac

Hunters on command. Sam never acts out of order without reason. The girl knows something Kassandra doesn't.

The black draconem dashes for Sam in a sudden burst of energy. Kassandra grips onto the upper neck spike tightly as the two giants collide.

"What is the meaning of this?" Lord Saule demands.

Sam overpowers the black draconem with one fell swoop of her claw, knocking it in the neck, causing the creature to collapse onto an operating table, crushing the corpse on it. Sam elegantly spins towards Lord Saule, sprinting for him, wings spread outwards to emphasize her size.

"No!" Llath shouts, standing in front of his leader.

Lord Saule begins to move his hands in strange patterns, creating symbols with his fingers. Sam doesn't stop.

"Sam!" Kassandra shouts, leaping off the black draconem who attempts to get up, dazed.

Through the chaos, the vazelead shouts, "He's building an army!"

A thick spike rips through Llath's back, raising him up. He lets out a howl of pain. The point is attached to a white scaled tail coming from Lord Saule's lower back. His body begins to twitch as a reverberating growling hums from deep within his core. The muscles and spine underneath his skin begin the pulsate, expanding as his body cracks. The human form he once was breaks apart as his head rises from the extending spine, stretching the flesh.

Llath is flicked from Lord Saule's spike while Sam continues charging towards her foe. She swats Llath's flying body against a nearby wall. Lord Saule's back stretches outward as his shoulder blades split apart, forming giant wings. His face extends out into a muzzle with sharp teeth as the skull grows. His skin begins to bubble, morphing into white scales as Sam raises her one claw, swiping downward. The blow hits Lord Saule's abomination body, sending him tumbling backward. He regains balance on his new clawed feet, staying upward as his form continues to mutate from human and into draconem.

"Sam, we must go!" Kassandra shouts, rushing towards her. She spots Llath on the ground, with a gaping hole where his stomach once was. He doesn't move.

Sam spins around, skidding, and hurries to her master. Kassandra snags onto the leather lace. She swings up onto the saddle as Sam takes flight, reaching the second level of the cave and hurrying back to the entrance.

Kassandra takes one look back to see that Lord Saule is gone and what remains is a massive draconem with its wings folded. Karazickle, the Drac Lord of the night. His claws smash against the spiral path, breaking it to pieces. The tail flails around, demolishing the laboratory as he begins the chase. There's a speckle of glowing gold hanging from this tail . . . It can't be.

Sam dashes in a strident sprint, flapping her wings to gain more momentum as they reach the cavern entrance. Loud thundering stomps echo as the Drac Lord of the night closes in. There's no way Kassandra and Sam have the strength to face Karazickle. They have to escape, yet he is faster, more significant, and can easily catch them.

They reach the cavern entrance as Sam leaps up to the skies, flapping her wings. She jerks backwards, yelping. Karazickle's jaws clench onto her tail, pulling her back. He throws her against the side of the mountain. Kassandra is barely able to hang on!

"You will perish for what you've discovered," Karazickle's deep, menacing voice booms. "The vazeleads are mine. For I will force them into an army of anger and hate, and they will remain oblivious. Your words of power do not affect their people. No human, nor nymph, nor any mortal will be prepared for the demise that awaits. The Drac Age will be reborn!"

Sam scurries to her feet and hisses, her throat vibrating, ready to fight. She is no match for Karazickle, yet they cannot outrun him. Kassandra would rather go down with a fight than die a coward. She pulls out her sword, raising it in the air as Sam stands on her hind legs, attempting to size herself up to the Drac Lord.

Karazickle barks and stumbles as if recovering from an attack. He shakes his head, revealing at the back of his skull is Llath. His mace pierces into Karazickle's head. The weapon radiates a smokeless white fire, blasting into the air and burning the scales on the draconem. The flame channels from a white flaming orb within the paladin's core, where blood pours out of the gaping hole in Llath's flesh. The paladin's heavenly power is barely keeping him alive.

Llath's voice is strident, shouting, "Karazickle, Drac Lord of the night, you will face humanity's justice for the terrors you've caused!" He raises his mace and slams it into Karazickle's scales. A blast of sparks and flame sputter from the attack.

Karazickle yelps. "Fool! For I am Lord Saule. Your people are disillusioned."

"Run, Kassandra! Warn the Council of Just!" Llath lunges the mace down once more, slamming it dead center into Karazickle's skull.

Kassandra knows they are no match for the Drac Lord. Llath can only hold his life force for so long through the will of the heavenly. She can either die here with Llath or attempt to warn humanity. The paladin knows he is a sacrifice for the greater good. With regret, Kassandra steers Sam clear of the Drac Lord. Sam flaps her wings, gaining momentum into the sky and leaving the tragedy behind.

Llath continues to slam his mace down on the Drac Lord, causing sparks to fly in every which direction. Karazickle cries again and again! For a brief moment, it looks like Llath may even get the upper hand on the Drac Lord, who tumbles several times, stunned from the vicious attacks of the paladin.

Karazickle lets out a fierce roar and throws his head against the mountainside wall, knocking Llath free. The blow is enough to cause the cavern's entrance to collapse, leaving nothing but snow and rubble over the cave. Llath descends as the Drac Lord swats at him. The blow throws the paladin violently against the rocks. He drops his weapon. The glowing orb from Llath's core fizzles out in a single blip.

The battle scene is a mere speck in the distance as Sam flies faster than she ever has before. The piercing icy winds bite Kassandra's face as she faces forward. There may be a chance that Karazickle follows, but unlikely. Llath managed to wound him before leaving this realm.

The discovery of the vazelead laboratory was a disgust of unimaginable heights. The sightings of draconem around Mount Kuzuchi proved to be true—Karazickle the Drac Lord of the night, and his tamed black draconem. The Drac Lord is alive and well, hiding amongst humanity as Lord Saule, leader of the Paladins of Zeal, member of the Council of Just.

The Drac Lord's haunting words echo in Kassandra's mind . . . *"The vazeleads are mine. For I will force them into an army of anger and hate, and they will remain oblivious . . . The Drac Age will be reborn!"*

He is building an army to strike back at humanity, and with the cavern's collapse, what proof does Kassandra have? Karazickle is capable of shapeshifting—another mystery of the Drac Lord's power. It gives him an astronomical advantage. Who will believe the accusations Kassandra will make? She's likely to give herself a death sentence, along with Sam, for making such bold claims. Yet, Llath's sacrifice cannot be in vain, for the sake of humanity rests on Kassandra's shoulders and she is unclear how to proceed.

Awake from the observing state. (Turn to Page 155)

The observing state dissolves with no clues, fragments, or anything related to the time loop. Malpherities also has nothing to share about the observation. You want to ask him questions about this hunter's life, who they were, and if history is inaccurate. You witnessed massive flying reptiles, dragons, really, and knights with holy power. How did all of this go missing in the sands of time?

Malpherities breaks you from your trance by scooping up the orb you dropped from the sand dune, the grains sifting between his claws. Time to go again. You can stop and ponder these witnessing states on your own time. Right now, you have to find those fragments.

And so, you take the orb, and your body melts into it. The cavern fades away as two portals appear. The orb remains still, unlike the other times you've fused with it. This is odd. Thankfully, you can still control the thing and guide it into one of the two portals.

The one on your left shows a child camping with his father by a fire pit. A bear is hiding in the woods. To your right is a laboratory with a fearful scientist held at gunpoint. Where will you witness next? The choice is yours.

MAKE ONE OF TWO CHOICES:

Enter the portal on the left. (Turn to Page 165)

Steer to the portal on the right. (Turn to Page 173)

ARCHEAN II

D ear child,

Humanity's stubbornness has allowed us to thrive beyond our primal counterparts. Colonizing a new world is by no means an easy task. Especially when we consider the Harvesters—gene freaks—that prey on Earthlings. They were once us. At the time of this letter, those behemoths pick us off like cattle to understand their own lost lineage. It's nauseating. We can only wonder what the old world must have been like before the gene editing split humanity. Time has a funny way of erasing history—with war. Understanding the details of how our people were divided seems more unlikely than ever now that we are so far from home on this new exoplanet.

My fellow crew members and I were on the seventh expedition to leave Earth, EX-7006 to be exact. We captured a number of the Harvesters' superior technology, bypassing their self-destruct systems. Humans are crafty. We've adjusted their ships to obey our command, letting us fly far beyond the solar system. I often think about home, where the remainder of humanity is struggling to survive from the Harvesters. It's impossible to know how the previous six expeditions went, as we cannot communicate with Earth anymore. Our crew operates as if we're the last of humanity, for the better of our species.

The exoplanet is named Archean II, as this planet is so young. There's much to explore, despite being smaller than Earth. We've seen fungus and other bacterial life growing around the waters. The rest of the environment is rocky, volcanic, or cold, depending on which part of the planet you are on.

Life has a cruel way of throwing a wrench into something good. Just look at what is being described on this paper. Our crew encountered some hostile radiation or creature during our travel to Archean II. This thing clung onto our ship, like some kind of spider web, as we entered hibernation, wrapping the ship in its embrace. We escaped, not without casualties. Now, Captain Ross, Lydia—who serves second in command—and I are left.

That damn green hue . . . I swear it was alive. A part of it attempted to follow our escape pods as we descended onto the planet. Something about the atmosphere caused it to dissolve as we entered the new world. We had never been so relieved in our lives as we opened the pod's hatch to see such vibrant red and orange colours in the sky and to inhale the rich air.

Earth is shrouded in ash, radiation, and violent storm clouds that block out the sun. Apparently, centuries ago, the war of humanity destroyed the planet, altering the weather drastically. I've seen pictures of the old-world Earth from our digital archives. The planet was a beautiful blue and green. Still, it is nothing like Archean II's two atmospheric purple moons and the orbiting twin sister planet. Both Archean II and its sister are far smaller than Earth, even smaller than Mars.

This world is certainly foreign to us with the red dwarf star and slightly lighter gravity, but we're adjusting. We believe it takes about sixteen Earth hours to complete a day and approximately one-hundred-and-fifty Earth days to finish its yearly rotation. None of us are astronomers, but we have measuring tools from the supplies we brought down with us. Our estimation is a safe bet.

We'd like to visit Archean II's sister planet. Realistically we cannot, as the spaceship was manually set to self-destruct during our descent, preventing any chance of the Harvesters tracking us. Just because we knew how to reverse engineer their ships doesn't mean that there aren't more layers to their tech.

Harvesters are smarter than us, faster, and more robust. They always have one more trick up their sleeve, and we aren't taking any chances. I wouldn't put it past them to have some tracking system in their ships as a fallback. Yet, time continues on, and we have never seen any sighting a Harvester. There's plenty of people back on Earth still, and our new planet is far, far away.

We've been here for over two Archean II years. A life of agriculture has a way of humbling you. Let's not forget humanity's future resting on your shoulders makes you reflect upon everything you've ever done. I've never had so much physical labour in my life. The tools we have help, but we can't rely on them forever. There are no backups, no repair supplies, and how long can the energy engines last? We barely understand how the Harvesters made these self-sustaining batteries work.

The four computers are protected in the main hall, archiving as much as we can. Personally, I'm uncertain about the lifespan of these machines—hence writing this message on paper. Paper! Our settlement is made of military tents—clearly not a long-lasting solution. We're learning to break down rock with fungus to fabricate concrete, but it is no easy task to forge bricks.

At the time of this message, Captain Ross and Lydia expect a baby in our new colony. I reflect on what my role is going to be. Our population will be small for many generations. The three of us have discussed expanding our people's chances of survival by conceiving more children with Lydia and me. This strategy will strengthen the human gene pool with two family trees. We'll focus on the second family lineage after Lydia births her first child with Ross.

Truthfully, I cannot believe we are having these cold, scientific conversations. Life on the run, back home, from the Harvesters, is all we knew. War, anger, fear, hate, violence, aggression, and primeval are everything we understand. Archean II gives us new hope to focus on nurture.

Unfortunately, on Earth, we never discussed strategic procreation to save our species. The topic had come up once during our mission briefing before we left the planet. It was okay then, as we had many crew members. I was fond of my crewmate Zoe before that damn green hue took her life. She was certainly someone I would have liked to have as a permanent partner on any settlement. It's just another wrench thrown by life. I still think about her.

In the back of my mind, I know we are humans. We dare the unknown; we are versatile; we adapt to our environment; the human spirit will live on. We are the founding parents of Archean II. Hope is alive and well in all three of us. Very few of our supplies were damaged during our landing. We continue to plant crops, preparing for the third season. My only sorrow for Archean II is that I will not live to see it thrive due to inevitable old age.

Writing with charcoal on what little paper we have is not ideal, but this personal letter will serve as the first physical historical document of our time here on Archean II. Again, who knows how long those computers will last. May you preserve these words and cherish them as humanity enters its new era.

I will show the newborn the location of this document when they are old enough. It resides here, higher from the ocean shores, just before the snow begins on the mountain. Here, in this cave, where I had first found those two chrome marbles almost two years ago.

There's a pattern of twos on Archean II . . . and I wish we had answers, but neither I, nor Ross, nor Lydia have any conclusion to what these two chrome marbles are. They appear harmless, as nothing has occurred when we brought them back to camp for inspection. There was nothing else in the cave either. Ultimately, we returned the marbles to the cave beside this letter, respecting their origins.

Whether it is life on this planet or simply a past visitor, we know these chrome spheres are no natural formation and we are not alone in the universe. When the newborn is old enough, they will pass down this message to all of you for future generations. It is what humanity has done since the dawn of time ever since we left the trees, further distorting our origins.

From your loving founding parents:

Alan McLeod, Ross Nesheim, and Lydia Ocano.

Awake from the observing state. (Turn to Page 163)

You wake from the observing state with no news to share with Malpherities. The ghoul also spotted nothing in this other life. Once again, you've seen a future landscape that doesn't resemble anything about the present. This one was a little less frightening, at least.

The two of you are determined to find any sort of clue, and you snag the orb, ready to go again.

Your body melts. The cavern dissolves, and two portals appear while you and the orb stay stationary. This is odd, for the orb usually gravitates towards one of the portals. You can still control it, directing it to go in either one of the observing states.

The portal on your left gives brief visions of a child's life. There's a forest, a campfire, and a bear. The portal on the right has a laboratory with syringes, futuristic guns, and people morphing into others. Which one do you take?

MAKE ONE OF TWO CHOICES:

Enter the portal on the left. (Turn to Page 165)

Steer to the portal on the right.(Turn to Page 173)

DESIGN

NATURE

DESIGN

LAVERY

KONN

KONN

LAVERY

NATURE'S DESIGN

People mystify me.

Yes, they're a part of nature, and yet they're the one animal that does everything in their power to force Earth to bend to their will. Look at our technology, language, culture, and cities. We migrate to every corner of the planet and try to change it, deeming it unfit for our needs. Our actions go against the root of evolution, which is to adapt to one's environment, not the other way around. Somewhere along our lineage, we decided we were better than Mother Nature. The amusing fact is we all return to her in the end, where we feed the soil to allow new and better life to flourish. I do genuinely believe that in the end, Mother Nature will reign victorious. People like me can aid her along the way. Whether it is by Nature's Design or my own free will, it is what I do.

People anger me.

Their arrogance fuels my desire to help Mother Nature. I fear the majority of humanity is unaware of the pain they inflict on the planet. People directly destroying the forests and drilling into the Earth's heart are proof of my claim. No well-adjusted animal deliberately damages their life source. Human beings' unawareness to acknowledge their downfalls makes me question if people have free will at all, like a parasite that kills its host. They are wrapped up in their 'civilized' work world that they fail to see the horrors they are causing, let alone the freedom to actively live their lives. Perhaps that is proof they have no will. Most people are pawns for the top few leaders. Maybe people aren't capable of free thought. It would explain the grotesque number of mindless followers popstars have.

People have use to me.

They can serve as a message. If some people lack free will, I may not be responsible for anything I do, just like the other animals. In that case, I am one of many, if not all, humans that are incapable of making a conscious choice. We are simply born the way we are by Nature's Design. It would explain my mindset and desire. The anger that grows inside me comes from a deep need to cleanse the planet of its pain caused by its inhabitants. Not everyone will understand, which is why I hid the first time I offered liberation—a mercy kill that aided the suffering. I was only six years old.

People wouldn't understand me.

The poor magpie was crippled after hitting our front window. The sound didn't grab my mother's attention, for she was too occupied with dinner, wanting to please my testy father. I went outside to inspect the animal, seeing that it had a broken wing. It lay beside the garden out front by the trimming shears, attempting to fly away with no luck. The magpie cawed in agony. It was the first time I had heard something cry like that . . . such a desire for the pain to end. Above, crows circled, ready to feast. You don't have to be very old to understand what was about to happen to the magpie.

Consciously or subconsciously, I decided to save the bird. No, I didn't take it inside where my mother would yell at me, telling me that Father would beat me for bringing a mangy animal into the house. Instead, I took hold of the rusty trimming shears and approached the bird. It froze, uncertain if I was a predator. I was its liberation, bringing the blade around the bird's tiny neck. The first clip didn't cut through the neck, and I will never forget the animal's cries. I cut a few more times and learned how dense bones are—and how dull the shears were. Eventually, the animal stopped moving, the head came free, and the crows came to feast. My mother never discovered what I had done. That day sprouted my purpose as I watched the crows peck flesh from the headless corpse. I knew I had done good. The magpie couldn't feel pain anymore. Pain is everywhere. Whether we have free will or not, everything feels it: the trees, the animals, humans, and the Earth.

A couple of years went by before I killed again; this time, it was a cat. The liberation was more violent and drawn out than the magpie. In the end, it was for the animal's best interest. The creature was being stalked by a pack of coyotes. The cat was homeless, thin, and unable to run. It was pure chance that I found the poor thing when I did, or perhaps it was Mother Nature's guidance. Regardless, the pack of coyotes was on top of the hill, watching. Knowing its soon-to-be fate, I strangled the cat in a puddle of water in the ditch of the road. Scratches, hisses, and bites did not bother me. I knew the good that I was doing. Once the feline stopped moving and I left the corpse, the hungry coyotes came to feast freely on the creature, who was saved from a more violent death.

People aren't like me.

My preferred method is head removal because decapitation is clean with the right weapon. Axes are effective tools, as my father had taught me while camping. I had saved a few more animals between the cat and my first human kill. My hate for humanity started with my father, seeing how he treated Mother, who only wanted to please him by providing a good home. Yet, it was never enough. He'd drink, arrive home late, and unleash destruction for reasons I cannot remember. It didn't matter. He'd find any excuse to hit her, or me.

Father took me on a camping trip, showing me how to navigate the wilderness and hunt. I enjoy the pursuit. The act of tracking, laying traps, and ultimately freeing the prey from grief surged me with new life. Yet, I didn't appreciate Father's methods. He deliberately attacked the animals, stalking them as if he were a predator who killed for fun. Father had trapped a buck and fired his rifle at it, missing the head.

The creature was bleeding with its leg in the trap, lungs filling with blood. He wanted me to give the killing blow, and I swung the axe into the creature's head, freeing it from the horrors my father had created. Father assured me that it was natural for humans to dominate nature. I disagreed and told him I didn't want to kill without reason again. The words upset him for the remainder of the trip. He repeatedly called me a pussy the more he drank the whiskey. He eventually slapped me and threw the first punch, telling me to fight like a man. A few more fists followed before I hit the ground.

Blood filled my mouth as I stared at the campfire below the starry sky. The punch brought my focus to the moment, realizing that I was now a victim, like Mother, like the buck, to this . . . human. He was only a man who deemed himself superior to Nature's Design. I wouldn't have it. The anger was ignited, giving me the strength to see that my father was merely a product of his environment, a piece of nature itself, as I was, as Mother, or the cat, or the magpie. We're all part of Mother Nature, each serving a purpose. Father's ultimate purpose was to create me, creeping up to him, with the weapon in my hand, as he drank.

He didn't even see the axe enter his neck as I swung down. His focus was getting the last drop of whisky from the wretched bottle. I didn't shake as my hands gripped the axe, still in his neck. Father sputtered a few times, getting up from his chair. I pulled the axe from his flesh, widening the wound. He collapsed into the fire, gurgling in pain. Power had shifted, and I realized that I could liberate *him* from misery. He suffered too, from the liquor and from his own chaos. With the axe, I hacked into his head with a sloppy strike. Then another . . . another . . . and another. Eventually, he stopped flailing in the flame, and I continued to chop until his head toppled onto the dirt.

The smell of burning flesh is one I'm not too fond of. Fire is destructive. An axe is clean. With Father dead, I watched the element scorch him. The axe dripped with his blood. Time ceased to be, and the flames withered, suffocating from the body's size.

A black bear smelt death, giving my father one more purpose on Earth—feeding nature. I stepped into the dark, watching as the large animal carefully gnawed on the body, avoiding the crisp, scorched flesh. I crept up and into the truck, locking the doors and hiding the axe in my father's toolbox, knowing that the act I had committed had to remain hidden. Human law and Nature's Design do not see eye to eye. An RCMP unit found me a couple of days later, and they didn't question my statement, for I was a starving, lost child. Nor did they find the axe. The RCMP only saw my father's half-eaten, charred corpse.

Strangely, my mother was comforted. She never expressed this joy to me. The woman cried when the RCMP returned with me and the tragic news of her husband. I could see the relief in her posture over the following days. She no longer scurried around the house like a beaten dog. There was relaxation in her motion, knowing that she didn't have to cook the proper meal or keep the house as tidy as my father demanded. Her subconscious behaviours were proof that I had done good, for my mother is pure. Vengeance can be a tool of mercy.

People fear me.

My anger grew well into adulthood. I became aware that my father was one of many dangerous men and women. I pieced together the harm inflicted on nature from large-scale agriculture and energy sectors to daily acts like carving your name into a tree. The horrific actions of humanity's ignorance take place all around me.

Prince George, my home, decided it needed some flare—a Hollywood-style welcome sign—to bring in tourism. They called it "Clean Up Prince George," saying that the flashy design would bring the town a new prestige. The mayor approved deforesting on top of a hill to build the horror: those poor animals and the dead trees. I wouldn't have it, and neither would my two friends. We formed the group *Mother Nature's Guardians* to defend her.

I don't think my comrades know the depths I am willing to descend to help Nature's Design. No one knows about my previous kills and how their deaths have been justified. Is my secrecy proof of free will?

I'm unsure. Regardless, I have done my best to keep my anger and wild actions hidden from everyone. My friends and I started small through letters, protests, and eventually leading to an attack on the logging site with homemade tear gas. It worked . . . for a week. The town was determined to make that damn sign.

We, Mother Nature's Guardians, plotted carefully against the mayor, wanting to send a message to him. The plan was to create shock by vandalizing his home, hopefully enough to make him end the killing of Mother Nature. I found a lone coyote pup at the deforestation site when we attacked the loggers with tear gas. The animal was wounded from one of the collapsed trees, making it exactly what we needed for the message. Still, I was conflicted. I wanted to heal the animal. I didn't. Just as I didn't nurture the cat, and just as I decapitated the magpie. Mercy kills serve both worlds. The crows were hungry, as were the coyotes all those years ago. This coyote pup served as a tool to free Mother Nature's pain from humanity's harmful actions. With that, I slit the pup's throat.

One of our comrades couldn't follow through with the plan, fearful of punishment. He was not fit for healing Mother Nature. The two of us initiated the vandalism on the mayor's home. We dropped the pup's corpse in the mayor's backyard with the spray-painted words "Clean Up Prince George Kills." My friend believed that was enough. I was not convinced and wanted to see if we could make a real impact. To my luck, the backdoor was open, and we went inside, where I sprayed more paint over the kitchen. Unfortunately, we did not foresee the mayor having a cat sitter. She and her boyfriend were in the home. There was an altercation, one that went too far. My comrade hacked a knife into the boyfriend's face as I chased the girl. She and I crashed through the glass backdoor, landing on the deck.

The poor girl's neck and chest had been sliced open by the glass. She was bleeding everywhere. I had to save her. Her suffering was caused by my own hand, and I had to make it right. So, I pulled the knife from the boyfriend's face and preceded to decapitate the girl. My friend did not understand what I had done.

It was for her own best interest. The blood loss would have killed her eventually. Even if she had survived, she would have been horribly scarred and unable to talk. Her death also served a greater picture, one that reassures my understanding of Nature's Design. The girl's demise was never part of *our* plan, but the opportunity presented itself. Killing the girl was such a tragedy to the town of Prince George that they finally understood the seriousness of our message—Clean Up Prince George Kills. The sign construction was cancelled.

People anger me.

My comrade and I were sent to prison, where I am today, writing this documentation. It is upsetting that I need to write out my justification as if my actions do not speak clearly enough. People do not understand why I do what I must. Perhaps it is Mother Nature herself who has willed me into existence, serving as her blade to cleanse the parasite known as humanity. Or maybe I have chosen this path. Then why don't I feel remorse for anyone or anything I kill? I understand the greater picture and each creature's purpose on Earth, which lets me see beyond the horrors of violence. Humans seem to think they can defy their natural course. That is what angers me and gives me purpose to ensure humanity falls under Nature's Design.

Vlad Borisyuk. July 3*rd*, 1990

Fragment: P

Awake from the observing state. (Turn to Page 229)

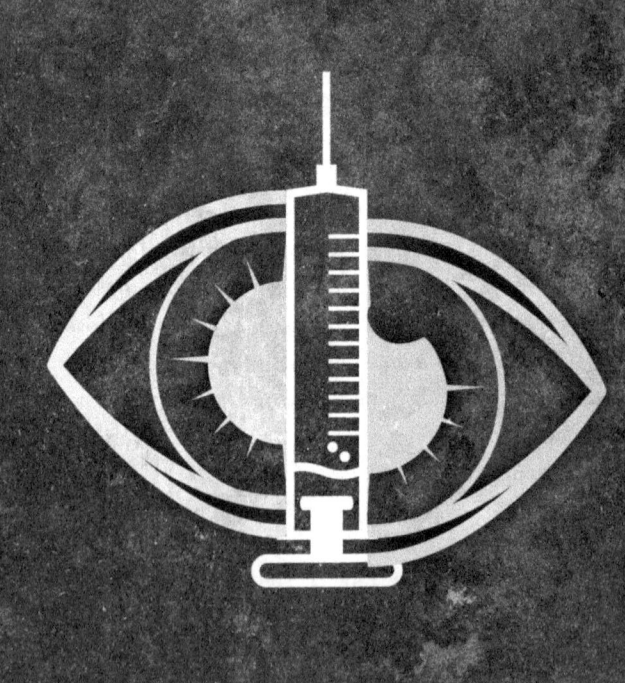

BIORINGER

BIOPUNK

Robbing a lab takes balls. For one, there's a high level of security. Cameras, AI facial identification, biomech guards, and DNA-locked doors on multiple levels. This, of course, is a government-run centre that ups the security ten-fold. To get into one of these labs, you must be *really* desperate or are just daring enough to oversee the risks for the marvellous rewards.

"Load it up!" shouts the robber.

She's drizzling in sweat from the top of her head all the way down. For good reason, as too many injections make the body unstable. She's also nervous. Her hands shake ever so slightly, holding the gun at point-blank to the white lab coat. His body is trembling, and he may have pissed his pants. It's hard to tell with his dark trousers, but the smell is there.

Moments ago, she bewildered him by entering the lab, biologically indistinguishable from his lab assistant. The AI facial identification cameras can see the whole altercation. Unless an unidentified person enters the lab, or guns fire, they aren't manned by anyone. And so, she's free to threaten the scientist to get the goods.

Threats aren't her preference, contributing to the sweats. Sure, this is a cold-looking all-white interior, but it leaves her burning. Her eyes aren't adjusting well to the brightness, even with the DNA Shift. Her visual spectrum is bloomed. She's far too used to the underbelly of the Society where the dark and cold are most welcoming to the scum and rejects. Like her, a robber. Technically, a bioringer, since the DNA Shift has completely reworked her genetic makeup. This isn't exactly the life she expected, nor did she think she'd be standing here in a government-run lab trying to get goods for the black market. But hey, when you don't fit into the Society's 'perfect' description of intelligent life, you become the very animal they deem unworthy. Everyone in the underbelly is. Unfortunately for the Society, there are more animals than there are of them—vermin are tough to kill.

"Ether," says her partner, Var, in his gravelly voice. "What the fuck is the holdup?"

She looks at Var's one blue eye—his real one—and the brown eye. He's some alternative fusion of his real rugged self and the bald, fair-skinned scientist her gun is pointing at. Those DNA Shifts are a real mind twist if you are unfamiliar with the physical and mental changes they temporarily produce. Thankfully, Ether is seasoned, and the half-scientist, half-partner in crime looking at her *is* Var. They just need to keep their heads on for a little longer to make it out of this laboratory in one piece.

"Old man, move it," Ether says, pressing the gun's tip against the man's skin.

The white lab coat cries, dropping one of the glass bottles from the steel counter. It smashes onto the floor, shattering liquids and spraying onto Ether's boots. The old man keeps loading more medical bottles into the chrome hov-box, trying to act like he didn't just drop ten thousand SCs worth of black-market trade—because he did. Social credit is a sound currency in the Society and its underbelly, which is even more reason why this robbery has to work for them.

"Fuck, Var. I'm trying," Ether says. "This old shit is messing it up. The hallway still clear?"

"Yeah, but we don't have a lot of time," Var says. He lifts his lab coat sleeve, seeing his sweaty arms pulsate violently. "The DNA Shifts have seven minutes tops, and then those cameras will lock onto us."

Great. Ether's fear is correct. Her body, too, is mutating. The muscles are moving back to their original state. The injections got them into the lab and passed the cameras and doors, which could now be their grave. They didn't come this far to be done in by some clumsy shit, technically named Dr. Mollberg, who can't load some bottles into a hov-box.

"If you don't pick up your pace, I'm going to cut your fucking hand off and grab the bottles myself."

"The injections are distorting your minds," Dr. Mollberg says. He grabs a couple of bottles at a time from the security drawer. His wrist, containing an essential fob cuff, passes a laser with each entrance, verifying his identity with a green light.

He continues, "The body isn't meant for the intense level of modifications you've forced upon it. You need my aid."

"Shut up, load the hov-box," Ether says.

"I'm serious. You're going to have withdrawals and long-term health repercussions. Let me help you."

"That's presuming we make it out of here, which we won't with your slow ass. Move!"

"Do you have any idea what you are doing?" Dr. Mollberg says.

"Getting a shit tone of SCs for these solutions, and you can go back to your pompous Society."

"Please. These bottles are only for governmental distribution. Unauthorized usage of DNA Shifts can be dangerous."

"Do I look like someone who cares?" Ether says, sweat drizzling down her face. Her cheek begins to pulsate, then her eyelid twitches.

"Hey!" Var calls out, loading up some vials from another cabinet into his utility belt.

Dr. Mollberg says, "You're going to—"

Ether cuts him short by saying, "Stop buying yourself time. Work."

Ether doesn't want to have a small chit-chat about her health. If she cared about that, she wouldn't have gotten into bioringing. Robbery isn't meant for long-term health, clearly, as both hers and Var's bodies are experiencing an unnatural trauma morphing from one DNA makeup to the other. The lab coat is right about one thing: it certainly mangles the mind. The robbers have made enough DNA Shifts in the past to understand how to navigate their ever-changing brains. And even then, her thoughts are never really her own. As it is now, she's never been this afraid. The neurological makeup of Dr. Mollberg's lab assistant is messing with her clarity and courage. Now, being locked in this oven-of-a-room is leaving her paranoid. She needs to get out.

"Okay, time's up," Var says, closing the cabinet and tapping the cuff on his wrist.

Ether lets out a deep sigh. Thank God he said something; it snapped her back to the now. She's *Ether*, not *Lia Catch*, the lab assistant.

The hov-box slides its lid closed, locking the goods inside. The seamless device floats off the counter before the scientist can drop the remaining two bottles. It hovers a few centimeters off the ground and stops beside Var, ready for them to get the hell out of here.

"Thanks, asshole," Ether says. She spins the gun around, pistol-whipping the man on the noggin. He drops the two additional bottles as he falls headfirst onto the counter. Ether snags them, checking the labels: GID SOLUTION. Genetic Injection Dose Solution. Perfect. She tucks them into the utility belt underneath the lab coat and holsters her gun. Those are why they are here. Not to mention, they're helpful for making DNA Shifts if you have a source sample of someone.

Ether and Var have planned this robbery for months and got their hands on Dr. Mollberg's and Lia Catch's DNA. Any sample will do to make the injection work. If you understand the underbelly of the Society, you can work your way through the sewer system, and well . . . it doesn't take a scientist to figure out how the robbers got the genetic samples.

Go time.

Var pulls out a couple of syringes from his lab coat, inspecting their labels. One states *Doc* and the other *Assistant*. Perfect, the final injections to save their skins. He hands one over to Ether for her to inject as he inserts the needle into the pulsating vein of his sweaty arm. She's hesitant to retake the solution, primarily due to the personality changes they induce. She doesn't like being scared. It's not her. Sadly, it is the only option.

The current injection is diminishing, and they'll shift into their authentic selves sooner than their clarity of thoughts will return. Var is looking more like his real self. That solution will morph him back into the fair-skinned whiner Dr. Mollberg within minutes, and no one will ever know the difference. Ether injects her solution and will be fully Lia Catch once more.

The lab doors open, sliding vertically into their hidden sockets. A young brunette woman walks in, sees Ether and gasps. The lab doors close. Var has already ducked underneath the island counter. Ether is too slow, and she locks eyes with the lab assistant who is struck with fear, looking at Ether—the half-version of herself.

They've been caught. There's a chance of recovery. Ether isn't going to be responsible for the fuck up. She whips out her gun, aims, and fires! The lab assistant presses the touchscreen fingerprint identifier to open the door as a blue plasma orb soars over the laboratory counters and burns into the girl's chest. The plasma soaks into her flesh, diminishing it into nothing. The orb leaves a gaping scorched hole where her heart should be.

The lab door opens as the Assistant collapses to the floor.

"Damnit!" Var shouts, hurrying around the counter and snagging the dead girl's body by the ankle. He presses the touch screen, closing the door. "I told you the cameras flag plasma orbs."

"I-I-I had to," Ether says. Fear is returning—the natural state of Lia Catch.

"You should have ducked."

"Fuck, Var. I can't take it back. Hide the body."

Var moves the body around the island counter and out of view. He takes a glance up at the small black dot on the ceiling, turning red. "It's over. We run."

Var dumps the body and taps his cuff wrist, initiating the hov-box to follow him. Ether stays close behind, and the three hurry out into the hall. Neither of the robbers wants to bite it today. They got the goods and want to get paid. They never will if they don't make it out of here *now*.

Did he take his dose? Ether thinks.

The bright chrome hall flashes blue and red while rows of tiny black dots on the ceiling lower, deploying small eight-millimeter-wide turrets, glowing red. Come on, injection—work! Red dots start appearing on Var's and Ether's bodies.

The cameras' weapons fire up with a high-pitch hum for half a second and then pause. Ether and Var keep running. They can't stop, even though it's pointless for how accurate those lasers are.

The injections have fully taken effect, and the guns start to power down. Their DNA has transformed. It's dumb luck or proof of a god. The barrels of the turrets raise upward, still deployed. The red and blue lights keep flashing with a loud beep echoing.

"Keep moving," Var says as they reach a fork in the hall. "The turrets will be manually overwritten at any moment."

Fast, loud thudding comes from around the left corner, their exit. The clanging metal stomping continues as tall, half-human monstrosity shadows appear—biomech guards. They're not going to make it out of here the same way, clearly. Var pulls out his pistol as the two hurry back the other way.

Ether fiddles with the bottle of GID strapped in her utility belt. She's fear-ridden. The DNA of Lia Catch is overthrowing her mind. She's got the solution. Even though she doesn't know much, she knows that too much GID without enough source DNA will water down the effects, even after injection.

No, she thinks. Trying to remember who she is. *Ether Coil. My name is Ether Coil.*

Several half-human and half-mechanical guards appear from around the corner. Their lean blue metal legs act as springs, giving them impressive speeds with each stride. The arms have been replaced with built-in plasma rifles, raised up, aiming at the two robbers who sprint away from the hall. The rifles light up with blue orbs, highlighting their sheening pale skin. The plasma orbs soar from the chambers and down the hall with deep pulse blips, reverberating.

One of the orbs hits Var in the shoulder. The power of the blast spins him on his heel several times, and he's about to tumble to the ground. Ether catches him and gets a good look at the bone sticking out of his scorched shoulder. Her mind runs two possible outcomes of this scenario. One is obvious and likely to occur if she doesn't take the second. The two of them will be captured by the biomech guards and taken to the Society's mediators, where their biological makeup will be extracted from the flesh and repurposed to make more GID.

She's thinking about her options. Lia Catch. Ether Coil. End up dead or feed Var to the biomech guards. Who is she? Ether has the GID solution in her hand right now, with the lid popped off. She's at a tipping point.

"IDENTITY. INVALID. CORRUPT," comes the disjointed inhuman voices from the metal vocal boxes of the biomech guards on their throats. "DOCTOR MOLLBERG AND LIA CATCH. VERIFY IDENTITY."

"Let's go!" Var grinds his teeth, standing, then tries to hobble away. His face is so alien, as is Ether's. His voice is unfamiliar, and yet the words are his without a doubt. This is Var, her partner.

"VERIFICATION REQUIRED." The biomech guards are several meters away, holding the charge in their plasma rifles, their metallic legs stomping.

"I'm sorry," Ether whispers and pours the GID solution onto the open wound. She slips the bottle into her lab coat, hiding it from view.

Var's eyes widen. He musters enough strength to push himself up. "You fuck! What the fuck?"

The solution seeps into the open half-burnt wound on Var's shoulder. His body sweats, veins pulsating, as the skin begins to tighten and sag in different areas, morphing into Var's. The irises shift from brown to blue, sealing the deal.

"Bioringer!" Ether cries. "Dr. Mollberg is back in the lab."

"INVALID." The biomech guards release their plasma bullets. One orb shreds through Var's leg, blowing the kneecap away. Another rips into his gut, and the third blasts the lower half of his leg off, throwing him to the ground.

"LIA CATCH. THREAT NEUTRALIZED."

"Thank you," Ether says, buttoning up her coat, further concealing her robbery equipment. "Please take proper procedures of his arrest." She leans down to Var, swallowing regret while taking his cuff, giving her command of the hov-box. Var looks up at her with heavy breaths, unable to talk through the pain.

She says, "He tried to take the supplies from Doctor Mollberg and me, taking me hostage."

"CONFIRMED. VIDEO EVIDENCE REQUIRES FURTHER ANALYSIS FROM MEDIATORS."

"Of course," Ether says.

The biomech guards aren't the swiftest and simply function as intended: Protect the scientists and neutralize foreign entities within the perimeter of the building. Var was just that. Ether is not, at least for now while the DNA Shift lasts. The real brains of security will be here soon, and she can't stick around to try and convince them that she is Lia Catch. They'll eventually find the actual corpse in the lab with the unconscious Dr. Mollberg.

She commands the hov-box to follow her as the biomech guards take the mangled mess of Var down the hall to the security sector. There, one of the Society's mediators will come for him, and he'll be made into GID.

As for Ether, she's getting the hell out of this mess. In the back of her mind, her real memory is feeding the screaming phantom. She betrayed Var, one of her own kind. The DNA Shift overpowered her own thoughts, and she will have to live with the regret for the rest of her life. No one said bioringing was a walk in the park. Var, like her, and every vermin in the underbelly of the Society, is forced to fight for survival. Turns out Ether is the real deal, and her own skin came first.

PULLBACK

Knowing who you are at the core is a rarity. We can spend a lifetime attempting to come to a half-baked conclusion. The question "who am I?" does fall under the philosophical realm and can be influenced by your genetic makeup. Our bodies change over time as we get older, metabolisms alter, adjusting our moods, is an example of what makes us, us. If you start adding DNA shifting to the equation, you're in for a whole world of trouble. Perhaps that is why the government has regulated the invention to prevent people from modifying their own DNA. If someone doesn't know the right mixture of Genetic Injection Dose Solution—GID Solution, or GIDS—to put in those damn syringes, the shifts are most unpleasant.

Ether Coil has experienced dozens of side-effects from short-term DNA shifting. She's lived long enough in the underbelly of the Society that she'll risk anything to get some SCs to survive. Her last robbery was a perfect example. The Society certainly doesn't like to acknowledge the fast-growing tumour below its 'perfect' utopia. Unfortunately for the Society, not everyone reacted smoothly to the government's Conditioning Human Initiation of Transcendence, known as the C.H.I.T. age. There's another ridiculous abbreviation to remember. Techies and futurists love them, and the Society is ruled by the brainiacs.

The government isn't aware of every biological makeup. The DNA shifts can be rejected; Ether Coil doesn't know all the history that transcended humankind to the Society, only the gist of it. She has firsthand experience with rejected DNA shifts, like with the last heist she performed with her former partner.

Var is the one word that enters her mind. Damnit, she sold him off to the Society just for some social credits. She takes a swift drink of

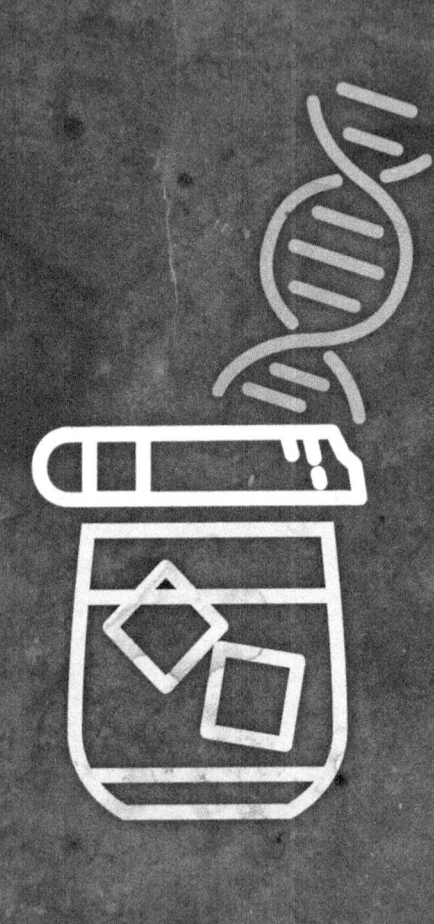

whiskey, finding it difficult to swallow. No. It's not the drink. It's the regret.

Would Var have done anything differently? Ether is uncertain, nor can she overthink it. She made it out with the GID Solution packets and is waiting to sell them to the businessman who hired her and Var to begin with. A businessman may be too polite of a word, but it'll have to do because slave driver is too harsh of a choice.

The bar is poorly lit. It's a hole-in-the-wall type of place. There are countless amounts of them within the underbelly of the Society. Thankfully the foundation of the city isn't monitored by biomechs, allowing the scum to exist. There are too many people down here for the Society to eradicate all at once. And so, Ether is one of a dozen or so reject barflies sitting and drinking away their miseries. The others are much like her, mourning the loss of someone or soaking in the misery of existence itself, knowing they'll never be deemed fitted to live within the Society. The bartender seems quite spry and energetic. He must be either too young to know the horrors of the Society or too naïve, obsessed with his silky dress shirt and tight black pants.

"Just one of you, huh?" comes a slur of a butch voice.

To Ether's right is the businessman himself, Blockchain. He takes off his wide-brimmed black hat and sits at the bar beside her. His large size causes the stool to creak, his thick legs flowing off from the circumference of the seat. "Where the hell is Var?" he asks with a sneer, exposing the gold and green microchip tooth coated in transparent protection.

"He didn't make it," Ether says while taking another swig of her drink.

"That's a shame," Blockchain says as he waves down the bartender for his own drink. "How are you holding up?"

"Sorry?" Ether asks, unsure what he means by the statement.

Blockchain nods at her nails digging into her forearm beside her rolled up sleeves. She stops the compulsive activity, feeling blood rush to her cheeks in embarrassment. Altering DNA also changes your skin, and you never find yourself comfortable in yours anymore.

"DNA shifts aren't easy, even if you are a bioringer."

"Oh, yes. It's a hell of a comedown." That's just scraping the surface. Ether doesn't want a complete psychological analysis of her being right now, especially with one like Blockchain, who is only ever out for himself. Ether has done plenty of DNA shifts in the past, as a bioringer does. She's dealt with the withdrawal in one way or another. Yes, it does completely rewire your genetic makeup, making you look and feel like someone else. She almost lost herself back at the robbery in the laboratory, where she lost Var.

"You live a dangerous life, kid," Blockchain says. "I wouldn't want it."

"No one asked you," Ether says.

"And no one asked us to live below the Society. You get what you get. Like those lab coats who got the better deal than people like us. It wasn't their choice that their DNA worked with the injections."

"They look remarkably human."

"The C.H.I.T. era created a lot of variations, not just the greats and the subs. That's why the underbelly exists. Real folks like you and I work in the shadows of that. Var did too, because we're real humans."

"Are we going to finish the deal, or not?"

"Right to business, I like that. Var was always a talker. This bar was his choice."

"That seems fitting. He liked the dingy places."

"You must, too, if you followed him around for all those years."

"Well, times have changed."

"Clearly. Looks like we will establish a new working relationship."

"Fair enough." Ether finishes the rest of her drink and taps the cuff watch—Var's former cuff watch—that activates the seamless chrome hov-box from under her stool, floating up towards Blockchain. The lid opens from the top edge, sliding into the walls of the box. Inside the hov-box are the GID solutions Ether and Var stole from the government laboratory.

Ether gets a shiver, looking at those wretched GID solutions. It relapses her back to the robbery, with Var taking the DNA shifts disguising them as lab workers. She barely kept herself together then, and clearly, the drinks weren't suppressing the comedown.

"Beautiful, you have done exactly as Var and I had agreed." Blockchain grins from cheek to cheek of his broad face. He places a duffel bag on the table and reaches for one of the GID solutions, causing the hov-box to close its lid.

"The SCs?" Ether asks.

Blockchain chuckles, stroking his goatee. "Not one for trusting, I take it?"

"All or nothing."

Blockchain reaches into his gunmetal blazer's pocket and pulls out a small disc. Social credits. The two dozen or so GID solutions within the hov-box will give Ether enough SCs to survive on for the next couple of months. She's in the clear.

Eagerly she reaches for the disc, but Blockchain pulls his hand back.

"Not so fast, kid," Blockchain says.

"But we had a deal," Ether says.

"Not quite. Var and I had a deal."

Ether's nostrils flare. She grips the empty glass tightly just as the bartender arrives with Blockchain's drink.

"Another drink, missy?" he says in a chipper voice. Oh, he'd sing a different tune if he understood Ether's anger.

"She will," Blockchain says. "On me."

"Of course," the bartender says with a slight bow.

Blockchain takes a sip of his drink with pride. He didn't even see Ether casually slide her pistol from the holster, keeping it tucked under her trench coat while watching the man drink.

"We're establishing a new business venture, kid. I'll give you half now and the other half if you complete another project of mine."

"Really?" Ether asks.

The bartender returns with her drink, and she takes a big chug of it, letting the harsh liquor burn down her throat.

"Really. You want to stay on my good side."

Ether casually places her pistol on her lap, finger on the trigger, aiming right for Blockchain's groin. "How about we stick to the original deal, and no one loses anything important."

Blockchain chuckles, saying nothing.

The casual nature fuels Ether's anger, and she cocks the gun. "Hand over the SCs."

"Kid, you really don't want to be doing that."

"Yeah? No one in this shithole bar is going to care if a fight breaks out. This kind of thing happens all the time."

Blockchain slowly pulls out a smooth chrome rod from his blazer and brings it to his mouth. The man takes a big inhale, sucking the vaporizer and exhales the smoke, leaving a lethargic acrid smell. He stares at her as the smoke seeps past his computer chip tooth as if expecting her to add to her words. She didn't expect this. He's so relaxed.

Ether says, "And I'm not concerned about your goons. Or whatever web of influence you have in the underbelly. I've dealt with biomechs and scum my whole life. What's another going to do?"

Blockchain sits upright and flicks his index finger casually, catching the bartender's attention. The man turns to face the two, his left forearm splitting open, revealing circuitry and metal underneath the skin. The mechanical parts shift around, assembling a bullet chamber with a glowing orb inside, pointed straight at Ether. Great, the bartender had to be a cyborg with a plasma rifle. No wonder he's so chipper. He can destroy anyone at any moment he pleases.

The bar silences as guns raise in the hands of the barflies. About a dozen and a half are now armed with weapons pointed at her and the hov-box. Only the twangy, outdated music plays as several moments go by.

Blockchain breaks the silence. "As I said, kid, we're establishing a new business relationship." He takes another mouthful of his liquor, finishing it and slamming it back down. "Var liked this bar, but he knew I owned it. He also knew that if he disagreed, his life would be on the line."

Ether bites her inner lip, causing it to bleed. Frustration runs through the sweat now building on her skin—another nasty side effect of DNA shifting. Var shielded her from the details of the relationship with Blockchain, which doesn't help her ballsy threat here. There's a reason why she never did the talking and rarely came to the meetings unless it was to pick up the payments. Blockchain has the whole arrangement neatly wrapped up. Var and Ether were simply his employees, and Var didn't want her to know.

She could go out guns-a-blazing, maybe get lucky with using the hov-box as a shield. She'd lose the GID solution and maybe a limb, or maybe her life. Cyborgs have good aims, stacking the odds against her. She doesn't like being cornered. If anything, she could eradicate Blockchain's manhood and then join Var in the void.

Blockchain takes another puff from the chrome cigar and says, "Now, you can't be frustrated with my sudden change in the deal. The prices for GID solutions fluctuate far quicker than you can imagine down here."

"We met the deadline," Ether says.

"Yes. I have no complaints, kid. You did well. But this is business."

I should just blow this fucker away, Ether thinks. Reason counters: she's still coming down on the DNA shift and is irrational. Her damn skin itches like crazy.

"We had a deal," is all Ether can say. She's trapped.

"We are making a deal now," Blockchain says.

Ether thinks about her options one more time. She can put her ego aside and agree to Blockchain's new offer. Or she can forcefully change their working relationship and likely go down in a good old-fashioned shootout in a bar. Her chances of survival don't look too good. Blockchain is a big man, and she doesn't think she can pull off a lethal shot in time. Thus, rendering her with only the option of accepting the new mission. She needs to pullback if she wants to save her own skin.

Ether casually holsters her gun and downs the rest of her drink in defeat. She eyes the bartender, expecting him to morph his arm back and give her another, but he keeps the plasma rifle up, not moving. Damn cyborgs, so disconnected from reality.

"Good," Blockchain says. He relaxes his posture, and the remaining people do the same. The bartender's rifle conceals back into his arm, and he arrives with a new drink, acting as if nothing had occurred at all.

"What do you want?" Ether asks. *I'm a damn coward,* she thinks.

"This mission is a little bit different from the previous. I need you to infiltrate a transport device."

"A transport device? Going through the underbelly?"

Blockchain puts the chrome cigar into his blazer pocket and then pulls out a bag containing a strand of red hair. "I'll make it easy for you with this to DNA shift. You will function as one of the crew members transporting the cargo and steal it from them."

Ether stares at the strand of hair in the bag. Var used to make the DNA shift for bioringing. She knows next to nothing about it and is unsure how to formulate the GID solution. Looks like she'll have to learn fast, as Blockchain isn't sympathetic.

"That's all?" Ether asks.

Blockchain passes the disc of social credits to her. "There's half in here for the work you've done now. It also contains detailed data of what you need to do and where you will find this transport. Do not be late."

"Great," Ether says, taking the disk and sliding it into the port on her cuff.

Blockchain nods at the cuff. "Try not to lose that as Var did. The disc contains valuable info."

"Yeah," Ether says. She's still pushing back the hate growing inside her. Goddamn Blockchain had to rub in Var's death to her. She was responsible for it, just like she's responsible for putting herself in this forced deal. She's a coward, fearful of risks. That mindset isn't going to help with this new mission.

She taps the cuff screen, opening the hov-box in defeat, letting Blockchain grab the GID solutions.

He says, "I look forward to continuing our working relationship and getting to know you better, kid."

"It's Ether Coil."

"Right," Blockchain says. He stuffs the remaining GID solutions into a duffel bag and gets up from the stool, causing it to creak. He buttons up his blazer, puts on his hat, and pats Ether's shoulder. The weight of his large hand pushes down on her despite her attempt to remain stiff.

Her new business partner exits without saying goodbye, leaving her alone at the bar. All the barflies continue on with their conversations as if nothing had occurred at all. Only Ether replays the frustrating encounter in her mind, reminding herself that she is indeed a weakling.

Well, she's not entirely alone. The hov-box serves as a ghostly reminder of her former partner. She has had no time to recover from the DNA shifts from the last heist either. This drink is the only thing reminding her that she is Ether Coil. Ether Coil is not a coward; it's just the DNA shift comedown making her fearful. That's all.

She may have lost her partner Var and the first arrangement with Blockchain, but the subsequent encounter will be different. Ether will take up the bioringing by herself, get whatever it is on that transport and redeem her name. All of that can be taken care of after this drink to suppress the DNA shift withdrawal. Well, maybe the following drinks will.

CYBERGAST

Ether Coil's hands shake subtly, holding the glass vial. There's a stutter in her exhale, a sign of nervousness and frustration. She can't push the new setup with her employer out of her mind. The bastard strongarmed her into doing another bioring gig before giving her the damn social credits she earned. This is all her former partner's fault.

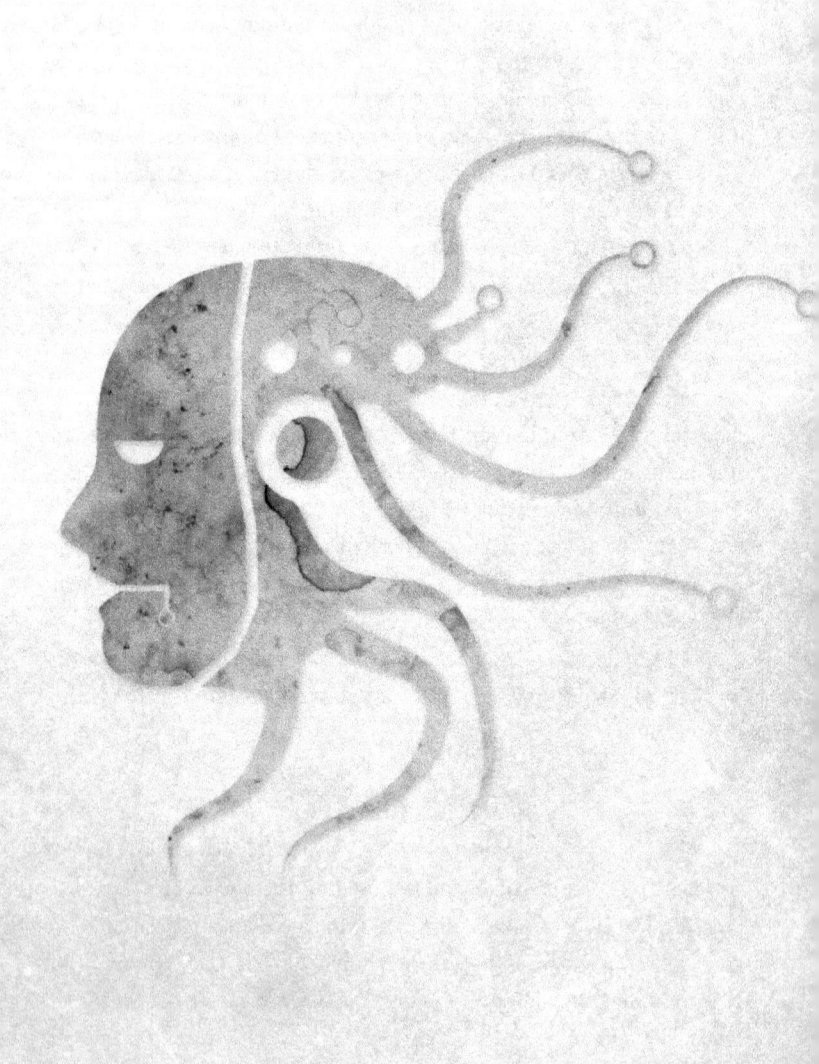

Yes, she misses Var, and her gut twists at the thought of what she did to him to save her own skin. It turns out his ghost is now haunting her, for he had never explained their relationship with Blockchain. All Ether did was work her ass off bioringing and got paid. Now that Var is gone—no thanks to Ether Coil's merciless choice—she's learning how complicated bioringing really is. For example, right now, she's attempting to prepare a DNA Shift to infiltrate a transport device and steal a valuable package for Blockchain. Her last two DNA Shift samples failed, so she's off to a good start.

Bioringing isn't for everyone. It requires plenty of stamina within the mind and body. The Genetic Injection Dose, or GID, is the crucial element that mutates a body from one physical makeup to another. Of course, there are plenty of other usages for GID. The Society transcended humanity by entering the infamous C.H.I.T. era due to it. It's old news, and no one needs to overthink the past because this is now the real world, and there is no going back. The amusing part is if you asked any historian about life before the C.H.I.T. era a century ago, they would have all told you the world was crumbling and a solution was needed. Now, look at humanity. No one presumed bioengineering would become so influential, effortless to produce, and end with deadly results of separating humans from post-humans.

So as mentioned, bioringing isn't for everyone. For Ether Coil, one of the many rejects whose DNA simply doesn't work with the transhumanism solution, you have to make SCs from somewhere. Bioringing is her skill, end of story.

Ether Coil is cutting off a small sample of the hair strand Blockchain gave her with a surgical knife. She needs to create the right formula that will temporarily convert her into the sample's individual. If you don't get the right mixture of DNA and GID, you will permanently shift into the person, damage your own makeup, or nothing will happen at all. All would have severe consequences on Ether Coil's life and this mission. Var was the one who prepared the DNA Shift injections, and now she feels like a fool for not watching him more closely over the years. Oh well, just like the pre-C.H.I.T. era, there is no going back, and humans adapt.

She curses under her breath, sitting in the dingy, small studio apartment that she rents from some pimp who sells cyborgs to lonely Johns. They may look convincing on the outside, but these sex workers are anything but the real thing. Injecting swine with GID solutions mixed with cyber parts can create compelling toys. None of that matters to Ether, for this is just a cheap place to rent where no one will look for her in the underbelly of the Society. She just has to accept that the walls are thin, and those moans are far too hoglike.

Var's familiar hov-box is here, serving as the reminder of how she fed him to the Society's biomechs. Thankfully, she won't be needing the hov-box for this mission. So, the storage bot rests, turned off, at the dark corner under a desk full of weapons and ammo. Two of the arms she'll be bringing: a laser-tipped blade and her pistol.

How did Var make the DNA Shifts so accurately? She has the equipment here. She has the DNA sample, the GID solution, and the nano builders. All three are the holy grail to becoming an effective bioringer. Yet, she is clueless as she uses a tweezer to drop the hair strand sample into one vial filled with protease to destroy the cell walls. Then comes the removal of the proteins. The hair dissolves into an orange-brown liquid within the vial, letting her mix it with the transparent GID solution in another. Instantly, the two liquids clash and create a neon blue. Still, she has little knowledge of what is happening.

The bright digital interface projects from her wrist cuff, rendering documents provided by Blockchain when they met at the bar. It's a profile of a man about Ether's age, the source of the hair strand. She'll be bioringing as him. She's never had to swap her birth gender. Apparently, it hurts like hell. Looks like there's a first time for anything.

The document appears to be an internal staff profiling from the government. Specifically, their transportation and shipment facilities that are located in the underbelly. The man's name is Robby Cord, he lives with his wife and two kids. His facial features are imperfect, the eyes aren't balanced, and his chin is weak. Clearly, he has a genetic disposition towards the Society's transhumanism solution. Noteworthy, for it explains why this transport device functions in the underbelly. Turns out you can still make SCs by working for the Society and not be part of their post-human paradise. You're just a bottom feeder, no different than Ether.

Good. Ether will bioring as Robby Cord and navigate through the transport device and . . . She swipes the projected hologram, moving Robby Cord's profile out of view and showing the following file. It's a photograph of an encased glass pod inside a metal shipping crate within a storage area. There's a naked woman in the specimen pod. The Society commonly uses these pods to move their experimental subjects around to further understand the human genetic makeup.

Based on the floor plans of the transport vehicle, the pod will be in the back storage of the vehicle. The sleeping woman in the pod has had her head shaven like most specimens. The photo has a title below it, saying: Emi Array. Handwritten words beside the photo from Blockchain say: HANDLE WITH CARE.

Interesting, Ether thinks. Blockchain mentioned nothing about a person. It was just a device to steal. A specimen pod is a large item to sneak out of a transport unit. Blockchain sure is going through a lot of trouble to have Ether infiltrate the transport unit and obtain this person. Is Emi his partner? Relative? Impossible to know. Blockchain isn't even his real name, believe it or not.

Regardless, this is her mission. She'll get the specimen pod out of the transport unit and get the rest of those SCs she rightfully deserves. Blockchain is a damn dirty businessman. What can she do, though? She has no other option other than to obey. She doesn't even know where to find more work. Besides, she must learn how to bioring on her own at some point. Now is as good as any time, starting with making DNA Shifts.

"Here we go," Ether whispers under her breath while adding a couple of droplets of the light grey nano builder liquid from a syringe into the vial. The little biobots behave as glue, so the DNA Shift sticks to the target DNA. Fingers crossed that this third mixture works.

She takes the completed vial and an empty syringe, carefully filling it, finds her vein, and takes a deep breath. On the exhale, she injects the needle and pushes the solution into her system. She keeps exhaling until there's no more air, feeling the adrenaline move through the body due to the uncertainty of what she has created. Making DNA Shifts is kind of like cooking, easy to add elements, but you can never take it away. Hence her previous two duds.

Several moments go by with deep, steady breathing. Her heartbeat is the timer, keeping track of when she injected herself. Her muscles twitch, the heart rate picks up on her cuff screen. Sweat beads on her skin. Yes, the solution is working. Unlike previous shifts, now she feels the muscles grow far larger, her bones are aching, her legs tremble, and she seizes up, sliding off the stool. Her body slams onto the floor and enters a fetal position.

She lets out an agonizing groan, knowing there was indeed enough DNA in this dose. There's no going back now. Ether exhales in deep, heavy breaths, spewing frothy saliva with each puff out, enduring the shift from Ether Coil into Robby Cord. The heart punches inside her chest. Blood visually pulses throughout her whole system underneath the skin. Her eyes turn pink and burn. The muscles grow and the bones extend, shrink, and mutate ever so slightly. They adjust her jaw, hips, legs, creating growing pains she hasn't felt since she was a kid.

Hair. Lots of hair. Whiskers cover her upper and lower lip and most of her neck. The hair shifts into a coppery tinge. Her stomach twists around as her innards ignite . . . hot. She's roasting from within. Slowly the mutations ease their intensity, and she can breathe at a steady pace with drool all over her face. The DNA Shift is complete, and she uses her shaky, sweaty arm to push herself up. She's weak and oddly hungry.

Ether Coil stumbles to the bathroom, almost crashing into her weapons table, to see herself in the mirror. Only she is no longer there, and she is looking at Robby Cord, the transport device employee. Well, mostly him. There's a few small traces of Ether left, such as the lips are narrower than Robby's and the fingers are more delicate. Still, the resemblance to the real Robby Cord is uncanny. And no, her junk didn't reform, for the dosage wasn't strong enough—she checked. Relief rushes through Ether; she did it! Ether made a DNA Shift and will be ready for the bioring gig tomorrow morning.

A third time the charm is accurate, and the solution reverts after seven to ten minutes as Ether reviews the documents Blockchain gave her. The shift back is more gradual and takes five minutes. Like the initial transformation, it's an awful experience. DNA Shifts shouldn't last longer than fifteen minutes in total. If they do, you'll create permanent damage to the DNA and never return to your original self. Her last mission with Var, as Lia Catch, made her fearful. This DNA Shift made her . . . angry. It must be the man's metabolism. It made her think faster, flooding her brain with useless mind chatter. She has far more vigour too. If only she could keep some of this energy. It certainly would give her an upper hand bioringing. But she can't stay like him forever. Eventually, she has to go back to being Ether Coil because she doesn't need this man's family to find her, thinking she's Robby Cord. Nor does she want to kill the real Robby Cord and take his identity. Killing is the last option, kind of like what happened with Var. It was her or him.

Ether has prepared a good four additional DNA Shift syringes for the mission. With any luck, she won't have to be on the transport device for that long. It's better to overprepare, as missions can go south. She memorizes the floorplans of the transport device to know precisely where Emi Array's specimen pod is and deems herself ready. It's game time.

She leaves the apartment complex in the morning to catch the transport unit before it leaves. Ether heads down the dark streets lit by the radiant glow of the ceiling tunnels dividing the underbelly and the Society. Vertical highways are leading to and from the utopia. Vehicles come and go past the dividing gate, watched by biomech guards. None of that is of interest, for the pickup location is located on the far end of the underbelly.

Ether got up early to prepare for the long hike towards the station through narrow alleyways and streets lit with dim blue and yellow neon signs of stores at the base of skyscraper buildings connecting to the ceiling. The pillar-like buildings form a maze of endless grunge, poverty, and shady dealings at every corner. People are just trying to survive down here, no different than Ether.

It would be unwise of her to use a cab or personal vehicle to get to the location. They can easily be tracked. The escape will be a different story. She's kept her cuff on a closed network, disconnecting it from the leading web of the Society and the underbelly. She can't risk being traced by any means.

She hides in an alleyway, spotting the station a vertical level down and a few blocks away. The gunmetal transport vehicle, the size of her entire apartment complex, is currently being loaded with metal crates. Each crate has its own interface with thumbprint activation. That makes this DNA Shift quite handy, presuming the fingerprints are fully converted. Her fingers . . . they were still too close to her own. That's a detail she can worry about later. The only thing Ether is missing is the uniform. She has to find Robby Cord. His shift should be starting soon.

Ether rolls up her sleeve and injects the DNA Shift. She's prepared for the hideously uncomfortable mutation, and the rush of chemicals runs through her veins. The bones ache like before. Her limbs tremble, and she falls to her knees. Eventually, the agony ends, and she can get up, covered in sweat. She looks in the reflection from her cuff to see she has entirely transformed into the ginger man. Now for that uniform.

The newly formed Robby Cord sets a timer on his cuff, keeping track of the estimated DNA Shift expiry. He exits the street and heads down a flight of stairs leading to the lower level. He crosses a bridge, moving over a steep fall into blackness. If anyone was stupid enough to jump over, they'd learn how many levels there are in the underbelly, and Ether isn't going to find out.

Across the bridge, she makes it to the station. She walks calmly, heading for the first glass doors leading into the building. The doors automatically slide away, letting the bioringer into the chrome lobby, complete with dim yellow lighting. Robby Cord should be in the back room preparing to start his day. If only he knew what was coming.

No one bats an eye as Ether confidently moves through the lobby, heading for the back room. It's past the black etched steel counter where two lobbyists work. She passes them, placing her thumb against the DNA check to unlock the back door.

Come on . . . she thinks. That fingerprint better work.

The DNA Shift wasn't fully accurate. They're going to know. I have my gun. I'll fuck these fuckers up. There's no way they're taking me hostage.

Ether is sweating. She checks her cuff timer. Five minutes.

Come on. Don't overthink this. It's just mind chatter. It isn't me.

The green light beams from the scanner run along the thumb, identifying her. Another second passes, and the door beeps. Success. Robby Cord has officially entered the station.

Go. Go. Go.

She navigates down the bright white hall and passes a middle-aged man dressed in the blue conductor uniform buttoned from neck to trouser. He smiles, clearly recognizing her. "Morning, Robby," he says in a bold voice.

"Morning," Ether says, voice deeper. The harsh change of testosterone in her system is working.

Keep going.

Ether makes it to the break room where the lockers are kept. Voices are heard further in the room. One feminine, the others masculine. There must be three or four of them back there. Ether cautiously approaches, knowing that she may run into the real Robby Cord. She takes each step slowly, reaching the locker room and keeping her head low as a couple more employees walk by.

Around the corner, the first row of lockers is clear. There's a door at the far end, presumably a supply closet. She creeps up to the second row, where two men and a woman change, getting ready for their workday. One of the men is Ether's height with coppery red hair. Bingo. Robby Cord. Their chat is all small talk and laughs as if nothing is abnormal. Little do they know that around the corner is a second Robby Cord, looking right at the real one buttoning up his blue uniform.

Ether checks the cuff. Three minutes. She's starting to sweat suspiciously.

Robby Cord finishes dressing by putting on the military-styled deep blue coat and buttoning it up. He says, "See you on the transport device." His pitch is eerily identical to Ether's.

He heads for the exit, towards Ether. She reaches for the leather handle of the laser-tipped blade under her armpit. Unsheathing the weapon activates the light red laser highlighting the chrome metal's edge. She presses her back against the locker as the footsteps reverb louder and louder from the approaching man.

One step, two steps, three steps. Now! Robby appears around the corner, coming face to face with an exact copy of himself. He freezes, mouth dangling open at the mirror in front of him. Ether lunges forward, snagging the man by the collar and pulling him over to the first row of lockers. She presses the tip of the blade on his neck, causing the skin to sizzle. His eyes are wide, but he says nothing. He may have no knowledge of what a bioringer is by the look on his face. Either way, he is spooked and is now breathing heavily.

Ether slowly brings the knife back and places her index finger on her lip, indicating he should keep quiet. He remains submissive as she drags him to the far end of the room. Wonderful. She raises the blade and slams the butt end of the weapon against his head, knocking him hard. He goes limp as blood begins to seep from his nose. Shit, Ether underestimated this body's strength.

She grabs Robby with both arms, carefully dragging him to the closed door. He's not nearly as heavy as she expected; this new strength is handy. Ether opens the door to find a storage room and pulls him into it, closes the door, and drops the man.

Wasting no time, she unbuttons the man's uniform until he is left in his boxers. She ditches her tattered clothes and dresses into Robby's, dropping hers onto the man's face. Ether is sweating like mad now, feeling dizzy. She checks her cuff's timer which has under a minute left.

Time for the next injection. She takes a new syringe, inserts the solution into her arm, and resets the timer. Her body shakes while she wipes the sweat from her face. It should calm down soon.

Fully changed, Ether exits the storage room and checks the knob to see if she can lock it. Unfortunately, no, it can't be. She goes back into the storage and uses her scraps of clothes to tie the man's wrists up. Next is his mouth so he doesn't cry for help. Ether tears her shirt, stuffing the scraps in his mouth, and ties him up. That's as good as it'll get.

Six minutes.

Ether leaves the storage room and marches down the hall heading for the hangar bay. A group of five other employees if also heading in this direction, letting her blend in with the workers. They move to the end of the winding hall and are met with a set of automatic doors. They slide clear, letting the employees exit the building and out into the open space of the hangar.

The view makes Ether almost miss the group of employees dissipating, marching towards their own tasks. She can't stand aimlessly out in the open. It's time to blend in with the other employees. Some are directing, while others are cleaning the dark gunmetal exterior of the transport unit. Based on those tasks, there's plenty of time before the vehicle leaves. She casually walks towards the transport unit, knowing the back room is where Emi Array is presumed to be.

Along the bay are twelve of those wretched biomech guards. They're everywhere with that iconic neutral blue and grey steel as if the passive colouring scheme reduces the hideousness of their naked torsos fused to circuitry. The plated deep blue digitigrade legs make them look like some kind of chimera terror. Then there's the pulse cannon arms. All in all, they're a pure menace to anyone who opposes them. The mere sight of the twelve patrolling the perimeter makes Ether's back twitch, reminding her of the last bioringing gig. No time to reflect on the past.

I fed Var to them, she thinks. *It's my fault. No. Keep focused.*

Five minutes.

One of the biomechs marches towards her as she approaches the transport unit. They're crossing paths, causing Ether's muscles to tense up. The mechanical legs slam onto the concrete with each step, ending with a hiss as the hydraulics adjust. Its lifeless blue irises look forward, utterly unfazed by Ether Coil—Robby Cord—who keeps walking at a steady pace.

Don't act unusual. Blend in. Blend in, she thinks. *Those pieces of shit took Var. No. It's my fault. I fed him. No. Stop thinking and just go. Wait, those eyes . . .*

Ether turns to face the biomech as it passes by. The lean, pale white torso is well-formed, and portions of the skin are red due to the irritation against the circuits and metal bolts along the waist and shoulders. Further up, the worn, grizzly face gazes ahead, not blinking.

"No," Ether mutters, recognizing the biomech. The blue irises and the rough face are clear reminders to her. It's her former partner Var. His long hair is gone, completely shaven and replaced with a metal dome, just like all the other biomechs.

Ether's skin turns to ice, stopping, and watching the biomech walk by. The sweat along her back and arms adds to the chill. She was so sure the Society mangles caught criminals for organ harvesting. Clearly not, for they have converted Var into one of their obedient units.

How much of Var is even in there? His face is dead. He's a biomech, not Var. It shifts her blood hot as she clenches her fists. No. She can't get emotional. Ether needs to keep rational thinking. Var is more machine than man now. The questions and anger are not Ether Coil. That comes from Robby Cord, the employee of the Society. She is Ether

Coil who must blend in and not be captured by the Society. If she is, she'll suffer the same fate as her former partner.

MERCY

Believing in a higher power is an excellent way to avoid responsibility. Ether Coil, for one, has never been a faithful person. Living in a post-humanism world, after humanity transcended from homosapiens and into the gods they are today, is enough for anyone with a rational mind to understand that there is no greater being watching over everyone. It all made sense until today. Ether is starting to change her mind. She's currently being punished for the betrayal of her partner. The dead can be brought back to life to haunt the living, as she sees this firsthand, facing Var, who's been harvested and reconfigured into a biomech.

His pale skin would tell you he is dead, but he moves. The eyes are lifeless, but he sees. The legs and arms are gone, but he walks with deadly pulse cannons fused to where his arms should be. The ghost of Var is back, reconfigured for vengeance.

Ether believed the Society harvested bodies only to understand organs and make GID. The situation doesn't seem possible. But Var is alive, sort of, walking past her. The rugged face is his, even with the metal dome that replaces half of his skull. He doesn't recognize her at all and marches around the bay. Even if he could identify her natural face, her DNA Shift into Robby Cord saved her ass.

Keep it together, Ether thinks. *What if he is in there? Should I try and rescue him? What about Blockchain's deal? The SCs. The specimen pod?*

Ether must stop the internal chatter; it is not her. She's Robby Cord, an employee of the Society. He's the one with the anger issues and the head chatter. She has to keep her mind focused on the goal if she wants to see those SCs. Damn Blockchain. Damn DNA Shift. Damn Var!

Keep it together.

The cuff states Ether has four minutes left before needing a new dose of a DNA shift.

She walks across the bay and over the bridge connecting the massive gunmetal transport unit to the station. Below the bridge is endless blackness, reminding Ether how far the underbelly of the Society can potentially go. If you're afraid of heights, it certainly isn't worth a look. Ether prefers to keep her head up, eyeing the vast underground foundation complete with concrete skyscrapers connecting to the ceiling and the luminescent lights from the vertical highways leading to and from the Society.

Ether chooses to enter through the side entrance of the transport unit instead of the large open side doors where workers are loading in hovering metal containers. She wants to get a sense of her surroundings. Through the doorway, she enters the vehicle. Ether's heart pounds and the perspiration drizzles down her body. It's the classic side effect of bioringing. The body fights against the temporary DNA Shift, attempting to return to its original state. Already she can feel the pain of the bones aching, attempting to become Ether.

Inside, under the dim lights, are various employees attending their tasks. Some have computer tablets, checking equipment and monitoring stats on various screens in the hall. Others are directing smaller crates into various rooms. The control center must be on the floor above. None of them notice who the sweaty infiltrator really is. Good.

Three minutes.

Ether notes the layout of the halls and reaches the far end of the transport unit, recalling Blockchain's documents outlining where the pod is. The hall leads to the significant open storage room where employees direct hovering crates. A few workers tap on the screens, commanding the crates to move vertically and stack on top of one another. Once landed, they automatically bolt to the one below with a self-screwing system, locking them in place, and eventually the bottom crate to the ground. It's far more efficient than a crane.

The screens attached to the crates all have the shipping information from the box number, weight, size, and of course, the items within the containers. She casually walks up and down the various halls, examining each screen. Somewhere in here is that glass pod containing Emi Array, whoever she is.

Ether pretends to examine the cargo as if she belongs. Truthfully, she has no idea what Robby Cord does and cannot overthink it. She needs to act fast and leave. Ideally, Ether can escape with the specimen pod before the transport unit leaves the bay.

After several more halls, Ether spots one of interest. Glass pods line the aisle, just like in the photo Blockchain gave her. These are specimens, dozens of them, all lined up neatly in the back. Naked, hairless people are sleeping inside each of them, strapped to the base of the pod with metal cuffs. Perfect.

This transport unit must be going to a laboratory based on the number of specimens here. She can't help but wonder if Var was put into one of these before they mangled him. Okay, no more reflecting. It's game time.

Either checks the cuff. She has less than a minute and pulls out another syringe, injecting herself with a third. The sweats and aches should pass. Her legs tremble slightly and her heart punches the ribcage ending in a sharp sting. It's the usual pain and no fret.

She taps on the computer cuff to double-check Emi Array's number in the documents. She cross-references each glass pod's touch screen she passes. One after the other, Ether finally finds the correct number. Inside this pod is the woman. To Ether, they all look the same—sleeping, hairless test subjects for the Society.

Then again, upon a closer look at the face, the woman must be a good ten years or so older than Ether. There's a long scar running around her neck, and Ether's best guess is that this woman is Blockchain's wife. None of that makes a difference, for Ether simply needs to get her out and earn those SCs.

On the touch screen, Ether taps the controls. The screen flickers, stating, "ID PRINT REQUIRED." Like with the hall door in the station, she places her thumb on it, and the screen scans the fingerprint, identifying her as Robby Cord. It beeps, giving her access, and she punches the interface buttons to enable the pod's hovering capabilities. After a few taps, the pod hovers off the ground and locks onto her. The screen states, "ROBBY CORD CONDUCTING" as it waits her next move. Time to get out of this wretched place.

"Another reject?" comes a man's voice.

Ether stiffens due to the commanding voice of the man. He's in the same blue uniform as Robby's, marching towards her. In fact, it's the same man she ran into in the hallway—a pointless observation.

"Yeah, it's no good," Ether says. Again, Ether has no idea what she is doing.

"They still haven't quite worked out all the gas quirks on those specimen pods, have they? Leaking the damn preservative gas," the man says, passing her.

"I know, it's crazy."

Keep going, Ether thinks while walking down the hall and towards the large open hatch doors leading back to the hangar bay. About three biomech guards patrol in the open space. Ether's eyes scan the bay back-and-forth, trying to find the easiest way to leave the station. She can't go out the way she got in, for it'll attract too much attention. There's got to be a back exit.

On the opposite side of the bay are wide open doors with a hallway leading straight into the alleyway. Workers are unloading crates from a smaller bronze truck hovering outside. The specimen pod follows her with each step, crossing the bridge connecting the transport unit, and onto the hangar bay to the far side.

Come on, come on!

Five minutes.

A stack of crates about twenty paces away hovers from a worker's command, revealing a lumbering biomech guard, moving towards the open doors. The hydraulics hiss with each step the blue metal animal-like legs make. It's ghost-Var once again. Of course, it would be. A day like today is potentially enough to make Ether genuinely believe in some higher force punishing her for leaving him. It's not like Var was a stellar guy, being a bioringer and all, but he meant something to her. Love? Nah, that's just a chemical imbalance and a primal need.

There's no stopping the interaction if Ether wants to get out of here. The biomech version of Var has now stationed himself right by the door, watching as more workers import hovering crates into the hangar bay. Each step brings her closer. Her muscles seize as the ghost looks right at her with its glazed-over eyes.

"THE SPECIMEN POD HAS BEEN APPROVED," comes the robotic voice from the vocal box located in Var's neck. The voice makes Ether ice cold. It's his voice, without a doubt, but more mechanical. It's haunting. A real live damn ghost.

"ROBBY CORD, STATE YOUR INTENTIONS."

"The specimen pod is broken. Leaking gas. It needs to be sent back." That lie better work.

"AFFIRMATIVE. I WILL ESCORT IT FROM HERE."

"No need for that. I've got it covered. Stay watch at these doors."

"NEGATIVE, ANYTHING BEYOND THIS POINT MUST BE ESCORTED BY A SECURITY UNIT."

"Walk with me then."

Don't look at him, Ether thinks.

"AFFIRMATIVE."

The two move down the hall, side-by-side, as the last of the workers walk past them. Ether takes each step slowly. Being with her former partner leaves her stomach in a knotted mess. Biomech guards are about a head and a half taller than humans, and with each step the metal legs hiss, reverbing against the now-empty hall. It's alienating the fact that Var is in there. He has to be.

Keep walking.

She gives in, looking over at him and staring at the pulse cannons that replaced his arms. He is more machine than man now. The robotic limbs, various metal plates, and cables fused to the remaining flesh are filling her with doubt that Var is alive. His eyes look forward, but they don't see the way a human should.

Just keep walking, Ether thinks. Sweat is dripping onto the floor, created by a mixture of fear and genetic mutation.

Ether cannot help herself; this is Var! She says, "When were you stationed at the hangar bay?"

"THIS IS DAY ONE OF DISPATCH."

"Where were you before?"

"I AM A NEW MODEL, RECENTLY ASSEMBLED FROM MY SOURCE MATERIAL."

Source my ass, Ether thinks. She cannot get pissed off, but already she is feeling the need to unleash a vengeful attack on the workers at this bay. Yes, they are employed by the Society, but none are directly responsible for what happened to Var; Ether is. She must keep herself in check.

The anger comes from Robby Cord and not her. It's the DNA Shift. Speaking of which, she checks her cuff and it says she has two minutes left. Shit. She can make it out of here and these emotions will be buried with mech-Var. She'll never be Robby Cord again. She can be Ether Coil, and those SCs will get her enough to lay low for a while and forget bioringing. Maybe she can start a new life. Apparently, unmodified humans can work for the Society. She has options.

Don't overthink it. Keep walking. Her muscles start to feel like jelly. The shift is weakening.

"So, how do you like your first gig?" Ether asks. There's no point in her continuing to talk to the biomech, but she needs to know if there's anything left of Var. It's a futile attempt. She's developed a loose form of hope. Perhaps it's the seed of faith.

"I DO NOT COMPUTE," the biomech says.

"It's your first day. You don't have any feelings on it?"

"I AM INCAPABLE OF SUCH EXPRESSIONS. MY DUTY IS TO THE SOCIETY."

"What about your source material? Didn't it come from somewhere, with feelings?"

"AFFIRMATIVE, THE LABORATORY ASSEMBLED ME FROM BOTH MECHANICAL AND ORGANIC MATERIAL."

"Do you have memory? Or is it all gone after being built in the laboratory?"

"AFFIRMATIVE. THE RECORDING LOGS WERE NOT YET ACTIVATED."

"Of course, they weren't. Is there a brain in you, or is it just a hard drive?"

"YOU'RE NOT AUTHORIZED TO KNOW THE BLUEPRINTS OF MY ANATOMY."

"Do you know what your organic material did before?"

"THAT IS IRRELEVANT AND NOT ACCESSIBLE BY MY PROGRAMMING. PLEASE WITHHOLD YOUR CURIOSITY AND REMAIN DUTY-FOCUSED."

My programming . . . The real him is in there, gated, Ether thinks. If only she had some way of dropping a hint of who she really is. Is it even worth it? Is Var even alive? Perhaps it is just remaining neurons holding onto memory imprints.

They reach the end of the hall, and the biomech examines both ends of the alley, making sure they're safe. There's the two of them and a driver who sits in the bronze truck out back. The biomech faces Ether, staring at her with those glassy eyes.

The alleyway is unnaturally bright. That DNA shift doesn't have much time left. She's got to act fast and get out of here.

"PLEASE RETURN THE SPECIMEN POD," the biomech says.

Fuck it, Ether thinks. She takes a step towards the biomech and raises her sweaty hand, pressing the palm against his chest, feeling a mixture of circuitry and flesh above where the man's heart should be. A moment passes, and there's heat from the flesh, but no heartbeat.

"PLEASE REMOVE YOUR HAND FROM MY SYSTEM."

System echoes in Ether's mind. That is simply what the biomech is. The flesh is used as additional components for the machine. They don't keep the memory. Even if they did and it was blocked by the programming, and he is in some strange comatose state, how the hell is Ether going to shut off a biomech and disable the program?

"That specimen pod going back?" comes the driver's voice from the front seat of the transport unit. He's smoking a drag, looking at her through the rear mirror.

"It does," Ether says. She takes her hand off the biomech in defeat, leaving an imprint of sweat.

Even if he has no heart and no mind, Ether is weighed down by guilt. Var's flesh is still alive and functioning. It's a part of him. The organic material still feels, and it's a part of Var.

"Load'er up then!" the driver calls out.

Ether is morally compelled while taking the specimen pod up and into the back of the truck. She slyly pulls out a new syringe. This awful feeling is the exact one she had while abandoning Var back at the laboratory. There's a chance she can redeem herself, partly. The powers that be are watching over her at this very moment as she injects herself a fourth time, judging the foundation of her character. If she leaves, the memory will haunt her just as the hov-box does back in her apartment or how the cuff's computer reminds her of him. If she shows mercy, she will be redeemed from this ghost.

What's it going to be? she thinks, exhaling and embracing the new dose. She feels far less animalistic fear being Robby Cord compared to bioringing as Lia Catch. Her muscles are gaining strength again, even through the mutation pain. Her vision is gaining clarity. The pistol is still tucked into her belt underneath the blue uniform coat, along with the laser-tipped blade. In fact, she feels a level of confidence in her spontaneous plan.

She taps on the specimen screen, disengaging the glass pod's hovering thrusts, letting it settle on the ground. Ether exits the transport unit and waves at the driver. "I'll be joining. There's extra notes I need to elaborate on."

"Isn't that in the logs?" the driver asks while closing the back door with a flip of a switch.

"Some things are better left unexplained."

"But it is in the logs, right?" He chucks the butt of his drag.

"Yes, don't worry about it," Ether says.

"ELABORATE," comes biomech Var's voice. "YOU HAVE DUTIES IN THE BAY TO ATTEND TO."

"Well?" the driver says. "Spit it out. I got to get back for another shipment."

"ROBBY CORD, EXPLAIN YOURSELF."

She can't just leave the biomech to exist. The Society will have won another battle if she does. Yes, life is about survival, and her choice back at the laboratory was quite clear as to where she stands, but she can still show grace. Her hands are near the pistol, walking up to the biomech, feeling the veins under her skin pulsate.

"ROBBY CORD."

Ether stops half a metre away from the ghost and pulls out the gun with one hand and the laser-blade with the other in one fluent motion. The blade swings upward with the red laser slicing into the vocal box and neck, sending sparks airborne. She pulls the gun's trigger, igniting the chamber and launching the bullet from the barrel and into the biomech's forehead. The metal shreds through the skin as a loud *BANG* bounces off the concrete towers, overpowering the nearby traffic.

Biomech Var seizes up. The eyes roll back as it attempts to raise its pulse cannons. The chambers glow bright and shrink, charging and de-charging in glitched spasms. More sparks fly out of the neck wound and the head as red liquid oozes down between the eyes. The arms go limp as the legs sway side to side, attempting to keep balance. Inside the head hole are circuit boards and some meat. Looks like there was brain matter left in the head after all.

"What the?" shouts the driver as he starts up the truck.

"Out!" Ether shouts, running towards the driver's door, pistol pointed at the man.

"Okay, okay," the man says while slowly opening the truck, raising his arms up.

"Out of the way!" Ether shouts, waving the pistol to guide the man clear from the door.

The driver is obedient and steps aside as Ether hops into the vehicle and engages with the controls. Holding the pistol with one hand, she bites onto her blade with the other, using her free hand to grip the polished black pleather controller. Like all hovercrafts, the U-shaped wheel has extra buttons along the central component and on the top of each handlebar.

Her boot presses on the acceleration, and the vehicle engages full throttle. The engines shoot bright blue flames as the vehicle soars from the alleyway. She holsters the gun, sheaths her knife, and takes control of the wheel with both hands as biomech guards storm out of the hangar bay, shrinking from the increasing distance. She swerves into a vertical highway, elevating her to the next level and merging with a horizontal lane.

These transport units are without doubt tracked. That driver will report the incident, the biomech powering off will send a warning signal to its superiors, and the gunshot will undoubtedly raise red flags to the street authorities. But she did it; she saved Var, or whatever is left of him. She abandoned him back in the lab, where she should have shot him to save him from the horrific conversion of becoming a biomech. It's all over now, and she can put her demons to the grave.

Ether eventually abandons the truck, parking it in an alleyway, and unloads the specimen pod. She unbuttons her blue uniform, throws it over the glass pod and takes Emi Array to the end of the road. She's out of here!

A pitch-black hovercraft speeds into place, blocking the end of the alleyway. The windows are tinted, preventing any view of the inside. Ether draws her pistol as the door slides open, revealing a large man in a deep blue pinstriped blazer—Blockchain. He holds onto his hat as the wind picks up from the hovering vehicle. To his left and right are men masked in metal human faces, dressed all in black, with far superior automatic firearms than hers.

"Get in if you want to live, kid!" Blockchain says in his signature gravelly voice.

Ether holsters her gun and hops into the vehicle. Emi Array's pod follows, and the men close the door as sirens echo throughout the three-dimensional highways. They're in the clear as the hovercraft accelerates forward.

Ether exhales, wiping the sweat from her face. The wipe pulls off some of the facial hair from her jaw and upper lip. The DNA Shift is starting to wither. She grips a handlebar on the ceiling and asks, "Were you just watching me the whole time?" Her voice goes up a pitch, another sign that her DNA is reverting.

Blockchain puffs on his chrome cigar while eyeing the woman in the pod. He says, "Yeah. I knew you weren't going to make it out of there on your own."

"Yes, I was."

"Right. That's why you had to make some hotheaded move and shoot a biomech."

"It was Var. I had to."

"You did," Blockchain says while placing a hand on the glass, directly over Emi's face. "I understand."

"Who is she?" Ether asks.

"My mother," Blockchain says.

"Really? She looks so . . ."

"Young? Yes. That's what the preservation gas does. It'll keep a body intact for years."

"And the Society hasn't done anything with her?"

"No. She's been sent from lab to lab, probably because of my attempts to rescue her. She slips out of my grasp every time. You just about blew it too with your little stunt."

"Well, I didn't. What's with her scar?"

"They've tried hamming one of those vocal boxes into her, turning her into a cyborg. But I busted the operation. Unfortunately, they got away with her."

"A biomech?"

"Maybe. Or maybe a hotel clerk. They keep people around for years at times, decades even, and pull them out when their DNA matches with a project they have in mind."

"So, it really isn't just GID and research."

"Nope, as you saw with your old buddy Var."

"Apparently." Ether sighs, looking out the window to the dark underbelly. There are no sirens. No one is chasing them. They're in the clear.

A burly hand bumps her arm. "Here," Blockchain says. "Those SCs."

Ether's eyes widen, seeing a small disk is in his hand. That's the glorious payment. Finally, it is hers. Her joy is reassured as she snags the disk from Blockchain's hand and puts it in her pocket.

"You did good, kid," Blockchain says.

As if that's supposed to mean anything to her. The asshole was the one who put her up to this ridiculous mission. She didn't want any of this! Still, Blockchain is a man of his word, based on their new business agreement. She got paid and the gig is done.

Blockchain was kind enough to keep Ether hidden until her body fully reverted to its original self. The muscle and bone aches were a bitch, just as they were before. She stares at the orange facial hairs on the ground as her physical form readjusts—goodbye, Robby Cord.

The two men with Blockchain give Ether new clothing, and the group splits, letting her return to the whorehouse of an apartment complex where her pad is. She holds onto those rightfully rewarded social credits tight as she enters her home. Oddly enough, those SCs weren't as rewarding as she had hoped. No. This mission had a far more satisfying component. It gave her a sense of redemption for liberating ghost-Var of his tortured existence.

His hov-box no longer serves as the symbol of her betrayal as she stares at the powered-off device, sipping on whiskey, recovering from the DNA shift. In a life of dog-eat-dog, she's in a temporary place of peace, for her mind has forgiven itself. She knows no gods are judging her. The seed of faith has died. The ghost, or biomech, has been put to rest. It turns out Ether can show mercy and isn't just an underbelly scum hunting for the next bioringing gig.

Well, at least for the next few months, until her social credits run out.

Fragment: A

Awake from the observing state. (Turn to Page 229)

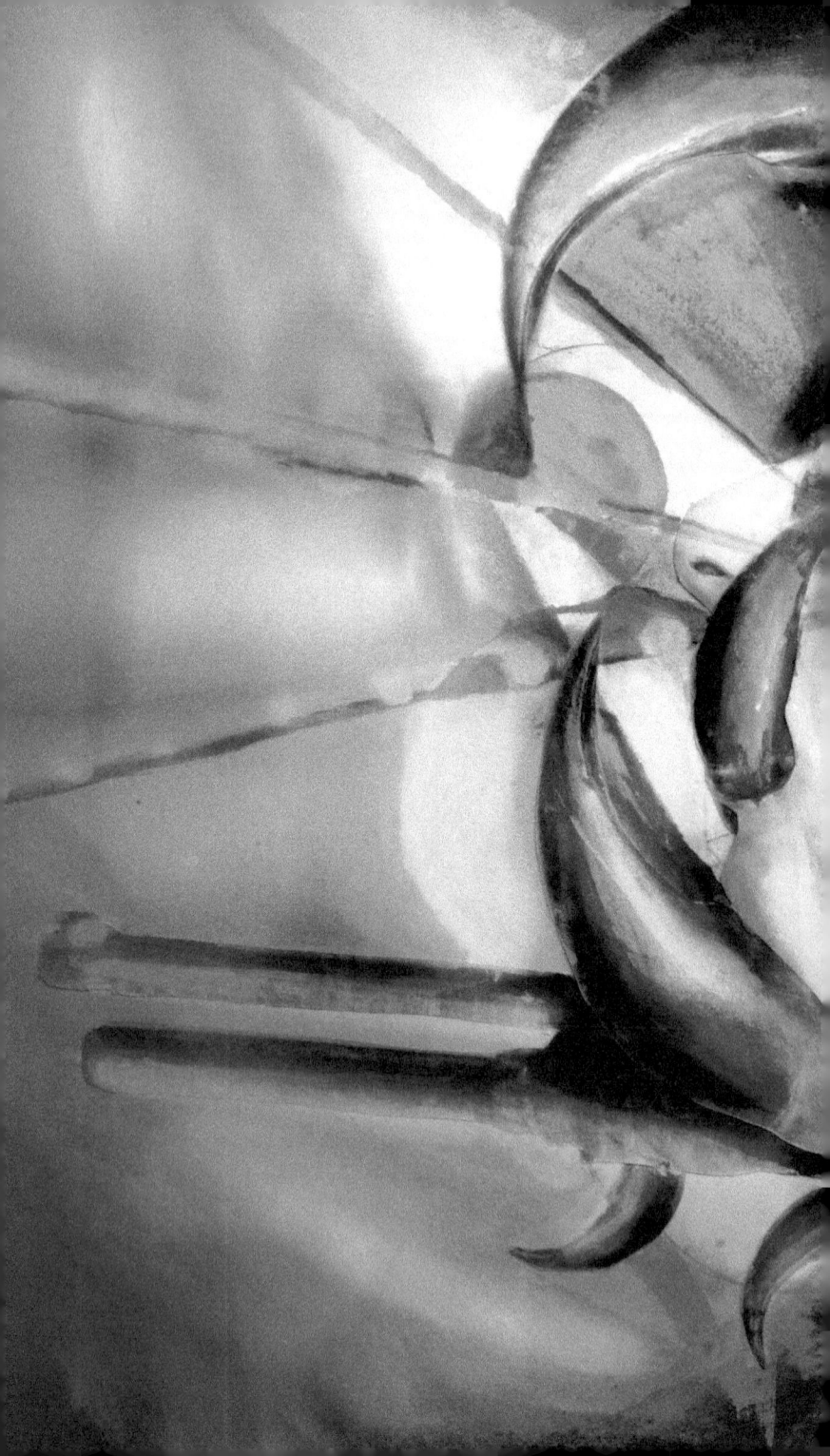

THE SMELL

One by one, we died. I watched my friends be torn apart like butchered pigs. The giant cleavers on the Bastard swung into them, slicing them up into unrecognizable chunks. At first, there were twelve of us, then there were six, three, and then just me. I'm not afraid to admit that I vomited multiple times, watching in pure fright as my friends were mangled alive. Eventually, I got to a point where I could not regurgitate anymore and have become desensitized to the atrocities and the funk.

The Bastard took every bit of dignity from my friends and me. We took shits in empty pots and drank our piss just to stay alive. The fusion of human bodily fluids and rotten corpses seeped through the vents. The stench was unbearable. We couldn't go anywhere inside the underground bunker, and outside . . . well, everyone knows you cannot go out there. That is straight-up suicide.

I'm not sure how the Bastard managed to get into the bunker, but it did. Thank God Dan was one of those end-of the-world-nut-bags, stocking up on canned foods and weapons. Unfortunately, no amount of preparation could have helped in this scenario. The whole world was mutilated. We don't even know where these bastards came from. Wild rumours sprouted before all communications were cut out.

Aliens, underground reptilians, demonic summoning, genetic super soldiers gone a-wall, you name it. Truthfully, I don't care. I just want to get rid of this god-damned pong.

When the Bastard first got in here, I thought about abandoning the bunker and risking going outside. The idea left my mind as quickly as those cleavers can slice through flesh. I remember seeing the footage on the internet. There are thousands, if not millions, of the bastards out there. Humanity has tried to kill them. Hell, twelve of us tried to kill one. Bullets absorb into it, making it howl like a dying dog, but it doesn't stop. It never stops.

Now I'm the last one in the bunker, gripping my shotgun tightly. When there were several of us, we formulated the final plan to trap it in one of the closed-off storage rooms. The Bastard managed to kill Nora and Pat during the scheme. Pat was supposed to be the bait, luring it into the storage, and we'd shut the air-lock door.

Nora and I got turned around to avoid the Bastard's sharp cleavers and ended up in the storage room. Poor Pat, he wasn't quick enough to dodge the attack. He did his best to stray it away while being sliced open in every which way. Nora was too loyal to Pat for her own good. She thought she could save him and blow the Bastard's head off, wherever the head was. The four cleaver-like limbs were the only distinct parts of its form. Its body changed shape every second, like watching a television with no signal, a static mess. I have to say, Nora went out guns blazing. If we lived in a different time, that type of death would be honourable. Now? it just makes me sad and creates another layer of funk.

We used to hypothesize what its strengths and weaknesses were. We were hopeful twelve-against-one would give us the upper hand. The result: one-on-one. Days have gone by with the Bastard on the other side of the door. I can hear giant cleavers slicing against the steel door from time to time. The Bastard likes to go for long periods of silence, hoping to psych me out. The only weapon I have now is starvation. It can't feast off the eleven dead forever. So, I wait.

I have several dozen cans of beans and crushed tomatoes, space-grade meat, and one box of bullets. The pots are full of my shit, and I have reverted to relieving myself in one corner of the room, with the mound ever-growing. Piss is for the other, drizzling towards the center of the room as I don't have any spare empty cans. This is no way to live. I've wondered if the Bastard would eventually leave, going back to the surface the way it came. Yet, we don't even know how it got in here. Maybe it is stuck, like when a fly finds a way inside a window screen and cannot get out.

Eventually, the clawing stopped. Another week went by with no sounds. This was the longest silence-session the Bastard has had. The last record was four days before it started scratching at the door again. I think. Days are hard to tell. The duration was promising. I cling to spite now. The Bastard won't win. Otherwise, I'd just blow my head off with this shotgun. The foul odor of the storage room was beyond anything I had experienced before. I wasn't sure how much longer I could stay in the small space. The combined power of malodor was killing me.

Scenarios ran through my mind—wondering if I should open the door or keep waiting it out. I still had plenty of food left. Drinking piss gets old . . . and that horrific sting lingered in my nostrils with a slow, elongated tingle after each inhale.

That was it. I couldn't live like this for much longer, or I would give in and shoot myself. The Bastard had won, and I'd face this thing head on. I wasn't sure how long I waited, but I mustered up the strength to stand. I had to get out of here.

I held the shotgun, pointed down, quietly approaching the door. The Bastard has good hearing. One step after the other, I reached the door handle, clutching the cold metal with my hand. With one deep inhale, I flicked the lock and swung it open. Shotgun raised, breath held while I scanned the blood-filled hallway. Nothing. Where was it?

My eyes were wide, not blinking, the further down the hall I went, checking every tossed-over boxes, the ceiling, in front and behind me. It was gone. The Bastard went back to wherever it had come from, leaving me as the only one to survive the cleavers, stepping on the remains of my dead friends. The stench out here was no better either; it lingers in my nostrils, forever present, unless I left the bunker and embraced death. Wait, the smell is worse, and closer. My trousers are moist and heavy.

Great, I shat myself.

Add that to the growing pile of funk.

Awake from the observing state. (Turn to Page 231)

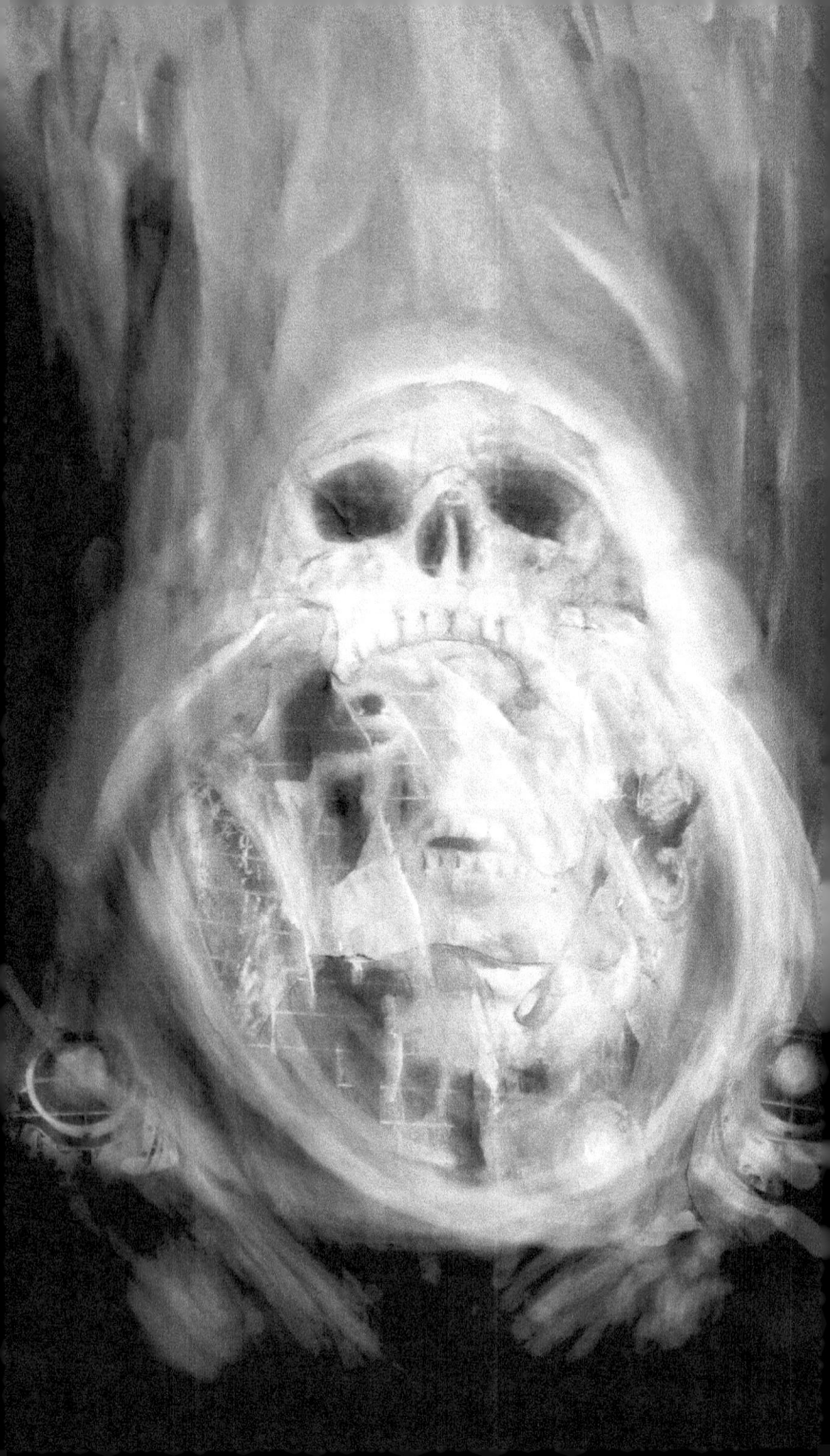

NATURAL COSMOS

.

. . .

. . . . . . thing on? . . . . . .

. . . wait . . .

. . . hello? . . .

There we go, it's . . .

. . . . . .

. . .

—orking now. I think. The red light is stabilizing. Okay. Our ship collided wit— . . .

. . .

.

. . . Shit, this recorder is busted. Not to mention, there's no telling how long my air tank is going to last. Damnit, Lorne, you've got yourself into a real mess this time. Look, the dashboard is shot. I can only guess the seconds from my breathing. And smart move, talking out loud here, wasting air. It's not like time matters anymore. I'm done for.

Wait, the light is dim, it is still recording. Damn right. Apologies for these ramblings. That little red blinking dot better stay on and keep my sanity in check. I can't believe I survived the explosion of the shuttle. If this thing is going to record, I hope that when my corpse is discovered, this audio log will make it to someone, somehow. Ideally, not in the hands of a Harvester.

Well, seeing as these are my last words, to whomever, I've gotta tell you that floating through space gives you a lot of time to think about life, what you did, and why you ended up here, and how you'll never have kids with the gal you should have made a move on.

Looking at the planets, stars, and ship debris floating around, makes you realize we're such a small spec in the larger painting. Nature's canvas, spanning across the universe. Biology, physics, chemistry—all of it is intertwined in the cosmos. The universe that doesn't care about our needs, as is the law of nature. To our knowledge, we were born from the planet Earth and surpassed many filters of evolution to bring us here, which makes us unique.

Now, we're even attempting to escape our home world and head for the stars, away from our own predators that evolved from us. Or we created them through science, depending how you want to define evolution.

.

. . .

.

What am I even saying? These thoughts are probably the result of a lack of oxygen, or maybe I am reflecting on my purpose in life, thinking about everything I should have done when I had the chance. Maybe I should have left the humans, found a way to serve the Harvesters and live a decent life. After all, I am a little spec of an evolution offshoot soaring through a vacuum. We're not meant to be up here, and we're not meant to modify our genes. Humanity has truly reached some fantastic feats.

Yet, here I am, gradually rotating on an angular axis, watching the aftermath of the Harvesters' attack on our escort mission. Damn organ-pickers, so persistent on making sure we don't escape Earth. We know that they were once human. How long ago remains unclear. Four hundred years? Eight?

The Lost doesn't have any answers. Whatever conflict that took place eradicated the old world and its history. Only the gene-freaks have record of what went on. They kept the tech. They were genetically superior, so who could argue? We can only piece together parts of our past from excavating the Lost. At the same time, the Harvesters continue to edit their genes, perfecting themselves. Their tinkering ways are what drove them so far from humanity, changing their forms and their minds, eventually seeing us as animals and themselves as gods.

Maybe their modifications are a part of nature. There is no good or evil, according to the cosmos. It doesn't play by any rules. Just look at that sun of ours; it shines so brightly. That is all it does with no favoritism.

Let me tell you, it sure is a beauty from out here, beyond the planet's smug. Earth isn't anything to look at. It is just a giant grey ball of clouds. From what archives we have salvaged from the Lost, photographs and paintings portray Earth as a vibrant green and blue. I can't even imagine what the surface must have been like or why people didn't care to nurture it.

Then to think that the sun will start dying in two billion years. In about four billion years our galaxy collides with another galaxy and everything becomes a real shit show in our cosmic region. It makes the fights we have with each other seem so meaningless. We humans live, what? A hundred years if we're lucky? We're nothi—

.

. . .

.

I'm not sure what else to tell you, whoever you are, listening. Oh, right, I still have a duty to serve. What happened here? Shit. Well, our cruiser made sure that the EX-7006 made it out of the solar system. I honestly didn't think that it would. Our distraction helped them initiate the gravity engines. The Harvesters won't be able to track the ship at that speed. Pricks. Score one for humanity.

Let me back up, in case my body isn't found by another human or even in my lifetime. The EX-7006 is unique to our previous launches into space. The crew is on a one-way trip to a new world. Which world? Well, if a Harvester is listening to this, then fuck you! You'll never find out. The brave souls on that ship are on the most vital mission of all. You're never going to know where the EX-7006 went.

The plan is a longshot. What other options do we have? You Harvesters are superior in every way. We can't out-gun you, nor can we reason with your superior intellect, or ego is what I prefer. Our only chance of survival as a species is to use our wit and get away as far as we can. That leaves the rest of us on Earth to perish unless we manage to send out more colonization ships to new worlds without being detected.

Maybe we will defy nature. My pal Alan McLeod believes we can. He told me, "We're humans. Defying nature is what we do." That stubborn bastard was so eager to make it onto the EX-7006. He's safe now, thanks to my crew. You pricks won't get him. I hope he is right about the human spirit. Hell, with his logic, it explains you gene-freaks and your editing. You were once human beings who defied nature too, then evolved, and are now preying on what you once were.

Go ahead. You'll eventually get all of us on Earth, and then what? You'll have nothing. EX-7006 made it out. Some of humanity has to be sacrificed, or in biological terms, naturally selected, for us to survive, and that's fine. That's the short version of why I'm hurdling through space. I could go into the details of why our captain decided to propel the shuttle straight into the Harvesters' ship, and why I seem to be the only one who survived, but what is the point? I don't think I will be making it out of here alive. My crew members' sacrifice is enough duty to humanity.

If you don't mind, I'd like some silence while enjoying what is the last view I will ever see, until the recording log glitches or the air tank runs out. I'll just stare at the great neutral cosmos, who cares not of who lives. It is both beautiful and sickening to watch. Seeing beings like the Harvesters just makes me think there is nothing out there for us but death and misery if we don't accept the wonder of neutrality within the universe. As individuals, our desires serve no purpose. As a collective, humanity has to find a way to survive, procreate, and resist, as we always do.

Hold on, wait . . . I see something. It's not one of ours. Definitely no asteroid. Oh shit, that's a H—

. . . .

. . . the red dot is flick— . . .

. . . they're coming for me. Those pri— . . . . . .

. . . . we made it ou—!

. . .

.

Fragment: N

Awake from the observing state. (Turn to Page 229)

A promising observation state! You and Malpherities are thrilled with discovering the letter fragment. The two of you have new hopes of breaking the loop and potentially the rip. It'd be wise to keep track of the strange letters you're seeing while exiting the observations. It'd be a shame to forget them . . .

Continue on in the Midway (Turn to Page 231)

The observation fizzles out, revealing the familiar cavern in the Midway. The orb slips from your hand as the power calms within your body. The ground is rumbling, and you struggle to maintain balance. Another crackling thunder comes from outside.

"That can't be good," Malpherities says, hovering towards the cavern entrance leading to a staircase up to the plateau.

You rub your head, still not fully adjusted to witnessing other lives. It's best not to get left behind, and you join the ghoul, stepping out into the brisk wind. The black ocean thousands of feet below is still violent with large waves.

Above, the swirling vortex is continually being sucked into the giant rip. The burning white flames along the edges of the rip flicker brightly, and you swear the edges have stretched further, spanning across the atmosphere of this strange world. The reflective space within the rip morphs in shape, showing wilderness, creatures, cities, and hundreds of other objects all mangled together in one big muck. Some of them you even recognize from the previous observing states.

"How did this rip happen?" you ask the ghoul who hovers in the middle of the plateau.

"This is what we're trying to find out, remember? It has to do with you. That's all we know," Malpherities says.

You are entranced by the intense visions within the rip. It's responsible for the violent winds affecting the endless ocean and creating massive tidal waves. Thankfully, no other waves have crashed into the plateau as of yet. There's another tidal wave in the far distance, about seven times larger than that first one. It certainly wouldn't be good for you or Malpherities if it reaches here. But it's hard to tell if it's moving in this direction or not.

"Is the Midway another planet?" you ask.

"More like another realm. You have the mortal realm where you are from, then there's Dega'Mostikas's Triangle, commonly referred to as Hell in most human religions. Then there are the Heavenly Kingdoms. And, of course, Death's Vortex, which is hovering above us. It'll disintegrate into that rip if we don't act soon."

You and Malpherities hurry back down the staircase and into the cavern as another rumble occurs.

"This time loop, is it part of the rip?" you ask.

"That is my best guess," Malpherities says. "As you can see from the rip, reality is morphing and twisting into all sorts of matter. The beings and creatures transforming are likely stuck in their own loop. I don't think we are the only ones trapped in this strange bubble, reliving our time again and again. The only difference is that we know it is happening."

"Kind of like Groundhog Day."

"Bingo. I, along with my ghoulish companions, can break out of space-time and remember past existences."

"Because you're part of that Death's Vortex, the resting bed for all souls?"

"You're a quick learner. This loop is slightly different. Hence, I cannot recall what clue I tried to give you before the loop mangled it into a candy box. Fragments remain in my mind. I know you, and I know how we've done this before."

"That's more than what I remember. I still have no idea who I am."

"The only thing you must recall is finding the fragments within this observing state. They hold the key to breaking this loop, and potentially the rip itself."

"And how did these fragments end up in these observing states?" you ask.

Malpherities reaches the orb. The golden glitter moves in and out of the darkness within the sphere. "I have a theory, Nameless One, that it might be related to how you first came to the Midway, in the version I showed you earlier."

"What do you mean?"

"We concluded you didn't die, and I sent you back to live your life. But something did pull you out of the mortal realm and into the afterlife when this rip was birthed. I think you are one of many that experienced an impact from the cosmological event, disrupting reality and everything we know."

"Okay, that really doesn't explain much."

"I know. It's a theory. Basically, it means whatever event occurred shattered in the ripple effect, impacting you and these other lives we observe through the orb. The fragments of the explosion, or the clues, are deep within their realities whether they know it or not."

"These other people we're witnessing are like me then, meaning they're important to the loop."

"Possibly, or collateral damage. We need to combine these fragments, similar to how we built this orb." Malpherities points at the object.

"I truly wish I could remember building the orb." Deep down, a part of you feels the familiarity towards Malpherities and the orb the longer you stay in the Midway. Maybe it is simply you being accustomed to the strange new existence. Or perhaps you certainly have been here before, many times, again, again, and again, reliving this loop. That's a concerning thought.

"Us making the orb is a minor detail," Malpherities says. "And of course, when you woke this time, you had to drop the damn orb down to the base level of the Midway. Very intelligent. You almost broke it."

"Give me a break."

"Unlikely. We're dealing with the end of existence year. There are no breaks. Now, are you ready to continue?"

"I guess we have to if we want to save everything from demise."

"That's the spirit," Malpherities says with a grin full of teeth.

"How many more clues, or fragments, do you think we have to find?"

"As many as we need to be able to break this repetition."

"Wait, if this is a time loop and you have most of your memory, when does this thing loop back to the beginning, when I was at the grocery store?"

"Oh, yes. Well . . . we are getting close."

"How close?"

"I was hoping you wouldn't ask, so you would react on your instincts to help find these fragments."

MAKE ONE OF TWO CHOICES:

Say, "Yeah, no that makes sense. I think going with my gut is best." (Turn to Page 237)

Say, "Malpherities, tell me." (Turn to Page 235)

Malpherities growls with irritation. "I suppose it doesn't matter, does it?"

"Why won't you tell me?"

"Well, I've told you in the previous loop. I was hoping this may be different. Each interaction with you I modify, trying to get a little further. It's trial and error."

"And how close are we to the reset?" you ask.

"We are two observations away from your final choice. Then the loop resets."

The words make your stomach sink. You're not sure if you have enough fragments to revert everything. There's also the fact that your memory will be lost when the time loop resets. Everything you've experienced up till now with Malpherities won't matter. Still, deep down, this is all familiar. Perhaps some of the memory is baked into your soul.

"We'd better find these damn fragments then," you say.

Grab the orb and find the next clue in a new observation.

(Turn to Page 237)

You pick the orb up and take a deep breath as the powerful energy surges through your system and your flesh melds with the orb. If this thing is made from your blood, it is part of you anyways, and you two are the same.

"We can do this, Nameless One," comes Malpherities's distant voice.

You and the orb leave the cavern, returning to the familiar white space as three portals appear from nothingness. The orb is being sucked into the portal on the right, which flashes massive sand dunes and remains of an ancient civilization. The middle portal showcases a dark dungeon with leather boots and whips. The portal on the left flickers visuals of a chimp strapped to a chair, lab coats, and mangled flesh.

MAKE ONE OF THREE CHOICES:

Take the portal on the left. (Turn to Page 239)

Take the portal in the middle. (Turn to Page 249)

Ride into the portal on the right. (Turn to Page 259)

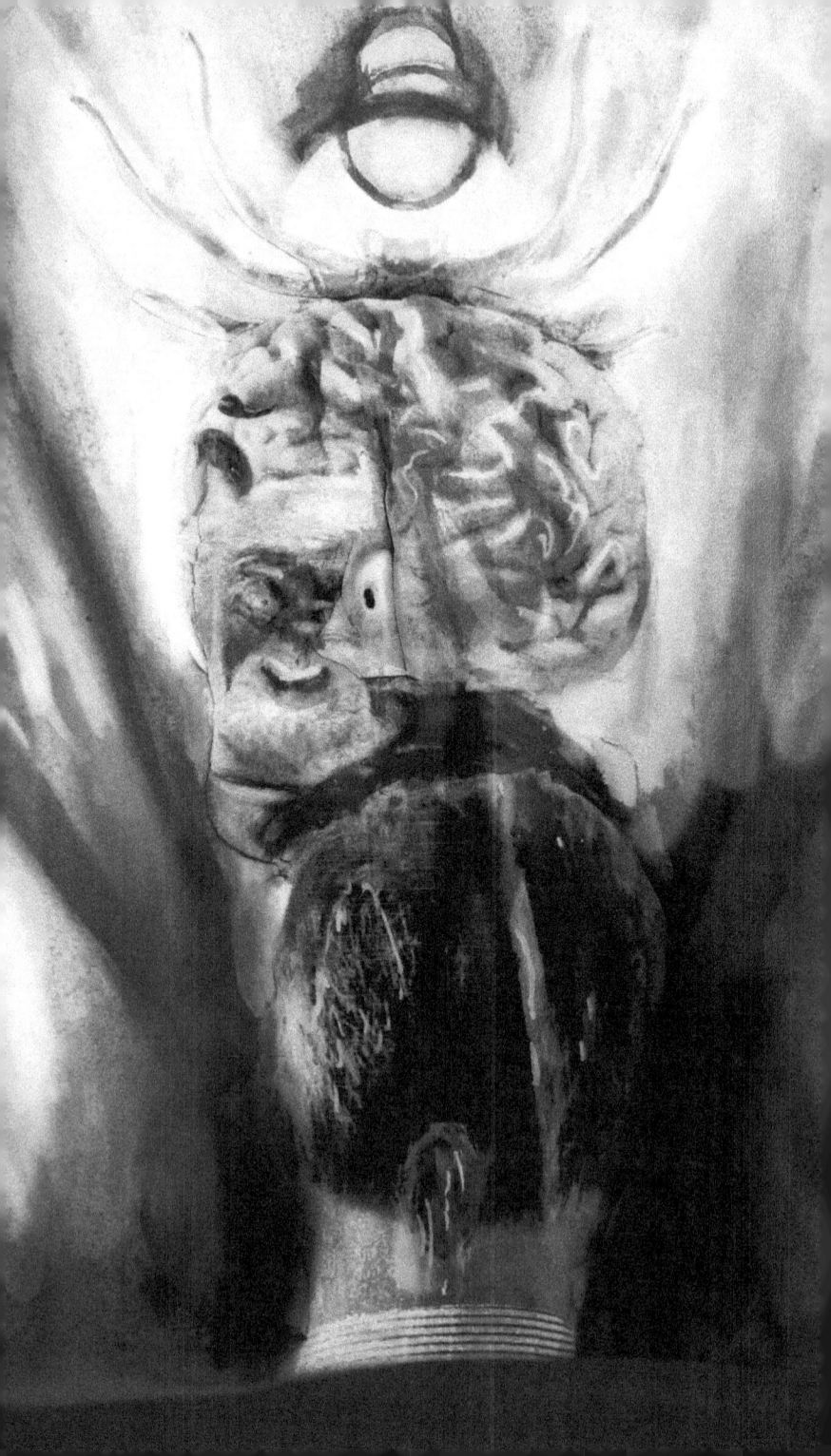

UNLOCKING IMMORTALITY

The key to immortality isn't a black and white answer. If it were, humanity would have unlocked the method long ago. Anyone brave—or delusional—enough to attempt finding the key to immortality must have a vast accumulation of knowledge in varying subjects. Or perhaps just access to the information. Each category raises unique problems. I ask myself fundamental questions to start:

1. Biology: Knowing our anatomy and how our bodies function is an important step. We're contained in this vessel during our time of being alive. Does immortality bring the flesh with it, or do we transcend into an ethereal, or digital, state? Big question.

2. Psychology: Our thoughts evolve. What we can comprehend as a child is nowhere near what we are capable of understanding at middle age. After, we deteriorate. Does immortality mean our minds are frozen from growth the moment the spell is cast on us? Or does our consciousness continue to evolve, eventually surpassing our human selves? Mystical terminology aside, it raises a prominent concern.

3. The Self: The modern world tells us that we exist in the brain, as the mind. Ancient philosophy claims we live in the heart. Spiritual leaders tell us we are the soul. What are we? Are we already

immortal post-death through the soul? Or are we only an accumulation of only microscopic creatures unaware of their higher self?

I can keep adding to the list. Ultimately, I leave that task to my colleague, Rand. He's more interested in derailing from our project's intention so he can question the unfathomable. We bonded on the discussion when we were both hired. It's fun to theorize, but quite frankly, I'd rather keep my job in the laboratory. Rand is willing to take the risk, thanks to the extra funds we got this year. The government was exceptionally generous with their grant. We've upgraded our stations, equipment, and even hired interns.

The buffer of cash sounds promising, but it means more pressure to complete our goal: Transcribing Neurological Pathways from Two Sets of Active Minds. Yes, it is a mouthful, but we aren't here to sex up our proposals. We're scientists. We discover and push the boundaries of humanity.

I generalize the project for the simple minds by saying we're in the process of sending thoughts from one brain to the other without the need to speak or read. We are creating a direct communication of opinions, feelings, and ideas. The concept birthed from the research done by Nichola Tesla. His World Power System proposed we can harness the energy trapped in the air, known as radiant energy. He proved the concept but lacked modern technology to access its full potential. We are close, and now we're taking it one step sideways by using the radiant energy as a superhighway to transfer data. The device will convert thoughts into the universal power, transmitting it to a receiving device. Similar to an adaptor for your computer and TV, transferring data from one type to the next.

The military is highly interested in what we are doing, hence the budget increase. If we pull it off, we can genuinely take humanity to the next phase of existence. The number of coffees and cigarettes I've had over the past couple of years is going to stain my teeth permanently. That will make a gal want to marry me. At least I'll be in the history books.

Personal sacrifice aside, we've made progress. We transcribed several thoughts from one primate mind to another through a quantum chip adaptor installed in the back of each subject's skull. One chimp sent the answer of a simple math problem to the other, taking a test, letting the receiving chimp answer a challenge it could not solve. The experiment was proof of telekinetic abilities.

Rand was ecstatic with our breakthrough and began hammering a bunch of algorithms into our deep learning software, saying the sending subject didn't just transcribe a thought to the receiving specimen but *entered* it. I told him not to get too excited with new theories. The chimps only sent and received a number. The experiment was *one*test of many we need to do with these primates.

If we can strap a couple of human test subjects and run the experiment, we could toy with Rand's theory of consciousness sending through the adaptors. The trials would be fun, and I would love nothing more than to test the tech on some human subjects. Unfortunately, we can't get clearing to do so—something about moral ethics and human rights.

Rand left, and so did the interns. I stayed behind to review the reports on the chimps further. As usual, I left the lab far too late and would be testy tomorrow morning. But hey, I am dedicated to the science.

Eventually I leave, tired and ready for sleep like any other night at the lab. I say goodbye to Tim, the night guard, who wishes me a good night. At home, I put my phone on the nightstand, keeping it on a ringer in case of an emergency from the lab. Thankfully, rarely do they call.

The phone hums—a text message. I ignore it and roll over to the other side, hoping I won't see the screen light up.

RING RING

Damnit. I spoke too soon. There is no sleep for me. I sigh, rolling over to pick up the phone, seeing the caller ID is Rand. I answer, "What?"

"Get to the laboratory fast. I've done it." Rand's voice is shaky, excited, and high-pitched. He has always been the jittery type, but this is different.

I want to ask him what he's doing back at the lab, but blurt out, "Can it wait until tomorrow?"

"No. I've done it."

"Done what?"

"Accessed our unlimited potential. Matter cannot be created or destroyed, right?"

"I don't need high school lessons, Rand, what is it?"

"Which means we cannot die. Our pieces are simply scattered with our body's death."

"Yes, theoretically," I humour him.

"We've seen matter exist in multiple states at once at a quantum level. This applies to many types of matter. Our minds, the thoughts, can exist with and without the body."

"What?"

"The adaptor, the chimps, the signal we saw today."

"I told you to drop this."

"I modified it."

My heart stops, realizing what Rand likely did. If he muddled with that adaptor, it would set us back months. We could lose the funding. "What did you do?" I ask.

"I've proven consciousness doesn't exist in our body, but only as a temporary state. It exists beyond these five senses caged in the flesh."

"Rand."

"Get down here."

Rand's mystical words convince me, and I put on a fresh pair of pants. My hair is a mess, and my breath probably reeks. I forgot to brush my teeth. If I have to scold Rand, the bad smell will make the down-talking more impactful.

I arrive at the Manageficient Enterprises laboratory entrance where Rand waits for me. I light up a smoke, saying, "What is this all about?"

"Finish that up. You won't be needing it anymore anyways."

"What did you do to the adaptor?" I ask.

"I ran the results of the sending subject through the computer to get more possible outcomes."

"Yeah, I know. You wanted to amplify the adaptor's signal. I told you it would scramble the receiving chimp's thoughts, probably causing a seizure to the subject."

"That's not what I meant, you're thinking linearly. Broaden your mind."

I specialized in quantum theory back in university, the comment is insulting, but I brush it aside. "Elaborate?"

"I installed an electromagnetic frequency unit, letting the adaptor suck in all possible wavelengths from the body. All particles have wave-like properties, which attracted frequencies that we didn't even know existed. They're frequencies of consciousness, the real us. I pushed them out into the radiant energy Tesla spoke of and freed consciousness from the flesh."

I stare at him blankly, thinking he is getting into some weird pseudo-science nonsense.

"I've unlocked the key to immortality."

I exhale the smoke from my mouth. "Bullshit."

"No, come see."

I flick the cigarette to the curb, and we enter the building side by side with our key fobs then pass the security desk where Tim should be. He isn't there and must be patrolling. We take the elevator, going down a half dozen floors to the laboratory. Rand is rambling on about some of the early inventions of Nichola Tesla that harvest power and how we are all directly connected to the universal free energy. Truthfully, I find it hard to listen to and phase-out of the conversation.

"Amplifying the wavelength module of the adaptor's signal has created a doorway for both our consciousness and subconsciousness to move freely into the ethereal space that surrounds us."

"When was the last time you slept?" I ask.

"Sleep is irrelevant now," Rand says as the elevator opens. He steps ahead of me. I spot blood running down the back of his neck, just below a freshly shaved patch in his skull where a hole rests, exposing some brain matter and bone. I'm no doctor, but he should be dead with one so deep.

"Rand?" I don't move, knowing something isn't right.

"Come," Rand says. "Don't let your human senses deceive you."

"Rand, did you install the adaptor on yourself?" I ask.

"I had to, who else could I try it on?" Rand continues to walk into the laboratory.

"One of the primates, you idiot!" My hand catches the closing elevator door. I'm not sure if it is the taboo scientific curiosity or because Rand is my friend, but I can't leave him and I follow.

The laboratory is trashed. The florescent lights dangle from the ceiling, flickering. Shattered glass is everywhere. The walls, floor, and countertops are cracked. Something big happened here. I wonder if Tim knows. Still, I continue following Rand. I need to know what he found.

I keep scolding him, saying, "You jeopardized our whole operation. You'll be removed from the project."

"That doesn't matter," Rand says.

My eyes are glued to the hole in the back of his head. It is quite dark, making me wonder how deep he jammed that adaptor in. I say, "Did you even think what the scientific community will say about you breaking moral ethics? No one will take you seriously."

Rand chuckles. "Please. We've been working towards such a primitive goal, humorously enough with primates, when the real prize was only a few thoughts away. The adaptor springboards our soul from this body. I've done it, it works!"

Rand leads me deeper into the laboratory, which becomes more unfamiliar with each step. Concrete sticks out from parts of the wall. Dirt and plants sprout from the cracks in the countertops. We never had plants in here. Melted metal is still burning on the floor, projecting red light into the darkening hall.

"Soul? Rand, we've concluded that the soul is just a combination of the body and mind. You're tired. Take some time off. We can try to keep this on the downlow. No one needs to know."

"Look at this place. You can't keep this hidden." Rand takes a turn and enters the testing room. "Besides, I have moved beyond simple human morals," his voice reverbs.

I turn the corner and enter the room. My eyes widen, hairs standing upright, as I stare at what lies, or has fused, to the testing station. A monstrosity of organic and human-made material. The two primates are intertwined with the metal that was once their chairs—a gory, morphic mess of flesh and steel.

"It's breathing," I mutter, not realizing I spoke out loud; my voice is dry.

The abomination sputters blood from an orifice on the side of its connected skulls as its single swollen, glassy, pink eye stares back at me.

"I boosted the adaptor signals a little aggressively at first." Rand's voice continues to reverb, becoming wraithlike, unlike my own. He smirks as one-half of his face droops. Did he have a stroke? "This is why I had to test the adaptor on myself. It was my only chance. You know they wouldn't keep me here after this mess."

I push my deep curiosity aside. Rand is sick, and the laboratory is a disaster. I must call security. I need to keep him distracted. "What happened here, Rand?" I ask as my hand slides into my pocket, ready to pull out my cellphone and get help.

"Don't call for Tim," Rand says, voice deepening into something demonic. His face continues to melt, including his eyes and hair. "He's already here. We all are. The adaptor has unified energy. All matter is the same and can be one."

The curiosity creeps up again, and my fingers loosen on the phone as I stare at the top of Rand's head. From the back of his skull, a black liquid-like substance channels upward to the ceiling. Torn shreds of spiky human flesh and bone along with scraps of a security uniform are flowing up and down into an unexplainable black space above, projecting from Rand's hole. Colours of the room smear out from the edges of what remains of the ceiling, continually shifting and stretching as I turn my head. The interactive colours and gory remains of Tim are oddly similar to when a computer screen is glitching out and you try to move a window. Stillness, only moving when I move, leaving a trail of the previous moment.

"The adaptor is the portal," Rand speaks in dual voices, one low pitch, the other high. He isn't moving. His mouth and whole body are static, also reacting to my movement against the continuing expanding black space from his skull.

My thoughts are active as I move my head. Yet, as I look down, my body isn't moving with me; it too is smearing. Weightlessness lifts me from my physical form as the darkness expands in space. New thoughts enter my mind. Emotions: fear, pain, terror. Senses overrule my better judgement: stale smells, cold, voices.

"The adaptor became a part of my body," the voices speak at once, coming from all corners of the room. "The adaptor pushed me through into the radiant energy. I am the portal. This is the key and the answer to all of our theories."

I try running, but . . . I . . . can't? I am simply a witness to new spaces—or memories. Tim's perspective of walking into work, Rand on the computer, and the chimps as they eat their treats are visions. I am absorbing them instantly, experiencing each memory simultaneously. The darkness envelopes all matter around my view. Tim's corpse, Rand, the chimps, and all space swirl into the blackness with me, shredding apart all that is physical. I feel them, their thoughts, I am them as they are me.

The negative emotions and senses dissipate to a state of isness. They were only a temporary uncertainty of what lies beyond our limited human-bound minds. I understand what Rand had become and what he wanted to show me. The beauty and the non-linear expressions are unexplainable. Our theories and questions about life after death were all wrong. There is no fault on us. We couldn't think in any other way in our previous state of existence.

We are now a part of the single consciousness found within radiant energy.

The unlocking of immortality.

Fragment: G

Awake from the observing state. (Turn to Page 273)

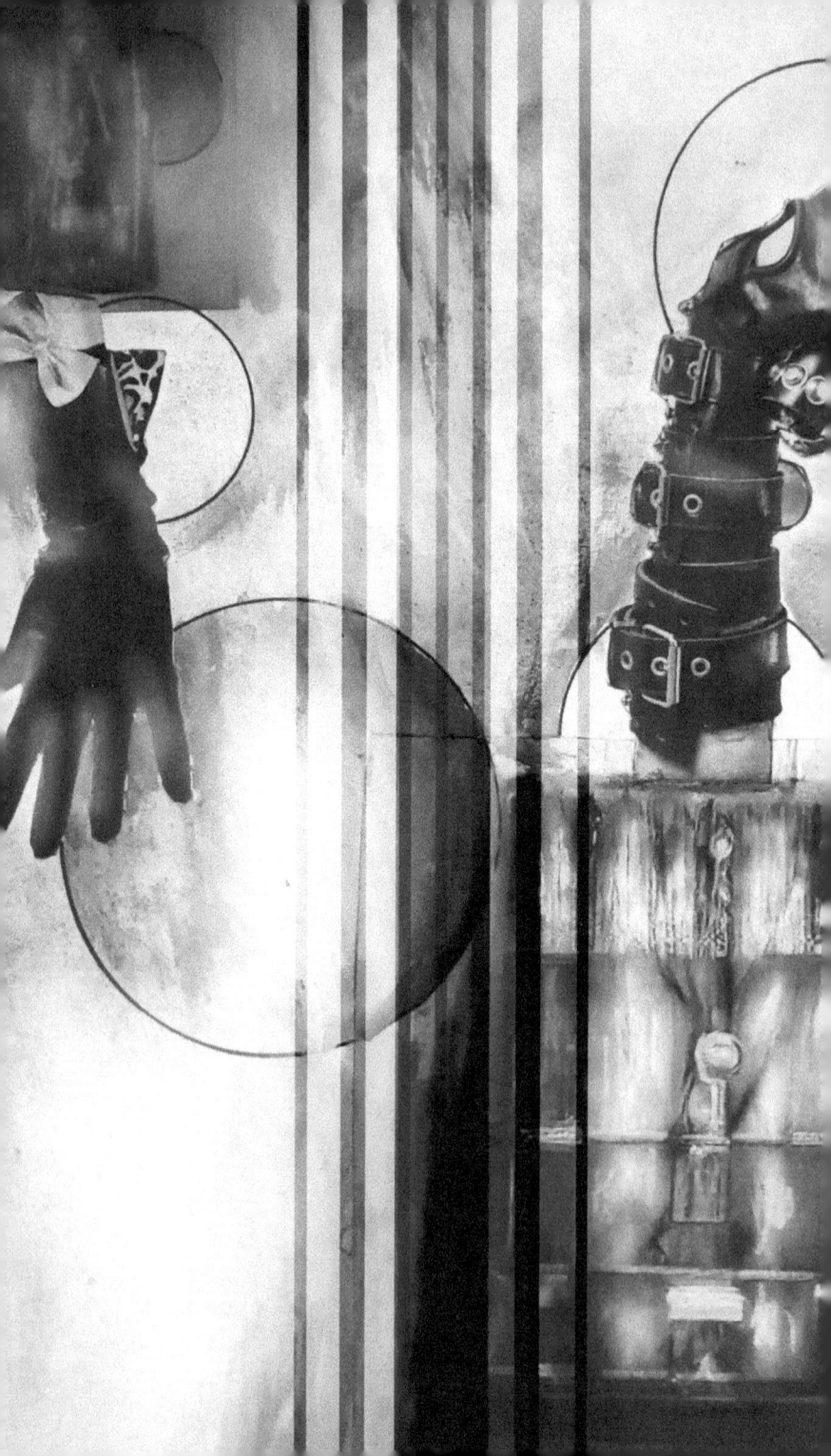

SWAY

Relationships are truly a complicated, exclusive club for two. Of course, that changes if you're into ENM, ethical non-monogamy.

Personally, ENM is not for me. I can't seem to stay in a club of two. Try adding a third, or fourth—my goodness! I'm far too attached to one; clearly, as I sit in the boardroom waiting for our next client, watching my ex-wife through the glass office walls.

Correction, Bridget is still my wife. We're processing the divorce papers. Look at her smile; I love that canine tooth that pokes out a little more than the rest of her teeth.

Working for her isn't helping me move on. Telling her I "lost" her pillowcases just so I can sleep by them each night doesn't aid the situation either.

My smartwatch says it's past ten, meaning this new client is already late. I take a sip of the best coffee in the world, JJ's, and try to calm my restless legs.

It's not the new client that's on my mind.

It's seeing Bridget day in and day out at the office.

It's the nerves of meeting my friend Danyal and his partner Wei later, reminding me to move on with my life.

It's been hell, ten months of hell.

A firm knock comes from the glass door, and there's Bridget. Her emerald hawk eyes are stern. She's in business mode, which never distracts me from her fiery orange hair that rests perfectly on her Alexander McQueen silk blazer. The high-end midnight blue material always pairs well with those black shoes. I barely hear her words, entranced by her presence. She says something about the client being here and to be speedy with it.

A lady comes from down the hall with a leather binder. Her high heels click, walking as if her legs are pencils, shifting back-and-forth due to the tight leather skirt. I'm drawn to her black gloves with little white bowties on each more than the ruffle cut-out blouse made of a deep velvety material. Those gloves must be by Cornelia James. I truly admire a high sense of fashion—just look at Bridget.

The new client and Bridget shake hands politely, and she enters the meeting room. Bridget gives me one last look, not of love—God I wish—but of 'chop, chop.'

I introduce myself as Booker, and she does as Olivia. Her voice has a rich, feathery tone to it. It's soothing. I shake her gloved hand, now noticing the cup of JJ's she put on the table.

Olivia opens the binder and shows me several pieces of paper with photographs of her painting collection. She explains her consulting business accumulated the pieces during a small tech firm buyout. The founder had an eye for good art. There must be at least two dozen unique works here. This is far more than I anticipated and will take time to understand the value of each one. Sorry, Bridget.

These paintings are spectacular. I'm drawn to an abstract piece with cubism influences. The harsh lines and geometric shapes in a gunmetal monotone colour scheme would look lovely in our—make that, my home.

Olivia says she needs these valued by next week. We discuss the usual: how old they are, who painted them, and with what mediums. It's the typical introduction, and of course, I must have a closer look at these works.

She mentions that knowing the value of the cubism piece is most important to her. She wishes to display it for a private party next Friday and wants to have the pricing available for potential buyers. I assured her that it would be fine. We set a time to see the paintings in her storage unit and I shake her hand, feeling the silky material of the glove again. It's quite pleasing on my skin.

As Olivia leaves, she says I have good taste in coffee, tilting her head at my JJ's cup. I blurt out that her choice in Cornelia James finger suits are equally great. I imagine the gloves flying off her hands and slapping me across the face. What a stupid thing to say to a new client! What are finger suits? Unprofessional. Oddly, she thanks me with a slight bow, clarifies that the gloves are by Dents, and she leaves the office in her pencil strut. What a delightful new client.

In the evening, I meet Danyal and Wei at their house. We catch up, with me blabbering about how the divorce is going. Wei says I need to take her belongings and throw them on the street. He's right. Me storing her belongings in the house lets her drag me around like her pet dog.

Strangely, I confess to them that I think I enjoy the control. It keeps me attracted to her, giving her a power that I cannot resist. Then I think about that client and her gloves slapping me. It's a captivating idea.

Danyal says he knows just the thing that can springboard me to move on. He's part of an invite-only club, Club Sway, where members express power dynamics for play and pleasure. Danyal says he is more than willing to vouch for me.

I know this is a BDSM club. It is something that I've wanted to try. Bridget and I had the usual ball gag and chains, nothing special. This is an opportunity to embrace my dominance fantasy.

I agree, and we set a date for this Friday.

Danyal warns me of the all-black dress code. Wei encourages me to embrace the subculture and is kind enough to lend me his PVC pants. These trousers happen to have five cleverly placed spikes right where you'd expect.

During the week, all I can think about is Friday night.

I'm nervous.

I'm unsure if I can go through with it.

I'm aware that seeing my wife smile through the glass walls every day isn't helping.

I'm doing my best to focus on Olivia's case and leaving the office to meet her at the storage unit is a brief exemption.

Once again, she's clad in a wonderfully stylish outfit. A clean, simple blazer with one exaggerated zipper, black pants, and a white blouse. No gloves this time. Drat.

We go through her collection one by one. I jot my notes, examining their conditions and taking photos. They're far more impressive in person, due to their size and detail.

Olivia jokes, saying I have no cup of JJ's today. I say I save the best thing for later in the day. She asks if that makes her second best.

I smile, realizing I'm getting too personal again, and try to focus on the pieces. She says she is surprised that my clothing is so . . . plain, considering my knowledge.

Olivia indeed has a good eye for finer things. She's right; I admire good taste but fail to wear anything beyond Hugo Boss. The brand is nice, but rather typical, and it's economically conscious too with the divorce in mind.

I shift our focus back to the art, feeling my throat tense up. Nerves? I don't know. I need to get back to Bridget—the office, I need to get back to the office. Olivia and I say our goodbyes. She gently squeezes my elbow in a friendly gesture that I welcome.

I return to the office and work on the appraisal. Bridget reminds me to hurry up with the client. Maybe I don't want to rush this one.

Friday arrives. Danyal and Wei meet me, bringing a police officer's hat to complete my outfit. I put on a black dress shirt and Wei's phallic pants. Bondage, law enforcement, and power control all make sense.

We head out to this underground Club Sway in an abandoned brick building east of downtown in the alley. I can already hear the thumping music outside.

Danyal leads us down a set of stairs to the entranceway, where two grizzly men guard the steel door. Danyal speaks, saying that he is vetting for me. One of the burly men informs us that the membership requires a hundred-dollar deposit and another hundred the following week, showing my dedication.

I'm unsure if I can go through with this. Two hundred dollars! Is that what it costs to get over my ex-wife? I don't think that's fair at all. People find all sorts of healthy mechanisms to move on, like fitness or travel. Perhaps working with your former lover isn't the best way to tend to your wounds.

Danyal, being the stand-up guy he is, offers to pay for the deposit. He sifts through his wallet as the clicking of heels echoes from atop the staircase, coming closer. The guards open the door for this lady behind us, and she steps forward, allowing me to get a good long look at the fiery orange hair.

My entire body turns ice, even in these airless plastic pants. This woman is with a taller, broad-shouldered chap. She is the right height, has the right coloured hair, and the beaming smile emphasizes her one canine tooth. I know her to be none other than Bridget . . . with some man.

Two hundred dollars and my ex-wife seals the deal. There's not a chance in the world I'm going in there. I storm up the stairs, hurrying down the night street, hearing Danyal and Wei shout my name. Boy, let me tell you, they were quite displeased. Danyal sent a massive wall of text to my smartphone. He emphasized how I must follow through with the initiation; otherwise, it makes him look poorly to the club.

Eventually, I apologized, typing out that I saw Bridget there. He is quick, texting that I need to drop it for my health. Bridget and I have the same taste in almost all aspects of life, making it difficult to avoid her.

Danyal and I text back-and-forth, me trying to explain my damaged heart and him telling me to come to the club. His name is on the line now, and there's a big birthday celebration for one of the co-founders next Friday. Guilt riddles me, and I agree. Next Friday it is.

On Monday, I keep working on Olivia's appraisal. After a few minor adjustments, the collection's value is finalized, no thanks to Bridget's constant pressure.

I fled in shame that night because I can't bear seeing my ex-wife clearly moving on.

I feel sick that she walked by, not noticing me.

I call Olivia to meet me.

On Tuesday, we sit in the boardroom, where I go over the estimates. I try to focus, but her full pinstripe suit pulls me in. Even the square earrings, one black and the other white, dangling from the lobes, are complementary.

Olivia notices my daydreaming and jokes, asking if I want to try the suit. I laugh with her. It lightens the mood while I go through each painting. We finish the loose ends of the appraisal, and she's ready to sell them at her event.

Before leaving, Olivia brushes her black hair behind her ear. She's looking down, tapping her leather binder, then, looks directly at me. Her following words are a surprise. Olivia asks me out for a cup at JJ's.

I'm stunned and stand frozen in my body. From the corner of my eye, I see Bridget in her office watching the two of us. I know she can read Olivia's body language, and I'm certain she wants this wrapped up. Those damn glass walls!

It only creates a more constricted prison.

It's exciting.

It's also draining.

It's . . . it . . . makes me come up with some clumsy excuse to decline Olivia's offer. She blushes, and I try to repair the exchange by telling her that I have her card. She masks herself in a smile and hurries out of the office.

What a fool I am. There's no way I'll ever tell Danyal and Wei. They'll never let me hear the end of it. My grievance sparks an act of spontaneous rage, and I throw out Bridget's pillowcases in a satisfying victory.

Friday arrives, and I suit up in my vampire-fighting police officer costume once more. Danyal and Wei meet me at my place, and we share a few drinks to lube up my mind. I need them. I keep thinking about declining Olivia. There's also a good chance that Bridget will be at Club Sway again, especially if it's a big party.

We leave home and arrive at the familiar staircase, with Danyal and Wei behind me. They're making sure that I cannot flee again. The guard gives me a stern look of disapproval. Danyal pleads, and the guard pulls out a white leather collar from a bag, resting on a table behind him. He tells me to put it on, saying it is part of the initiation. I ask why, and he says it's to identify me amongst the members.

I buckle the collar around my neck, initiating my membership into Club Sway as the guards open the door. Wei, Danyal, and I enter the club.

Pulsating, heavy, distorted beats blare from the amps at the far end of this dungeon. Black lights highlight the lobby while coloured ones signify different rooms where groups play scenes together. Some are tie-ups, others role play, and some involve pain with floggers and other creative devices.

A few of the doors are shut for private fun. A dancefloor is at the far end by the blaring music. In the middle is a common area, where most members mingle. There's a central pillar with a table of snacks and water resting against it. On the wall, I notice a remarkably familiar cubism painting.

There, off to the side, I see Bridget's striking hair. She's got her arm wrapped around that same gentleman. He's taller than me and far more fit. I clasp my gut, feeling the fat in disgrace. A breakup has a way of declining your physique through ever-gripping misery. At this point, I want to turn and run.

"Welcome, darlings!" comes a strident, feathery voice. My ears tingle.

That familiar voice is reassuring as I turn to see Olivia approach us from the dark. She is wearing a birthday hat on top of her black hair

BEYOND THE MACROCOSM BY KONN LAVERY

and is the only one with a hat, which contradicts the complete black PVC dress and the flogger in her gloved hands.

She gives Wei and Danyal a hug and does a double-take of me. Her smile doubles in size. "Booker?"

"Hello," I say. "Is this party for you?"

"How did you know?"

"Wild guess."

I glance at Bridget once more and push it aside. She may be here, but I'm no longer part of her club. We can co-exist, and she won't have me under her spell. I'm ready to embrace a new kind of exclusivity and say, "Happy birthday, Olivia."

Awake from the observing state. (Turn to Page 305)

PROMISES IN SAND

We aren't meant to live forever, for our bodies deteriorate long before our minds do. Over enough time, our thoughts begin to slip away before we are even aware. We strive to justify our death, avoiding the grim fact that we are mortal. Religious texts speak of gods, philosophers ramble, and many people wish for an afterlife—all have been discussed in immense detail by every civilization.

Dying is so vicious. I refuse to believe that we were meant to have our vast intellect for a short amount of time in this world. I refuse. Hence, the belief remained strong that I could achieve immortality. I had faith that I could defy the pathetic acceptance of death, like so many others. There is no afterlife superior to the world we live in. If there were, why would we be placed here for such a short time?

My search was held on by faith. I suppose you could say that makes me religious myself, in the sense that I believed that there was a method to reach immortality. I believed that there was some truth found within the stories passed down for generations. Too often, words of gods and mythology from a distant time are only fables explaining what alchemists eventually achieve.

My interest in everlasting life began when I first heard a specific story as a boy. These rumours spread from village to village over Life

River. The elders spoke of a lost civilization that once ruled the deserts to the east. The people worshiped a living god, one who granted eternal life to their loyal followers. No one alive had ever seen this civilization, or ruler. The rumours didn't spawn from my village. We heard it from another, and that village said they heard them from another who had first heard the story from travellers—further distorting fact from fantasy.

Still, this story failed to leave me as I grew into a young man. My father wished me to marry the neighbouring village chief's daughter to establish a strong bond. I was hesitant, as my mind was fixated on these rumours. I wanted to learn more about them. Why? I've asked myself the same questions for years. The fascination with beating death began with the passing of my mother. It was further amplified after my sister left this world. Both kissed death due to Life River's six-year drought.

My father told me to keep our faith strong. He said that the gods would keep us together if we believed in them. The years went on with little rain. I didn't see any reason to believe in these beings who lived beyond the sky. Maybe that is why I care about immortality, or maybe I fear my own death. With that uncertainty, I chose to be the master of my own faith. Why should I worship these supposed gods who punish us with droughts and pain?

I wanted to believe in something better. This is where I began my search. The story I heard as a boy must have come from a truth from somewhere. I exited the village, leaving my father in fury and despair. He said I had betrayed our family, for I was his only son. I am sorry, Father.

I travelled down the river by canoe, pushing onward. My journey took me to the other villages to learn of their knowledge. One village after the other, they each explained slight variations of the story.

One group said the civilization is still alive and well, hiding in the mirages of sand in the eastern deserts. Others told me that these people are long gone, buried below the dunes. One consistency they had was about the leader. A queen who showed no mercy to those who refused to kneel before her. The story goes she held the key to immortality with a single kiss. The tale distorts, as some villages said the queen was still alive and resided amongst people after her civilization's collapse. They said that she was determined to regain her throne. Others said she perished in the sands. I kept note of every story variation in my journal, hoping to piece together one truth.

A particular villager made a haunting statement. He said, "if you seek immortality from this queen, she will devour your life and curse your soul."

I took note of that unsettling message too.

The last village led me to someone new. An old woman was living far from the other villages south of Life River, beyond the jungle coast and near the deserts of the east, just by the rocky plateaus. I hoped she could provide answers rather than more altered tales. My water supply was running low, and I had little food. On occasion, I found a lizard or a snake that I could catch and cook. Through days of travel, I located the old woman's hut atop the highest plateau. My feet were sore, and the skin exposed to the sun was burnt.

The old lady hunched, sitting on a wicker chair outside a hut by the fire as the sun set. She smoked a pipe and could manage her home well despite having a cloth cover her eyes. It was safe to say she was blind. I wonder if she was expecting me through attuned senses because she smiled and said she was glad to see me. The woman offered me water and warm soup, replenishing my strength. I explained to her why I was there. She cut my explanation short.

"You wish to leap past the limitations of your mortal body," she said, stroking her metal bat amulet. Her voice was raspy and cold. She didn't blink as the wind picked up.

"Yes, that is correct," I said.

The old woman said that the shortcomings of man were surpassed by one civilization out east, the same one the villages spoke of. The army was once the dominant force in the lower region of the world, controlling all of Life River. They ruled for thousands of years under a single queen known as Queen Valturus. She was merciless to all who refused her kiss of immortality.

The loyal army obeyed every command she made in exchange for their eternal life. Her piercing green eyes were enough to pull in the most willful men. Add the gift of immortality as an addition to her charm, and men would commit notorious acts for her. Pillaging. Murder. Torture. There were no depths too far for them to descend in the name of their queen.

The army was feared by all men of the known world. No kingdom dared to fight. They could only pray to their own gods that Queen Valturus wouldn't come for them. She was the visible proof of a living goddess, unlike these other religions. She defied time and never aged during the thousands of years ruling.

I asked the old lady what happened to Queen Valturus and her army.

"Her army was washed away by the sands of time," the old lady said to me.

I didn't buy it. "How could one be immortal and be washed away from the sands of time?"

"Look for yourself," the old lady said. "Find the civilization out in the east over seventeen great dunes from this plateau, by the two limestone rocks. The remains of her achievements will be found."

"There's evidence of their collapse?" At the time, I was beginning to doubt the power of this civilization and Queen Valturus.

She smiled. "Immortality doesn't make you all knowing of betrayal from within."

"Of course. May I stay the night?" I asked, hoping to avoid the winds and cool desert night.

"You may, only if you provide one favour for me when you reach the Queen Valturus's fallen empire."

"And what is that?"

"Her temple resides in the center of the kingdom, where you'll find her throne. The queen has a red amulet resting on her necklace."

"And you need this amulet?"

"It is the key to immortality," she said. "The amulet is made of pure blood through centuries of draining her own. You must obtain it for me so I can consume it and restore my youth. Bring me the amulet, and I will bless you with life."

I thought about her request and nodded in agreement before internally committing. Yes, I should honour my word, even if I didn't fully believe it. Deep down, I knew I had no reason to believe this woman.

She spoke, "If you don't, you will die of the poison within your soup."

My heart stopped, stomach tightening from her words. The old lady must have known the internal struggle I was experiencing. Or she knew I would be gullible enough to eat. I was a young fool and too trusting from my life in a secluded village.

"You're lying," I told her.

"You can wait four days and find out for yourself what scorpion poison can do to a body. Or bring me the amulet."

Then, I realized my desire for immortality rested in fear of death and not in the loss of my mother or sister. I didn't want to challenge her bluff. "We'll share the amulet?" I asked.

"I promise you I will uphold my end of the deal for immortality," she said with an expressionless face.

"How do you know so much about this civilization and their queen?"

"The same way we all know the mythology of gods in the sky. Stories passed down for generations, my dear boy. You learn to use your ears more when missing a sense."

"You're sure, seventeen sand dunes east, by two limestones?"

"The kings of the earth were immoral with her, and those who dwell on the earth were intoxicated with the wine of her immorality."

Her words were not reassuring and further bound my quest for immortality by a leap of faith. If I'm not mistaken, her disturbing words were reference to a religious scripture. I didn't have time for riddles!

I wanted to kill her right there. Unfortunately, she had hidden the remedy to the scorpion poison, and I had to obey. We had a forced deal. I stayed with the old lady that night, waiting for the winds to pass by. My dagger was close to my chest, ready for use if she tried to do anything suspicious. I couldn't trust her at all and questioned this deal.

Nothing occurred during the night, and I left early in the morning. The old lady wasn't in the hut or anywhere near her home when I woke. Without hesitation, I left, wasting no time to get to the ancient civilization. I climbed down the plateau and walked over the first sand dune—sixteen to go.

The travel was long, tiring, but I was determined to carry it through. I was unwilling to bend to the fact that I was mortal, even with the scorpion poison in my veins and hate brewing in my heart for the old lady. The limitations of my human form weren't going to take me away. The sheer will I had alone kept one foot in front of me, going up and down the hills.

With all my water gone, I lost count of the hills. Was I on hill eight or hill fifteen? I did not know, but I kept walking for any sort of clue to this lost civilization. I had taken rest under one of the sand dunes to avoid the scorching sun during peak hours and travelled most at dusk.

The following dawn, I continued, hungry, thirsty, but unbendable. Eventually, the body refused my will and I collapsed, rolling down to the other side of a hill until my head shredded against something sharp, stopping me. My face was covered in sand and blood which I wiped clear from my eyes. To my joy, it was a limestone rock that I had hit, beside a second, just as the old woman had described.

The two stones had carvings in it from a language I could not identify. This had to be the civilization, for there was nothing around for miles other than this square block. With frantic excitement, I dug around the limestones. Through several scoops of my hand, I moved aside enough sand to trigger some opening because the sand began to fall into darkness.

I stepped aside as the hidden door slid away, revealing a staircase into the unknown. I entered the hall leading underground. I had no torches and relied on the light from the entrance to take me to the other end. The path was long, leaving me in pure darkness, hoping I wouldn't trigger another hidden lever. A dim light appeared, leading to a large underground opening where beams of light shot through cracks in the rocky ceiling. Finally, this had to be Queen Valturus's lost civilization, hidden below the sands of time.

Indeed, it was. I made it to the other side of the tunnel. Her triangular temple was easy to spot in the circular enclosure. I was not tempted by the mounds of gold, silver, and gems found at every corner of the roads. Skeletons scattered the sandy streets. The skin and bone on their necks all had puncture holes in the same spots. There wasn't an explanation for why they all had the exact same wound. Maybe it was related to their deaths. A few without holes were missionary men, based on their clothing and the sacred cross.

There was no sound other than my own feet echoing against the empty roads. The limestone buildings were left perfectly intact with paint, windows, doors, and hinges, lightly coated in sand and dirt. The kingdom's frozen state reflected my own quest.

The temple's entrance was atop a long and wide staircase. Covered in sweat, I reached the top and entered the building. My first step on the entrance's stone floor trigged the ignition of torches on the walls. They burst to life two at a time, one on each side, leading straight to the end. I drew my dagger and cautiously moved into the hall, hoping I wouldn't trigger a more deadly button. At the far end of the temple's black interior was the blood-red throne where the corpse of Queen Valturus rested. The throne itself had to be as tall as two men. The marble had perfectly carved linear lines, painted bright red, on and all around it, leading to the back of Queen Valturus's heart. It was an impressive sculpting achievement.

There weren't any booby-traps, nor signs of other adventurers. I stepped cautiously down the hall. To the sides were cradles with small corpses resting inside. I couldn't bear to look at the infants and continued, reaching Queen Valturus's throne. The once living god was a still corpse. I wondered how she died, who betrayed her, and if her blood truly offered immortality. The corpse was peaceful, sitting on the blood-red marble. She was far smaller than I had thought. Her hands gripped the armrests, head leaned against the smooth back, mouth dangling open. Puncture holes were on her neck, like the others.

Her hair was still attached to the scalp in a tattered mess, and the skin was pressed tightly against the skeleton, as no meat remained. The red amulet rested on her gold and red breastplate. I carefully stepped forward and reached for the amulet. As my hands got closer, I could sense a radiating power coming from the item. Then, I knew it had the power of immortality. I had never felt such a force come from something so small.

My fingers glided against the smooth stone. Carefully I lifted it and the chain over Queen Valturus's neck. Her body was stiff, but the chain moved with ease over her head. It was almost too easy. There was no grand climax or foe I had to fight. The blood amulet was mine.

After a night's rest, I returned to the surface through the entrance, leaving the civilization behind. There wasn't much to the empire, and I wish there were more answers as to how it submerged beneath the sand. The old lady said there would be proof there. Perhaps time indeed did wash away the civilization under the dunes.

This was the third day, and my time was limited to beat the inevitable poison. A part of me questioned if the amulet would bypass the poison or if it simply prevented aging. I decided not to risk it and would return to the old lady.

The travel back was equally tiring, if not more, but I had to press on. In the back of my mind, I couldn't help but wonder how obtaining the amulet was so easy and why the old woman didn't do it herself. Perhaps she couldn't handle the great travel. She was blind, after all.

Each step I took was more demanding than the last. It was as if this amulet had some sort of power over me. I resisted, pushing against this invisible force that rested in my poncho's pocket. I had to reach the old woman and get the remedy. Maybe it wasn't just the amulet, but the scorpion's poison was finally taking effect on me. I couldn't waste time to find out.

I reached the old woman's home near the end of the fourth day. She sat in her wicker chair outside her hut by the fire, as I found her before with the setting sun, creating a sense of déjà vu. She smiled at me as I approached. Again, she had to have an attuned sixth sense, for how would she know it was me?

"Did you find answers to the civilization's collapse?" the old lady said.

"No, but I got the amulet. Give me the remedy."

"You didn't look hard enough," the old lady said. "You're too eager, as is your quest for everlasting life." She extended her hand, saying nothing more, expecting me to hand the amulet over.

"Not until you show me the remedy," I said.

The old woman lifted a glass vial from her poncho containing a green liquid claimed to be the remedy. "Now, give it to me."

I extended the amulet to her, feeling it resist with excessive might. I ignored it as best as I could and placed the gem in the palm of her hand. It started to glimmer. The powerful force made one last pulse, rippling through both our bodies and pushing the rocks around us.

"Well done," the woman said, handing me the vial.

I snagged it and pulled the cork off, tilting it upside down to let the liquid pour into my mouth. The remedy had a bitter sting, but I forced it down, praying it would rid me of the scorpion's poison. I exhaled after the last drop, waiting anxiously for it to work.

The old woman clutched the blood amulet tightly with her hand, causing the exterior to shatter. I took a step back in shock, watching as fresh blood oozed out of the broken gem. I fully expected it to be hardened if it was made of ancient blood. She raised her hand and poured the blood into her mouth. It drizzled into her throat, over her lips, neck, and down her wrists.

"Share some!" I shouted, reaching for her hand.

The old woman swatted my hand away with her free arm, throwing me back due to her unnatural strength. She hissed while pulling off her blindfold, revealing emerald eyes. Her skin lifted up, tightening, as her wrinkles faded. Her hair glistened and gained newfound volume as she sat upright from her previously huddled state.

Her piercing gaze locked onto me as blood dripped down her chin. She stood from the wicker chair, throwing off her old ratty poncho, arms extended wide as she embraced her newfound youth. The muscles of her form shined in the setting sun while the surface of her body rose smoke ever so slightly until the light vanished, leaving us under the night.

It wasn't like anything I had seen before. This was real magic, not some presumed power of gods living above us, casting droughts. I knew then that I was staring at Queen Valturus, a living goddess.

"Queen Valturus," I said.

"Sweet, sweet, trusting boy. You've been so loyal, obtaining my strength."

"But, you were at the temple. I saw you."

"So naïve as you were with the soup. For your eyes lay witness to the betrayer of my civilization."

"Betrayer?"

"Do you not remember the tale? I'll finish it for you. The betrayer and her followers took my kingdom, resentful of my drunk power and quest of creating superior children. They formed allegiances with holy men, naïve to their hate for us. You can relate, my dear. I escaped to save my own life, withering away here. At least, until you arrived and were willing to take a leap of faith."

"What are you?" I asked.

"There are many names I've gone by, none of which are the label human. The undying. The eternal. Goddess is the name I prefer."

The living goddess was real. I couldn't believe what I was seeing as I stared into her hypnotic bright green eyes.

"You have proven yourself, boy. Let me reward you as promised," she said, taking a step towards me in a slow, confident stride.

"You'll grant me immortality?" I asked, stepping back.

"Of course. Through only a kiss . . ." Queen Valturus said, placing her hand gently over my jaw before I could back away. She had me locked into her dazzling irises. I couldn't look away. I tried. Over and over. I couldn't. She had me under some spell with that gaze. I wanted to live forever, and she was willing to offer it to me through a kiss. How dreadful could her lips be? Yet, I felt only fear.

"Please," I managed to say. My tone was dull as drool seeped from my lips. I fell to my knees as she stopped mere inches from my face. Her eyes did not leave mine. They're . . . a green that encompasses all of nature found within Life River. She was life. She was immortality.

Queen Valturus held my head up with her index finger and leaned down. I extended my head to her, ready to kiss the beautiful being. Her mouth opened, and her canine teeth extended into fangs. The emerald eyes widened as she grazed past my lips and swooped down to my neck, biting it with immense force.

I tried to pull away . . . but . . . her strength! It was overpowering as she sunk her teeth into my flesh, the jaws locking me in place. I felt dizzy. My limbs weakened . . . I surrendered to her as my skin turned pale. Blood oozed out of my system. Victim to her control, I hung lifelessly until she freed my body, and I fell into the sand.

"You'll rise at midnight, my child," Queen Valturus said, licking the red liquid from her chin. "Your newfound immortality comes at a price. This gift will make you like me—forever living. Unlike me, you cannot pass this gift on. That is mine alone. Stay clear of the sun and the holy." She brushed the hair from my face as the warm blood seeped from my open wound and onto the rocks.

She stroked the bat amulet that dangled from her neck. "Fear is natural. Step past it, for your human body is dying now. You'll emerge as a new form, a stronger, more resilient being."

I sputtered and managed to speak. "What is this?" It wasn't a clear statement. I certainly could have made the question more direct.

"I am your new God."

"I . . . I . . . what?" I had many questions in my mind. Was the betrayer good? Why should I avoid the sun? What was I to become?

What did she have planned? I couldn't say any of it as the life seeped from my body.

I died that day. Fear overwhelmed me as I attempted to breathe. Eventually, nothing entered my lungs, and the remaining blood left my body. As Queen Valturus said, I was reborn that night into something new. Now, my senses are more attuned than I could have ever imagined. My strength is unmatched by any man. I feed off people who are fearful, killing them to maintain my own life force through their blood.

The humans in the European kingdoms refer to us as vampires. They deem us horrors who leech off the good of this world. Now that I am one, I know this to be false. I simply need their blood to live, but I will never die. I am a better version of man, immortal as long as I stay clear of the sun. I can watch the centuries pass around us in darkness. If I do not feed, I will only wither into an old man, similar to Queen Valturus, and eventually a corpse, like her loyal followers lost below the sand. Only they aren't dead; they're conscious and resting. Her blood will reactivate their damaged states if she ever wishes it. I wonder if she will return for her children slumbering in the cradles . . .

However, Queen Valturus doesn't seem concerned about resurrecting her army. She has found a new appreciation for life after living in her old body. She wishes to live and experience rather than dominate and has left me to my own devices. This brings me to my original thoughts about the mind withering. She lacks the fire she was said to have in the stories. She no longer wants to dominate like the fierce goddess the story spoke of.

My initial concern of humanity's limitations was correct. Humans are, unfortunately, stuck in their limited forms—even a vampire's mind ages, if they were once human. We, or they, have amazing brains and frail bodies. For us to grow beyond, we have to accept the most frightening transformation through death. Queen Valturus can offer it to us if we are loyal to her. Perhaps Father was right, and I should have taken the simple life of marriage, unifying the two villages, and dying of old age. My mind and body would have been one. There is no going back, and I am forever.

I took the risk.

I believed, and I was right.

Now I pay the price . . . watching the world live and die. Live and die. Live . . . and die again.

Awake from the observing state. (Turn to Page 305)

Another clue! In the back of your mind, you can't help wonder if these observing states all happen within the same dimension as similar names and places are mentioned. Again, you don't have the luxury of time to ask Malpherities every little detail. The observation completes, and whatever happened after that obscure event with the chimps at Manageficient Enterprise matters not. It's only a memory as you return to your body in the Midway.

You pick up the orb and take a deep breath as you're about to experience another's life. You and the orb fuse, the cave turns white, and two portals appear. The one on the left shows a man writing a letter in an upper-class bar while drinking whiskey. His nose twitches repeatedly. The right portal shows a mountain landscape with a cabin and a family in the icy weather.

The orb is gravitating towards the portals, but no specific one. Remember, you can direct the sphere to where you wish to go.

MAKE ONE OF TWO CHOICES:

Take the portal on the left. (Turn to Page 275)

Guide the orb into the right portal. (Turn to Page 297)

DEATH SHOT

My hand shakes. The tip of the pen taps the paper, leaving marks of nervousness. Dot. Dot. Dot. I am to compose the most important message I will ever create. I don't write handwritten letters. The big boys upstairs must like keeping it old school. I'll play by their rules. After all, they'll determine the verdict of my soul. Here we go . . .

TO WHOM IT MAY CONCE—no, that's not personable enough . . . I know!

DEAR ANGEL OF DEATH, respectful, but too crude.

DEAR ARCHANGEL, there we go. Civil and direct.

A person can only make one first impression. I learned this from curating world-class art exhibits. If you walk with a little insecurity— BAM—you're pegged as prey, and the agent will walk all over you; stutter while making a deal, and you can forget about sticking to the budget. Seriously, it's a cutthroat industry. A handwritten letter is no different than a formal email or an alignment meeting—confidence, firmness, and clarity.

Yet, I am struggling, despite having done this a million times. I never thought I'd be making a case to justify my life, correction, my soul. I didn't believe in an afterlife because I'm practical. All of this is just wack. God, I wish I could get a line. Maybe I'll just ask the big man himself in a postscript: *P.S. PLEASE PROVIDE ONE RAIL ON A GOLDEN TRAY.*

The shock of rocking a coke binge, the Death Shot, a white light, and awakening here in the afterlife are on replay in my head, which is why I can't focus. The blinding light—what a cliché. Death is a big load to swallow.

"He's an archangel, right?" I shout through the crowded bar.

The round-faced man in front of me, puffing his cigar, takes it from his mouth and lets the smoke seep upwards. The century-old fashioned figure elegantly sips on his whiskey before answering, "Haven't you ever read the scriptures, boy?"

My hand squeezes the pen. I am frustrated and weak. Why can't this guy throw me a bone? My question is a yes or no answer.

"I have," I finally say after a pause, sipping my whiskey.

"Then what would possess you to ask?" the man chuckles. "You know the answer."

"I want to make sure this is right!" I snap. "This Michael guy, he's the top dude to talk to?"

"*Dude*? Please. You vegetarians are all the same."

"I'm vegan, but that has nothing to do with this."

"Bushwa! It does." He points at me with his index finger. "Know your onions. Adolf Hitler was one of you."

"What? That's not the point. I just want to write this damn letter."

I feel agitation crawling up my back from attempting to talk to a man from over sixty years ago. Understanding his jargon isn't easy. Come to think of it, he is the only person I've seen from a different era. Everything here seems relatively modern, in a demented surreal way. Hell, I spotted a Starbucks when I first woke from the blinding light. Churchill must be in a culture shock. I want to ask him, but I don't see a point in doing so. He seems testy, as if there is a layer of desire hanging onto every word he speaks, like me.

He adjusts his bowtie and says, "It's not normal for a man to deny the animals God gave us."

I point upward. "Look how the good God treated us."

"You vegan-tarians are all wet, or whatever new terminology you came up with in the future. Or *come* up with, I should say." He smiles, knowing I am frustrated.

"It's just vegan," I mutter. "Look, that's got nothing to do with the letter. Should I address Michael?"

He leans back in his highchair, losing focus on me, gazing at the bar several tables away. His glass is still half full. He's distracted by two greasy suits in a heated discussion and a flirtatious couple whose hands can't wait to undress the other.

A young man behind the counter is wearing one of those high-class, five-star, top-dollar vested uniforms, all red and pinstriped. The only customization the bartender has is his pencil-thin wax-twirled mustache. One must wonder how long he spends each morning getting those curls just right. It makes me look like rubbish, waking up from OD'ing, hair every which way, and looking whiter than a corpse.

Woah. Glimmering emerald eyes pull me away from the exquisite bar. They belong to a pretty-pasty gal in a tight black dress, sitting alone. What a babe. I hadn't seen her when I first got here. I was probably in too much of a panic to notice. We lock gazes, and she doesn't blink.

One of the suits slams his fist, throwing me from the beauty-trance. He points aggressively at the other suit, raising his voice, which is muffled from the bar's noise. The look on his face says he is pissed.

I look back to the pretty-pasty girl. She is gone. Strange.

"My . . ." the man across from me says, licking his lips. "Say, whatever happened to that delicious bartender?"

"Sorry?" I say with agitation seeping from my voice. The speed of the conversation can't get to me. I'm impatient because I need to prove that I don't belong here—gluttony my ass. Tolerance and discipline are essential, just like any negotiation when I was alive. I can do this. Take it slow. Patience. I *will* get to write this letter.

"That bartender was an emotional rollercoaster. Loved it," the man says.

"I wouldn't know. I just got here, remember?"

"Oh, right. You're new. A future-man!"

I raise my hands, playing along. "That's right." Finding common ground is vital when you're in an alignment discussion. Like any art deal I've done, I'll *relate* to him. Hopefully, he buys it.

"You're too casual to write a letter of such importance," he says. "Do I have to remind you who you're talking to?"

"No, I know who you are." I rub my brow, wanting to get back to this stupid letter. My hand begins to shake. Yep, that is the withdrawal. As for the increasing weakness, I am not sure. Stress, I guess.

He puffs on his cigar and blows the smoke into my face, leaning closer on the round table. The candle in the middle emphasizes his wicked grin and the two sharp canine teeth. "Say it then."

"Winston Churchill," I say, not blinking through the cigar smoke.

My eyes begin to tear, but only a little. I remain cool because Churchill has the information I want. He knows it and isn't giving it up easily. As to why, who knows? Regardless, never did I think I would be sitting in a bar with one of the most significant figures in modern history.

He sits straight, puffing his chest, looking for a good ego suck. Time for me to get down on my knees, metaphorically. I won't blow him. That's not my thing. Well, maybe I would if it meant getting out of here. There's an exchange for the postscript: *P.S. PLEASE PROVIDE ONE RAIL ON A GOLDEN TRAY; IN RETURN I'LL OFFER A BONE-LIPPING FOR THE BIG MAN.*

"Sir Churchill," I say. "Is Archangel Michael the one I should be addressing the letter to?"

"Sure," Churchill says. His posture relaxes, seeming to approve of my newfound tone. "Or you could address God if you want."

"Right! He takes care of all souls, doesn't he?" Now there is traction. I can finally finish this introduction and start explaining my case.

"Let me ask you this. Do you think you're the first person to try writing to God for being wrongly accused?"

Churchill has a point. I wasn't anyone special on Earth. All I did was curate art. At the end of the day, when compared to all the souls in human history, one would say my contribution was pretty small. Then again, the people here seem to be around my time era, except for Churchill. He is the odd one out.

"The letter will get lost," I say, rubbing my nose. The frustration grows. I know I need a quick bump, just a small one. I'm a victim of jimmy-legs, and my brain feels squeezed dry. The motivation to talk lessens with each passing moment. Depression? No. It's like a lack of will to go on. It's got to be the realization that I'm in purgatory—such bullshit. A drug habit is no reason to judge someone's entire life's work unworthy.

Churchill licks his lips. "Yes, you're in such misery?"

I take a deep breath and manage to say, "No shit."

"No one wants to be down here, boy. No one believes that they would have to think about every little mistake they've made. Yet here you are, all twitchy. I've seen this behaviour before. The defeat. The desperation. The *need*."

"Fuck," I mutter to myself, fighting to gain strength.

Churchill licks his lips again, sweating like a pig. "I could sniff it a mile away. Delicious," he squeaks the last word.

That woke me up. "What?"

Churchill's tone returns to normal as he says, "You know who else was a drug addict?"

"Who?" I ask, humouring him.

"Adolf Hitler."

"Christ," I groan, leaning back in my chair.

"See? Vegan-tarians—all the same."

Again, with the dietary choices! I lose my cool and shoot back, "Oh yeah, lard-ass, what about you? Let me guess, gluttony?"

Churchill puffs on his smoke. "That's not exactly relevant."

I look around the bar, eyeing the folks drinking and chatting. All of them fit in in terms of time. The hair and fashion match. "Okay, Man of Mystery, tell me why you are the only one that's ancient?"

"I beg your pardon?" Churchill asks.

"You called me 'future-man.' You're aware that you're the only person from your time, right?" I fold my arms, collecting my energy. Take that, withdrawal.

Churchill's eyes stray from the table, locking onto a couple of gals striding through the crowd. One is a cute little thing, crying with mascara running down her face. The taller friend holds her tightly. A slight grin forms on Churchill's face as he brings his cigar up for another puff. He's gone, sucked into the simple pleasures of man.

The women disappear into the crowd, and Churchill's trance ends with a jolt. He faces me, muttering, "Tasty." He swirls his whisky and says, "Listen, you seem to have it all figured out. I'm going to finish up and go back to my room. Have you seen the tellies we have?"

"You didn't tell me why you're here," I say.

Churchill downs the last of his whiskey. "No, I didn't." He stands, waving goodbye. "That's for me to know and you to guess."

"Hey," I say as he turns, walking away. "Hey!"

Nothing.

"Thanks for the drink," I say, taking a sip, defeated.

I got some info, at least. Churchill was the only one willing to talk to me in this damn bar. No one else gives a shit about my frustration. I suppose they see people dropping down from Earth all the time. Every wanker and his dog are in denial when finding out they are rejected from the good life post-death.

The intensity of my withdrawal lessens with each passing moment. I take a deep breath and have another drink of whiskey, collecting my thoughts.

"You should watch yourself," a silky voice says from behind me.

I look over my shoulder—nothing. I spin back to see that pretty-pasty gal walking over to the empty seat.

"May I?" she asks, gliding her elegant hand onto the wooden back. Her other hand has already placed her drink on the table.

"Be my guest," I reply, finishing the rest of my whiskey. "What'd you say?"

"You should watch yourself," she says, casually taking a seat, one arm on the chair. Her posture complements the confidence she has in that revealing dress. I like it.

"What makes you say that?"

"That isn't Churchill," she says.

"Who is it, then?" The words entice me, but I stay collected. I want to see what she is about first.

"His name is Mo," she says coldly.

"And who is this Mo guy?"

She takes a drink of her whiskey and says, "Motus 'Mo' Devoro. He's a demon, and he's hungry for misery."

"A demon?" My voice goes up, exposing my emotional responses. The news is jolting, even now, being among the dead. "I thought this was a place for people to redeem their sins?"

"It is, but angels and demons can come and visit. The afterlife is their domain, not ours."

"Huh, that explains why he's the only old-timer here. Everything else seems to be modern."

"You're quick."

"So, where is the real Churchill?"

"He was here at one point. His time was up. Didn't you get the welcome package? It talked all about the famous residents."

I pat my pant pockets and check my leather coat. Nothing. "I must have lost it. This whole thing has been kind of a blur."

"I'd say. It happens to most newbies. I saw you stagger in here, all scared." She smirks. I think she likes me or wants something. I'll let this play out.

"And . . . are you human?" I ask.

"Yeah. Don't worry. I'm not going to feed off you or anything."

"Feed?"

"Mo feeds off emotions, mostly negative ones. That's why he was so friendly to you. He does that to everyone who first comes here. He did it to me until I clued in."

"Wait? Is that why I feel so . . ."

"Weak? Like your will to go on is being sucked out of you?" She takes another drink.

"Yeah, that."

"Mo would be why. He's like an energy vampyre. A vampyre with a *Y*. Ever hear of those?"

"Sort of. I thought that was all bogus."

"It is with humans, not with demons, or fallen angels. Just stay away from Mo. He'll get nice and fat off you until you're dry as a raisin."

Well, that explains what 'Churchill' wanted. He was dangling a carrot, metaphorically, in front of me and gorging himself on my delicious misery. What a piece of shit. "No problem. So, does everyone know who he is?"

"Pretty much. Everyone gets a good laugh watching the newcomers get drawn into Mo's enchantment as he feasts off their sorrows."

"How nice of you all. You'd think he would pick a more realistic disguise."

"It worked on you, didn't it? The whole Churchill act? A recognizable figure, credible, he shouldn't exist. It's all masking the true bombastic character he is."

"That's predatorial."

"He'll treat you nice too, buy you a drink, hear your concerns, and even help you out a little. So be careful." She leans closer, clearly more interested in me. "What'cha working on anyways?"

I turn the letter over. The mystery of my note is the only thing I have over Pretty-pasty. I don't know who she is or what she wants. She could be using me too.

"I'm just writing. Mo gave me the paper and a pen."

"Let me guess, a letter to God?" she says, twirling her black hair.

She's good. I reply, "Let *me* guess, you tried writing one to God too?"

"Can't say that I have. But others have. Want me to look it over?"

"I'm trying to figure out who I can address the letter to. I thought about the Archangel Michael."

"That's too high up. You'll never get his attention."

"Yeah, Mo said something similar." I scratch my nose. God, I need that bump.

She downs the rest of her whiskey in a single go. "How about I get us another?" she asks, eying my empty glass.

I now realize that my whiskey is gone from stress-guzzling. Another one would be nice, and so far, Pretty-pasty was good company and easy on the eyes. "Sure," I say.

Pretty-pasty gets up to fetch some drinks, leaving me with the letter, wondering who I should write this to. Maybe I can acknowledge someone further down the chain of command.

Heavy footsteps rise to my side. A deep raspy, "hey bud," follows, tingling my ear. The smell of smoke and dirt fill my nose. To my left, the sensations have derived from a hairy beast-of-a-man whose hand is large enough to crush my skull.

"Yeah?" I ask, feeling agitation from the revolving door of people coming to talk to me. What am I, an entertainment monkey?

"You lookin' a lil' desperate," he says.

"Who says that?"

"I got your snow."

My breath holds. Yes. The need. The desperation. Dealers sniff us out. Drug hounds go in for the kill. "How much?" I blurt out, not thinking about who this guy is, or remembering that the coke addiction got me in this mess. Even in purgatory, the temptation follows.

The man brushes his pointed goatee, saying, "Cash doesn't work the same around here."

"What does?"

"Souls."

Wait a minute, that's a ghastly currency! "Are you some demon?" I ask.

Before the man can answer, Pretty-pasty grabs a couple of drinks from the bar and starts making her way back.

"Think about it," the drug hound says, pushing a small note against my elbow. The scent of smoke fades as the heavy footsteps dissipate from the white noise of the bar.

I look at the note, seeing it is a room number, *"Suite 66"*.

Pretty-pasty arrives, sliding the glass over.

"Thanks." I stare at the whiskey, judging it. Souls are required for coke. A demon feeds off emotions. What does Pretty-pasty want? "Is everyone here preying on newcomers?" I ask.

"Everyone? No. You just walked into one of the more immoral bars."

"Great. And how do I know you're not a parasite too?"

Pretty-pasty raises her glass. "That's a risk you're going to have to take." She has a drink, not losing eye contact.

Pretty-pasty is right. I don't have any allies. Hopefully, I don't need to make any, and I can get out of here. For now, the gal doesn't seem threatening. She's what I'd consider a low-risk interaction, which is a colleague you can use down the road. It's a tactic I mastered in the art of negotiation. Maybe I can leverage her if I need help.

Pretty-pasty points her index finger at the note. "You should probably address that to Michael's executive assistant."

"Yeah?" Alright! Pretty-pasty proves useful. "What's their name?"

"Bonni."

I take a quick sip of my drink, flipping the paper over and jot down, *DEAR EXECUTIVE ASSISTANT BONNI.* Bingo.

"What's the address to Heaven?" I ask.

Pretty-pasty almost snorts out her whiskey. "Cute," she sputters.

"Seriously."

"Just put Heaven. Or Heavenly Kingdoms."

"Think that's good enough?"

"Honestly, I have no idea. I haven't heard of anyone who has successfully written a silly letter to redeem their sins."

Great. A blast of defeat scorches me. Her words are discouraging. Yet, I know damn well that I don't belong in purgatory. Drugs aren't like consuming food or wealth, and I keep thin because of my veganism lifestyle and *not* the coke. I can elaborate on the vegan life in the letter. That's got to be worth some points. Worst case, if it fails, I can track down that drug hound and get some snow. If I'm destined to be down here, why not? In fact, I could even use a bump just to power through this letter and end my jimmy legs. They haven't stopped bouncing.

Pretty-pasty's eyes widen. "God, you're bleeding," she says, leaning over to me.

A droplet of red falls on the table, coming from my nose. I touch my nostril, feeling more blood.

Pretty-pasty pulls out a handkerchief from inside her bra and leans over the table, dabbing my upper lip and nose with the warm cloth. She keeps pressure on my face for several moments. I can't see her eyes over the handkerchief, so I stare at her cleavage. The view isn't bad.

"Thanks," I say nasally.

"Don't worry about it. Look, you might have been some hotshot amongst the living, but down here, you're a newbie. Take it down a notch and ride out your punishment. Plus, it isn't so bad. They have booze."

I say, "And just get plastered, waiting for our time to end?"

"Not quite. You need to work still. There's a head honcho demon who runs this place."

"And what type of work is this?"

"Exports."

"Exports of?" I ask.

"Agriculture. Meat."

"Figures."

"There's demand in all sorts of realms. Like Dega'Mostikas's Triangle," Pretty-pasty says.

"Dega-what?"

"Hell, or three hells. It's not bad, really. I do the work, like most people. The labour is intensive, but you get great discounts on meat."

"Are you trying to recruit me?" I ask.

"No, trust me. I'm just letting you know how it works."

"And why is that?" I ask.

She looks to the ground, biting her lip. She's nervous. The moment passes, and she stares at me with those hypnotic eyes. "Let's just say friends are a rare thing around here."

There we go. Pretty-pasty is lonely. A simple concept I didn't even fathom. There must be all sorts of creeps in purgatory. She thinks I'm a decent guy and decided to take a risk talking to me, as I am her. She longs for something pure, and all I want is pure cocaine and a ticket out of here. Interesting. I'll keep this tidbit of information in my toolkit.

"But why not humour you?" Pretty-pasty checks the handkerchief for more blood and deems me cured of the nosebleed. She jumps off her stool and scoots it closer to me. Her molasses smell compliments her good looks. "Let's see what you got."

No longer worried, I pass her the paper. "I only have the first line," I say, taking a drink and scanning the rest of the bar.

I can't get that drug hound out of my mind. He has coke, and I need to lose this withdrawal to think clearly. One bump would fix it. Most of the shakes and sweat are gone, but I know it will be back. Times of stress doesn't help either. I can barely think, thanks to the withdrawal and this afterlife nonsense. A small line would get me right.

The drug hound. Souls. Coke. Pretty-pasty. Trust. My scheming mind is brewing up a vindictive plan, one that I am not proud of, and I feel rotten just thinking about it. Unfortunately, I am good at shifting people around and stepping on them, which my assistant was all too familiar with. Using folks isn't a skill to be proud of, but you know, it gets the job done.

Plus, these damn jimmy-legs. Oh great, the sweat is coming back. Hey, Pretty-pasty has a cute dimple, I didn't see that before. Okay, no. I'll push the moral concerns aside and run this plan through. That doesn't mean I'll go through with it, it's just an idea. The plan is something like this: the drug hound has coke in exchange for souls. I probably want to keep mine and can charm Pretty-pasty into befriending me. Then, I can sell her off and see how much coke that gets after we write this letter. Wait, no, thinking it through makes me sound awful. I'm talking about selling someone's soul. That's evil with a capital 'E.' I don't even know *how* to sell a soul for some coke. I can't . . . or can I? Pretty-pasty is just some bar trash, right?

The diabolical plan spins in my head the more Pretty-pasty and I chat. My pocket houses the drug hound's note, continually reminding me that coke is only a soul away. Morality is eating away at me. Then, moments go by where I forget about the plan. Pretty-pasty and I laugh. I tell her about the crazy agents and painters I dealt with while alive. We exchanged names. Truthfully, I can't remember hers. Something about 'Pretty-pasty' sticks. Plus, I'm too focused on making her laugh with my life stories, and my own needs.

She is smiling and asks me why I think I was wrongfully accused. I tell her straight up, "I had a bad cocaine habit."

"Had or have?" she asks, still smiling.

"Have, I suppose."

"I'm going to guess that's how you died too?"

"Half right."

"Oh?"

"Yeah, I was at an afterparty from an opening for Oscar Elvira."

"Wait, *the* Oscar Elvira?" Pretty-pasty asks.

"Yeah, you know him?"

"Of course, I love his contemporary work! Some of his post-modern futurism stuff didn't live up to his quality, you know?" Pretty-pasty sounds genuinely excited. Cute, passionate, and a great taste in art. This isn't helping my dilemma.

I clear my throat, keeping calm. "Totally. So, I was schmoozing it up with a couple of big agents from France. It turns out they were coke fiends too. My assistant, Clark, and another artist joined us in their executive suite hotel room. One of these France guys pulls out a nasal spray—cleverly disguising liquid cocaine. He asks if we'd ever done a Point-Blank."

"What's that?"

"Well, it's supposed to be like a Kamikaze shot but with a drop of coke."

"Sounds intense."

"It's not really if you're into the drug. Taking it orally doesn't hit you the same. Anyways, we all did a Point-Blank, a couple of rails, more liquor, and kept living the party life. Later, the time came for some more Point-Blanks. The French agent brings out a bigger bottle of clear liquid. Man, I had no idea where they got all this coke. We were thrilled and decided to use bigger glasses, like eight ounces big."

"Woah," Pretty-pasty says, clearly impressed by how I partied. She must be of the same life.

"But I needed a smoke. Foolishly I left to the balcony, letting my guard down, thinking they'd just pour another Point-Blank."

Pretty-pasty plays with her hair saying, "Big shot art dealer, the master of people-skills, let his guard down?"

"Shut up, we all did that night. One of the agents joined me outside while the artist went for a piss. The other agent and Clark were pouring the shots. I don't know what happened in that kitchen, but Clark had been trying to undermine me for months."

"You think he poisoned you?"

"He gave me liquid cocaine. He wants my job and probably got it by making an expensive deal with that agent. Coke isn't cheap. We all gathered in the kitchen, cheered, and downed our Point-Blanks in one go. Instantly I knew that shot wasn't a Point-Blank. That was a damn Death Shot. A one-way ticket to Hell."

"Purgatory."

"Whatever."

Pretty-pasty gently touches my arm. "Sorry, newbie."

"I wish I could just beat the living shit out of Clark."

"That would be wrath. Then you'd have no chances of getting into Heaven."

"Right," I say, staring down at the paper.

Pretty-pasty says, "Now that I know how you died and about your coke addiction, maybe we can spin that in your letter. Shall we?"

"I'm vegan."

"Okay?"

"I do good things! Coke is just a party supply."

"Alright, Mr. High Ground," she says, grabbing the pen.

We start writing. Time is a blur. Pretty-pasty brings us more drinks as the barflies dwindle. The two of us are some of the last folks here. We're pretty piss-faced, which only fuels the itch for coke. Great. At some point I took the pen back and wrote the last few words.

"Done," I say, my legs are still bouncing up and down.

"Woohoo!" Pretty-pasty says as we clang glasses.

The letter is a beauty. Drunkenness aside, I am sure of it. We even elaborated on my ethical eating choices and how it helps the planet. Proving I *have* done an unmeasurable amount of good by saving animals. "Glad you came around," I say. Regret starts to clog my throat. I'm not sure if I can even go through with selling her off for some blow. I still don't know who she is. But the itch . . . it's getting worse with each drink.

"Say, why are you here?" I ask.

"Me?" Pretty-pasty says, blushing. "I made some bad choices."

"Seems pretty human."

The bartender shouts that they're closing up. It's now or never. I could either fumble around and try to make it another day in purgatory, mail my letter, and wait. Or, I can get some snow, get that last fix, and mail out the letter. If this letter works—and it's a damn good letter—I won't be hanging around here with Pretty-pasty anymore. If it doesn't . . . well, I know where I can get coke again.

I clear my throat, pushing doubt down. "Hey, listen. Do you want to come back to my place? I haven't exactly been there." I pull out the note from my pocket to show her. "I kind of ran into this bar in a panic when I arrived."

"You did," she slurs, taking the note. "You wrote your address down but lost the welcome package?" She raises her thin brow. We enter a stare-down duel of trust. Did I fuck up? Moments pass.

She snorts. "You're so stupid."

The victor: me. I shrug smoothly. "Hey, I'm a newbie. So, where is that exactly?"

"I'll show you if you'd like?" Her voice is tender while passing me the note. If only I could have both the blow and the girl.

"Yeah," I say, staying cool.

"It's on the sixth floor," she says, hopping off her stool with a slight tumble. She doesn't look embarrassed and recovers. "I'm good."

"You sure?" I smile. Oh no, I'm liking Pretty-pasty. Now I'm unsure if I can even go through with this. The sad part is, I actually did lose that welcome package that had my number and key.

Pretty-pasty and I leave the bar in a drunken swagger, arm-in-arm. She is proving to be the kind of girl I would have hung out with when I was alive, maybe even girlfriend material. Then my nose itches and a cold sweat brews. Of course, when I start to experience reason, the desire creeps back up into overbearing demand.

I'm a chained slave to the drug, being pulled into the darkness once again. It doesn't help that Pretty-pasty is leading me right to that temptation with no knowledge of it. I could come clean. I could.

We walk out of the bar and into the outlandish winding halls, covered in bastardized religious symbols and otherworldly wiggling appendages. Animated paintings . . . or ghosts and breathing rugs, are they alive? With so much to see, I lose my train of thought and am barely able to keep track of where Pretty-pasty is taking me—a turn here, and a staircase there. Next thing I know, we are at a red door with golden letters *66* nailed to it. This is it. She turns to me.

"Well?" Pretty-pasty says. "You got your key?"

"I . . . uh . . ." Shit, I didn't think this far. Instincts kick in, and I boldly grab the doorknob. It twists, and to my luck, the door opens.

"You sure this is your place?" she asks, following me inside the dark room.

"Yeah, of course," I lie. "I just lost the welcome package."

A spotlight beams down on a black table with a golden tray, housing a mound of cocaine. Hot damn. There is no furniture or decorations, only an open space that leads into blackness. The door slams shut, and we both cower. Pretty-pasty, visibly shaken, backs up into me. I grab her. By the door, the drug hound stands, all hairy and smoky.

"So, you do want some snow after all?" he says with a toothy grin, revealing his fangs.

"Yeah," I say, thinking that Pretty-pasty would start to freak out now. She looks worried, almost confused by everything. Maybe she is more desperate and drunk for friendship than I thought. Now I feel even worse.

"Good," the drug hound says. He points to Pretty-pasty. "Yours?"

"No." I let go of Pretty-pasty. "The—" I choke from the swelling guilt pushing back up into my throat. I don't think I can even finish my sentence.

Pretty-pasty is looking at the drug hound and me, back and forth, several times.

No, this isn't right. I can't. "I—" my words are cut short by Pretty-pasty.

"Wait. You asshole, were you going to sell me off?" She pushes me hard, and I manage to keep my intoxicated balance.

"No, wait," I say, trying to justify my remorseful actions.

"That's not a surprise," the drug hound says. "From a vegan-tarian."

"What?" I say.

The drug hound's body bubbles. Bones crack. The flesh rips, moving and fusing anew as the skin colour morphs. His whole form warps into the indistinguishable Winston Churchill, better known here as Motus "Mo" Devoro. Hell, even his clothes mutate too, like some sort of magic act. That cunning prick, of course, there is shapeshifting. I'm out of here.

I stomp towards the door and Mo.

"Leaving so soon?" Mo says, licking his lips. "Already I can sense the frustration in you . . . the emotion. You're so close to what you need, are you not?"

I look over my shoulder to see the pile of cocaine, then Pretty-pasty, who held her one arm, looking at Mo intently.

"You coming?" I ask her.

"Eat a dick," Pretty-pasty hisses with a pink face. She's pissed. I'm messing this up. Maybe if I get us out, she'll come around.

Mo stands closer to the door. "No one is leaving until a deal is made."

"Says who? Nothing is binding us," I say. "No deal."

Mo laughs. "What makes you think something needs binding?"

"I don't know. What about those contracts and deals with the devil?"

"You mean in Hollywood?" Pretty-pasty shakes her head. "You are such a newbie. Mo isn't going to let us leave."

I scratch the back of my neck, looking at the pile of coke and then Mo, who is grinning, showing off his two sharp teeth.

"So, how does this work?" I ask, folding my arms.

"Well," Mo says. "It's quite the scene. First, we need to tie her down and carve a plethora of demonic symbols into her flesh. Then, I cut my hand, raining blood down on her, fusing her to me."

"That sounds horrible!" I say.

"It's either you or her," Mo says. "I'm not letting you both leave. But I am a fair dealer. I give in return."

Pretty-pasty and I lock eyes. She is furious. That scowl. My guilt.

The victor: Pretty-pasty. I can't go through with this. There must be a way out of here, for both of us. I need to think. The drunkenness is making me slow. I need that bump. Wait a minute. Yes. The scheming mind is doing its work.

"How do I know this is real coke?" I ask.

"Fair question," Mo says, gesturing to the pile. "Give it a try. My goods are top shelf."

Fool. I'll feed this fixation and get my brain firing on all cylinders. I've pulled off crazy deals in the past after a quick one. I wink at Pretty-pasty while walking over to the golden tray, hoping she trusts me.

My eyes widen while walking. There must be about a quarter of a million bucks sitting on this table, the equivalent of a soul. Wow. I've never seen this much at once.

Mo takes a deep, satisfying breath. "My, my, so much pent-up excitement from you both. Please, embrace a line. We'll get to business after."

Gross. As I get my fix, old Mo here is sucking off my energy like a baby on a tit. I can feel his misery-slurping lingering in my body. It's weakening me. I push the sensations aside, realizing I need to stay focused. Without hesitation, I snag my hand-written letter from my pocket and roll it into a beautiful thin tube as I section off a fatty with the note.

Sorry, big boys upstairs, down I go on the white road with one big SNIFF. God yes! I missed that. Who knew purgatory would have access to such greatness? This is good stuff. Almost too good. Another rail wouldn't hurt. I line it up and take another loud SNIFF. Wow. The drunken slur is fading fast. A familiar buzz hums through my veins, nurturing my poor malnourished addiction. Come on, brain, start scheming a way out.

"And done!" Mo says with excitement. "Pleasure doing business."

I spin around, bug-eyed, with white powder all over my nostril. "We haven't started the deal!" I snap.

"Pleasure was all mine, asshole," Pretty-pasty says.

"What?" I say, flabbergasted, realizing Mo wasn't talking to me.

Mo has a one-page document in his hand with a red splotch on it, right beside a black signature. Pretty-pasty is holding onto a pen and that bloody handkerchief in the other. Mo is breathing heavily as sweat drips onto the floor. My heart rate is increasing from the drugs and boiling fear. That paper . . . the blood. Did they just?

"Wait. What? The note . . ." Words aren't coming quickly like they usually do with coke. I'm stifled with disbelief. Mo and Pretty-pasty lied to me. Selling a soul *is* like in the movies. A simple contract binds it with blood. I am the fool who was so desperate to get that bump. I wonder if Pretty-pasty was planning this from the beginning. She was so genuine, like she really needed to connect with someone. But who has handkerchiefs stuffed in their bra? Plus, she approached me, like Mo did. It doesn't matter now.

Pretty pasty narrows her eyes, saying, "Still think your letter is going to do you any good? Being bound to a demon?"

"Fuck you!" I shout, not buying into what just happened. "I'm out of here." This can't be real. I take my first step to the door, yet my legs reject my instructions as I stare at the doorknob that is too far from reach. No. My legs . . . don't listen to me. I snag one, trying to lift it with all my might. Nothing.

Mo holds out his hand. "It doesn't quite work that way."

I don't know what to say and just stare at my leg with intense crushing tunnel vision, thanks to the coke buzzing through my mind.

"You're my tasty little treat!" Mo squeaks, walking towards me. "Your anger, oh my! So succulent."

Pretty-pasty twists the handle on the door.

I shoot back to reality and yell before she leaves. "Hey, lady! Do you think God is going to let you go into Heaven after this? You're stuck down here with the rest of us."

She looks at me with those magnetic eyes, saying, "I knew that about me long before you arrived."

"I was going to get us both out."

"No, you weren't," Pretty-pasty says. "I know addicts, no matter how cute they are."

"Fuck you," I say through my teeth.

"You asked what I did to get here?"

"I don't care," I say.

"I did this kind of thing, any deal to take a shortcut."

"So, it all worked out great for you," I say.

"I guess so. No more agriculture work after selling a fresh soul. Sorry, newbie." Her lips press tightly while stepping out into the hall, leaving me alone with Mo.

Mo's skin is so moist as he downs his good misery-stake. "Oh yes, we'll keep this lovely feast rolling. You'll be a shrivelled up little prune," he says.

My heart continues to pound, punching against my ribcage. The drugs melt into the fear, the anger, and the desperation, creating a boiling stew of raw human energy. The kind of dessert a demon of the afterlife would love. Will I live? Will I die in purgatory with Mo feasting off every drop of life I have? What happens then? Questions swirl around my mind a million miles a minute.

The demon is turning red as two horns erect from the top of his head. His body slowly morphs into a demonic version of the drug hound, presumably his natural form. I swear that tub is getting fatter the longer I stand here, withering away to an almost mummified state. I feel so dry.

Then, those advantageous two rails provide me with one last buzz of brilliance. Yes . . . oh yes. That resourceful mind is doing what it does best. I can escape Mo's feeding. That soul contract might be trickier. I never did get to read the fine print. This plan better work.

Mo is close to me, moaning, getting fill of the energy buffet for one. My body is weak, and my legs aren't responding, but my upper half is. The mound of cocaine is so close. The temptation that offed me, prevented me from getting into Heaven, and locked my soul into a dance with a demon, is now the key out of here.

I'm still by the table, and I loosen my grip on the letter, widening the circumference, and exhale slowly, removing all oxygen. Ready. The demon's yellow eyes slowly open as I calm my emotions, watching as I bring the paper to my nostril. Mo gasps as I divebomb into the mound of white benevolence. The powder flies up the vast chamber, through the nasal cavity, and blitzes my brain with exemption pearls.

"Wait!" Mo shouts, spit flying from his mouth. "No!"

The demon's food-spell ends, and he raises his claws upward. My arm freezes, his power over my soul locking my limbs and spine first. My breathing begins to whither as I suck in every bit of coke I can, lungs stretching beyond capacity as Mo shuts them down.

Come on, white mountain! Those little shards of mercy are running rampant inside my bloodstream. Mo has locked my whole body. How long have I been frozen now? The ghost of the Death Shot haunts me, with a familiar yet overbearing sensation I once feared: dying. Yes. I remember . . . I see . . . numbness. The cliché blinding light!

Awake from the observing state. (Turn to Page 361)

ICE FACE

The winter can kill you if you're not careful. Living outdoors every day is something our ancestors did all the time. Now we defy the elements and live all over the planet. Some of these regions are pretty remote. Canada is no exception to this. Our country has plenty of dangerous wilderness all throughout the provinces. If you don't know what you're doing, you can get yourself killed. If it's not the weather, there's plenty more out in the wild that will get you. Bad luck? Likely. Motivated revenge? Unlikely.

An example of dangerous wilds would be the Canadian Rockies. It is home to a tourist town known as Banff. It's a fun place with shops, eateries, hot springs, ski resorts, you name it! With that, my family made a tradition of leaving the small town Fort Nelson for a cabin getaway north of Banff, higher up the mountains. A lot of people head for the Rockies this time of year. I get it.

I'll admit, I do enjoy the escape. When it's minus thirty degrees outside, sitting close to a burning brick fireplace in the middle of nowhere is a great way to 'Zen out.' I just try to forget about all that went wrong.

Usually, I have a bad memory for things, short term, but this is well engrained into me. I'll never forget this incident at the cabin. I'll back up. The tradition originates from my grandparents, I think. They built the cabin and my dad inherited it after they passed. We spend Christmas and New Year's here all the time. Even Uncle Tom and Aunt Jenny join us. Dad used to come, but that's another story I'll get to.

For years it was no problem. Despite the natural cold that can kill you, we tough it out. There's been talk around the neighbouring cabins and even the Banff locals. They whisper of a legend in recent years. It's not like other tall tales you hear; it's about a creature specific to the region and specific to this time of year. They call it Ice Face.

Ice Face wanders the wilderness, lurking in the snow and waiting to strike people. Some people say it's just an updated version of Bigfoot's story. I don't think so. It has motive, unlike Bigfoot. For example, anyone who sees Ice Face dies. Their body is later found frozen in the snow, with bloody icicles running down their orifices and their skin shred apart. The story goes that Ice Face is a hideous being, jealous of people's warmth and flesh. Ice Face is entirely cold, jagged, and unwanted, which made the being go mad, becoming one with the snow. They say Ice Face sings a song before taking you.

You ever hear of that ice mummy discovery years back? Scientists think it was the Neanderthal that was shot in the back by an arrow and froze to death. My guess is that something similar happened to Ice Face and turned them into the monster that they are.

Either way, Ice Face sings.

"Nice Face. Nice Face. Such a warm embrace for Ice Face."

I'm not sure how much anyone would buy into the tall tale from locals. Quite frankly, it doesn't make sense. How do people know the song if Ice Face kills everyone who hears it? Then again, what tall tale follows logic? People go missing in the wilderness all the time, all year round. Again . . . the weather will kill you. If you manage to survive that, then there are bears, wolves, cougars, and wild men in the mountains. And what does Ice Face do in the summer? I can't help but wonder where the true story comes from. I'd like to know; maybe it could explain why some people go missing, like my dad.

This time of year hits me hard. It's not because of Ice Face or family reunions. It's because it's the anniversary of when Dad went missing. I was much smaller then, probably a good eight years ago when I was seven.

Eight years ago, smartphones were still kind of a new thing. Cell reception was notorious in those devices way up in the mountains. It wasn't like they could call for help right away. I remember hearing him go down the rickety wooden staircase, getting dressed, turning on his flashlight and heading outside. The door closed with an extra click. I thought he was off to use the outhouse. He never did come back.

At first, I presumed I had simply fallen asleep and didn't hear him return from the snowy evening. Later in the night, I got up and went downstairs to pour myself a glass of water. That would have been about the time Dad should have come back. I saw Uncle Tom and Mom in the living room, sitting by the amber of the dying fire. They both were drinking hard liquor. Uncle Tom was adjusting his shirt, startled to see me.

Mom said I'd best get some sleep if I wanted the presents from Santa tomorrow as she fixed her messy hair. I thought nothing of it and went back to bed, passing the foyer to see the front door was locked. Thinking back to the incident, I think Uncle Tom and Mom were unfaithful to Jenny and Dad. Deeply reflecting, I can't help but string a malicious sequence of events through my mind.

The following day, I wanted to be thrilled about opening presents. The most memorable gift I received was the horror of Dad being nowhere. Uncle Tom went back into town to alarm the authorities. Mom had a permanent scowl on her face, retreating to her whiskey as the sun rose. Aunt Jenny and my brother, Wesley, simply cried with me as we pretended it was only a dream.

I try to tell myself that Dad isn't dead; he is simply missing. Maybe he found out about Uncle Tom and Mom and decided to book it. I like to tell myself that. Uncle Tom, Aunt Jenny, and Mom moved on. Maybe dealing with death is something you learn to do when you're older. That or the life insurance money eases some of the worries. It's a mystery how they claimed that, since there was never a corpse. My brother accepts it, but he's darker now. It's the loss of innocence.

Either way, we continued the tradition every year. This holiday we all went to the cabin with Uncle Tom and Aunt Jenny. As per usual, Mom cracked open her whiskey once we arrived, and the three adults started drinking. They eventually get boozed up enough that they give Wesley and I a small glass each year.

The day carried out as usual with cooking, chopping wood, hot cocoa, and we all went to bed. Uncle Tom had to use the toilet, and since Dad's disappearance, we always go with an outhouse buddy. It's safer that way, especially with all the wildlife and the weather, which we know will kill you.

I was Uncle Tom's outhouse buddy. We bundled up, grabbed our flashlights, and went outside. The icy wind bit our faces as we marched through the fresh snow. It crunched with each step we made as our feet sunk a good two feet deep. The wind howled and was easily mistaken for wolves under the starry night.

I stood by the outhouse while Uncle Tom went to do the deed. It's a burning cold out there, but I stood my ground as everyone does for anyone that has to go. I've thought about asking Uncle Tom about him and Mom, but there's no point. Mom hasn't dated since Dad, so I can only presume their affair was still at large. I've never told Wesley, I don't think he could handle it. Then there's my concerning theory, which I'll never bring up.

The thoughts got the better of me as the wind picked up, making me shiver. Usually, I can focus on 'Zen'ing out,' and the cold doesn't nip. Not this time, I knocked on the outhouse door for Uncle Tom to hurry up. He finished his deed, and we began our hike back to the cabin.

That's when we heard it.

"Nice Face . . ."

The song. It started as a soft, gentle whisper with the first two words.

Uncle Tom and I exchanged glances, both wondering if the other person had heard those two words. The wind rocketed, almost knocking us to our asses, sending a howling whistle through our ears. Through the high-pitched bites, we heard the remaining verse.

". . Nice Face . . ." The whisper grew louder into a raspy voice. It was loud enough you'd think it was someone yelling into your ear. The voice continued to escalate into a growling high shriek that complemented the wind. ". . . Such a warm embrace for Ice Face."

"All right, get inside," Uncle Tom urged.

His hands were shaking as he held the flashlight, making our path disjointed. I held mine with both hands, now second-guessing everything I once thought was real. Ice Face. There's no way we heard that verse.

Uncle Tom stopped in his tracks. His flashlight flickered a couple of times just as the protective case of the bulb cracked, and the light went out. He hit it a couple of times, trying to jolt its life again with no luck. My flashlight began to dim. I swore I had just replaced the batteries. It faded into nothingness, and we were left in the soulless dark.

"Nice Face. Nice Face. Such a warm embrace for Ice Face."

"L-l-l-e-e-t's ge-e-et a move o-o-on," Uncle Tom said in a shaky voice. I don't think it was the cold. I think it was fear.

We began marching in the snow, trying to follow our previous footsteps to the cabin. Most of it had snowed over, making it impossible to figure out which way we came. We thought it was a straight line, but it's easy to get disoriented when you're in the dark surrounded by a blanket of white. We walked close together, acting as our lifelines, knowing how dangerous the Canadian winter nights can be. Our hearts thumped in rhythm with each step we made, marching for several dozen paces. I thought that was the distance to the cabin, but I was dead wrong. We kept walking.

Uncle Tom stopped again, and his eyes squinted. "Bill?"

Uncle Tom had to have been hallucinating. I looked around and couldn't see anyone else in the snow. We were in an open patch of snowy hills. No trees were nearby to be mistaken for human shadows.

"Waaaarrmmm," the high-pitched voice swirled through the gust.

Uncle Tom gasped, stumbling back. I turned to see what startled him. In front of us, the snow began to rise upwards as if it were being vacuumed into the air. It rose to about six feet as more snow hurled aloft, compressing into the shape of a man. The figure took its first step forward, causing the entire body to rattle, snow trickling off its chest.

"Nice Face . . ."

Uncle Tom grabbed my arm, and we booked it as fast as we could, running back to the outhouse. Or at least where we presumed the outhouse to be. We couldn't find it. I glanced back, seeing that the snow had finished compiling the humanoid with hands, fingers, neck, and a face covered in icy shards. Ice Face. Ice poked out of where the ears should be. Icicles ran down the eye sockets and mouth, shielding the black void inside the three holes.

We weren't watching our step and slipped on a frozen decline, tumbling onto the ice, and sliding away from each other. I was the first to attempt to stand, looking around for Uncle Tom. He was a good fifty paces away from me. I slid on the ice again, falling onto my hip.

Ice Face descended into the snow. Only his upper torso and head peeked out, slithering through the blizzard like some giant cobra in the sand. His speed was unmatched, and he made it to Uncle Tom before I could even stand. Ice Face rose from the snow, walking towards the man, the body clattering with each step.

Uncle Tom tried to scurry backwards, but he froze purely in fear as Ice Face's form expanded into an enveloping sheet of white and ice, soaring straight into him. The tiny shards of ice ripped into his jacket, shredding through the fabric and piercing into his skin. The frozen water ravaged his face, ripping through his cheeks, nostrils and biting into his eyes. Blood oozed out his wounds and face, quickly freezing in the weather's cold embrace. He wailed in sputtering bellows as the snow blanketed his body, entering his mouth and shooting out his nose and ears.

The snow slithered off Uncle Tom's corpse, reanimating into the humanoid form. I wanted to run. But I couldn't, for I was also frozen in fear. Instantly I knew that I was next for Ice Face.

The monster took its complete form, with the icicles forming above the eye sockets and mouth. They eventually started to crack, paving way for new snow piling delicately onto the face, forming intricate details under the moonlight. The face was distinguishable.

"Dad?" I said.

A gust of wind blew by, causing Ice Face to disintegrate. The snow particles blew away as the icicles collapsed onto the ground. My flashlight flickered and beamed bright over the scene, giving me a clear look at Uncle Tom's dead body with bloody icicles running down his face.

Awake from the observing state. (Turn to Page 361)

Nothing. It's just another observing state that proves to have no value. You return to the Midway with your feet stepping onto the sand. The element is oddly familiar too. Maybe you've been standing here too long.

"Anything?" Malpherities asks.

"Nothing this time."

"Then go again."

You snag the orb and melt into it. The room washes away, leaving you in white space as two portals appear. The portal on the left shows flashes of a church, shining armour, and inaudible demonic whispers fading in and out. The orb gravitates towards the portal on the right showcasing an artist's studio, gallery, and a man with a knife behind his back.

MAKE ONE OF TWO CHOICES:

Steer the orb into the left portal. (Turn to Page 307)

Let the orb be pulled into the right portal. (Turn to Page 345)

BLOOD WILL

PART ONE

God's trials never end. To be a loyal follower, one must devote themselves entirely to the church. From birth, through childhood, and into adulthood, sins are ever present. Learning to avoid temptation is a task every priest must endure. They must walk through the fire to prove themselves to their Heavenly Father. The Devil may tempt those who stand too close to the shadows, straying from the Lord's light, ready to sink his claws into the unfaithful.

Thus, each of the four seminarians kneels in the chapel, rehearsing prayers for God's protection. Their eyes are sealed shut, hands held together, facing the large stone cross at the end of the church's sanctuary. Their teacher stands in front of the cross, joining them in prayer behind the oak podium. His long red and black robe drapes onto the marble flooring.

"Oh Lord, protect us from evil.

Embrace us with heavenly grace.

And deliver us from the evil one."

The four seminarians and the high priest speak in synchronization. Their monotone voices reverb off the marble walls, with the only other sound coming from the crackling of torch fire. Any sniffle or sigh would be heard by all and deemed punishable.

The prayers repeat, twelve lines before the end, starting from the original verse. The four seminarians will not stop until the high priest commands it so, as with every day. His dry, wrinkly hands grasp the podium. Unlike the four trainees, his eyes remain open, watching his loyal subjects.

Specifically, his gaze falls on the girl named Imperia. The only way she is aware of his glare is because she keeps her eyelids ever so slightly open, watching her instructor. She feels the power of High Priest Jochen's looming glare all throughout her body.

He's not looking at her performance. His gaze latches onto her creamy skin, rosy lips, and her lavender irises. It's the only skin exposed in her holy black and white gown with her silky black hair resting on the cloth shoulder pads. The glare was acceptable moments ago, but now she is concerned, for he doesn't shift to her three colleagues. She mustn't be praying well enough.

Oh, Lord, protect us from evil, Imperia thinks with more focus, presuming that in return it will make her pray more effectively. Her forehead scrunches, trying to focus her mind, heart, and body on the task as she connects with the Heavenly Father.

Child . . .

The voice is a faint whisper yet originates far closer than the exterior vocals provided by the five chants. It can only be a lingering strange thought in the depths of her psyche. Imperia focuses with more might than she ever has in prayer when suddenly an "amen" comes from High Priest Jochen.

Child . . . You follow so loyally. Why?

The voice is crisper and comes from the back of her skull. God is speaking to her directly. Could it be true? She is unsure, as the words don't seem to be what she'd presume the Good Father would say. God wouldn't question her loyalty. She brushes off the strange words.

"Rise, you have all done well today," High Priest Jochen says, raising his hands.

Imperia and her three comrades stand from the marble floor, eyes open. They await further command under the soft, dim light projecting from the torches mounted on each of the six white columns in the chapel.

"Each of you complete your lesson with a thank you prayer to the Lord, for he has blessed you with another day of life. Then you may dismiss yourselves for the evening and retreat to your private studies. I would like a summary from each of your findings in the morning."

"Yes, High Priest Jochen," the students say simultaneously.

Imperia, the last of the four seminarians, leans closer to her colleague beside her. Another girl with brunette hair who is no older than she. Imperia whispers, "Kaylor, what are your study focuses tonight?"

Kaylor tucks her jaw-length hair behind her ear, saying, "Most likely the same verses we learned this morning. I don't think I quite grasp them correctly."

"That is fair."

"And what of yourself?"

Left-hand path.

Imperia's limbs tense from the words. "I, well . . . I think I will—"

The other two seminarians begin whispering a prayer, distracting Imperia from finishing her thought.

"We best make our thanks to God," Kaylor says, cupping her hands.

"Of course."

The seminarians close their eyes as High Priest Jochen says, "Imperia, may I have a word with you?"

Imperia glances at the other three seminarians. The two boys and girl look at her briefly and return to their final prayer, mumbling away. Imperia blushes, unsure if she should be pleased or embarrassed to be called out directly.

"Of course, Father," she says.

The girl lifts her long gown and hurries to keep pace with High Priest Jochen, marching from the podium and through the arched doorway leading to the back of the church.

"High Priest Jochen, what do you wish to speak to me about?" Imperia asks.

He doesn't answer until they reach the far end of the hall and into his private quarters. He closes the wooden door behind her and smiles. The wrinkles on his face curve up to the curly grey hair on his balding scalp.

Imperia hasn't been in the High Priest's quarters too often. Only when she was first appointed to the church, and since then, only if she hadn't correctly followed God's rules. Now, here she is again, looking at the familiar oak bookshelves with tomes and the cross mounted on the wall behind the desk, just below the semicircle stained glass window.

"Dear Imperia, I am afraid you are not keeping up with your studies as well as your colleagues."

Imperia looks down, feeling her back turn ice cold. "I'm so sorry, Father. I will do better."

High Priest Jochen extends his hand, lifting her face. He caresses her cheek with his thumb. "I want you to study here, in my quarters."

"Here? I have all of my notes and books in the basement and—"

"Go gather them," High Priest Jochen interrupts, freeing her from his hand.

"Of course," Imperia bows.

"Do so immediately."

"What of the finishing prayer, to thank the Lord?"

"We will do so together."

Imperia notes the L-shaped room, with the dark corner to the right of the door which contains the priest's bed. The dark corner is hard to see, but not nearly enough room for her to bring up her own mattress. "Will we be studying throughout the night?"

"Of course," High Priest Jochen says. "No need to bring your personal belongings. We'll make do."

Child . . . You follow so loyally. Why? Embrace intuition.

A blazing light blooms from outside the church, highlighting the stained glass. One would presume it was morning due to the spontaneous light casting orange and yellow hues. It beams up from the ground, reaching for the sky at a rapid speed as a thundering boom comes from outside. Small pebbles of dirt and rock fall from the ceiling and onto the marble floor.

"High Priest Jochen, what is happening?" Imperia asks.

"Come now, back to the sanctuary," High Priest Jochen says. He urges her to move, snagging her upper arm, forcing her to move in front of him.

I bring the gift . . .

Another loud rumbling comes from outside of the church. A deep snap whips through the air right outside as the two reach the end of the hall. One of the stained-glass windows in the chapel cracks as dust and wind blow by the entire building. The structure rumbles, causing one of the two spears mounted at the entranceway to fall, rattling on the marble ground several times before resting still.

There is always a choice.

High Priest Jochen reaches the podium while staring at the damaged glass as the blooming light fades outside, leaving the five under the warm torchlight. Imperia retreats to her three comrades, moving closer to Kaylor. The two hold each other's arms tightly, waiting anxiously to hear their teacher's commands.

"Has he sent a sign to us?" asks a boy, Tyrmus.

High Priest Jochen raises his hands and says, "Do not alarm yourself. It is a sign from God."

"From God?" Imperia asks.

"What is the glow?" Kaylor asks, pointing to the subtle orange hue from outside through the stained-glass behind the stone cross.

"Trust in God's ways, my children," High Priest Jochen says. He squints, looking up to the ceiling. "Trust in God's ways."

"What should we do?" Kaylor asks.

Imperia lets go of Kaylor and looks at the cracked window. The stained glass splits vertically along the middle perfectly over the Son dying on a cross with his crown of thorns. She walks down the aisle, slowly approaching the broken glass.

"Imperia, please stay still. Let God guide us."

Imperia stops in her tracks. "Of course, High Priest Jochen."

"Return to your quarters. The Shield and I will witness the gift from God."

Such a loyal disciple. Do you have a choice?

Imperia feels a throb pulsate through her forehead. This voice won't leave her be. She says, "What makes you so sure it is a gift from God?"

"Imperia. Such an immature question to ask. Only the holy comes from above. Anything below is deemed of sin."

"Including us," Kaylor says.

Imperia's gut twists. She saw the light beam from below. How can they be so sure it was from above? There's no reason to challenge High Priest Jochen's words. He knows far more than her. She wishes only to exceed in the church, and her foolish question makes her clearly inept in the ways of God and what she has learned. No, that cannot be the case. She clearly saw the light beam from below with her own eyes. She is certain.

Imperia says, "And we're sure it came from above when the light projected from the ground? May we inspect this gift or ill fortune?"

High Priest Jochen's lips press tightly together. She's pushed him too far. His wrath and her punishment are set aside as the chapel doors burst open, sending a cool breeze against the flickering torches. Three warriors in silver armour finished with gold-coated edges, red-feathered helmets, and sheathed swords march down the red carpet. Their silky gold and red tabards of the holy cross sway side to side on their chests down to their knees with their prideful stride.

This is the Shield. They kneel before High Priest Jochen, gripping their swords in synch. The woman in the middle speaks in a naturally gruff tone. "High Priest Jochen. What are your orders?"

High Priest Jochen keeps his gaze on Imperia. He says, "We will inspect the sky sign. Lead us, Evelune."

"Of course," Evelune says. The three Shields rise from the ground and lead the five priests out of the church. Imperia and Kaylor lock arms together with two of their colleagues in the back and Tyrmus walking with High Priest Jochen in front, following the Shield. All of them feel the anticipation of what the gift from the sky could possibly bring. Only Imperia knows it couldn't possibly come from above. The light beamed from below, then the sound erupted.

Only blind monotony can be found above . . .

The voice won't go away. Imperia fiddles with her nails in nervousness as the group exits the church. She can't help but wonder if this isn't God nor the Devil, but something else entirely. She has no reason to think such thoughts, but she's felt the Devil's temptation before through sin. This is not sin, nor is it God's common words found in prayer.

Her foolish thoughts are pushed aside as Evelune and the two Shield lead the priests down the stairs of the church, passing the garden under the moon, approaching the glowing orange hue behind the building.

"Be cautious," Evelune says. "We haven't inspected it thoroughly yet, awaiting your command, High Priest Jochen."

The group turns the corner and stops to see no crater as one would expect from a sky gift. Instead, the entire ground is scorched charcoal grey, getting progressively darker towards the center. The patch is jagged with dirt where the grass once was. Small spits of flames dance wildly in a circular arch, forming symbols of swirls, rectangles, circles, and other simplistic shapes on the ground. Each group of flames is evenly spaced. These flames are neatly grouped together to form symbols none of the priests have seen before. The patch of dead earth radiates hot air. An inner circle of greater flames blocks the view of the core. This is entirely unnatural.

"Pentagram! The Devil!" Tyrmus exclaims, stumbling back, almost hitting Kaylor and Imperia in the noses with his elbows.

High Priest Jochen raises his hand. "Remain calm, my children. This is no pentagram, but something else."

Imperia is now certain this is no gift from God. This clearly came from below, a place of evil. The Devil is a genuine possibility now. Simply being near the scorched ground she can sense the presence of something watching her, deep within her soul. Her hands tremble, losing herself in the dance of the flames.

"This place is unholy," Kaylor says. "But how?"

"God deems us unfaithful," one of the seminarists says behind Imperia.

"Don't be so quick to judge, Izahl," High Priest Jochen says, stepping around the circumference of the scorched earth.

What are you, child?

The pressuring aura of the unholy ground morphs into a pulling sensation. Imperia surrenders immediately, gravitating towards the inner circling flames. Her first step is slow and unnoticed by her comrades. Several steps more she reaches the scorched ground, with her sandal stepping onto the ashes.

Evelune is the first to notice, baffled more than anything, and observes Imperia taking another step into the circle, now with both feet on the scorched earth.

"Imperia!" Kaylor exclaims.

"Step back, Imperia," High Priest Jochen commands.

Imperia doesn't listen, as the gravitating force is too much to bear. The voices fade to silence as they continue to make demands.

Come to me . . .

"Yes," Imperia whispers.

Open your eyes, child.

Imperia feels the heat of the fire from the edges of the circle. The flames are ever closer with each step she takes, gently kissing her hands. This power is all too inviting, numbing her mind and worldly senses. Her hand extends, index finger pointing furthest, ready to embrace the flame.

A cold thundering clamp snags her shoulder, yanking her back from the flames and dragging her from scorched earth. All sound returns and her vision sharpens, realizing that Evelune has pulled her free from the unholy circle with a firm gauntlet.

"Seminarians, get her inside, now," High Priest Jochen commands.

Evelune passes Imperia to Kaylor and Izahl, who hold her with both arms. She is weak and unable to control her legs which remain lifeless as if she'd taken a hot bath. It takes several moments for her to gain control of herself. Her colleagues guide her from around the back of the church and into the chapel.

"Imperia, what happened to you?" Kaylor asks.

"I . . . I don't know." Imperia gently shrugs her fellow students off her arms and takes her first steps. "I'm not sure. I must pray on this."

Izahl says, "That would be wise, sister."

"Will you be okay?" Kaylor asks.

"Of course," Imperia says. "I think I have to get my belongings."

"What for?" Kaylor asks.

"High Priest Jochen requested that I study in his private quarters."

Izahl says, "I think High Priest Jochen has far more pressing matters to worry about tonight. You must get some rest."

Kaylor says, "You'll feel better in the morning, after a prayer of protection from God."

"Yes, course," Imperia agrees.

The four seminarians retreat to the basement, moving down the spiral staircase and into the stone halls. Izahl is the first to retreat to his quarters, and Kaylor reaches hers next. Imperia enters hers at the end, after Tyrmus. The creaky door reverbs in the stone hall as she opens and closes it. She plants herself on the metal frame. The hay mattress pokes at her thighs, piercing through the black cotton. She is used to the rough texture. Imperia and her three colleagues are not worthy of the luxurious feathered pillows and stuffed mattresses with soft sheets. They must earn their right through the trials of God. Embracing pain will allow them to flourish and understand that indulgences such as a soft bed are only temporary pleasures. At least, that is what she tells herself. She must remember why it is essential to be here.

"Lord, give me strength," Imperia whispers. She closes her eyes, bringing her palms together in preparation for another prayer.

I bring a gift to you . . . Child.

"Lord, if this is truly you, please give me insight into what you offer."

I am the forger of choice. Child. Do not be alarmed. Following the ways of old will only lead you to monotony. Do you not think?

Now Imperia knows she's not speaking to God. This voice . . . belongs to the Devil.

"Shield me in your everlasting love," Imperia prays quickly. Her hands are shaking.

Child. Even the house of the Creator cannot protect you. Why do you fear me?

"Oh Lord, deliver me from the Evil One."

There is no evil one.

Demon, Imperia thinks. She must be encountering a demon, which is beyond her skillset. She has to inform High Priest Jochen. He will shackle her and perform a righteous exorcism through words of power. Her spine tingles, and her throat tenses in fear of what her fellow loyal followers of God will think of her. Perhaps she mustn't tell High Priest Jochen. This will be her secret. She will be faithful in the power of God's protection.

What type of life immersed in fear and submission is worth living?

"Father, douse me in your everlasting love. Amen." Imperia opens her eyes. She breathes steadily through her nostrils, filling her sense with the musty, tight air mixed with the burning wax from the candle on her desk across from her. She exhales and repeats the breathing cycle several times to discover there is no more voice. The demon has been defeated. She can always rely on the power of God.

Imperia smiles, thanking God several times. She blows out the candle and slips into a deep sleep, letting all thoughts dissolve, knowing that she has been victorious through her faith in God.

PART TWO

Escaping internal demons is worth celebrating, at least until they return. Night after night, the whisper continues to speak to Imperia. The words don't appear just during the day. Now they've seeped into her dreams. She's attempted to push the voice out of her mind countless times through prayer with no results. She's attempted every protection verse she knows, repeating the words of power, and somehow, none of them afflict the mental demon.

You're worth so much more . . . the haunting whisper says. The scratchy reverb of this being endlessly loops through her mind, gradually fading into silence.

She prays, *Father, in the Heavenly Kingdom, protect me in your eternal embrace. May the Holy Spirit shield me from the temptations of the earth.* She repeats the phrase every time the haunting voice run through her mind.

God . . . The Creator has abandoned this plane. I will never abandon you. If only you will embrace me.

Every night . . . *God, please answer me!*

And then her night terrors begin. This voice guides her through dreams, for God does not reply. Her quarters in the chapel basement crumble below her she floats beyond this plane. The visions are brief in this other place. It's a barren, rocky wilderness, red, and has a foulness of rotten meat and metal, stinging her senses. Blood.

The following mornings, Imperia buries herself in her studies with the other seminarians. Since that fateful day of discovering the scorched earth, Tyrmus, Izahl, and Kaylor have been unaffected by the patch behind the church. They follow High Priest Jochen's command as he trains them in the ways of a priest and to strengthen their relationship with God.

Each new prayer the seminarians perform is under High Priest Jochen's watchful eye. If a poor effort is noticed, there will undoubtedly be penalty because none shall disrespect the word of

God. This worries Imperia, whose mood shifts drastically over the week, becoming more agitated as she plucks at her skin and fingernails. Despite everything she has tried to hide this mental whisper, she can't defeat it on her own. Now, she sits across High Priest Jochen's desk, who listens to her ramble about invisible demons.

"And these voices . . . What are they telling you to do?" High Priest Jochen asks.

Imperia's legs shake as she keeps fiddling with her fingernails. "It's not voices. It's a voice."

"Right. Now describe it to me."

"It started since that scorched earth appeared behind the chapel. It's persuasive and asks these questions that stray from the path of God."

In the back of Imperia's mind, she cannot help but wonder what happened after they found the fiery circle. The flaming symbols and scorched earth were clear signs of something unholy. High Priest Jochen and the Shield have remained secretive about what they discovered.

She wants to ask High Priest Jochen about what they uncovered. It would be pointless because he would provide the same answer over the past weeks. He'd say, "A foolish attempt from the Devil that was abolished by God's holy ground." Deep down, Imperia knows it is a lie.

It's clear how hastily High Priest Jochen had commended the Shield to cover the scorched earth with fresh dirt. They tossed grass seeds on the ground, attempting to bring new life. They poked shovels and pitchforks into the ash, trying to remove the burnt earth. Each new dirt tossed onto the patch turns grey and dark, with the same symbols scorched into the earth reappearing.

High Priest Jochen asks, "And you are simply hoping you could defeat this whisper on your own?"

"Apologies, High Priest Jochen. I never meant such disrespect. I only wanted to prove that I follow God's will without question."

"Yet you fail."

Imperia looks to the ground, clutching her fingers tightly together to the point that the nails dig into her skin, puncturing the flesh. Feelings of hatred for herself boil under her skin, knowing that she is too weak to handle this demon on her own.

Weak? comes the familiar whisper, tingling behind her ear. She twitches, scratching her lobe, hoping it will go away.

"Is it talking to you right now?" High Priest Jochen asks.

Or are you simply better than this façade?

"Yes," Imperia says, feeling her eyes start to water. Her lip quivers, and she presses them tight together, swallowing her building emotions.

Child . . . I brought you a gift. Why do you not embrace?

"What is it telling you?"

"To stray from God."

"Specifically?" High Priest Jochen asks.

"No. It says it—"

Stop, fool! the whisper shrieks, interrupting her words. *Why do you reject my gift?*

Imperia shakes her head, trying to push the pest away. She pauses and thinks about her answer. The whispering voice is enticing. What type of gift could it possibly bring her, and why her? Imperia comes from no royal bloodline and has risen to nothing.

"I, well. It says I am a no-one," Imperia says. "It says I am nothing."

High Priest Jochen leans closer, cupping his hands. "The voice says you are no one?"

"Yes, that is correct. And I fear it may be right."

"Nonsense, my child. You offer much to God. And you can offer much to me."

Dismiss the snake.

"That is untrue, High Priest Jochen. No disrespect, of course. I've been here my whole life and am still struggling with such basic prayers of protection. This demon is a clear sign of it."

"Demon, or the Devil. Your parents brought you to the church at a young age, knowing that you could offer something better for the Kingdom of Zingalg. Something beyond a life of peasant work, like your family." High Priest Jochen pauses, leaning back in his chair. "What did it say that made you feel inoperable?"

"It's every night. Each slumber it reaches me in my dreams."

"Dreams?"

"Yes. My soul leaves the world entirely. Each night, after I pray to God for aid, I rise from my body. Everything I have experienced flashes before my eyes. I get clear visuals of key moments in my life."

"Such as?"

"When I was young, an infant really, my parents surrendered me over to the church. The Shield came and beat my father. And my mother . . . They—"

"But you're too young to remember such things. You know this is an illusion created by the demon?"

"Perhaps. But it feels so real. It shows me memories of being a child of the church. Sister Batilda lashed me more times than the others. She was ruthless, saying my idiocy would get me nowhere. I don't pray well enough, High Priest Jochen. I just don't pray well enough."

"Sister Batilda only does what she must. The trials of the flesh are a natural process when following God's path. Your soul is full of fire, and we are aiding in neutralizing the heat to better serve the one true Lord. You must walk through these tests, knowing that the pain is temporary and God's eternal love will hold you forever."

"I try, Father. I just fear I am as good as I will ever be."

"And that is the demon talking."

A gentle knock comes from the door, catching High Priest Jochen's attention. He stands, brushing his gown. He says, "If you'll excuse me."

The door creaks open, and Tyrmus steps in with his hands tightly gripping some scrolls and books. His eyes are shifty, looking at Imperia and then High Priest Jochen.

"I have a private study session to attend to with your colleague Tyrmus," High Priest Jochen says.

Imperia stands up, saying, "Of course."

The two seminarians lock eyes as she walks past him. His face was sad, possibly the same as hers. Tyrmus hasn't shown any signs of talking to the demon, though. Something else is concerning the boy. It doesn't involve Imperia; that is what High Priest Jochen is here for. She exits the quarters, retreating back down the hall. The wooden door closes and locks, echoing against the stone walls as she reaches the chapel's sanctuary.

Her mind wanders to Tyrmus again. She dares not toy with her first instinct.

And yet you do . . . the whisper says.

This is a holy temple, a place for God and all things good. High Priest Jochen has led them this far, and she cannot imagine him misguiding them. Then again, just before the scorched earth, High Priest Jochen also wanted Imperia to participate overnight in a private study session. Could she be so naïve?

Yes.

Imperia shakes her head violently, storming down the sanctuary, heading for the front door, passing Izahl and Kaylor, who pray together at the front pew. The footsteps catch Kaylor's attention, and she breaks her focus, watching as Imperia passes her.

Outside, Imperia hurries down the steps and marches along the grass. She needs to see this circle again. She's looked at it plenty of times over the week, but she must look at it again. If it is some supposed gift from this voice, why is High Priest Jochen hiding it?

In the garden, Sister Batilda is taking a stroll with Evelune and two Shield members. The nun breaks her discussion, glaring at Imperia hurrying past the garden to the end of the church.

"Young lady," Sister Batilda says in her shaky voice. Her wrinkles highlight the natural scowl that is imprinted on her face. "Young lady!" Sister Batilda says again.

The lady's demoralizing voice freezes Imperia in her step, knowing that she will be met with the whip if she does not listen.

Greedy hands route themselves in comforting words of the Creator.

"Imperia, come here now," Sister Batilda says.

Resist the false prophets, and the gift is yours.

Sister Batilda will certainly lash her now. Imperia waited too long to respond. And now that High Priest Jochen is aware of the voice, she fears her future at the church will be bleak. Her only chance is to embrace the gift . . . what could it be?

Her first step is slow, breaking the disheartening chains of Sister Batilda's words. The following steps are more manageable. She's enticed by the whispering voice's gift. She's resisted it for so long, and surrendering to it is liberating on her soul, removing hundreds of stones off her back.

Show me, Imperia thinks, trying to talk with the voice.

Child . . . I embrace you.

Imperia picks up her pace under the cloudy sky as thundering booms erupt in the heavens, hinting at the sign of rain. It is possibly a signal of something much more powerful.

"I command you!" Sister Batilda shouts.

Imperia doesn't look back, free of the nun's spell, and disappears around the corner of the building, facing the scorched earth. Small patches of grass are on freshly laid dirt. The plants are brown and lime green. Even with healthy soil laid over the top, the plants do not grow, unlike the rest of nature surrounding the chapel. Black scorched lines remain where the flaming symbols and inner circle once were. This is unholy ground.

Show me, and I will embrace you, Imperia reasons with the voice.

Walk . . .

She obeys, moving a dozen paces and pressing her sandal into the ritual circle, causing her hairs to stand. Her vision saturates while staring at the centre of the circle. The new dirt rapidly shifts from brown to grey. The scorched lines heat up, glowing hues of red and orange. Dead centre is the darkest portion of this circumference which is blacker than any regular charred object. It's so dark that no light reflects off the space. It's unnatural and is the driving force guiding her as she moves towards it, passing the inner circle's glowing red outline.

Walk . . .

"Imperia!" comes a muffled voice.

It's difficult to tell who's calling her name because her senses are narrowed into this black void. Her peripheral view blurs, and her focus sharpens on the black centre. The sound of the wind softens as the faint voice continues to call her name.

"Imperia!"

Come to me . . .

Imperia is only a couple steps away from the harsh transition from charcoal to black. The scorched centre moves, pulsating, like a beating heart. It's slow at first, and with each step closer, it begins to pump faster. With each pulse it makes, the earth tumbles aside, revealing a hole.

"I am," Imperia says in a monotone voice.

The animated black hole expands with dirt tumbling in. Deeper inside the pit, a pale finger reaches out from the darkness. It rises slowly with the sharp grey fingernail pointing to the sky. It bends, aiming directly at Imperia.

Child . . .

"Imperia!" the gruffly voice is loud and clear. Evelune snags her shoulder and pulls her back from the hole, spinning her around to face her, just like the first night.

"Imperia, Sister Batilda needs to speak with you." Evelune's eyes scan Imperia's purple irises like she is some sort of creature.

The thundering skies dissipate with the sun shining through the clouds, directly onto the two of them. Imperia's vision returns to full colour, and her hearing becomes crystal clear. The strange trance is over, and she realizes her entire body is sweating from head to toe. She glances over her shoulder to the black hole to see nothing. It's only scorched earth.

Evelune looks around and leans into Imperia's ear. Her breath is hot as she says, "I hear it too."

Imperia almost gasps. She was so close to uncovering the whispering voice's gift. Everything she experienced from this being was powerful and defied everything she had practiced at the church.

God has never been so direct before. Whether it is a demon or the Devil, Imperia knows she is not alone, for another listens to the whisper.

PART THREE

They didn't speak of it again, for Sister Batilda awaited. There is no reason to ponder the four words because the two know that punishment from Sister Batilda and High Priest Jochen would be too severe. Their faith would be put into question. Their bodies inflicted with pain. Imperia is comforted in knowing she is not alone anymore. Another hears the whispering voice.

Since the arrival of the scorched earth, Imperia struggles to resist it. The visions flood her mind every night, ranging from flashes of her past to the hellish landscape with red dirt. Every day she wonders why she continues to deny it. She could freely give in and embrace this mysterious gift.

The Shield captain had freed Imperia from her trance in the unholy scorched earth. The seminarian was too focused on discovering what the whisper's gift was and ignored her faith, surrendering entirely to this being below the earth; what a fool to do such a thing! She has no knowledge of who the whisper is. Evelune hears it, and what does she think of this voice?

The days go on, turning into several weeks with Sister Batilda and High Priest Jochen refusing to let Imperia go to the back of the church. They ordered the Shield to build a wooden fence around the ritual circle and keep piling more dirt, rocks, and grass seeds to remove the unholy ground. As always, everything rots. The rocks crumble, turning to dust and paving the way for the new dirt to turn grey. Then the scorched symbols appear from nowhere.

Imperia knows a dark secret about the unholy ground that her higherups fail to realize. That toxic earth keeps an otherworldly being below. It refuses to leave, and Imperia is its reasoning. She is reminded

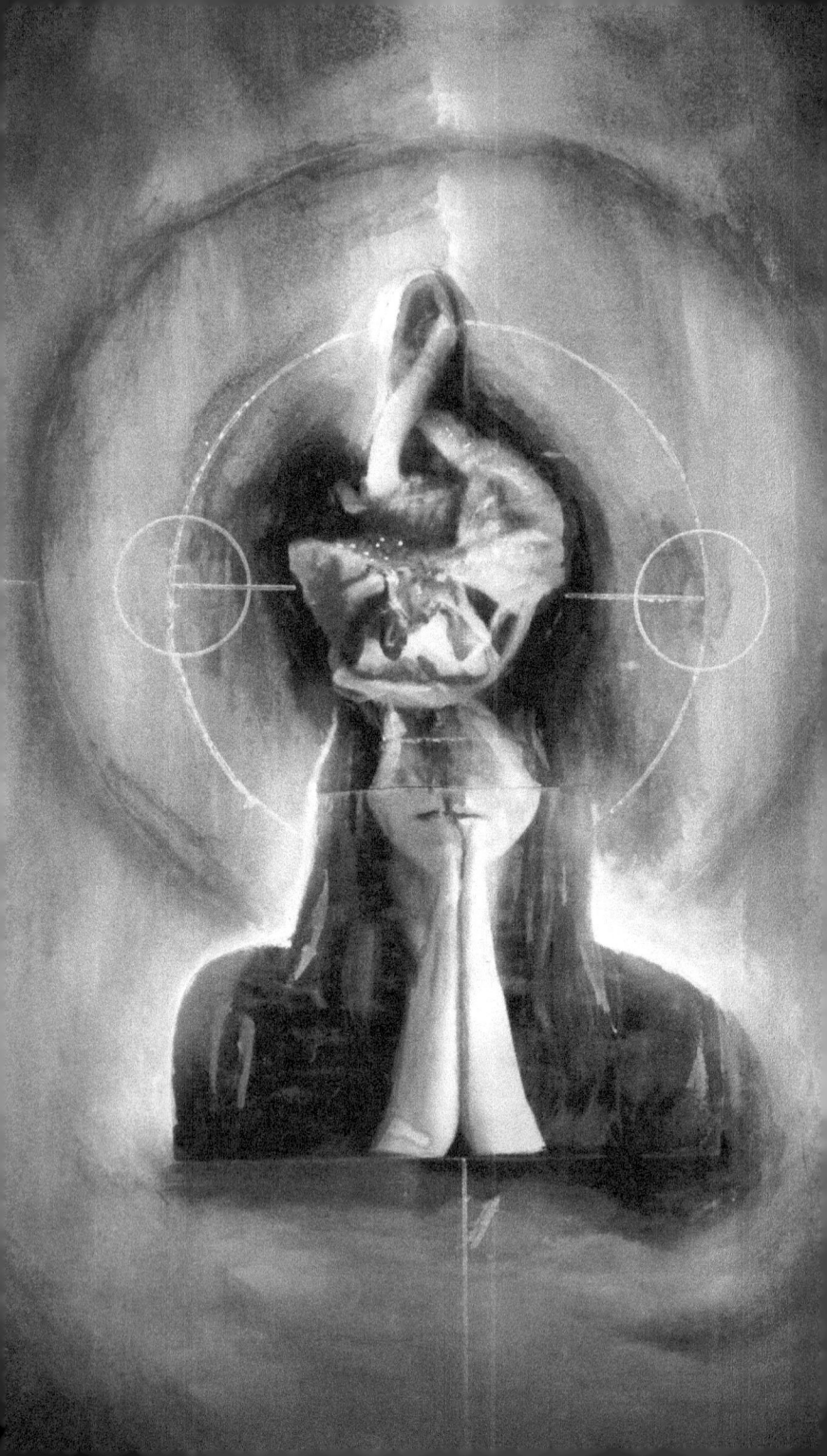

by the whisper each day to return to the circle. It speaks before she enters her nightly slumber, making her pray to God for protection.

I need blood . . . embrace your gift, the whisper says.

"God, answer me."

She must remain resilient and focus on her training with the other three seminarians, Izahl, Tyrmus, and Kaylor. They have not fallen into any strange trances or shown signs of talking to the demon. It proves that Imperia is weak, despite the whisper's encouraging words.

High Priest Jochen shares his lectures every morning. The seminarians watch and study as he commands the room. The town of Nevertroll comes by each Sunday to hear his words of empowerment, love, and of course God himself.

When the townsmen of Nevertroll leave for the day, that is when High Priest Jochen invites Tyrmus to private study, as he's been doing for weeks. Each passing day the boy's eyes are a little darker, his skin is increasingly faint. Whatever is occurring in the priest's private quarters has beaten Tyrmus into a whimpering dog.

As for Imperia, she no longer sleeps in her quarters in the basement. She is under the close eye of Sister Batilda. Each night after Imperia finishes her evening study and prayer, she lays down on the cot in the nun's spare room. Sister Batilda tends to stay up during the evening to finish the duties around the chapel, letting her keep a close eye on Imperia.

Child . . . Why do you fear me?

Imperia slips into her dream, being met with visions of blood. Flashes of the scorched earth appear under a stormy night. The charred remains of the fire represent symbols that glow amber. The central black void pulsates. The sky rains red, splattering onto the soil heavily.

Child . . .

The blood rain pours faster. Lightning strikes as the black void caves in, creating a hole.

Child . . .

She shoots to life as icy water envelops her face, gasping and shivering. She rises from her bed, seeing Sister Batilda holding a bucket of empty water. The lady stares at her with the same permanent scowl of distaste.

"Your dreams are becoming violent once more," Sister Batilda says. "Pray to God for protection again, weakling."

I thought you trusted my word? So boldly walking to me before.

Sister Batilda storms out of the room, slamming the door and leaving Imperia in a freeze. The owls hoot outside, and the crickets chirp under the starry sky behind the closed planks of wood, keeping the window shut. The sound is reassuring that Imperia is a part of this world and the whisper is not.

At least that's what she tells herself. She wants to believe in the church, she keeps resisting these words, but she saw the being in the scorched earth. The demon is alive.

I am no demon, child.

What are you? Imperia thinks. No. Here she is, reasoning with the demon again. She will be disciplined by Sister Batilda, who will clearly see if she slips from God's grace again. She'll sense it.

I am your new God.

Imperia replies, *Only the Father, the Son, and the Holy Spirit can—*

The whisper shrieks before Imperia finishes her thought. *The Creator abandoned all mortals. I do not!* The voice returns to a gentle tone saying, *Do not fear Sister Batilda. We will take care of her.*

Imperia sits at the edge of her bed and rings the water out of her hair, shivering. She is certain to catch a cold throughout the night if she doesn't warm up. As usual, Sister Batilda offers no aid. The seminarian must rely on praying to God . . . or asking the whisper. It's so easy to give in because it's the only one who answers to her.

What am I to do? Imperia asks, curiosity consuming her.

You are to be my eyes, ears, and tongue in this world, the whisper says.

Why me? Imperia asks.

The whisper says, *You do not belong in this chapel. Your mind does not operate like the others. You know you are not them, and for that, I see the potential in your independence.*

She replies, *You wish me to not follow them and follow you? How is that any different?*

The whisper chuckles, *This is why I chose you. You see, child—*

Imperia interrupts. *I have not been a child for half-decade. I am a woman. And so are my three colleagues. It's nonsense to see it in any other way.*

Yes, you are a woman. Women hold power. Independence flourishes in adulthood, even in the youthful kind. Yet, my eyes have seen centuries and eras come and go. I've witnessed the Creator, the original name of your God, give birth to the mortal realm in which you reside. I've been here from the beginning and hold the right to call all mortals children. For compared to a god, you are nothing.

So, I am useless. Whether I follow God or whatever entity you claim to be. Imperia pulls the sheet off the cot and wraps it around her shivering body, attempting to warm up. She rises, walks to the window frame and slides the plank of wood off the window, keeping the wooden shutters together, and gets a whiff of fresh air to try and clear her mind.

A mortal is nothing without guidance. You're wild animals. You're lost souls astray. Imperia, I don't wish you to follow. I wish to offer you my guidance.

Guide me to what? Imperia asks.

Child, I am not freed from irrational emotions. I have made grave mistakes in my life. You cannot force preachers of free will to obey you; you must work with them. We all wish for independence from our personal chains. The Heavenly Kingdoms, Dega'Mostikas's Triangle—or Hell, this realm, all of them have restrictions that prevent us from embracing our true powers. They burden our beings with rules. I wish it no more. I wish every soul to be free to stand and master their own lives. I can offer this if you prove your trust in me.

And how do I prove such trust? Imperia asks.

You must mend me. Return to the ritual circle, douse me in blood to heal my wounds, and I will gift you a power that is beyond your wildest imagination.

Imperia is tempted by such an idea. She never thought of herself as someone who could rise to power. She's always been humble, following God, despite her fiery nature. Her parents surrendered her from a young age to the church, ingraining the holy words into her mind. She cannot imagine living any other way. She could have independence. What would that mean to her?

She spots Evelune walking with the two members of the Shield, leaving the garden. Their holy church tabards drape over their torso and several pieces of armour, each gripping the handle of their sheathed sword.

Child, can't you see that High Priest Jochen has put the Shield on guard duty since I have arrived. Don't you wonder why he keeps the earth gated? Don't you wonder what more I can offer?

I do, Imperia says.

I will show it to you once you come to me.

Evelune and the Shield leave the garden, proceeding along the side of the church. Evelune looks to the open window, spotting Imperia.

I hear it too. Evelune's words run through Imperia's mind.

The whisper says, *I bring you an ally. Independence may be the path you pave, but you will gain followers. Some are not destined to take the first step. This is my gift to you. Now come to me.*

Imperia waves at Evelune. The Shield stops while the two patrolling members leave her behind. She walks towards the window. Evelune stops, looking up at Imperia, about half a person higher at the window.

"We don't have long," Imperia says. "Sister Batilda will back soon."

"How have you been feeling?" Evelune asks.

"Not well. High Priest Jochen and Sister Batilda are persistent in making me better. But . . . I don't know if *better* is the right word."

"I don't believe so." The Shield looks to the back of the church where the gated scorched earth rests.

Imperia asks, "What did you mean when you said you hear it too?"

"The voice. Ever since I pulled you out of the burning circle that fateful day."

Children . . .

Evelune and Imperia tense and stand straight, staring at each other. Their silence confirms that they both can hear the word.

"Do you trust it?" Evelune asks.

"Sorry?" Imperia asks.

"Do you trust the voice? They speak of another way. They speak of you."

"Of me?"

"Yes. At first, I thought I was going mad. Clerics don't have the same foresight into the word of God as you seminarians and priests. We can only master simple words of power. I know no defence to withstand it. I thought it was evil at first, deeming it the Devil. The more I listen, the more reason it offers."

"I share the same feelings. I've witnessed the prideful sin of High Priest Jochen and fear of more he hides. I know what Sister Batilda is. I question if my parents surrendered me or forced me to the church. I question everything."

"I've only been the hand of God, never questioning my role. I fail to even know who I am. There must be a better way."

"The voice claims to be a god. Yet we are told there is only one God and there are plenty of false prophets serving the Devil and cannot be trusted."

"The blanket statement is a perfect way to shroud any other form of thinking."

Imperia feels her stomach twist, and her heart sinks to the knotted mess in her gut hearing Evelune speak such ill words of their faith. The concerning part is she feels the same about their ways and the people within the church. She is simply coming to terms with the reality she lives in, and it is not easy to digest.

"What are we to do, Imperia?" Evelune asks.

"Sorry?" Imperia asks.

"I have embraced the voice. This god, whatever it is, it's words of guidance I cannot deny. I have asked it what it wants of me so I can find my own path, and it has told me to follow your lead."

"Me?"

"Yes, we will free you from Sister Batilda's and High Priest Jochen's grasps. The Shield are loyal to my word. I will convince them. But, please, I must know what your first command is."

Footsteps rise from down the hall beyond the closed door, making Imperia's ear twitch. She grabs the wooden shutters, and while closing them, she says, "Take me to the circle."

Evelune nods as Imperia closes the wooden shutters and slides the plank in, locking them. She scurries to the bed and lies down as quietly she can to prevent the metal frame from squeaking. The door to the room unlocks, swinging open and casting an orange light in the room from the torches in the hall.

Imperia's eyes are shut, pretending to sleep. She breathes steadily through her nose and out her mouth, feeling the blood run wildly in her. Footsteps move towards her bed and around the cot. Sister Batilda is watching her, judging how she sleeps.

She will be the first to go, Imperia thinks. The thought surprises her, for she thought it would be the whisper's words. It is sinister and something that God would not have taught. The supposed God of the Bible would also not have allowed many things that the church has been responsible for; just look at Tyrmus.

An independent thought . . . good, my child, the whisper says.

The footsteps fade away, and the door closes with the long creek, followed by a click. The muffled steps move down the hall, leaving Imperia safe in darkness. She sighs with relief and relaxes her muscles, ready for sleep.

I await your arrival, and we'll set forth the new faith. One birthed of the left-hand individual's path, letting their soul guide them. You will be the teacher, as I am yours.

I am coming for you, Imperia thinks. *With blood.*

PART FOUR

Free will is the gift given to all mortals when they are brought into this world. The ability is an active practice that must be disciplined daily to reinforce its strength. If choice isn't made into a habit, then the tides of life will wash you aside, locking you into the will of another.

Each passing day Imperia is reminded how she has failed to practice her free will, following the path of God directly under the supervision of High Priest Jochen and Sister Batilda. They have been her guide in telling her what she wants and needs to do to live a fulfilling life. Everything they say is, of course, under God's plan, not hers.

Now she has woken to the years of lies. According to the holy book, the whisper is said to be a demon, but it speaks reason. What type of God would let her live a life like this? Her fellow seminarians are also victims of torture. Poor Tyrmus . . . She's heard the sounds behind the closed door. He's only High Priest Jochen's sinful toy.

Izahl and Kaylor have been indoctrinated, embracing everything High Priest Jochen offers. This all ends now. Imperia plans to shatter the chains of conformity and rise to the seat of power. Her will shall be, under the watchful guide of this . . . whisper.

What is your name? Imperia asks, sitting in the garden on a stone bench beside the statue of the holy mother, Mary, under the cloudy sky. The weather hasn't cleared in days ever since she accepted the whisper.

I will share with you, child, the whisper says, *once you have freed me. But I guarantee I am not in any of your books, not anymore.*

Why is that? Imperia asks.

History has been long mangled and rewritten since the days of the Paladins.

During the Drac Age?

Yes. The Creator was refashioned into God. The Heavenly Kingdoms turned to Heaven, and Dega'Mostikas's Triangle simplified to Hell. I, among many others, was erased entirely from the scripts. It will not be

long before the Drac Age is shortened into a tall tale. So, my name matters little now.

Imperia decides to leave the question at that. Since she accepted this whisper into her life, as Evelune of the Shield has, the horrifying dreams have fizzled out. Her sleep is restful, and she is accelerating in her priestly practices. High Priest Jochen and Sister Batilda have been impressed. Little do they know that she is simply acting for the old fools to give her freedom again. This is her will in action.

"When do we strike, Imperia?" Evelune asks. She stands in her full suit of steel armour beside the bench, still wearing her churchly tabard draped over the breastplate. "My two men are compliant, understanding that this sign is beyond High Priest Jochen and his corruption."

"Tonight," Imperia says, still gazing at the statue of Mary. "We first strike Sister Batilda. The whisper demands blood, and we will deliver it. You will lure Sister Batilda out of the garden, inform her of your security checks as you do every evening. Once I arrive, you execute her."

"Of course."

"Be careful, as we must savour her blood."

"I will perform the task with precision," Evelune says.

"Make note of the priests' words of power," Imperia says.

"I am aware of a priest's God-given capabilities."

"Cut off their tongues if needed. They can't smite you if they can't pray."

"We will do what is required."

"I want your two men to seize High Priest Jochen," Imperia says.

"What of the other seminarians?"

"Have the Shield bring them too, we'll gather at the back of the chapel and let them witness what we create. We will give them a choice, either kneel before me as a sign of loyalty and follow in this new free will, or die protecting their enslaving faith."

"Of course," Evelune says. "I will inform my fellow clerics."

"Good."

Evelune leaves Imperia in the garden. Now, all the seminarian needs to do is wait. She doesn't even have to lift a finger on anyone. The Shield will implement her bequest. Those holy warriors are a force to be reckoned with. They aren't a paladin but are highly skilled in the art of a blade, and priests are no match for them.

See, child? Independence draws those to follow, the whisper says.

I don't wish to lead cattle, Imperia replies.

No, you mustn't. Then you will be no better than the very thing we are dismantling. You must guide them, as I guide you.

The sun begins to set, disappearing beyond the forest of Zingalg. The gloomy clouds highlight a bright red along their edges, prophesying the horrors to be unleashed upon the blind followers of God tonight. From the opposite perspective, Imperia sees it as a celebration, representing blood for the whisper and the rise of choice.

She carries out the rest of her priestly tasks during the day, acting as a good seminarian under the watchful eye of High Priest Jochen. Sister Batilda doesn't even bother to acknowledge her. Her attention is brought to Kaylor, who she beat several times. Imperia is unaware of why. She has lost interest in the daily activities of her fellow colleagues.

High Priest Jochen takes Tyrmus into his private studies most nights. Izahl retreats to his quarters for his private studies. He's either utterly unaware of every dreadful event occurring in the church or buries his head in God's books. His time will come, as will Kaylor's, and as will Tyrmus's.

The night is born, and Tyrmus exits from the back of the chapel and joins Kaylor, whose one cheek is red from Sister Batilda's wrath. Both walk hastily, looking down to the ground in shame. Imperia pretends to pray at the front pew, watching Evelune and Sister Batilda exit the foyer and down the stairs, retreating to the garden.

Come to me, the whisper says.

She snags a silver goblet from one of the shrines along the wall just under a stained-glass window of Christ himself on the cross. His face is frowning, as it should be. Her storming down the sanctuary towards the front doors catches the attention of Kaylor and Tyrmus, who were just about to head down to the basement. The two simply watch like the sheep they are. Imperia is supposed to retreat to her quarters like them.

She exits the sanctuary, through the foyer, out the main door and down the staircase into the breezy night. Evelune and Sister Batilda have entered the garden, strolling peacefully.

The seminarian hurries across the grass, approaching the garden. She slows her pace, spotting Sister Batilda and Evelune standing by the holy Mary statue. She breathes steadily through her nose and out her mouth, feeling the focused energy of excitement channel through her. Removing this wretched woman is her will in action.

"Imperia?" Sister Batilda says, noticing her approach. She steps towards Imperia. "What on earth are you doing here? You are to retreat to your private studies."

Evelune slowly walks behind Sister Batilda, drawing her sword.

Come to me.

What if Imperia is making a mistake? She's betraying the Good God and will undoubtedly burn in Hell. If this is indeed a demon toying with her, she will be enslaved by it if she frees it from the scorched earth. Killing Sister Batilda would be punishable by death.

Evelune draws her sword entirely, creating a *schwing*! noise.

"Evelune?" Sister Batilda spins around as Evelune thrusts the blade into the nun's gut. The metal rips through the internal organs and pierces past the heart and the spine. The old lady gasps, blood drizzling down her face. The state of shock prevents her from saying anything as Evelune slides the blade free from the body.

Sister Batilda collapses onto the stone ground with blood seeping out of the front and back holes. There is no turning back for Imperia. She must embrace her newfound path.

Sister Batilda starts mumbling a prayer . . . words of power.

"Slit her throat," Imperia says, leaning down with the goblet.

Evelune places the sword against Sister Batilda, whose wound is miraculously healing. The cleric carves into the throat, opening a fresh

337

wound with warm blood pouring down into the silver goblet. The old woman gurgles, sputtering red liquid under the brim of the cup and onto the ground.

Come to me . . .

The two victors are no longer enslaved. Imperia raises the silver goblet that drizzles red liquid down the bowl's outer rim, dripping onto the floor. She marches out of the garden under the moonlight, just as screams come from inside the chapel.

"The Shield has engaged," Evelune says.

After exiting the garden, the two pause, watching as Izahl, Kaylor, and Tyrmus hurry out of the chapel, down the staircase and towards them. High Priest Jochen's head flails violently as the two Shield force him to walk, gripping his arms.

"What is the meaning of this! This is blasphemy," High Priest Jochen shouts.

The Shield let go, and one throws a swift boot into his back, knocking him down the stone staircase, tumbling to the ground. Both men pick him up, dragging him across the path and onto the grass. Blood runs down his scalp as he looks up at Imperia and Evelune.

"Treachery! You have betrayed God and walk the path of the Devil."

"Dear sister Imperia!" Izahl asks. "What is going on?"

Kaylor is crying. "Why does the Shield harm God's followers?"

High Priest Jochen starts chanting, "Father in Heaven, grant me protection to—"

Imperia interrupts with a shout. "Silence, priest! If you resist, we'll cut off your tongue."

High Priest Jochen clenches his teeth, glaring at her.

"Imperia?" Izahl asks again.

"My fellow colleagues," Imperia says, holding the goblet high. She walks in a slow, confident stride towards them. "You will have the choice to embrace your true gift or perish with this ancient, enslaving religion as Sister Batilda has."

High Priest Jochen's face twists into a hateful scowl. "You will burn in Hell for all of eternity for what you are committing."

Imperia ignores High Priest Jochen's curses and says, "Bring them." She leads Evelune, the Shield, and the remaining followers of God to the back of the church to the gated circle. The grey scorched earth remains with small patches of dead grass laying on top. The blacker lines that form the ruins and inner circle light up red with Imperia's presence.

"Evelune, the key," Imperia says.

Evelune sifts through the pockets on her leather utility belt and pulls out a ring of keys. She unlocks the gate and swings it open. It creaks with an elongated squeak, letting Imperia enter.

Come to me, child.

She takes her first step into the scorched earth, sending a wave of heat through Imperia's mind. The energy is less harsh than the previous two times she entered the circle. This heat is comforting, and she embraces the energy flowing through her body, electrifying her form with an immense sense of power. Her vision constricts into the centre of the scorched earth, seeing the darker black outlines are now radiating an amber hue. In the centre, where the blackest portion is, the dirt pulsates with tiny pieces of earth tumbling aside.

Come to me . . .

"Stay here," Imperia commands Evelune while proceeding further into the circle.

Evelune, the Shield, and their captives watch as Imperia boldly steps onto the scorched earth. They don't blink, wholly spellbound by what they are witnessing.

Each step Imperia takes, she feels the gravitation of the center grow. She accepts this energy and feels no resistance with her stride. The pulsation moves faster, pushing the dirt aside, and revealing the black hole in the middle of the circle.

Long fingers poke out of the hole with jagged nails. They reach for the sky, curling and extracting in rhythm with the pulse. Imperia reaches the centre, looking straight down into the hole to see the base of the large fingers disappear into the void, making it impossible to see its complete form

Bathe me in blood, child. Give me the strength of mortal life.

Imperia pours the blood from the goblet into the hole directly onto the hand. The throbbing slows as the red liquid drizzles onto the old pale skin.

Drink the blood with me, the whisper says.

Imperia obeys and drinks the remaining droplets from the goblet. The energizing force within her system compresses into her core, where her soul resides. The earth rumbles from the black void. Not quite an earthquake, but it's enough to raise concern in the mortals awaiting Imperia's next move.

Raise me from this hole, child.

Imperia obeys, setting the goblet down and reaching into the pit. Touching the cold, dry fingers, Imperia understands the sheer size of this hand. It's monstrous and clearly belonged to a giant. She moves her hands deeper into the darkness, feeling the superficial palmar arch.

Raise me!

It takes all her strength to lift the goliath hand out of the hole. She roars with might, lifting the blood-drenched hand from the void and earth. This massive hand has an additional thumb on the opposite end, totalling six fingers, each reaching for the sky.

Imperia almost loses her balance as the torso-sized palm slams against her chest. The arm-length fingers aid her, pushing against her shoulders to lift itself higher. As it climbs, she comes face to face with a reptilian eyeball in the centre of the hand, blinking at her. The hand moves higher up Imperia as the two work as one, raising it above her head. Dangling flesh and bone reside where the wrist should be above her skull.

Come to me.

Instinctually, Imperia rotates the massive hand and herself to face her witnesses. Her limbs shake from holding the weight of the object. She looks up at the flesh and bone at its base. The innards of the hand contain small red bug-like creatures scurrying inside, slipping between and out of the muscles and tendons. There are dozens of them, moving out of the way for Imperia to place her head inside.

"By the power of God! Protect us from this unholy ritual!" High Priest Jochen rambles. "Seminarians, pray with me. God as our witness!"

Tyrmus obeys, and the two priests attempt to perform words of power. Evelune nods at her two men, and they hit them with the blunt end of the swords, knocking them dazed. Tyrmus tries again, and the Shield grabs his throat, strangling him.

Imperia places her head inside the hand, letting the warm insectoids and moist flesh surround her. The hand easily slips onto her head, covering her in blood and meat, encasing her in darkness. She can feel the scurrying of the tiny creatures all around, entering her mouth, nose, and ears.

She wishes to scream, now wondering if her slight thought of reason before Sister Batilda's fate was true. Is this a demon that has consumed her? Her vision returns before she has time to reflect. In the blackness there's a small golden circle glimmering.

The shape grows, coming closer to her. It radiates light from the core of its smooth surface. Etched in the circle is a modified holy cross, with an open hand in the middle. It has two thumbs and an eye, just like the one mounted on her head. Along the edges of the hand and eye are countless tiny engravings in it, similar to the scorched symbols glowing in the ground.

Three is the symbol, child, the whisper says.

What do you mean, three? Imperia asks.

The golden circle envelopes her, followed by the reptilian eye, and then more darkness. A second golden circle appears, growing and passing her, and then a third.

The mind, body, and spirit are what make you, symbolized endlessly throughout history. See behind the curtains of the masked Father, Son and Holy Spirit. With these three unified, your will is unmatched.

The final eye passes her, and her true vison returns, letting her see her witnesses and the church. In the core of each of the six beings in front of her is a glowing golden triangle formed by three radiant orbs—the source of the symbols. The trees, grass, and even the wind have a radiating glow with more tones and hues than she could ever imagine.

The energy centralized in her core divides throughout her body, giving her the strength needed to wear this massive hand on her head. Her legs no longer shake, and she can move freely.

Guide them, my child. As I will guide you. For I am the Weaver, shaper of worlds and bringer of free will.

Of course, Imperia obeys, raising her hands up high to be vertically parallel with the monstrous hand helmet that she wears.

"My fellow seminarians," Imperia's strident voice causes the witnesses to stop everything and focus purely on her in awe and fear. "You have the choice to walk the left-hand path with my guidance under the watchful eye of the Weaver. Or you can follow the poisonous lies of High Priest Jochen and his false god."

"God will punish you if you follow this demon!" High Priest Jochen shouts. "This is the test of God! Test of your true will! Do not bend or give in."

"Kneel before the Weaver and me and prove you accept the path of free will. We will be your guide you as you become your own. Accept us, embrace us."

"By the power of God, I smite the!" High Priest Jochen shouts.

Tyrmus is the first to kneel, breaking High Priest Jochen's focused word of power.

"No, no, no!" Kaylor shakes her head fiercely with tears pouring down her face. "God! Please protect us!"

Izahl is the second to kneel. Evelune follows.

"This is your final chance, fellow seminarian Kaylor," Imperia says.

One of the clerics places the sword against Kaylor's neck. The second cleric places the sword against High Priest Jochen's.

"God Almighty!" High Priest Jochen shouts.

"Protect us!" Kaylor cries.

Imperia brings both hands down simultaneously. The Shield draws their swords back, sliding against the flesh and slicing into the tendons. Blood spews onto the grass as the two priests topple onto the floor beside the loyal followers. The two clerics kneel as thunder cackles in the distance.

I bring you the gift, the Weaver says.

Is this it? Is my destiny to lead these people? Imperia asks.

There is more. I bring you the proper guide, the one that once directed me. Together, we can make a better world. Lean back into the hole, child.

Imperia obeys, turning and kneeling into the hole. Deep inside, there's a book with a cover made of charcoal stone. Swirls of gold and red surround this tome. It's as massive as the hand mounted onto her head. Truthfully, she is unsure if she can carry it, even with the newfound strength.

Lower me, the Weaver says.

As one, Imperia and the Weaver lean into the hole, and his fingers snag the massive tome. Imperia groans, using her arms to push them up from the dirt, and the two raise the book high. The Weaver grips the tome with both thumbs wrapped around the object resting on his palm.

The Book of Consulo is the key to bending all creationism. It is ours, and we will undo the tyranny that the old world created. As you guide your new followers, we will learn its ancient words, child. These followers will rediscover their free will, unifying their mind, body, and spirit.

Imperia extends her hands out as rain trickles down, washing away the blood tainting the ground. The five loyal followers do not move, awaiting the next command.

"My fellow Shield and priests!" Imperia shouts. "We bring truth to the New World. We are the Aureate Rise. For we have climbed from the depths of blood, torture, and suffering demonstrated by the ancient religions. We will weave our own path of will."

Fragment: E

Awake from the observing state. (Turn to Page 361)

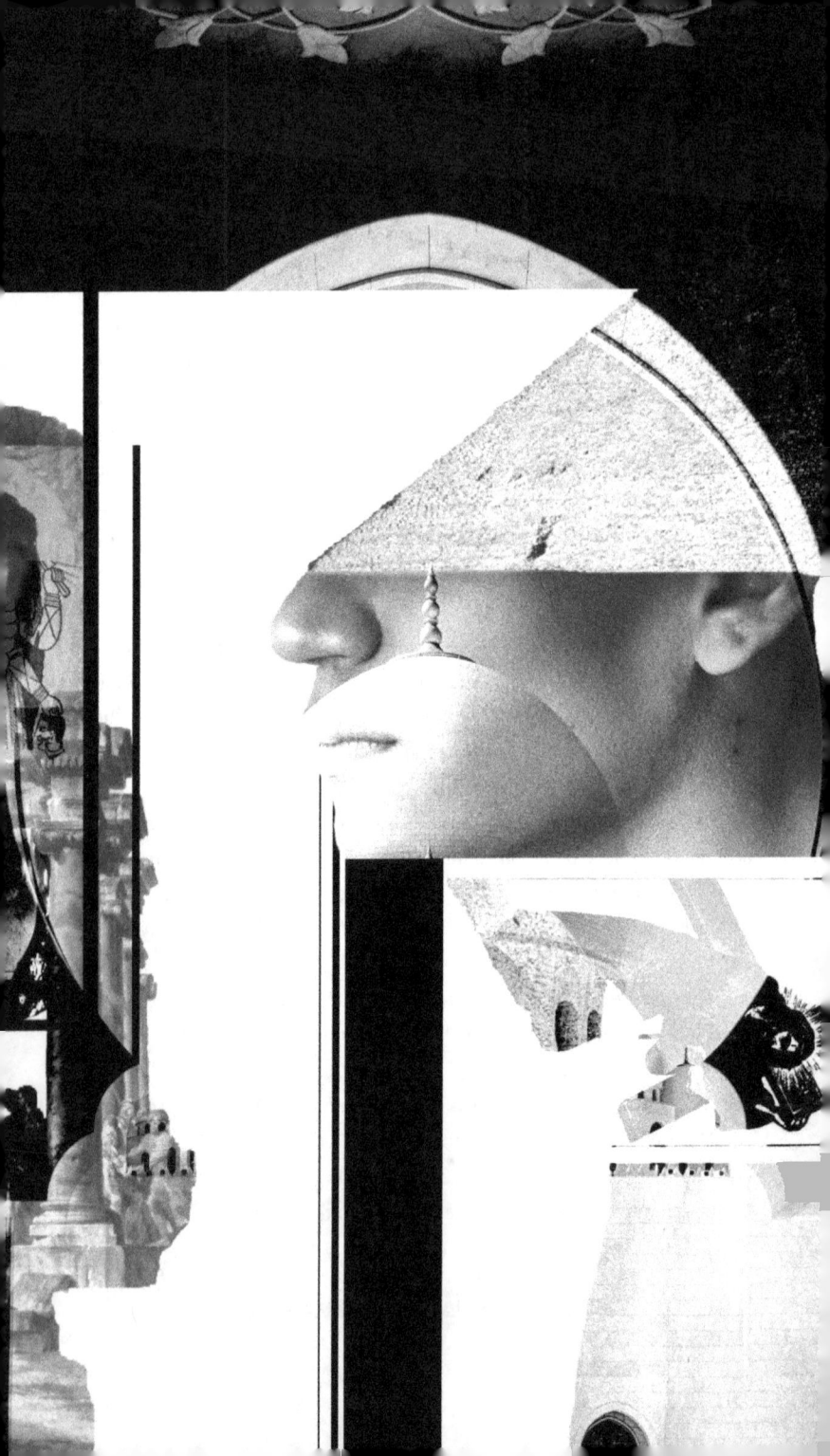

POST RELIGIONISM

D oes the artist guide the work, or does the work guide them? Sure, creativity is a discipline with a toolbox of theories, but still, there is an external force that drives a person to pursue the arts. I've learned from an early age that the paintings spoke to me. Some people might write this off as "the gift," or I'm being vague like all typical "artist types." Maybe I do have a gift. It doesn't change the fact that I worked tirelessly on improving my craft to be a successful commercial artist. Craft can be taught. One's drive is something deep within each and every one of us. For me, it's what truly aids the best paintings. It always has. Drive, or inspiration, all comes from the muse.

School was never an easy area for me in both high school and postsecondary. Don't I sound like a cliché? A troubled artist who struggled through school. Well, it is true. Like the usual creative types, we are outcasts amongst the regular kids who enjoy football or whatever sport is equivalent in their country. I don't care. What matters to me is channelling this muse that directs me. If I don't, my skin burns and my stomach twists up inside. Have you ever been in such mad love that you couldn't control yourself, and if you tried you became sick? That's the drive I have. There are visions, sounds, even smells that I must compile from the human senses and express through the two-dimensional plane of the canvas.

You know, there was once a time where civilizations viewed the artists as a higher class. Their muse was what drove societies forward because it was seen as a direct link to god, or gods, channelled through the artist and into their work. The modern world is different. We focus on tastes and less spirituality. Thankfully, I've understood the difference between inspired art and commercial art. Even though the muse is the drive, it's worked in my favour. I've never been a spiritual person, but I accept where the muse leads me, and I wonder about my sanity, thinking about how these ancient artists once "channelled the gods."

As a kid, my parents let me explore my creative outlets, nurturing my skill. It helped that my father is a professor and my mother is a professional fine painter. I had a few friends in high school, but my artistic abilities far surpassed my classmates. It alienated me from the others; even though some admired the work, they didn't feel they could talk to me.

College was where my true abilities shined. My classmates admired and respected me, and I wonder if they feared me too, for I made their work less important. The instructors paid close attention, noting how I tossed aside their key examples of good art, such as Oscar Elvira's work. His post-modern futurism paintings didn't live up to my aspirations. My teachers noticed my internal inspirations—the muse's inspirations—as I was simply channelling it.

It sounds ridiculous, but the muse mainly spoke in vision form, both day and night. You know when you daydream? Your thoughts wander a little bit, going to places you might not usually think of, and then you're suddenly blasted with an array of emotions, feelings, and visuals. Well, that is how the muse speaks to me. It always has.

Postsecondary was when the muse started using phonetic words. I wondered if this had any relation to my drug abuse. But please, everyone in college was using some sort of drug. Whether it was doctor prescribed or the street, from those notorious Crystal Moths, everyone had some form to boost their creativity. I was no different, and the muse encouraged it.

They were simple words such as "murder" or "love" or "fueled happiness." I don't always know what the muse means with these words, but the visuals supporting them repeat the words over and over until I snap out of the dream. I awake in sweats and jolt to life while on the bus or in the classroom. That's when I know the muse has given me a new direction, and I must act, or it'll pain me too greatly.

I've explained this to my classmates before, and most of them write it off as ridiculous new-age bullshit, or I need a medical doctor. That is fair because we are taught to be creative professionals and use skills to problem-solve the blank canvas. Of course, I use these theories because I think the muse can't be around all the time.

One boy did take me seriously. Callan was his name. Fair-skinned, intelligent, witty, with a deep alluring voice, everything that I admired. In fact, his interest made it clear as day to me that I was not fond of women. We related on many topics such as our preferred artists, political beliefs, and even the petty things like who we didn't like in our class. Gossip was one of our many pastimes. We loved observing who was sleeping with whom and who was jealous because of it. If anything, we were like those bratty girls in high school with their own secret club.

We also inspired each other and encouraged one another to focus on our work. I explained to Callan about the muse and where it led me. It took me to places I was not comfortable painting like "murder" themes, or if I believed I lacked the skill to do it. But Callan pushed me to expand my artistic horizon. I would critique his work too, and he'd flourish.

Obviously, I developed an emotional attachment to this boy. I wanted to tell him, at least until I saw him grow fond of a girl in our class, Jeong was her name. One night, out of blind passion, when we were working alone in the studio, I grabbed his hand and confessed my growing love for him. I pulled him in for a kiss. He resisted and told me that is not who he was, and he was serious with this . . . Jeong of his. I tried to reason with him, but he yelled. Even then, his voice of rejection was attractive to me, drawing me in. I tried to kiss him again, and he pushed me. I felt foolish, ashamed, for what I had done and stormed out that night.

The next day we pretended as nothing had happened. He critiqued my work as I did for him, and my criticism was harsher, telling him that he didn't know what he was talking about. I suppose I regret my anger towards Callan, but emotions are part of the human experience, and I use them. I channel them. Good and evil are all mixed into the work that I do. It shows I'm able to harness this energy and manifest it into something within the world that's both critically acclaimed and commercially successful. It is far more than could be said for any of my classmates in postsecondary, including Callan and his Jeong.

We all graduated. Callan moved on, and so did I. I had my flings and eventually found a partner while growing my career internationally. The commercial success was when my work started to change. The power of the muse was so potent to the point where I shifted into the passenger seat, watching my body animate against my will. I was an observer, seeing what it could inflict onto the canvas. I never questioned it, judged it, nor feared it. I was merely a vessel for something greater.

It frequently painted strange symbols, creating ritualistic styled collages. The muse took influences from all around the world. Hieroglyphics from Egypt, ancient Aztec structures, North American indigenous sculptures, you name it. It was like a strange fusion of every culture and faith mashed into one mosaic. No culture stood out from any of the others; each equally represented and complimented the other.

Post Religionism is what my critics commonly classify my work as. The new style of art blew up. Much like Andy Warhol with pop art or futurism in Italy, I created a new trend. There were imitators, but I was the original, and the best.

Years after college, in Toronto, I was in the middle of giving my artist statement for the grand opening in front of a room of two hundred people. Through the mash of attendees, I spotted Callan way in the back. He had a son, a younger daughter, and a lady I presumed to be his wife. I didn't recognize the woman, and it did not matter, Jeong or not.

I froze, just as the muse spoke to me. I was blasted with darkness, rivers of red, and shores made of muscle surrounded with spines representing trees. The smell was rotten meat and metal. It was horrific. I had never seen such a violent vision from the muse before. I was petrified as the whispering words spoke: "obtain."

Obtain was not a word that I would use for the visuals that I had. It happened so rapidly that I jerked onstage. My manager came up beside me, and she touched my arm, making sure I was okay. She was aware of my past abuse with substances, and I presumed she thought I was having withdrawal. However, I have been clean for many years, and that was not the case. It was simply the muse reminding me who was in control.

I finished my artist statement breaking into sweats and hurried offstage so the gallery could finish their opening ceremony, and I could wash down this strange array of emotions with a swift drink. Wait, no, there was a second and third as well. I'd never felt so disturbed by the muse's visions before.

"Dasco!" came that familiar smooth, deeper voice that rides from the bellows of the man's belly. The dominating voice always drew me in.

I maintained my posture, turning to face Callan who smiled at me. I said I was pleased to see him. I wasn't. Callan introduced me to his family and explained that he had gotten into real estate. He was excited to see me again, grabbing my arm. His wife and children carried on to the gallery and the two of us walked around the room. I felt the need to apologize for my past behaviours, letting him know I should have never acted so immaturely. Callan was calm, collected, and did not mind.

The muse struck again as I looked at the man. Callan's eyes were dead centre as his skin stretched across the wall, peeling the flesh open, showing the muscles and bones underneath. It wasn't a wall but a massive canvas. He tried to speak, but the elongated muscles prevented him from moving, and the eyes simply jerked back-and-forth watching as red paint splattered onto his face, eventually covering his entire stretched skin in shiny red.

"Dasco?" Callan said.

I shook and assured Callan I was fine, just as I heard another whispering voice say to me, "passion paint."

I had a sickening hunch about what the muse wanted for the next piece, and I couldn't. Thankfully, my partner came by, and I introduced them. We exchanged small talk, not going into our past other than we went to school together. My partner does not need to know that this was someone I was once fondly in love with.

The rest of the show was a success, and I sold several pieces that night. My partner and I said our goodbyes to as many people as possible. We caught Callan and his family on their way out. He invited us over for dinner, and I agreed. Truthfully, I wasn't the one speaking. Deep down, I wanted to tell him no, and I never wanted to speak to him again. But I didn't. I don't know if it was me or the muse.

In fact, I flipped it on Callan and invited him and his family over to my loft. Everyone thought this was a splendid idea. The date was set, and the wheels were in motion. As the muse took control, I started slipping into the background as a watcher of my flesh and blood. In my studio, I began to work on the new pieces for my next series.

The gallery and my partner assured me that I did not have to keep making pieces as the current opening was doing so well, and there was no need for a new series. I did not listen and was submissive to the muse's will. I made three, each one using more reds and progressively adding tactile elements onto the canvas. It started with layering the acrylics, gluing materials onto the surface, and then applying sharp and pointed components, like the spine trees I saw in the vision.

After a week's time from the opening, Callan and his family were in my home as my partner and I prepared dinner. There was the usual chitchat, discussing which foods we liked, where we've been around the world, why my partner and I will not adopt, and why Callan chose to have a family. The talk mutated into college and my work. My partner and Callan's wife took over the cooking, letting Callan and I retreat to my studio, where I could show him what I've been doing.

I wanted to scream. I was, inside, in this darkness, viewing through a small glass window. Callan and I spoke about our art and how he wished he continued his skill. He asked me about the muse and if I still believed in it. I made up some bullshit answer on how creativity is simply work, and we have tools, much like a carpenter or welder. I didn't want him to know how powerful the muse had become and how weak I indeed was.

I felt sweat bead across my skin and my heart thump as Callan moved closer to the paintings. My blood ran hot, and my vision began to saturate into only red tones. The whispers of the muse spoke on repeat, "passion paint, passion paint, passion paint."

Then, I realized that the muse had slipped a knife into my back pocket from the kitchen. I didn't know my physical senses had numbed so notably. In this dark observing room, looking through the window, I could only watch in dismay for what it was about to do. The muse took several steps closer to Callan, who examined the work in progress. Its hand reached for the knife in my back pocket and held it tightly, walking ever closer.

Callan lifted his whole hand and glided it against the canvas. He got too close and yapped, pulling his hand away. I froze. Or the muse froze as Callan examined his sliced hand from the uneven surface. Callan apologized for getting blood on the work.

Passion paint.

The muse relaxed its control, and I shifted from the darkness and into the front seat of my body. Finally feeling the sweat under my pits, the coolness on my back, and the warmth of the knife handle in my sweaty palms. I put the blade in my back pocket and grabbed Callan's hand. He seemed startled, eyes wide but obedient.

I pulled the man into me, and he closed his eyes, leaning forward, mouth open, ready for me to embrace his skin. I rotated his body, shocking him, and guided his bleeding hand like a brush over the canvas. The muse channelled through me, and we acted as one, just like when I was younger. Callan's blood smeared over the canvas, avoiding the sharp tactical components. I grabbed the brush in the jar of water with my other hand and saturated the blood, forming the symbols that the muse desired. Callan's eyes didn't move, mouth still dangling open. His face turned pink as I released him.

He stuttered incomprehensible words, unsure if he should apologize, be offended, or what emotion he felt. I thanked him and asked if he would like to return to the kitchen to his family. He nodded, wiping sweat from his face and taking the lead out of the studio.

I'm no fool and am fully aware there is something more between Callan and me. Not that matters much, I suppose, for he only served as another tool for the muse. I left the knife in the studio and returned to the others. We had dinner, laughed, and said our goodbyes. Callan and I acted normal, as if the shared moment in the studio didn't exist, just like we had done in college.

I felt nothing of it. Since my foolish feelings for him, I've had many lovers and can suppress my emotions for him. The focal point of my concerns is the muse's power. Its forcefulness and hostility are something I have not experienced before. I wonder if it was my past emotions merging with the muse to create this violent takeover.

I continue to work on the piece with Callan's blood, painting around it with genuine mediums, wondering to myself if there will be another aggressive overthrow. It could make a permanent invasion, committing notorious acts. Until then, it is my guiding light, and I am simply the vessel for it to express its needs as we continue to build its mosaic of post religionism.

Awake from the observing state. (Turn to Page 361)

Malpherities looks at the giant rip in the sky. His nostrils flare, letting out a stress-induced sigh. "We do not have a lot of time, Nameless One. There are still fragments from the other observation states we can get. We must be quick in the next loop." Malpherities extends his hand to the black ocean. "Be my guest."

"I just jump in?" you ask.

"That's correct."

"Both of our memories are going to be erased?"

"Yours will, of this event. Mine is a bit more, uhm, sophisticated than yours."

"Thanks."

"I'll remember portions, but not all. This loop and rip are unlike anything else."

"Before, when you showed the other me running from the ghouls, the black ocean took me back to my old life?"

"To your previous life, yes. Things are different now, as you can see. The Midway is disrupted, being stuck in this loop. The liquid locked in with us is also on repeat, meaning it can only take you back to where the loop begins, in that grocery store."

"What if I sit here?"

"You always fall in. Whether willingly jumping or due to the plateau sinking. Just jump already."

"Okay. Great. I will find the other clues."

"I believe you will."

"The loop, it'll take us back to making the orb?"

"No. Just when the loop begins. You'll drop right where the event starts. Like a scratch on a vinyl record which skips back to where the scratch is, not to the previous moment. Once you find the clues, I am certain we will be able to break this cycle."

"And how we made the orb?"

"We made it, Nameless One, before the loop began and after our first encounter. How much does it matter when we're stuck here? Best jump in, you'll be in for a real mind twist."

You step closer to the edge of the cliff. The black waves below move back and forth from the ever-increasing wind. It seems like a farfetched idea, but everything so far has been arcane. Malpherities hasn't steered you wrong yet. You need to figure out how to revert this chaos, and it would be wise to jump in.

With that reasoning, you take one more deep breath and leap from the rocky ground soaring into the ocean. You fall for several moments, feeling the icy wind against your face. Down and down you go until you finally collide with the liquid.

Instantly you sink into the ocean with bubbles rising in every direction. All light ceases to be in this dark liquid. You continue to plummet faster, as if something is sucking you in. You keep moving at such an accelerated rate that your entire body stretches out.

The physical form elasticities so far that it ceases to be, and you transcend beyond all limitations of the flesh, projecting from the Midway. Spirals of vibrant colours flash before you with endless sacred geometric patterns all around. Radial light beams come from the sucking source, pulling you into the white until all imagery is gone.

Lightness.

Your soul is gently dragged down to a vibrant blue sky with birds flying around fluffy clouds in the distance. Down below are buildings and familiar streets. You recognize this place. Yes! This is where you live.

The force keeps dragging you further. Your vision moves directly above one particular building where you commonly buy groceries. You move through the roof, past the ceiling with the wires and vents, and into the grocery store.

The observation state fizzles out as your five senses return. You're fuzzy, with a slight headache. Everything you just went through is fading from your mind. The feelings are still there, but you can't grasp the events anymore. There are brief blips, but they too quickly disappear.

You're at the store, as you usually are when you need items. Day-to-day_/\/\/__

Finish your thought in the real world. (Turn to Page 13)

Malpherities raises his eyebrow. "You do?" His tone is a bit unenthusiastic, for you know how to revert the rip and fix the time loop, or so you think.

At this point, you are uncertain if you have enough information to even assemble anything. You're assembling something, right? Maybe you didn't see any fragments Malpherities keeps talking about, and they weren't real clues. It could be a figment of your imagination. There certainly have been plenty of bizarre observations in these other lives that you could have presumed you found clues where there weren't any at all.

"I do," you say. "I've seen enough of the observation states, and I know enough of the clues to piece everything together."

You and Malpherities look up. A monstrous roar bellows from above. Within the rip, a giant reptilian monster with wings spanning for a mile morphs from the mirror image of the black ocean. Its white scales are twisting and turning with the reflection of the waves, attempting to break through the rip.

Malpherities says, "What is your plan, Nameless One?"

This loop . . . started with you in the grocery store. Yes, you're piecing an idea together; no thanks to Malpherities. You were sucked into this place and woke beside an orb. The sphere was made of the same black liquid as the ocean and melts when you touch it. The ghoul mentioned that you and these other beings you've witnessed are somehow related to this strange cosmic event. He said the orb was made using your blood. Then, there are the golden bowls. The orb has gold glitters.

Of course! It's a wild idea, but if the orb lets you witness other lives and make choices, it must be responsible for the time loop to break.

"We have to make the orb!" you shout while running to the tipped golden bowl.

"We make the orb?" Malpherities asks.

"You said my blood helped this, right? And I'm the anomaly within the universe, so the clue must be me."

Malpherities watches as you hop onto the next platform and snag the golden bowl with your right hand that has the cut from Malpherities. Already the metal begins to melt in your hands, swirling with the blood. Now you just need the liquid.

"Malpherities, grab some of the liquid from the pool!" you order.

Malpherities obeys, scooping some black liquid into his claws and soaring to you. The golden bowl melts rapidly, and you use both hands to keep all the metal and blood from falling out of your grasp. The blood and melting gold turns burning hot and bubbles in your cupped palms.

It's all come down to this moment with the golden liquid and blood, which starts to release a yellow glow as Malpherities arrives, raising his claws. You groan in pain, trying to ignore the instinct to release the liquid. You focus on the fact that the universe is collapsing to push through.

"Pour?" Malpherities asks.

"Is that how we made the orb the first time?" you ask.

"You're catching on."

"Must be in my memory somewhere. Do it."

Malpherities carefully pours the black liquid into your hand, blending the blood, the glowing gold, and the black all into one mess.

Some of the mixture drips onto the ground, only several drops. The three liquids stir together on their own, rapidly thickening and bubbling. This trio become a glittery deep red muck, compressing and hardening.

The searing amplifies, and your whole body begins to violently jitter. You use all your might to keep your hands steady, yelling through the boiling pain as the object compacts. Your hands expand out, making way for this clay-like object. You can morph it, sculpting the object into a ball.

The glow softens, and a translucent outer layer forms around the orb as it cools down, containing black liquid and golden swirls within. The familiar energetic hum rushed through your body with no pain, and your fingers start fusing with the orb.

"We did it!" you say.

"The orb is restored," Malpherities says.

Your fingers melt into the object, then your hands, and your arms start to follow. You say, "This will do it, right? The time loop will break with the brand-new orb?"

Malpherities says, "The clues are your guide. Make the choice, Nameless One. You have the power within you to turn everything anew."

That's not concrete. You take one last deep breath, feeling the gravitational pull of . . . something. The Midway isn't blooming into white like the other times you've touched the orb, a promising sign. You are sucked directly into the sphere. The body is absorbed into the object, numbing any sense you have left.

You're in pure blackness for a moment until a radiating light glows from far away. The light casts view onto a spectral of all colours shifting in shapes and sizes, creating sacred geometric patterns moving endlessly inward as the light pulls you in.

The sensation of warmth, peace, and cosmic understanding feels right. You can comprehend the unity of everything on a microscopic level, intertwined within the universe. The world is very much alive. This must be everything resetting.

Through the beam of white light, you continue to descend until fluffy white clouds appear. Blue sky follows shortly after with birds flying around. Directly below is the familiar grocery store where you were shopping just before you were pulled into the Midway.

Further down, through the roof and ceiling of the grocery store, you gently land in your body. All of your humanly wits and sensors return and you raise your hand looking at seeing they are no longer damaged. Well done!

Although, you do have a blasting headache all along your skull with a pulsating beat. It's brief, lasting three thumps, but it is enough to make you blink and rub your head. All of the memories you had in the Midway are blurring. It's like a distant fuzzy memory that you try to recall but cannot.

You're certain you lived through those other lives, right? Maybe not. Perhaps it was all a dream. Someone said something about your memory being wiped . . . You can't even recall anymore, feeling the blips of visuals and sensations slipping deep in your very core. You're failing to recall anything that happened prior to this moment, despite the familiarity and your gut feeling. Strange. You were shopping for groceries just like any other day. You certainly know that daily_ /\/\/__ Finish your thought. (Turn to Page 13)

You wake from the witnessing state and drop the orb in the sand, just like every observation. Despite the number of lives you've experienced, you have not grown accustomed to the jolting energy that enters and leaves your system from that damn orb. Taking a deep breath, you gather yourself and remember that you are here, in your body. Living multiple lives can take a toll on the mind and spirit.

"Well?" Malpherities asks.

"Nothing," you say.

"Do you wish to go again?" Malpherities asks. "Then again, I've seen this play out before."

"Right, the time loop," you say.

"You got it."

"What choices do I make?"

"It varies, depending on which loop we're talking about. If I tell you, it will muddle your choices now."

Another thundering crackle echoes throughout the ocean landscape. You see glimpses of the rip from the cavern entrance. That rip is certainly getting larger since your last two observation states.

"Okay, let's go again," you say, snatching the orb. "There's still time!"

Malpherities is silent.

Another boom erupts outside. The tremble rumbles deep in your core, travelling underneath your feet as a massive shockwave slams against the plateau. Black liquid splatters from every cavern entrance on each level within the plateau.

"Tidal wave!" Malpherities shouts while being thrown against the cavern wall. The stalactite walls crack and split as sand and dust are thrown in every direction. The orb, half-melted into your skin, rips from your hand and tears the flesh right off, leaving you with a bloody mess of what was once your fingers and palm.

You scream in pure agony, clutching your twitching hand as the orb soars through the air and smashes against a half-cracked wall, shattering on impact. The gold glitter smears against the rock while the black liquid runs down to the ground. You can see portions of your ripped skin droop down with the liquid.

"Malpherities!" you shout.

The ghoul doesn't hear you as more deafening rumbles erupts, causing you to fall. That's right, you are falling. There's so much chaos that you barely even notice that the cavern's ceiling crumbles to pieces, and the rocky pillar is collapsing onto itself, crushing each level below you.

Black liquid splashes against the rocks as you tumble around. It's impossible to tell if you hit the ground or a wall as you're tossed around with the shattering rocks. Some of the black liquid from the waves soaks into your clothes and hair. You try to keep your eyes shut, knowing very well what the liquid can do.

The smashing and falling end, and you're at the base level of the cavern. Liquid drizzles through the cracks while others form pools within the debris. The plateau is in ruins. Parts of the walls are flipped upright while others have been reduced to rubble with boulders crashing into the ocean. Portions of the ceiling remain intact directly above you. Beyond the remains, the massive rip in the sky is clear, consuming the atmosphere and sending violent winds all around.

Miraculously, you didn't sustain any injuries during the collapse. Your ripped hand is covered in dirt and rocks, sticking to the bloody mess, scathing relentlessly. You stand up just as a stalactite comes soaring down towards you. You leap out of the way, tumbling onto the ground and rising to your feet.

There, several paces away, you spot Malpherities. His arms flail wildly in a pool of black liquid.

"Hold on!" you shout. You briefly wonder how the ghoul is drowning in the liquid when he manages to hover everywhere else. It doesn't matter. He needs help.

You leap from rock to rock, avoiding the steep angles of the uneven surfaces. A few hops later, and you're one more away from the ghoul. This boulder has a little foot room, and you hang on tight to it, wrapping your arms around the cone-shape top. Your bloody hand stings mercilessly while your arm shakes, trying to remain strong.

This rock is the only way to get to the ghoul, and with a deep breath, you spring from the boulder, soaring through the air. It's a far jump from this rock to the next with a sheer drop into the ocean. You land on the even ground with one roll and spring to your feet, running to Malpherities.

You reach out your good hand as the ghoul extends his claws. The sharp appendages land in your hand, piercing your skin and shredding the flesh. You grunt but resist letting go, and with a mighty shout you pull Malpherities from the pool of black liquid.

"Thank you, Nameless One," Malpherities says. The liquid drips from his form, piercing through the black and blue smoke below his waist. "As you can see, I cannot swim in this element."

"Obviously." You raise your bloody hands. "The orb is smashed."

"As it always does," Malpherities says.

"What do you mean?"

"The orb can't exist. We create it from the beginning, before the loop. It's kind of a chicken and the egg scenario."

You bite your lip, trying to think of some sort of answer. Looking around, you spot a golden bowl toppled over on the ground beside a half-shattered black matte pedestal.

"The clues, Nameless One! This is why they are important. We have reached the end of the loop. It's going to reset."

"What am I supposed to do with them?"

"Use them now. Use the fragments and break the loop before we sink."

MAKE ONE OF TWO CHOICES:

Say, "I don't have enough clues. We have to go through the time loop again." (Turn to Page 353)

Say, "I know the answer!" (Turn to Page 357)

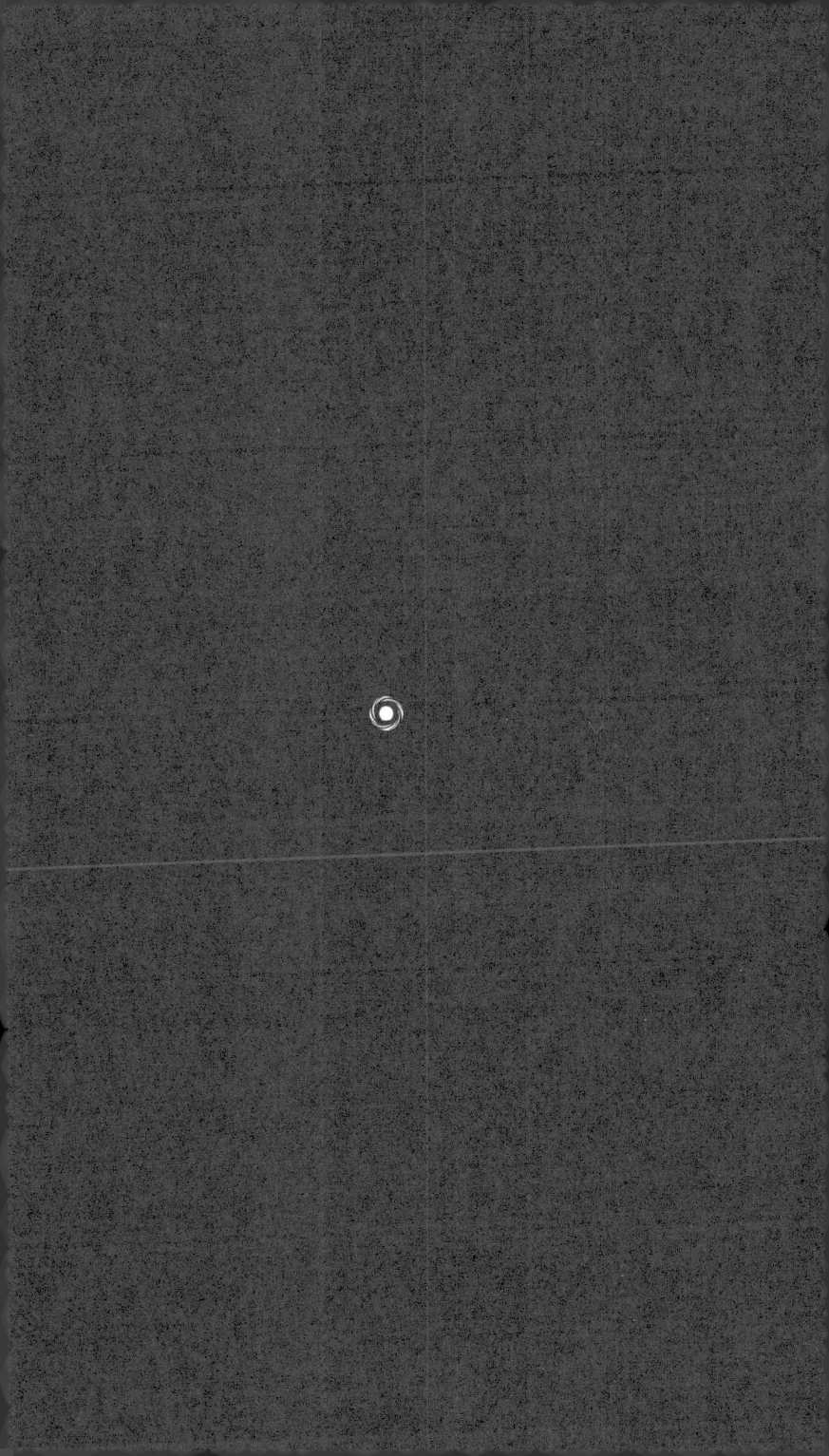

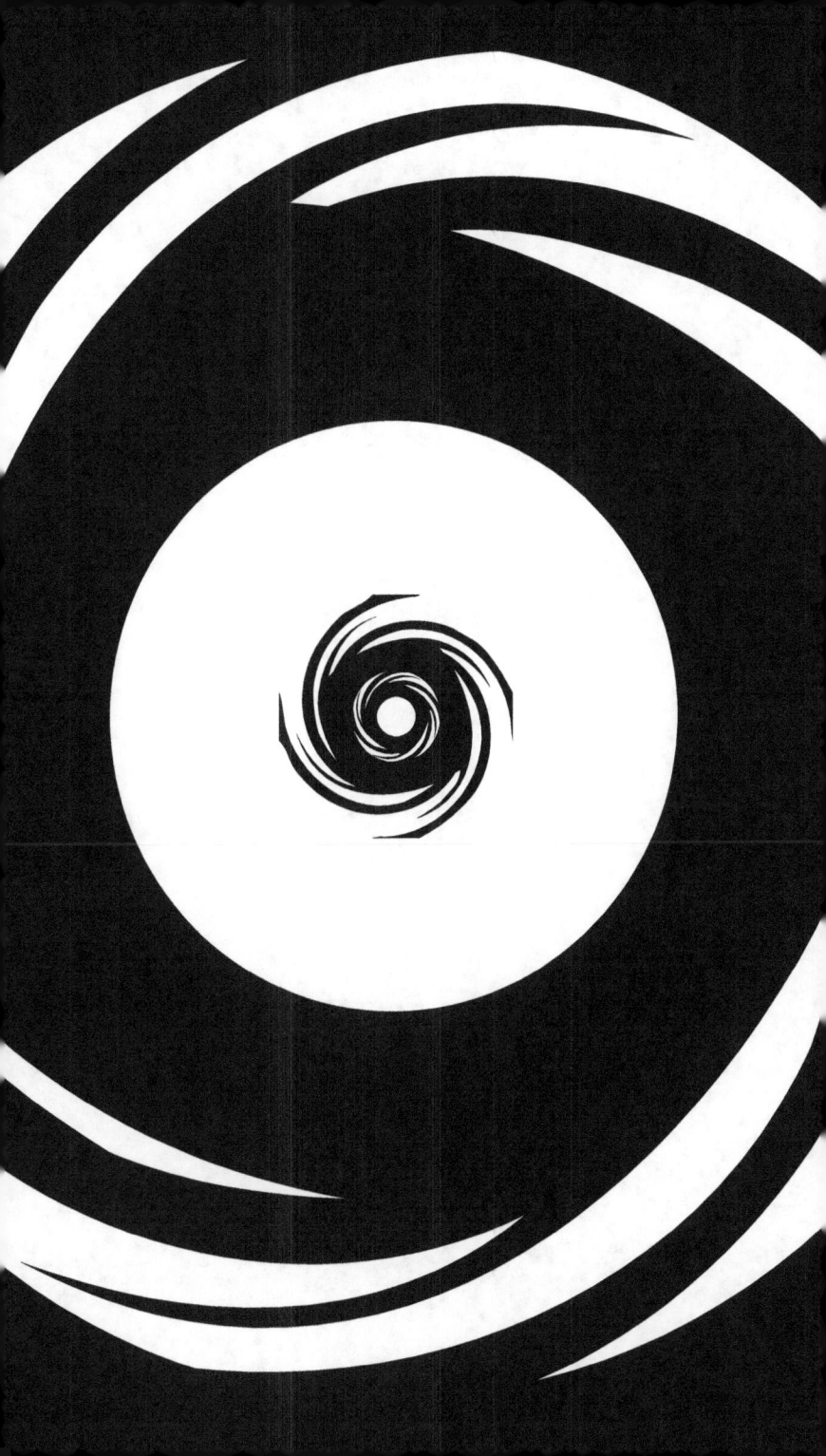

NUT
GRAPE
Chewz

NUT
GRAPE
Chewz

NUT
GRAPE
Chewz

NUT GRAPE Chewz . . . Scrap that end part.

NUT GRAPE . . . NURT GAPE . . . TURN GAPE?

. . . TURN PAGE!

Your feet lift several inches off the ground as you raise your hands into the air. A sudden surge of power jolts inside your body. Your hair becomes static, standing in all directions as a distorted aura ripples around your body. The cut from Malpherities and your ripped skin heal instantaneously while this mysterious energy zaps blue and white bolts between your fingertips.

You let out a victorious roar and shout, "I choose!"

Malpherities smiles, a genuine one showing his bright razor-sharp teeth while watching you hovering above him. "Nameless One! You've done it. You've embraced choice!"

You can conquer the world. No, scratch that; you can command the universe. The godlike experience channels through every portion of your soul, making your physical form obsolete. Even the other lives you may or may not have lived in the time loop matters little now that you are here, right now, experiencing the Midway under your free will.

Cracks suddenly etch in the open sky, coming from nowhere. They extend, appearing in an arch shape, forming a dome in the sky leading to the black ocean. These cracks expand rapidly and eventually shatter, floating off into the air until they dissolve seconds later.

Malpherities raises his claws, shouting, "The loop is broken! Nameless One, well done."

Yes, indeed, the loop is broken. Instinctively, you know already. You also know precisely what to do next with this newfound power: sealing the rip.

"Seal the rip!" Malpherities says a little too late.

"Already got that," you say while bringing your electrifying hands together. The lightning in your fingers concentrates into a ball between your hands. Pressing your palms together, you angle the sphere up towards the rift's endpoint. The shape blasts a beam of bright white light smashing into the fiery end of the rip as you guide it towards the center, fusing the two sides together. You aim the ray towards the other end, closing it entirely.

The wind calms, letting the clouds fly off gently in all directions while the ocean settles. You free your arms, letting the orb dissipate. Next, you wave your hands, focusing on all the broken rocks that were once the plateau. With only your free will, you move your hands up, lifting the rocks and reassembling them into the cavern, pillar, and the plateau above.

Your thought is enough to command the plateau back into existence. Even though you do not know all the individual pieces of how to reassemble this thing, you visualizing the end is living proof of your mind's power. These two miraculous actions make you realize that everything here is controlled by your thoughts.

Next, you soar high into the air, above the plateau, and twirl your fingers above your head, repairing Death's Vortex. The swirling reanimates the black and blue clouds, speeding up the whirlpool motion, moving endlessly into the dark central void. Those familiar hands and faces start phasing in and out once more.

Everything seems to be back in order.

In fact, there's so much power within this newfound free will that you question the Midway itself. Everything and anything you imagine can happen.

Malpherities is on top of the plateau and says, "The power has been within you all along."

The other two ghouls you previously saw distorted from the cavern are alive and well. A third joins them, floating up onto the plateau beside Malpherities. They look up at you in awe, not blinking in wonder.

Malpherities takes a bow.

The ghoul was right. The power has always been within you. This godlike state gives you the ability to create, undo, destroy, redo, and fabricate. The possibilities are endless, and all of them exist within your mind. Yet, so many questions remain about the Midway.

What was the rip?

What is your name?

Where are your memories?

When and how did you and Malpherities make the orb with your blood that started the loop?

You never did get that latter question answered. Then again, do you really need an explanation? He could have visited you in your dreams, pulling you into the Midway and babbled on about the dangers of the rip. Then you two tirelessly forged the orb with your blood, sweat, and tears for ten sleepless nights. Maybe the two of you made the orb at an arts and crafts class with school glue and felt fabric and a small dab of your nose bleed. Or, how's this . . . you pulled the sphere out of your ass. It could be any of these answers, for it is all of these versions. Each iteration co-exists in the chasms of your mind.

That's probably not the answer you were looking for, is it? I bet you wanted this book to guide you to some grand conclusion in a neat linear format, trying up the story arch about how everything is linked to the Macrocosm and the mysterious rip. Well, too bad. This book is chaotic and messy with no straightforward narrative, just like the real world and the random mangled nonsense that it is.

The paragraph above sounds like this story got written into an escapable corner filled with endless plot holes, doesn't it? Not quite, because there's good news. This is where you get to decide how the story ends.

Do you fly away like some superhero, with a cape, of course, off to a distant universe to fight more evil? Or do you celebrate with the ghouls in an all-out party? Maybe you blow them up, and this book is an antihero origin story. Who doesn't love a good antihero tale? This is your mind and your world. All of the stories within these pages exist inside your thoughts in their own unique way. It's all thanks to these letters magically converting words into worlds and engraving them into your memory. Reread the book, and you'll experience new variations of these lives.

As for your name, the Nameless One, you know your own damn name. Malpherities knows it now too. The same goes for your memories.

Let's look at the origins of that rip in the sky, shall we? Apparently, you have seen this rip before in a previous life. It is the source of all the mayhem. Maybe you did initially die and were thrown into the Midway. Maybe it is just an extraordinary cosmic event, as Malpherities originally said in that volume. A more exciting theory is that a bald supernatural villain named Victor Destroyamaximus hatched an evil plan to have you act as his servant with this new godlike power and harness five magical coloured lollipops. The likely scenario is that the rip is emblematic, and you picked up this book and are still reading it. The rip, supervillain, or these words have allowed you to meet Malpherities, go through other lives, and discover the depths of your imagination.

Your mind is a marvellous place, processing everything you are experiencing and filtering it through your senses. With your free will and thought, you're able to break through those limitations and live any life you want through your psyche.

The lives you have observed within the Macrocosm are stuck on a linear path, seeing their existence straight to the end, unlike you. You can turn the page. This is your free will in action, and you're experiencing the results of it. Being a participant is not nearly enough while living in your world. Participants can be locked into rules, following a game that suppresses creativity and makes everything stale. You do not have to follow the game. You have saved the universe for the fantastical, bizarre, and extraordinary beings within this volume. You've practiced your own ability to make a choice by deciding how this book ends a handful of pages ago.

We're only here for a short time before we transcend from the flesh and likely into Death's Vortex. While we're alive, we have the power within ourselves to choose how we want to live. Everyone's journey is different the moment we are born with unique restrictions, rules, and terrors that can quickly manipulate us and dictate our path. We're living in the present whether we like it or not, meaning we can buckle into the shotgun seat, observe, and let someone else drive, or we can participate, demonstrating our free will.

You chose the latter. You played along many times, navigating through the strange Macrocosm within this volume. Then, you've actively broken the rules to get to this page. Hang tight; only a handful of words are left until you reach the true ending. You can go back, read the volume again and catch any details or shorts you may have missed, or you can place it down.

When you do put this book away, and leave your imagination, live your life through your own choices for the truest you.

THANK YOU FOR READING BEYOND THE MACROCOSM.
WOULD YOU CONSIDER GIVING IT A REVIEW?

Reviewing an author's book on primary book sites such as Amazon, Kobo and Goodreads drastically help authors promote their novels and it becomes a case study for them when pursuing new endeavors. A review can be as short as a couple of sentences or up to several paragraphs, it's up to you. You can find review options on Goodreads or Bookbub or your preferred online distributor such as Amazon or Kobo.

ALL WORK

Mental Damnation Series

- Reality: Part 1 of Mental Damnation
- Dream: Part 2 of Mental Damnation
- Purity: Part 3 of Mental Damnation
- Mortal: Part 4 of Mental Damnation

The Macrocosm

- Rave
- Cultivate: Seed Me Relapse Edition
- YEGman

Short Story Collections

- Into the Macrocosm: Short Stories of the Dark Cosmic, Bizarre, and the Fantastic
- Beyond the Macrocosm: Interactive Short Stories of Dread and Wonder

Rutherford Manor Series

- The White Hand: A Rutherford Manor Novel
- Fire, Pain, & Ruin A Rutherford Manor Novel

Audiobooks

- Cultivate: Seed Me Relapse Edition Audiobook
- Into the Macrocosm Audiobook
- Rave Audiobook
- Fire, Pain, & Ruin A Rutherford Manor Audiobook

Novel Scores

- Frequencies of the Macrocosm Score
- Missing Head Highway Rave Novel Score
- World Mother: Seed Me Novel Score
- Sounds of Society: YEGman Novel Soundtrack

All publications are listed on konnlavery.com/publications

ABOUT THE AUTHOR

Konn Lavery is a Canadian author whose work has been recognized by Edmonton's top five bestseller charts and by award programs such as indieBRAG, The Wishing Shelf Book Awards, Literary Titan, and Dan Poynter's Global Ebook Awards. His work has also been curated into the Edmonton Public Library's Capital Press collection.

He started writing stories at a young age while being homeschooled. After graduating from graphic design college, he began professionally pursuing his writing with his first release, *Reality*. He continues to write in the thriller, horror, and fantasy genres.

His literary work is balanced alongside his graphic design and website development business. Konn's visual communication skills have been transcribed into the formatting and artwork found within his publications supporting his fascination of transmedia storytelling.